Praise for Xio Ax
The Girl with Stars i

"Written with an expertise in—and deep reverence for—the music industry, *The Girl with Stars in Her Eyes* is a brilliant standout. Axelrod's writing sings sweetly, transporting the reader to gritty clubs and brightly lit stages, making us feel the buzz of Toni's burgeoning stardom even amidst the tangle of her heartache. Sharp, propulsive, and sexy. Once I started, I couldn't put it down. Antonia and Seb are imprinted in my book-loving heart. I genuinely, truly, relished this book."

—**Christina Lauren**, *New York Times* and #1 international bestselling author

"Xio Axelrod has quickly become one of my go-to authors, and *The Girl with Stars in Her Eyes* a favorite of 2021!"

—**Jennifer L. Armentrout**, #1 *New York Times* bestselling author

"Xio Axelrod's writing is like music—sensual, sweet, and utterly powerful. With captivating connections, swoony scenes, and characters so vivid you'll swear they're real, you'll be putting Xio's stories on repeat."

—**Sierra Simone**, *USA Today* bestselling author

"You will lose sleep and fall in love with a book you never knew you needed. *The Girl with Stars in Her Eyes* is a stunning and magical novel full of swoon-worthy, complex, and deserving characters who I need in my life. Xio has found a fangirl in me and I bow in her greatness!"

—**Carrie Ann Ryan**, *New York Times* bestselling author

"I devoured *The Girl with Stars in Her Eyes*! It's so incredibly good! Axelrod's richly complex characters and her authentic world of up-and-coming musicians deliver a truly captivating read. I couldn't turn the pages fast enough. Xio Axelrod is an auto-buy for me!"

—**Karen Rose**, international bestselling author

"Written with an easy grace and vivid style... I was fascinated with the music scene, something I know nothing about but which was brought to bright life in this engaging, vivid page-turner."

—**Kristan Higgins**, *New York Times* bestselling author

"Xio Axelrod writes compelling, emotional stories that keep me engaged to the very last page. Simply put, her books rock!"

—**Jennifer Probst**, *New York Times* bestselling author

"*The Girl with Stars in Her Eyes* [will] linger in your memory like a favorite song that makes you smile as soon as you hear the opening chord. Xio Axelrod proves again why she's a rock star in romance."

—**Avery Flynn**, *Wall Street Journal* and
USA Today bestselling author

"Xio Axelrod has a wonderfully poetic way with words. In *The Girl with Stars in Her Eyes*, Xio weaves a lush, evocative rock-star fairy tale full of emotion and heart."

—**Kristen Callihan**, *New York Times* and
USA Today bestselling author

"Xio Axelrod hits it out of the park! Toni Bennette is the rock star heroine we need right now. You'll be yelling encore at the end of *The Girl with Stars in Her Eyes*."

—**Kwana Jackson**, *USA Today* bestselling author

"Xio Axelrod consistently delivers the kind of story that will make your heart sing."

—**Farrah Rochon,** *USA Today* bestselling author

"Wonderfully fresh and original! This book will pluck your heartstrings with an aching riff."

—**Sarina Bowen,** *USA Today* bestselling author

"Sexy, achingly heartfelt, authentic, and original! With a compelling ensemble of interesting characters, Xio Axelrod brings Toni and Seb—and their music—vividly to life. This book is the true rock star!"

—**Laura Kaye,** *Wall Street Journal, New York Times,* and *USA Today* bestselling author

Also by Xio Axelrod

THE LILLYS
The Girl with Stars in Her Eyes

Girls
with Bad
Reputations

XIO AXELROD

sourcebooks
casablanca

Copyright © 2024 by Xio Axelrod
Cover and internal design © 2024 by Sourcebooks
Cover illustration © Sabrena Khadija
Internal design by Ashley Holstrom/Sourcebooks

Sourcebooks and the colophon are registered trademarks of Sourcebooks.

Published by Sourcebooks Casablanca, an imprint of Sourcebooks
P.O. Box 4410, Naperville, Illinois 60567-4410
(630) 961-3900
sourcebooks.com

Cataloging-in-Publication Data is on file with the Library of Congress.

Printed and bound in the United States of America.
LSC 10 9 8 7 6 5 4 3 2 1

For dB. You were full of more light than you knew.
And for tía Lillian, who always marched
to the beat of her own drum.

"I believe in individuality, that everybody is special, and it's up to them to find that quality and let it live."

~GRACE JONES

PROLOGUE.

KATHY: 15 YEARS OLD

KATHERINE YOLANDA LARRINGTON DIDN'T KNOW how it was possible to be so angry and yet not feel anything at all. She was numb from her fingertips to her toes. Her hands shook, and her head wouldn't stop pounding. It was an insistent rhythm that she heard in her ears and felt in her throat.

Outside, the rain dripped like sweat from the heavy clouds that hung low in the sky. Inside, people meandered from room to room to room, talking in hushed voices. Their words were as empty and lifeless as her brother's body in its shiny, black coffin.

He was so young.

Such a tragedy.

I'm so sorry for your loss.

Our deepest condolences.

Kathy wished they'd all gone home after the funeral and left her family in peace. These people were ridiculous, gray-faced and hollow-throated, as if *they'd* been the ones to get the call.

There's been an accident...

The black dress that had been laid out for her that morning had wrinkled in Kathy's sweaty fists. Every time someone said Zach's name, she had to stop herself from tearing the fabric. It wasn't supposed to be like this. Zach had been two months away from graduating from high school, ready to head to college and freedom from their mother's iron will. Her eye fell on a copy of the funeral program that one of their guests had decided to use as a coaster.

> Zachary leaves behind his loving mother and father, Gisele Larrington, AB, AM, PhD, and Geoffrey Larrington, PhD, and his doting younger sister, Katherine Yolanda Larrington.

The gentle hand on her back made her jump. "Hey, pumpkin." Her father leaned against the wall next to her. She didn't have to look up to see the worry lines on his forehead. They'd been there all week. "How are you holding up?"

Kathy's throat was sore from crying. She managed to nod, wincing when dry fingers slipped over hers. Her father ran his thumb over her fist until it relaxed.

"Have you eaten anything?" He made a small sound of disapproval when she shook her head. "Honey, you need to eat. I know it's hard, but you have to keep up your strength. Zach wouldn't want you to waste away."

Kathy turned to him at the mention of her brother's name. "Then he shouldn't have died."

It was so wrong to say, especially to the man who had loved both of his children beyond reason. The pain in his eyes seemed to double. Triple. Bend toward infinity.

"Dad..."

She watched him swallow another cup of grief and wondered how he hadn't overflowed with it.

"It's okay, sweetheart."

It wasn't. "I'll get some food if you will."

The ghost of a smile curled the corners of her father's mouth, and it was like someone had pressed their thumb, hard, into the hollow of Kathy's throat. She couldn't get her lungs to work.

Eyes widening, her father squeezed her hand. "Come on."

They moved through the clumps of visitors and staff. Dressed in black, their faces blurred together. Their platitudes were as distant as the sound of a passing train. When they reached the hallway, Kathy was pressed against the wall. Her father's hands on her shoulders were the only things keeping her upright.

"Breathe, sweetheart."

She tried. As he massaged her arms, pressing soft kisses to her forehead, Kathy came back to herself in small increments. The smell of the food served for the repast mingled with a hundred colognes and perfumes worn by the mourners. Hushed voices punctuated by the occasional laugh brought her back to where she didn't want to be. Whatever had been choking her—grief, panic, rage, or all of the above—the only thing she managed to latch on to was the rage. She needed to *do* something. Hit something.

"Do you want to go lay down? People would understand."

Kathy didn't give a shit about *people*. "Yeah, okay. For a little while." She turned toward her room. When her father turned with her, she stopped. "I'm okay. You should go be with Mom."

"You sure?"

"Yeah. I just need a break, that's all."

In his eyes, Kathy could see how much he needed one too. She also knew he wouldn't leave her mother alone to deal with their visitors.

"All right. I'll come check on you later."

He hugged her, but Kathy couldn't feel it. She was cold and walked down the hall toward her bedroom like her feet were encased in blocks of ice, each step heavy and slow.

They'd closed all the doors to the bedrooms. All except one. As Kathy reached her brother's room, she stopped, half expecting him to yell at her for being nosy. The room was still and quiet when she stepped inside, everything as he'd left it.

A treasured poster of the Foo Fighters concert he'd gotten VIP tickets for still hung on his wall. A neat stack of books sat on the edge of his desk, stark against the chaos of the rest of the surface. And strewn everywhere, drumsticks.

Kathy closed the door and locked it, drawn to the corner of the room that held Zach's practice kit. She picked up the pair of sticks lying at the foot of his bed and clutched them to her chest as she approached the set. Under the gray of the clouds outside Zach's window, it stood like a broken, black skeleton.

Climbing behind the kit opened the floodgates to her memories. The first time he'd let her sit and watch him play and the first time he'd let her tag along to a band rehearsal. Kathy hadn't understood Zach's fascination with drumming until that day.

KATHY: 11 YEARS OLD

"Let's try that Mutemath song the bride requested." Pete, the leader of Zach's trio, lifted his guitar strap over his shoulders. The bassist nodded and made adjustments before the group started up again.

Kathy didn't know the song, but it had her head bobbing and her toes tapping.

The air in Pete's garage had a metallic quality, as if she could smell the electricity flowing into the amps and between the players themselves—all powered by the same current.

"To the bridge!" Zach called out, turning to make eye contact with the other musicians.

They effortlessly floated through the song, sounding every bit as good as any band she'd heard on the radio. Kathy couldn't stop watching her brother play. He was a blur of movement behind the drum kit, all anchored by his blinding smile and the sheer joy written all over his face.

When the song ended, she clapped. "That was badass!"

"Thanks, lil' sis," Zach said, grinning.

"It would be even better if we could find someone to play keyboard," Kevin, the bassist, said.

"Maybe your sister should take it up," Pete said to Zach. "Make it a family thing, yeah?"

"Well, Kayla is a genius." Zach turned, his smile warm. She always loved his private nickname for her. "I bet you'd pick it up in no time."

"You ever thought about it?" Pete asked hopefully.

Kathy shook her head. "Not really."

"I'm surprised your mom didn't make you take music lessons," Kevin said.

"Oh, she did. Violin." Kathy cringed at the memory. "At school, I had a choice between that and piano, actually."

"And you chose the violin?" Pete asked, his brows lifting.

"I wanted to play guitar or bass or...something cool." Her gaze returned to Zach as he tightened one of the drums on the shiny chrome and wood kit, her fingers tapping against her crossed legs.

For a moment, she pictured herself in his place. Pictured her hands gripping the wooden sticks that were too long for her small hands, the very tips of her shoes pushing against the pedals, all in sync.

As they worked through the song, she felt the rhythm moving through her, down her arms to her fingers and down her legs to her feet. She tried to anticipate what Zach would do next—tap that drum, play that cymbal—and found that she could for the most part.

When he did a quick and complicated fill, she got up and moved closer to try and work out how he'd known where and how to place it.

Kathy was standing right over him when they finished.

"Ever consider the drums?" One brow arched, Zach grinned at her from over his shoulder.

Kathy blinked and stepped back, watching as her brother climbed out from behind the kit. "Come here. Let's try something." He beckoned her.

She obeyed, wiping her hands on her jeans as moved beside him.

"Here." Zach held out a pair of drumsticks. "Take these."

She did and let him steer her to the stool, which he adjusted for her height. Sitting down, she took in all of the different drums and cymbals in front of her.

"Play something simple," Zach told the others.

The musicians began a song Kathy recognized, an old Beatles tune her dad loved. She began to tap the sticks against the rim of the snare drum, feeling uncoordinated but in love with it already. Looking up when the music changed key, Kathy snapped out of it, realizing where she was. Her fingers fumbled the sticks, and she dropped one.

The music stopped.

"I'm sorry, I don't really know what I'm doing," she said, ready to slink away.

"Doesn't matter." Zach smiled softly at her. "We all have to start somewhere. Give it another try, and this time don't be afraid of hitting the skins. It'll seem loud to you, but it's all right."

"Play whatever you feel," Pete added. "We'll follow you."

With everyone watching her, Kathy was caught in the eye of a hurricane of uncertainty. But as she sat there, a pattern emerged from the chords. She gripped the sticks tight in her fists and let the rhythm take over her heartbeat.

"Can you tell where each verse begins?" Zach yelled over the sounds. Kathy nodded. "That's your one-count. Start there"—he pointed to the pedal at her right foot—"and just let go."

Kathy stomped her foot down on the kick drum pedal, sending a resounding boom throughout the room. She struck the snare drum with the stick in her left hand and the hi-hat cymbal with the one in her right, bouncing it the way Zach had done in the recording for his YouTube channel the week before.

"Almost," Zach instructed. "Kick on one, snare on three, hi-hat on one through four."

She followed his instructions and soon got the hang of it, hitting and kicking harder each time until the kit reverberated throughout her body. Kathy closed her eyes and just...played. She barely noticed when the bassist began to play along, and then the guitarist, until her brain caught up to the fact that she was doing it. Playing. With a band.

The beat steadied her, and Kathy clung to it. Let it anchor her. Every stomp of her foot and crash of the cymbals drove away the thoughts swirling in her head.

It wasn't perfect, but it was...amazing.

Kathy tried to keep the tempo steady for as long as she could until her hands cramped, and she had to stop. She was sweaty, breathing heavily, and her thick curls were plastered to her head, but she had never felt so alive.

"Damn, girl!" Pete's smile was bright as he looked at her. "I think you might just be a drummer."

Beside her, Zach beamed. "I knew Kayla was a natural!"

"Uh, Zach?" The worried look on Kevin's face dampened the pride fizzing in Kathy's veins. "Didn't your parents have a thing tonight?"

"When don't they? Oh shit!" he exclaimed, ignoring their mother's rule about profanity. "We better get home before Mom grounds me for life."

Checking her phone, Kathy winced. They were super late. The dinner party started in half an hour, and it would take them almost that much time to bike back home. Their mother would definitely ground Zach for this, especially if she found out he'd brought her to band practice and not left her at the library like he'd promised.

"Tell her it was my fault," Kathy said to Zach as they mounted their bikes. "I lost track of time studying."

Smiling, Zach shook his head. "Nah, Kayla. Nah. Then she'd nail us both. I'll take the hit. At least that way she can still claim to have one perfect child."

KATHY: 15 YEARS OLD

The door to Zach's room swung open. Kathy looked up to find her mother standing there, her hair neat and her dress tidy with none of the fatigue that seemed to plague Kathy's father and herself. The only thing that gave her mother away was the pinched corners of her mouth. She was livid.

"Katherine Yolanda? What do you think you are you doing?"

Kathy removed the headphones and set them on the snare pad. "I was just coming back."

"Your father said you were lying down because you were tired," her mother said. "Instead, I find you in here...disturbing Zachary's things."

"I wasn't—" The denial faded from Kathy's mouth, the fight snuffed out as quickly as it had arisen. Nothing she said would matter. "I'm sorry."

"I know you miss him, but this isn't the proper way to mourn your brother."

But it was. Drumming meant everything to Zach. It was the one thing they'd shared that was just theirs.

"You've got rhythm in your heart, Kayla. Don't let anyone drive it away."

"What are you going to do with Zach's stuff?"

For a moment, her mother's features contorted with genuine emotion before her usual, implacable mask slipped back into place. "We...haven't decided."

Kathy almost sagged with relief. Given how much her mother hated Zach's drumming, Kathy expected his kits would be immediately donated or, worse, tossed into a dump somewhere. She stood and smoothed her dress.

Her mother made a sound of disapproval. "You're a mess. Clean yourself up before you come back downstairs. I'll have another dress laid out for you."

"Okay." Kathy walked to the door, stopping when her mother blocked her way. She lifted her chin. "Mom?"

"I made mistakes with your brother, gave in to him too much," her mother said, her gaze distant. "I never should have agreed to let him take a gap year. If I'd only stood my ground, he would have gone to school. Would have become a doctor." She smoothed a hand over Kathy's hair, pushing back a curl that had sprung loose from the tight bun. "Did you know he wanted to be a surgeon when he was a child?"

Kathy felt her head move from side to side. "He didn't say."

"No, I don't suppose he did. Once he got it in his head that *music* was his calling, he—" She made a choked sound that swallowed whatever she was about to say and searched Kathy's eyes, frowning when she didn't seem to find what she was looking for. Then she reached down and pulled the drumsticks out of Kathy's hand.

She hadn't realized she still held them. Her mother studied her face for a long moment, and Kathy tried to stand a little straighter.

"I won't make the same mistakes with you."

CHAPTER 1.

KAYLA SWIPED HER ARM ACROSS her forehead in a feeble attempt to wipe away the rivers of sweat pouring down her face. Her butt was asleep, her thigh muscles were screaming, and her right hand had begun to cramp, but—goddamnit—Katherine Yolanda Larrington was exactly where and *who* she wanted to be. Zach would be proud, she hoped.

Perched behind a set of shiny black Neusonic drums, Kayla surveyed her domain like a queen on a throne. She had a commanding view of her surroundings. To her right, Toni Bennette wielded her guitar like a knife, slicing and dicing through the melodic verses. To Kayla's left, Tiffany Kim punched through her bass riffs like a woman on a mission to reverse the blood flow of every person in the audience.

Their slot in the Dragonfly Festival lineup was short, only twenty-five minutes, but they'd resolved to make every single one of those minutes count. To leave an indelible mark on the crowd.

Tiff swung her long twists over her shoulder and flashed Kayla an open-mouthed smile, entirely in her element.

Kayla grinned back as she gripped her sticks a bit tighter and slammed them down against the skins. Lifting her chin at Tiff, she snapped her wrist, hitting the snare drum with crisp precision that felt as natural to her as her own heartbeat.

At the front of the stage, Lilly Langeland used her otherworldly voice to whip the crowd into a frenzy. She sounded incredible tonight. Honestly, she had been getting better with every show, her confidence growing with every encore, but this crowd was their biggest yet. If Dragonfly was anything to go by, their upcoming tour was going to be epic.

"I can't hear you!" Lilly screamed into the microphone, setting alight the sea of forty thousand souls scattered across the field. "Get those hands up, Delaware!"

Lilly's newly anointed acolytes obeyed, raising their hands in the air and screaming at the top of their lungs. Earlier that morning, rain had poured in slanted sheets over the crowd, turning the once-green field into a veritable mud pit. They didn't seem to care, lost as they were in the music.

It didn't matter that the Lillys were so far down the list in the festival's lineup that you needed a magnifying glass to read their name on the posters. People danced, sang along with the covers they knew, clapped for the songs they didn't know, and gave themselves over to them.

Lilly spun around to face her, signaling Kayla, Tiff, and Toni to play the song's outro.

Kayla settled into the groove, closing her eyes and listening to the others. They gelled so well. Like they were always meant to be—these four women playing this song in this place at this time.

As their penultimate song finished, Kayla let the roar of the crowd buzz through her sweat-dampened skin. She had just enough time to grab a towel and swipe it across her forehead before she had to jump right back into action, setting the pulse of the crowd with the ticking of her drumsticks against the hi-hat. Immediately, heads began to bob. Kayla watched the sea of hopeful faces as they waited to hear which song it would be.

She and the Lillys could keep them suspended like this forever. It was potent magic to wield.

"Thank you for being here," Lilly shouted. "For being present and at this moment with us, it's been incredible. *Tusen takk*, DragonFest!"

Kayla took the cue for what it was and dived into their final song of the night. She loved the pickup intro to "Juliet's Got a Gun" and zeroed in on the four-four downbeat, in no particular hurry. Happy to ride it out for as long as Lilly wanted.

Lilly didn't make them wait long, spreading her vocals over the layer Kayla, Tiff, and Toni had created for her. Icing on their cake.

They ripped through the song, fueled by adrenaline and the frenzy of the massive crowd. By the time they reached the end of the four minutes and change, Kayla was flying high. She finished with a clean double-stroke roll over her toms, smashed her crashed cymbals, and silenced them with her fingertips before standing to raise her drumsticks in the air as Lilly bade the crowd good night.

Kayla's leg muscles quaked as she climbed from behind the kit and made her way offstage, tossing her used sticks to a few outstretched arms at the front of the stage.

"Hot damn, this place is on fire," Tiff said, grinning as they made their way to the artist area. "Festivals are fucking fantastic." She looped an arm around Kayla's neck and pulled her close, causing them both to stumble as they walked.

"That was pretty cool," Toni said, understated as ever.

Kayla looked up and saw their number-one-fan-slash-manager, Seb, barreling toward them with a big-ass grin on his face.

"That was fucking awesome," he exclaimed before sweeping Toni up into a bear hug.

"Careful," Toni warned, laughing into their inevitable kiss. "I'm all gross and sticky."

Seb waggled his eyebrows. "Just the way I like you."

There was a collective groan, albeit good-natured. By now, they were all used to Seb's jokes.

GIRLS WITH BAD REPUTATIONS   13

The pair were sickeningly in love. Kayla was happy for Seb—for both of them—even if jealousy did rear its ugly head from time to time. Not that Kayla wanted either of them. She envied the kind of unwavering love they seemed to have for each other. The way they appeared to be true partners offered a stark contrast to power dynamics she'd grown up around.

Her parents loved one another, of that she was certain. But her mother was a force of nature whose will could blow through the people around her like a gale-force wind. She was well-meaning, but Kayla had found it increasingly difficult to live up to her expectations, especially after they had lost Zach.

The way Seb and Toni worked and loved in tandem gave Kayla hope.

As Tiff pulled Kayla to her side and praised her skills, Kayla thought, for now, what she had with these people—people who loved and supported her unconditionally—was more than enough.

———

Of course, her phone would ring just when she had wrestled her sweat-soaked leather pants down to her hips. She made a mental note to silence the thing for at least an hour after showtime from now on. Just about everyone she needed to hear from was within shouting distance anyway.

Also, whose bright idea was it to play in leather pants in the middle of a freaking heat wave? She cursed past Kayla for her lack of foresight.

Thankfully, the caller gave up, and Kayla's phone fell silent. She struggled her way out of the leather and had just pulled up the zipper on her comfy jeans when the damned phone started up again.

"For fuck's sake," she grumbled as she reached around the privacy screen and plucked it from the makeup and hair products that littered the countertop. Kayla's heartbeat quickened when she saw the name on the caller ID.

"Mom?" she asked as soon as the call connected. "What's wrong?"

"Katherine. Why would you assume something is wrong?" Her mother's tone caused an automatic straightening of Kayla's back. She could almost picture the stern expression in her sharp features.

We don't call each other, Kayla wanted to say. Instead, she asked, "How are you?"

"I am well. Busy but that isn't cause for complaint. And you?"

Relieved it wasn't an actual emergency, Kayla parked herself in a chair and turned to the mirror to fix her hair and makeup. A group of reporters usually awaited the bands after their sets, and the Lillys had agreed to attend those pressers as a unit. With their former bandmate Candi stirring up trouble, they didn't want to give the press any fuel for the fire.

"I'm busy too."

"I see." Her tone was cool, which was the best Kayla could hope for. "I have news."

"You wrote another book?" Kayla could almost see the illustrated cover, having been the inspiration for her mother's Little Miss Yolanda series. The books had cast a long shadow over her world. Wildly successful, they were in school libraries all over the country.

In interviews, her mother had never hidden the inspiration she'd found at home in her daughter. Her perfect, straight-A student, reading-at-a-college-level-at-the-age-of-nine prodigy. But Little Miss Yolanda was the pride and joy Kayla had never been for her. She had been too willful, too stubborn, *too much like your brother*.

"I…yes, as a matter of fact," her mother replied. "I have a book tour coming up. The usual."

Kayla shivered. There would be Little Miss Yolanda ads everywhere.

"But that isn't why I called. Your father is retiring." There was an awkward pause while Kayla processed the information. "They're honoring him with a banquet."

She couldn't quite wrap her head around her mother's words. Her dad *loved* teaching. It was his whole existence. "Is Dad all right?"

"He's perfectly fine. I… *We* expect you to be there, Katherine." Her mother spoke as if they were already arguing.

"Of course, I'll be there," Kayla replied, bristling. She took a breath to calm herself. She would not let a simple phone call with her mom devolve into its usual exchange of snide remarks. "When is it?"

"I'll send you the details once they are finalized." She sounded… relieved? Surprised? Did she really think Kayla wouldn't attend?

"Okay, thanks."

There was another long silence as Kayla waited for her mother to ask how she was, what she'd been up to, if she needed anything. She knew she wouldn't.

"Where are you?" her mother finally asked, her voice on the edge of reproach as if she were prepared to disapprove. "It sounds like a train station."

"I'm…at a park." It was a partial truth. An unexpected wave of guilt swept over Kayla. She hadn't been up front with her parents about her life for years. Once her grandfather's trust was released to her at twenty-one, she stopped pretending to toe the Larrington family line. Whenever her father asked, she simply said she was taking time to find her way. As long as she was safe, that was all it took to satisfy him, and she adored him for that. As far as her parents knew, Kayla was still in LA. She hadn't confided in her dad, not wanting to put him in the position of dealing with the fallout from her mother.

"Katherine Yolanda?" Her mother's impatience cut through Kayla's thoughts.

"Sorry." Kayla refocused. She closed the flap to the tent that served as a makeshift dressing room and moved to the quietest corner. "Sorry about the noise. I'm at...a thing."

"Is it a *music* thing?" It was a particular talent to pack so much disdain into such an innocent word.

If her parents were to learn about the Lillys, Kayla knew her mother's reaction would be disastrous. The kind of cold disappointment only noted author, celebrated lecturer, and legendary university president Dr. Gisele Larrington could deliver. It's what had driven Kayla to leave home as soon as she'd turned eighteen. And it was why they rarely spoke anymore.

"Mom, I have to run." Kayla wasn't willing to lie outright. Better to cut the conversation short before it went south.

"You know, phone calls work both ways," her mother said. "You could try calling your own family sometime."

"Mom."

"Your father misses you."

"I know. I'm sorry."

"You apologize, but nothing ever changes." She sighed, and Kayla could almost picture the purse of her lips. "You're just as selfish as ever."

And there it was.

"Mom, I really do need to go." Kayla sighed at the state of her hair. Between the sweat and the humidity, there was no use trying to suppress her curls. She pulled them up into a high ponytail, fussing with the tendrils around her face before giving up. Like her mother always reminded her, they would do whatever they wanted to do.

"At some point, you need to take responsibility and get your life in order," her mother continued to vent. "Not ignoring everything to go watch some concert."

Kayla reapplied her lip gloss and stuck it back in the pouch, zipping it up before tossing it into her bag. The counter was littered with jars of foundation, tubes of lipstick, and various compacts left behind by some of the other performers. She didn't want her stuff getting mixed in.

"You father should have gotten rid of them," her mom said.

The drums. She was talking about Zach's drums.

Kayla knew her own triggers, and she wasn't about to let this one derail her.

"Mom, I can go...*watch* whatever concert I want. I'm twenty-six years old. When will my life become my life?"

It hadn't been easy to leave home, and it wasn't easy to stay away. Kayla loved her parents, but she knew she'd never be enough. She'd never be Zach.

"It *is* your life," her mother said. "Do what you will. You always have."

There was a knock on the tent's flap before a head poked through. "Hi, are you with the Lillys?" a guy asked, his earpiece dangling from a clip on the collar of his bright green Dragonfly Festival crew shirt.

Kayla pushed the button to mute the call, panic squeezing her chest. She nodded. "Yeah."

"We need your group in the press tent, stage left, in five."

She nodded again and had to take a breath before she raised the phone to her ear. Kayla waited for a beat to unmute it, wondering if her mother had caught anything.

"Hello?"

"Sorry, I'm here."

A pause. "I'll let you go."

"Okay. Thanks for calling. It's...good to hear from you." Kayla cringed. God, they were like strangers.

"It would be nice to hear from you too, Katherine," her mother replied. "Take care."

She hung up before Kayla could respond.

"You too." Kayla pocketed her phone before grabbing her bag and heading out.

A few minutes later, she was sitting in the press tent with her bandmates, adrenaline still pumping through her veins. Her phone pinged. Cursing herself for forgetting to mute it, Kayla pulled it out.

MOM: Here are the details for the event next month.

Kayla was looking them over when another text came through.

MOM: Whatever you're doing with your life, keep in mind that it reflects back on your family. Never forget what Little Miss Yolanda always says: Be Your Best Self.

Silencing her phone, she stuck it in her back pocket. Be your best self.

Christ, how she hated that damned mantra.

Little Miss Yolanda was a figment of her mother's imagination. Her perfect child, hand-drawn to her satisfaction, had only a passing resemblance to Kayla. Her very real daughter. Having to deal with her mother's far-reaching shadow and unrealistic expectations was a later issue. This was Kayla's time.

CHAPTER 2.

TYRELL BALDWIN JERKED INTO CONSCIOUSNESS, awakened by the arctic blast of the AC and an incessant sound, like nails driven into his skull. He hadn't set the alarm before he went to bed the night before. He had been back in his childhood home for months, yet Ty still found it difficult to sleep through the night. So, if it wasn't an alarm…

"Whaaaaaat the shit?" he groaned, rolling over in the lumpy twin bed. Blinking, Ty looked for the source of the noise. He realized the piercing, rhythmic tone was coming from the other side of the closed door. It wasn't until the fog of sleep cleared that his brain registered what it might be.

Jolting upright, Ty sniffed the air. The unmistakable smell of something burning raised his alarm bells, and he scrambled out from under the covers. Shoving his head and arms through a T-shirt, he swung open the door and ran in search of the source of the disturbance. In the hallway, the sound was infinitely louder, stabbing through the air like an ice pick to his eardrums.

The door to the bedroom opposite his was open, the room empty. He took the stairs down to the first floor two at a time. His granddad's tiny Nicetown rowhome was no more than eight hundred square feet. It only took a few seconds for him to trace the acrid smell, and the beeping smoke alarm, to the kitchen.

Hunched over the open oven, his grandfather cursed under his breath as he pulled out a baking pan. Wisps of smoke curled out from the charred remains of whatever he'd been cooking. He tossed the tray onto the stovetop with a disgusted grunt.

Ty couldn't make out what it was—or rather, what it was supposed to have been. Small, blackened lumps sat in two rows on the tray's ruined surface. He made a mental note to pick up a new one the next time he went to the discount store.

"Pop-Pop?"

His granddad turned around, a look of surprise on his face before the expression morphed into a frown. "Dammit, I didn't mean to wake you," he said. His shoulders sagged as he turned back to the failed baking experiment. "I wanted to have these ready for you when you woke up."

Ty smiled to himself. In his absence, his granddad had become obsessed with cooking shows. Since moving back home, Ty had spent many evenings on the couch by his side listening to him complain about ingredients and techniques as they binge-watched his favorite series, claiming, "I could make one better than that."

It was such an odd change to come home to, one that hit Ty particularly hard—high on the list of developments he'd missed. And for what?

One false accusation of plagiarism and three years of academic progress had evaporated into the ether—time and money he would never get back. No reputable school would even consider him as a candidate for admission. Ty tried hard not to be bitter about it. He'd been lucky not to have to pay back the scholarships, but the whole experience—with schools, with law enforcement, and with the legal system—had forever changed him. It had changed his relationship with Pop-Pop too. Like Ty, Van Baldwin wore guilt like a coat on his shoulders, even though he had nothing to feel guilty about.

If Ty had listened harder, had heeded his granddad's advice and spoken to the dean before confronting his accuser, things would have turned out very differently.

"What were you making?"

Pop-Pop took off his baking mitts and slapped them down on the counter, defeated. "Croissants." He shook his head ruefully. "I don't know what I did wrong."

Ty walked over and inspected the pan. It was dire. "Hmm. Do you still have the recipe?"

Pop-Pop nodded and turned toward the smart device that sat on the counter on the other side of the sink. He swiveled the tiny screen toward Ty and pointed. "I followed the instructions step-by-step. Watched a few videos, just to be sure." He kept shaking his head as he spoke. "They make it look so easy."

Ty peered over his grandfather's shoulder. He perused the instructions, then looked back at the oven. "I think I know the problem."

Pop-Pop waited expectantly. "Well?"

Ty pointed. "See there? It says to turn the oven down to 375 halfway through baking." He indicated the temperature gauge. "You still have it at 400."

"Damnation," his granddad hissed. "How did I miss that?"

"Easy mistake," Ty said. "Sometimes, it's the small things that trip us up. We can try again." He turned the oven off. There was no need to waste gas. Pop-Pop's pension was modest, and it would be a while before Ty would be able to contribute his fair share, much less pay back everything that had been spent on legal consultations.

Even if his record were to be cleared, Ty's life had been derailed. All his dreams were swept away in a puff of smoke, along with his academic scholarship. The university knew there had been no case, but they still treated him as if he was tainted. He'd accused a legacy student—a girl with the name of her family emblazoned on a wing of the university hospital—of filing a false claim. Of cheating.

Meredith Stanwick had been a friend, he'd thought. They'd even hooked up a few times when studying had turned to teasing and teasing to flirtation. And yet, to cover her own ass, she had falsely accused him of assault.

Assault. *Him!*

It had stung more than he'd ever thought possible.

Ty would never forget the whispers and glares when he'd walked into the dean's office to see what options he had left. As if he had some culpability in the events that led up to his arrest and weeks-long stay in jail. Local news—with the help of a newly elected, overzealous district attorney hell-bent on appearing tough on crime—had sensationalized the story beyond recognition. It didn't matter that Ty had eventually been cleared of any wrongdoing. The stain remained. Even the neighbors gave Ty a wide berth when he walked down his own street. People occasionally recognized him in stores. On the bus. In the library.

Ty wasn't sure he'd ever feel clean again.

"Hey." His granddad's warm hand on his arm pulled him out of his downward spiral. "You look tired. Still having trouble sleeping through the night?"

"Not every night," Ty lied.

Pop-Pop gave his forearm a gentle squeeze. "I'm sure it'll get easier over time."

"I know." Ty hoped so anyway. He hadn't been able to shake the nightmares that woke him up most nights. Dreams of what might have happened to him had the truth not come out.

"You have your whole life ahead of you," his granddad continued. He lowered himself into one of the chairs at their small kitchen table and gestured for Ty to sit.

The wood was chilly against the bare skin of his legs, reminding Ty he wasn't wearing much.

"There's a hoodie on the hook behind you," Pop-Pop said.

Ty reached back and grabbed it, grateful for the warmth of the soft fleece and for his grandfather's caring, attentive nature. "Thanks."

"You'll warm up sitting by the oven." He reached over and flicked the switch on the electric kettle. "We still have some banana bread I made the other day. It'll do for breakfast, don't you think?"

"I sure won't complain." Ty smiled. "But let me get it. I'm too old for you to be serving me."

"Don't expect me to argue," Pop-Pop said, chuckling. Ty could feel his eyes on him as he moved about—getting plates from the cabinet and pulling the banana bread out of the fridge.

"What's up?" he asked as he grabbed a couple of mugs.

"I was just wondering how things are going with the new job."

Ty froze for a moment but forced himself into motion. This was a touchy subject. Ty's grandfather didn't seem to understand how much things had changed for him. Part of that was by design.

"Things are about the same on that front," Ty answered, hoping he didn't sound as frustrated as he actually was. "Now that I have my CDL, the sky's the limit," he said, aiming to sound cheerful.

He opened a cabinet to grab a couple of mugs for their tea, his gaze alighting on the row of prescription bottles there. Ty knew how angry Pop-Pop was about what had happened to him, and he didn't want to add to his stress. The blood pressure pills were one of those new developments that had occurred during the whole ordeal, along with some issues with Pop-Pop's memory. Ty had no doubt that he'd been partly responsible for his granddad's declining health. The stress of the arrest and the back-and-forth with the university weighed heavily on them both.

"Commercial driver's license," Pop-Pop muttered. "I don't understand why your school won't just let you pick up where you left off. You worked so hard to raise that tuition money. It took you a little longer than you wanted before you could start college, but you did so well once you got there."

"I know, but—"

"You could get a teaching job with a bachelor's degree. You only need a few more classes, right?"

"Pop-Pop."

"I know you said they claimed there was a grant freeze, but we hear all the time about the university's endowments and donations, especially from their famous alumni," he added.

"For science," Ty corrected him. "Math and engineering. There isn't much money earmarked for the humanities. Plus, there are people with way better résumés than mine." *And no criminal charges*, Ty thought, gritting his teeth as he cut into the bread with a little more force than necessary.

He placed a thick slice on each plate and turned to put them on the table.

"It's because people don't read anymore. We need people like you to show them what a joy it can be." Sighing, Pop-Pop reached over and opened a drawer, pulling out a spoon before closing it. "You'd be a wonderful teacher, Tyrell. Or a professor, even."

Ty made the tea and brought their mugs to the table before sitting down. "I don't know what to tell you, Pop-Pop. I can't make money appear out of thin air. Going back to school just isn't in the budget. I shouldn't have picked such a useless undergrad degree to begin with."

He grabbed a napkin out of the holder and tossed it down, irritation burning away the remnants of his fatigue. Ty was tired of circling around this particular argument.

Pop-Pop scowled at him. "Don't start with that again. You have a passion, and passion is never wasted when you apply it to your life. To your work. To your relationships."

"Passion can't put food on the table, gas in the car, or…" *medicine in the cabinet*. Ty swallowed those last words. Exhaling a long breath, he handed his granddad the small container of raw sugar they kept on the table and watched as he added precisely one and a half teaspoons to his tea. He forced a smile, chastising himself for getting his granddad worked up so early in the morning. He needed to take a different approach.

"Pop-Pop...look, I wish I had the luxury of studying, of working in my field, but it's not in the cards right now."

"So that's it, then? You're gonna be a truck driver?" His granddad pursed his lips. "Get the milk."

Ty turned in his chair. It was a small kitchen, and he was able to open the fridge without even getting up. He'd dreamed of eventually earning his doctorate, perhaps landing a position at a small, liberal arts college and moving on or near campus. He'd take his grandfather with him. Give him a taste of another kind of life, away from the cracked sidewalks and constant noise of north Philadelphia. Somewhere quiet where he could work on his puzzles, or enjoy bird-watching, or bake in peace.

None of that seemed possible now.

"I'm not going to drive trucks," Ty said, reaching across to pour a dash of milk into his mug. He waited.

"A little more."

Ty obliged and then added a splash to his own. "I could, with the license I have now, but my buddy Aaron is a manager at a touring company. I'll be driving tour buses."

"Like the red buses downtown?"

Ty shrugged. "Maybe. Or charter buses, whatever comes up."

His granddad shook his head mournfully. "Such a waste of your wonderful mind."

"It's not a waste. I'll earn decent money and probably meet some interesting people. It's fine for now."

"My father was a bus driver."

Ty looked up from where he'd been picking at the corners of his banana bread. "What? You never told me that."

"I never really got to know him. He died when I was four. I have vague memories of sitting with him at family gatherings and asking about the buses. How fast they traveled. How many people he met." Pop-Pop took a sip of tea, nostalgia and melancholy coloring his expression. "I was the youngest of the nine kids Calvin and Leola had, and she was nearly forty when I was born."

"How did I not know any of this?"

"My fault," his granddad replied. "After your father passed, I guess I stopped talking about the family. It's just been you and me."

"Against the world," Ty finished, smiling at their personal mantra. He reached across the table and covered his granddad's hand. "If I haven't said it lately, thank you."

"Whatever for?"

"For raising me. For supporting me." He swallowed, his voice growing thick. "For believing in me, believing me when I said I was innocent."

His granddad scoffed, covering Ty's hand with his other one. "There was never a question. I knew there was no way you would cheat on an assignment. And no way in hell would you ever raise your hand to a woman. I've never known you to lose your temper, even when those kids at school used to pick at you. That DA was in a rush to judge you, and that school was in a rush to sweep it all under the rug. You embarrassed them. And if you ask me, you should sue the lot of them."

Ty sat back, removing his hand. "We've talked about this. I'm not interested in being any more of a spectacle than I already have been."

"But they owe you."

"Maybe, but it's not worth it to me," Ty said as he stared down at his tea. "I just want to get back to my life, such as it is."

"And drive buses like your great-grandfather? You could be doing so much more, should be doing so much more. They already robbed you of a year and a half of studies. You shouldn't let them steal what's left." Pop-Pop's hand shook when he lifted it, and Ty watched as his granddad hid it under the table. He couldn't hide the trembling in his voice.

If only Ty could wipe that anxiety away with a wave of his hand.

"According to Aaron, some of the jobs are really interesting. He once traveled on tour with an opera company and said they rehearsed on the bus while he drove." He smiled. "Imagine that. Paganini on tap."

As he'd hoped, Pop-Pop's face lit up. "Now that would be something." He broke off a piece of bread and popped it into his mouth. "So is this banana bread by the way. Try it and tell me what you taste."

Ty obeyed, picking up the whole slice. He bit into it, preparing to fake his delight. An explosion of banana flavor hit his taste buds, along with chocolate, walnuts, and… "Is that maple syrup?"

"I used maple sugar."

"Pop-Pop, this is seriously delicious," Ty said around another mouthful. "You should finish writing that cookbook you're always tinkering with. This is amazing."

"One of these days," he replied, eyeing Ty over the rim of his mug, "we'll both be doing what we should."

CHAPTER 3.

"STOP STEALING MY FALAFEL BALLS." Kayla pulled the paper bag closer and swatted Tiff's hands away.

"Hog," Tiff said, grinning. "They're too dry anyway. I don't know how you eat them without any tzatziki or anything." She wiped her hands on her sweatpants and picked up her bass.

"I like them like this."

"Weirdo."

"Is food all you guys ever talk about?" Toni descended the stairs into the brand-new studio that had been set up in the basement of Lilly's house.

"What else is there?" Tiff asked.

"I don't know," Toni replied. "World events? Sports? My Union are playing your Red Bulls this weekend.

"Sports?" Kayla snorted. "You really are a Philly girl."

"When in Rome." Toni smiled. She lifted her chin toward the drum set. "Is that new?"

Kayla wiped her hands on a towel and picked up her sticks. "Pretty, aren't they? Lilly let me house them here, since this is home base." She loved the way the light picked up the iridescent flecks embedded in the black paint of the drums.

A plexiglass semicircle stood between Kayla and the drum kit and the rest of the room. The basement was long, but the ceiling wasn't very high. The barrier provided a buffer between Kayla and the others so they wouldn't be overwhelmed when she played. As it was, they all wore headphones during rehearsals.

"I love the color," Toni said.

"Right? I can't wait to take them for a spin." The kit had a perfect combination of style and functionality. The configuration, five drums of varying sizes, plus two cymbals, was fairly basic, and Kayla had brought along a couple of roto toms to augment it.

"Where's Seb?" Tiff asked, directing the question at Toni.

"He had some stuff to take care of at the apartment. He'll probably drop by later."

"How goes living together?" Kayla tightened the head of the snare drum. "You haven't killed him yet?"

"Not yet," Toni replied, smiling. "It's been good. Everything moved so fast, you know?"

"But it's okay?" Tiff asked. Toni nodded. "Cool, cool. If he gets out of line, let me know. I'll put the fear of God in him."

Toni laughed. "I'll let you know."

"She's not kidding," Kayla said. "Tiff might be cute and tiny, but don't get it twisted. The girl is a viper."

As if to demonstrate, Tiff slowly raised one leg impressively high into the air, her foot sideways as she balanced on her standing leg. "I have a particular set of skills," she said in a gruff voice.

Kayla and Toni laughed.

"Do I even want to ask?" Lilly appeared on the stairs.

Tiff dropped her foot to the floor. "I was just telling Toni I had her back if Seb ever forgot himself."

"I see." Lilly's cool gaze passed from Tiff to Toni and back. "If Seb ever does anything stupid, he'll have all of us to deal with. I don't think you have anything to worry about, though."

"Damn right," Kayla said. "Hey, what's this I read about Candi's new group?"

"Her *what*?" Tiff asked.

"She has a new band." Kayla dug out her phone and pulled up the article she'd seen earlier that morning. They were months removed from the night Candi had stormed the stage during their industry showcase, drunk and out of control. If there had been any chance of them letting her back into the fold, it evaporated with every sour note she'd played. Every stinging accusation.

Kayla wanted to keep Candi and her media circus firmly in their rearview mirror. But she wasn't naive enough to believe their former bandmate would simply disappear from the scene. Whatever else she was, Candi was a talented guitarist.

"Here. Look." She passed her phone to Lilly, who had walked over to the partition.

Lilly read it silently before handing it back. "We didn't expect her to disappear, did we? I'm glad she's found an outlet for her talent."

"Good luck to whomever gets to work with her," Tiff muttered. "Wait, Zeph is in her band?"

"No kidding?" Toni asked. "Zeph is incredibly talented. They intimidated the hell of me when I auditioned for you guys. I'm honestly surprised they'd want to work with Candi."

Groaning, Tiff rolled her eyes. "YMI probably threw a ton of cash at Zeph to get them to sign on."

"What Candi does now is not our concern," Lilly said as she walked over to the vocal mic. "We have a week to get in shape for this next run of festivals."

"Are you unhappy with the set?" Toni asked.

"No," Lilly quickly replied. "It's okay, but we're going to need more songs."

"Yeah, that's what I figured." Kayla glanced at Toni. "The set will need to change a bit from gig to gig."

Toni nodded. "I've been fiddling with arrangements. I feel like a lot of the songs fall into the same feel and tempo."

"Yeah," Kayla said. "We definitely need to switch things up. How about some newer covers?"

Lilly nodded as she picked up the microphone, rolling it between her hands as she thought. "I liked the Metric track you were tinkering with last week," she said to Toni.

"I'll see if I can come up with a new arrangement," Toni offered.

"What if we gave one of Aurora's songs the indie rock treatment?" Tiff asked. "It would give you a chance to show off that otherworldly head voice of yours."

Lilly's eyes lit up, and Kayla felt the atmosphere shift. They all knew that look on the singer's face.

"All Is Soft Inside"? Lilly asked, turning to each of them.

"You read my mind," Tiff said as she poised her bass on her thigh. "Toni, can you handle the high harmony?"

Toni nodded. "If you're comfortable with the alto."

"You know it."

Kayla donned her headphones and settled behind the drums, her fingers wrapped around the sticks and her legs bouncing in anticipation. She loved moments like this, when the four of them embarked on a new musical journey together.

Over the next three hours, Kayla lost herself in the process. By the time Seb appeared at the edge of the room, she was drenched and grinning.

They'd been working on their first single, "Hurt U." Toni's, Tiff's, and Lilly's voices soared over the outro.

Lilly held up a hand, indicating a gradual fade-out, and the three of them obeyed.

Kayla reduced her volume in small increments, Toni and Tiff following suit until the song came to a natural end.

"That's what I'm talking about!" Seb shouted into the silence that followed. "Gorgeous. Love it."

"God, that was awesome," Toni said, removing her headphones.

"Take that, Candi," Tiff declared. "We fucking rock!"

Seb winced. "I see you heard the news."

Kayla shrugged. "She has her work cut out for her with that new band if she wants to compete with us."

"Seriously," Tiff said. "And good luck to any label that's willing to put up with her toxic ass."

"What even is Fortune Favors Records anyway?" Kayla asked.

"Oh," Seb said, turning to Lilly. "You didn't tell them?"

Lilly closed her eyes and took a breath before looking at him with a subtle shake of her head.

"Tell us what?"

Lilly turned to Kayla. "It's a new label under YMI."

There was stunned silence before Tiff exploded. "What the actual fuck?"

None of them had any love for their label, which had been taken over since they signed with them. The new owners, a set of twins who'd made millions in Silicon Valley, had zero knowledge about the music industry. Kayla doubted either of them had ever touched a musical instrument or stepped behind a microphone.

She didn't mind the quiet twin, Daniel, but his brother... *Argh*! Andre had a sadistic streak and seemed to enjoy pitting Candi against the band whenever he could. She didn't doubt this was all his idea.

"YMI signed Candi's new outfit?" Toni asked. "That's..."

"Their business," Lilly interjected. "Ours is showing everyone what we're capable of, because you can be sure that Candi will take every opportunity she can to outshine us."

They looked around at each other, each wearing a look of determination.

"All right," Seb said, clapping his hands together. "Enough about she who shall not be named. You've got a tight schedule coming up, between shows and interviews."

"Interviews?" Kayla asked.

"Sure," he replied. "There will be journalists at each event, TV, print, and web. Speaking of that, we need to talk about wardrobe."

"Are you telling us what to wear now?" Tiff asked.

"Not me." Seb held his palms up. "YMI. And it's more like a… suggestion."

"The last suggestion they made had us in a fuck-ton of makeup wearing aluminum foil dresses," Kayla said.

"Thank God the photos from that shoot got scrapped," Toni said.

"They'll show up one day to haunt us." Tiff shuddered. "I mean, I look good in anything, but that photographer sucked."

"You'll be working with a totally different stylist," Seb said. "Someone independent."

"And YMI is okay with that?" Kayla asked.

"Jordan made sure they would be." Seb leaned against the wall near Toni, who reached out and squeezed his hand in greeting.

"How did our illustrious attorney manage that?" she asked.

"She's cheaper." Seb winked at her.

Kayla wiped her arms down with a towel and draped it over the back of her neck. She was hungry, thirsty, and tired in all the best ways. "If it gives us more control over how we present ourselves, I'm all for it."

"Agreed." Lilly stood and stretched. "Who's hungry?" Setting her mic back on its stand, she climbed the stairs to the main floor, and the others trailed behind her.

Everything in this house was larger than it had been in Lilly's Brooklyn brownstone. Kayla took a deep breath as they entered the expansive kitchen. The scent of garlic filled the air, making her stomach grumble. She pulled a stool out from the island and sat.

"What did you make for us?"

Lilly was washing her hands at the sink. "It's a lamb stew."

It smelled decadent. Under the garlic, Kayla detected rosemary and thyme.

It reminded her of one of her mother's favorite dishes. Kayla shook off the melancholy that threatened her happy mood. At some point, she'd need to make travel arrangements for her dad's retirement dinner.

Kayla wondered how her mother felt about her father's decision to leave his position at the university. She didn't imagine it had been received well. Being half of an academic power couple was a large part of her mother's identity.

"I picked up the bread you asked for," Seb said. "Want me to slice it?"

"Please." Lilly pulled the butter dish out of the fridge.

"Be right back. I'm going to get changed," Tiff said before bouncing out of the room. During the renovations, she had relocated from Lilly's basement into her own room in the three-bedroom brownstone. What was meant to be a two-week stay had turned into a year. No one questioned it. Tiff wasn't good on her own, and Lilly had a penchant for adopting strays.

Kayla was watching Lilly ladle the stew into five bowls when a thought occurred to her. "Why is YMI so willing to let us choose our own look now? And why did they not insist we record in New York? Something doesn't add up."

"Now that you mention it," Toni said, "I was wondering the same thing. It's hard to believe Andre is suddenly so hands off after what he pulled at the showcase, not to mention everything else."

Kayla cringed, thinking of everything that happened that night. Andre had put them in an untenable position, insisting Candi take the stage when she was barely capable of standing up on her own, much less performing. Were it not for Toni, it could have been the end of the Lillys.

"You think he's up to something?" Kayla asked.

"Do snakes slither?" Seb replied. "He knows the four of you have something to prove, and you know how much he enjoys drama."

"So *that's* why he signed Candi's new group," Kayla said.

"What do you mean by something to prove?" Toni asked Lilly.

Lilly set the bowls on the island and opened a drawer to retrieve some spoons. "To a lot of people, Candi was the only reason anyone paid any attention to us. She told us she was the draw, and that was true to an extent."

"That's bullshit," Kayla said, her blood beginning to boil. "We killed it at DragonFest. You saw the hashtag."

"We did, but Lilly's right," Toni said. "Before I decided to audition for you guys, most of what I'd heard was about Candi. The spoiled rich girl playing at being a rock star. I didn't even know she could play or what you guys sounded like. It was all about her."

Kayla gritted her teeth. "Well, it's not like that anymore."

"No," Seb agreed. "The conversation has been more about your music, and your reputation grows with every performance. That's what you need to focus on over this first leg of the festival circuit."

"We can't control what Candi does or even what Andre and YMI do," Lilly said.

"If we could, I'd shove my bass down Andre's throat." Tiff stormed into the room and tossed her tablet onto the counter, barely missing one of the bowls of stew. "Look at this shit."

The group crowded around as Tiff pushed play on a video. She stood back, her arms folded and her cheeks reddening. Someone had recorded one of Candi's live performances.

Kayla recognized the second guitarist, Zeph, and was surprised that they would work with someone as volatile as Candi. But it took a few moments for Kayla to realize what she was hearing.

"Is that…?"

"Jesus Christ," Seb muttered before turning away.

Lilly stood silent and stone-faced, staring at the screen as they all watched.

"But that's our song," Toni said, and Kayla took a moment to revel in the fact that Toni considered herself a full-fledged member of the band now.

Candi had left an indelible mark on the band, and not in a good way. It had shown a lot of courage and strength of character for Toni to step in and make a space for herself in their family.

And she had. Kayla loved what she'd brought to the table, particularly on their originals.

She couldn't believe Candi would stoop so low as to perform "Hurt U" at her shows.

Lilly and Seb had spent weeks working to perfect the track, tweaking the lyrics, and cultivating the sound until it straddled the line between indie rock anthem and radio-friendly pop song, just as YMI had demanded.

They had all resisted the idea, no one more vocal about it than Candi, until Lilly sang it in full voice for the first time, and they realized it was a perfect way to introduce the band to the world.

Candi had some nerve.

"Lil," Seb said, turning to her after the video ended. "Don't let her get to you."

"I'm not," Lilly replied, her voice as cold as a shard of ice. "Does she have plans to release it?"

Tiff thumbed away at her phone. "I don't think so. Nothing comes up in search."

"That's good." Seb let out a slow breath. "Okay, we can work with this."

"Yeah?" Toni asked.

"Absolutely." He was already pulling out his phone. To Lilly he said, "Jordan will handle it."

Lilly nodded, her shoulders relaxing a tad. Her face had grown red, and the edge of her hairline was almost white. "Eat before the food gets cold."

"Let me call Jordan first," Seb said.

"Eat." Lilly snapped her head toward him. Despite her anger, her voice had grown quieter.

Some kind of silent communication passed between them before Seb sighed. "Yeah, okay." He stuffed his phone away and sat down, pulling a bowl toward him.

The tension in the room eased as the group ate. Bread and butter were passed around in silence.

"What was that Muse song Candi used to love to do?" Tiff asked. "The one where she came up with that killer arrangement."

"Hysteria"? Kayla dipped a piece of bread into her bowl.

"Muse? I don't know a lot of their music," Toni said.

"You'd love this one. It would give Minx quite a workout." Her cheek stuffed with food, Tiff grinned at her.

They glanced around the table at each other, the air suddenly buzzing with a different kind of energy.

"That was Candi's showpiece," Seb said, his lips twitching.

Beside her, Lilly leaned back in her chair and looked at Toni. "Yep." Her lips curved into a subtle smile. "It *was*."

CHAPTER 4.

ON THE SUBWAY, TY KEPT his head down and his eyes on his phone. He scrolled through the local news and told himself he wasn't looking for mentions of his name or what had happened. It had been months since the local news stopped regularly reporting on the alleged scandal, but Ty's background had been presented to the court of public opinion for judgment.

Orphaned at twelve, picked up for shoplifting at thirteen, and raised in a rough part of town. For some, it was enough evidence of his predilection for crime. As if loss and poverty could only lead to one outcome for a young Black man. Nothing was ever mentioned about his scholarships or the 4.0 GPA he maintained through three years.

He forced himself not to look her up. He knew what those articles would say. Daughter of a prominent family, valedictorian, majoring in American Literature. Victim.

It didn't matter that the lie Meredith Stanwick told had nearly cost Ty his freedom. Her last name was enough to make her immune to any backlash.

As far as Ty knew, she had suffered no consequences. He guessed her family had thrown more money at the university to keep things quiet. Maybe they'd agreed to build another library. Cold, hard cash was, after all, the most efficient detergent for dirty laundry.

To avoid temptation, Ty closed the browser. He needed to break this endless spiral of self-pity. Needed to get out of his own head. If nothing else, Pop-Pop deserved better from him. Van deserved a grandson who pulled his own weight and didn't wallow in what could have been. This was Ty's reality now.

After this last letter of rejection from yet another college, it was time to move on.

We're not sure you'd be a good fit for our community.

Ty's granddad was getting older and would need someone to look after him. To provide. Ty hoped working for Aaron would give him the fresh start he needed. A year, maybe less, and then he could figure out his next step. And the next. Until he found a path through life that didn't leave time for him to dwell on what had been taken from him. *Denied* to him.

The subway slowed, stopping at the next stop. Ty jerked when a hand swiped at his back pocket. He looked up just in time to see the man slip through the subway doors, which closed before Ty could even stand up.

He checked his pocket, knowing the weekly subway pass he'd put there would be missing.

"Shit," he muttered to himself, relieved when he remembered his wallet was in his messenger bag, tucked safely between him and the side of the train car.

Across from him, an elderly woman frowned and shook her head.

Lady, I've just been robbed, he wanted to say, but he turned away and leaned his head against the window. The view of the tunnel was black with rhythmic streaks of orange as they sped past the lights.

Life was unfair. No one had learned that lesson better or more efficiently than Ty. He'd pick up a replacement pass on his way home. Another twenty-five dollars he couldn't afford.

As the train came to his stop, Ty stood and popped in his earbuds. Bach's preludes accompanied him on his walk from the station to the depot, temporarily distracting him from his dumb fucking luck.

Ty's luck seemed to change when he received his morning assignment to drive a high school choir to the Academy of Music.

He dropped the kids off and parked the bus in a nearby lot where he listened to the latest audiobook from N. K. Jemisin and munched on some of Pop-Pop's banana bread. It was a nice, quiet afternoon spent doing something he loved, and the time flew by quickly. By the time he deposited the choir and their chaperones back at their school and pulled the bus back into the depot, it was nearly five o'clock.

Ty turned in his log, clocked out, and was eager to head home when Aaron called out. "Tyrell! Just the man I was looking for. Have I got the perfect gig for you!" His boss waved Ty over to his office.

Reluctantly, he went.

"A rock band?" Ty asked for the third time.

Aaron grinned at him from the other side of the desk. "An all-girl rock band. I've never heard of them, but the contract is for three weeks, with the potential for a second leg."

"Three weeks?" Ty knew he sounded like a parrot, but he was trying to picture what traveling with a rock band would look like. Sound like. There would be no Paganini, that much was certain. And three weeks away from his granddad sounded like too much. He hadn't been back with him for that long. "I don't know."

"It pays triple our base."

That was certainly worth considering.

Ty narrowed his eyes. "Why me?" It seemed like a pretty lucrative gig, and the ink on his CDL was barely dry.

Aaron ran his thick fingers through his thinning, sandy-blond hair. Sometimes it was difficult to believe they were only a few years apart. Aaron seemed so much older. So much more grounded than Ty.

"To be honest, you're the only guy I trust to handle this professionally," Aaron said. "There's a strict no-fraternization clause in the contract, plus some other stipulations about drinking. Drugs. That sort of thing."

"Ah, I see." Ty nodded. "Well, I have no real vices, unless you count books. And contrary to what you may have heard, I know how to keep my hands to myself."

"I know that." Aaron pursed his lips. "Look, I realize things are a little rough for you right now. To be honest, I'd take the gig myself, but I can't be away from here for long stretches."

They were practically alone in the depot, only faint sounds from the maintenance bay drifting into the office.

Aaron leaned in. "Not to mention, Ella would have my ass if I were to go out on the road with all those sexy women, clause or no clause." He straightened and winked. "Besides, who knows? The job could turn into something more permanent. Nope, this is for someone without strings."

"I'll need to talk it over with my granddad, but it sounds doable."

"How is your gramps?"

"He's good. He thinks he's Ainsley Harriott, but he's been a lot better lately."

Aaron quirked a brow. "Ainsley, who?"

"He's a British chef. Pop-Pop's been baking up a storm lately, tinkering with the recipes he finds and adding his own twist to them," he said, unable to stop his grin. "It's kinda cool, actually. Keeps him focused."

"That explains why you always bring the tastiest snacks. I can only imagine what he'd make for you to take on the road with you." Aaron rubbed his hands together, smacking his lips.

"I haven't said yes."

"All-girl band," he stage-whispered. "Best gig ever. How could you say no?"

Ty laughed, but that part didn't matter to him. It would be a lot of time. Time away from home, but also time to regroup. Time to study on his own, perhaps. Maybe he could do an online degree.

He pictured the long hours on the road and wondered if he'd be able to listen to some audiobooks. Maybe he'd finally catch up on all he'd missed while he'd been dealing with the mess he'd made.

The money wouldn't hurt either.

Yeah…okay. It might be doable if his grandfather could manage without him for a while. Maybe Ty could ask their neighbor, Miss Peggy, to look in on him from time to time.

"I'll think about it," Ty said.

Aaron sat back in his seat. "Okay, but don't take too long. I'm still tempted to take it myself."

"And Ella?"

Aaron's shoulders slumped. "Ella, right. I do like breathing."

"Having a pulse is also preferable, yes," Ty added, grinning.

"Generally speaking, the whole 'staying alive' thing is a pretty powerful argument for me to keep my ass at home."

———————

The scent of chocolate greeted Ty when he got home, and he smiled, remembering the brown butter pecan cookies his granddad had mentioned. He walked down the hall toward the kitchen and stopped in the doorway.

"Something smells yummy."

His grandfather stood in front of the window over the sink, staring out at the back patio.

"Pop-Pop?" When he didn't answer, Ty walked over to him and laid a hand on his shoulder. "Van?"

Startled, his granddad turned his gaze to Ty's. For a second, he frowned before he seemed to return to himself. "Oh, hey."

Ty scanned his face. "Hi. Are you all right?"

His granddad shrugged off the hand on his shoulder. "I'm fine. I was just thinking up a new recipe."

"I called you three times."

"It's called being lost in thought," Pop-Pop snapped back as he walked away. "I'm not some old man you have to keep asking about his health."

Frowning, Ty followed his granddad across to the fridge. "I never said you were."

"We're low on butter," he said, peering at the shelves. "And I could use another carton of eggs."

"No problem," Ty said, still watching him closely. "I can pop down to the corner and grab them."

Pop-Pop stood up and looked at him, clear-eyed. "Make sure the butter is organic. Non gomo."

"Gomo?" Ty asked.

"You know." His granddad waved a hand. "When they mess with cow hormones. None of that."

"Oh, GMO. Okay." Ty smiled. "Anything else?"

"No. Take twenty dollars out of the pot." He pointed at the coffee can filled with petty cash that they kept in the cabinet next to the toaster.

Ty opened the lid and took out the bills. "Hey, Pop-Pop? I wanted to run something by you."

"Sure, son. What's up?" Crossing his arms, he leaned against the counter and faced Ty. "Something wrong at work?"

"No, nothing like that," Ty replied as he put the can back in place. "If I were to go away for a short while, would you be okay on your own?"

"Why wouldn't I be? I'm perfectly capable of walking to the corner to buy my own butter and eggs."

Ty dragged a hand down his face. He should have known

Pop-Pop would say something like that. "I know you are. I just didn't want you to be...uh..."

Van arched an eyebrow expectantly. Ty was messing this all up.

"Aaron offered me a gig driving a tour bus for three weeks. It's out of town."

His granddad's eyes brightened. "Yeah? I think that would be fantastic."

Surprised, Ty stared at him. "You do?"

"Yes!" Pop-Pop opened a cabinet and pulled down the stack of mixing bowls. "Get out on the road and see something other than these walls and this city."

Ty hadn't considered that. "It would only be for three weeks." He didn't want to think about anything longer, not until he felt assured that Pop-Pop would be okay without him.

"Hell, I could use a break from your documentaries. Why does everything have to be about learning?"

Ty grinned. "Not everything. We watch some sci-fi too."

Pop-Pop grunted. "I'll binge all my reality shows while you're not here."

"You do that." Ty turned for the front door, feeling lighter than he had in months.

"Don't you worry," Pop-Pop said to his retreating back. "I'll catch you up on all the Real Housewives when you get home from your trip."

CHAPTER 5.

KAYLA HANDED THE PORTER A crisp twenty dollar bill and thanked him for helping her with her bags. The train from Newark to Philly to meet the others for the start of the tour had been blessedly empty and had given her a lot of time to think.

The Lillys had spent the last ten days rehearsing and perfecting their sets and were about to embark on their first real tour across the country. Even without Candi, they were gaining more and more fans every day. If their manager had anything to say about it, their names and faces would be plastered across every available screen in the continental United States before the end of the summer. Katherine Yolanda Larrington wasn't sure how to feel about that.

Little Miss Yolanda would certainly disapprove, but Kayla would be living her best life.

Zach would have been thrilled. It should have been him behind the skins, with his own band. Instead, he was gone, and Kayla was living her brother's dream.

But no matter what she called herself or how many times she switched hairstyles and slathered on makeup, her parents would eventually find out what she was up to—who she was now—and her mother was not going to be happy about it.

Kayla resolved to tell her parents the truth when she visited. She just hoped it wouldn't lead to another argument with her mother or, even worse, spoil her dad's celebration.

The interviews Seb mentioned were another problem altogether. If her parents' colleagues discovered their prodigal daughter was a college dropout playing drums in a rock band, it could damage her parents' reputations immeasurably. Kayla could almost see the teaser reel for *that* interview.

"Kay-kay!"

She turned to find Tiff bounding toward her. "Were you on the same train?" Kayla was pulled into a bone-crushing hug that smelled of leather and vanilla. "I wish I had known. We could have sat together."

"We're going to be stuck together in a tin can for three weeks," Kayla replied. "Be grateful for that last bit of solitude. It might get rough."

"Nahhhh," Tiff said, releasing her. "Peas in a pod, that's us."

"And Toni? And Lilly? And sometimes Seb? Probably Jordan at some point? The driver? Do we have roadies?"

Tiff scrunched her nose. "Okay, yeah, it might be tight, but we'll have a blast, I promise. I've been waiting for this my whole life." Her enthusiasm was adorable.

Brushing a lock of hair out of Tiff's eyes, Kayla smiled. "I know. And I'm glad we'll be in this together."

"Because you loooooove me," Tiff singsonged, squeezing her again. "You wanna daaaaaate me."

"Oh my God, I can't breathe, you loon." Laughing, Kayla shoved her away. "You're so weird. But it's true, I do love ya. Don't think I could date you, though."

"Why not? I'm funny, hot, and I play bass like a motherfucker."

"You are, and you do, but no offense, you're a lot of work."

Pouting, Tiff seemed to think about it. "Yeah, okay. True."

Kayla patted her cheek. "Still love ya, though."

Tiff glowed before turning to look around the walkway. "Where is everyone?"

"Seb said to be at the 30th Street entrance by ten, didn't he? To meet the van?"

As she spoke, an enormous black bus pulled around the curb and into the pickup zone, its hydraulics hissing as it rolled to a stop. The door opened, and Toni appeared. "Hey, guys!"

The bus was ten times larger than Kayla had expected. Judging by Tiff's wide-eyed expression, she was just as surprised. The thing looked relatively new and must have cost YMI a pretty penny to rent for them.

Toni hopped down onto the curb. "What do you think?"

"Uh, wow," Kayla replied, squinting up at the sleek exterior.

"Isn't it just so sexy?" Toni bounced on her toes, clapping her hands together with excitement. "Wait 'til you see the inside."

Tiff seemed frozen, staring up at the bus with glassy eyes.

Kayla and Toni exchanged a look.

"Tiff, hon? You okay?" Toni asked in a concerned voice. She laid a hand on Tiff's back.

"Yeah," Tiff said, her voice rough. She cleared her throat. "Yeah, sorry, I... It's just..." She blinked, and a tear slipped down her cheek. "Sometimes, I feel like I'm living someone else's life. Like any minute now, someone's gonna tell me there's been a colossal mistake—that I'm not supposed to be here—and then snatch it all away."

"Oh, honey," Kayla said. She and Toni moved in to hug her at the same time. "You are living the life you were meant to live. We all are now."

Toni leaned back. "Kayla's right. You are such a badass, Tiff."

Tiff gave her a watery smile. "Well, duh. I know that."

Kayla grinned. "Hell yeah." After one last squeeze, the three of them separated.

Tiff swiped at her cheeks, laughing as she shook her head. "Sorry, I didn't mean to get all mushy over a fucking bus."

"Trust me, I get it," Toni said, reaching for one of Tiff's bags.

"I'll take care of those," a voice said from behind her.

"Sebby!" Tiff tackled him, and he laughed as they hugged. "I haven't seen you in forever."

"It's been two days," Seb said, grinning as he lifted her off her feet. "But that's forty-eight hours too long." He set Tiff down and slid an arm around Kayla. "You ready for this?"

Kayla slipped her arm around Seb's waist and rested her head on his shoulder. "As ready as I'll ever be."

He kissed her cheek before letting go. "Excellent, because this is the start of something. I can feel it."

"Me too," Toni echoed.

"Where's Lilly?" Tiff asked.

"Flying back from Oslo," Seb replied, checking his phone. "In fact, she just landed. We'll swing by and grab her before we head out." He walked over to the open door. "Hey, man. Can you help us load up?"

"One second," an unfamiliar voice replied from within.

"Is that our driver?" Kayla picked up her cymbal cases and walked them to the side of the bus. The cargo door swung up as the latch was released.

"Yeah," Seb replied.

"Sorry about that. I had to check in."

Kayla turned as their driver joined them and paused to look him over, surprised. She'd expected him to be old and grizzled, but he definitely was neither of those things.

"Guys, this is Tyrell Baldwin," Seb said. "He's our driver for this leg."

The man standing in front of them was a lot to take in. From the shock of asymmetrical locs atop his head to the tie-dyed T-shirt clinging to his toned upper body to the black utility kilt around his tapered waist, everything about his look was a statement.

Tyrell gave them all a shy smile and a small wave. "Nice to meet you."

Tiff pushed forward, shoving Kayla and Seb out of the way. "Hi, Ty. I'm Tiffany. My pronouns are she and her, and you can call me Tiff." She held out her hand, and they shook. "Nice to meet you too."

"Hey, Tiff. Ty. He/him."

When he turned to lift Kayla's bag into the hold, Tiff turned to her and bit her lip, her eyes wide. Tiff fluttered her hand as if she'd been burned. "So hot," she mouthed silently.

Kayla had to refrain from rolling her eyes. Not that Tiff was wrong—Ty was gorgeous, but it was more than his flawless ebony skin or his dark, expressive eyes. Here was someone comfortable in their own skin, someone who didn't care what others expected of or thought about him.

Or maybe not.

A small frown had formed over Ty's dark eyes, and he stiffened as if bracing himself for a snide comment. Kayla understood that feeling all too well.

Wary eyes met hers, and Kayla realized she was staring. She mentally shook herself and offered what she hoped was a welcoming expression, glad when his shoulders relaxed incrementally.

"Sorry, I'm Kayla," she said, offering her hand. "She and her pronouns for me too. Cool earring." She pointed to his left ear.

The earring was in the shape of a pen. Ty lifted a hand to it as if he'd forgotten it was there.

"Oh, thanks." He nodded, his expression friendly and open. His hand was surprisingly soft when she shook it, his fingers long, and his grip firm but gentle. Her gaze snagged on the clear, iridescent polish that lacquered his nails. She'd almost missed that.

Ty's gaze swept over her.

Kayla could practically feel his assessment. Knowing they'd be on the road most of the day, she'd thrown on her most comfortable pair of black jeans. She also wore one of her favorite Blondie tees, and her favorite pair of Chuck Taylors, black leather. The Chucks had been a gift from Zach and served as a kind of talisman when she embarked on new adventures.

As he hefted another bag into the cargo area, Ty pointed his chin at her feet. "Twins."

"Huh?"

He lifted his foot, wiggling it to show an almost identical shoe to hers, though considerably less worn in.

Kayla smiled.

"Well, look at that," Tiff said. "You made a friend."

When he looked up at her again, Ty's grin had transformed his entire face. "I practically live in them."

"Same," she replied. Pointing at his earring she asked, "Do you write?"

Ty lifted one shoulder. "I dabble."

"Are you a songwriter?" Tiff asked.

"Nah, just awful poetry," he replied, grinning.

Tiff laughed. "They're often the same thing."

"Do you have a favorite?" She heard herself ask him.

"A favorite poem?" His brows lifted with surprise. "That's a tough one. Lately, it's been 'A Dream Within a Dream' by—"

"Edgar Allan Poe," she finished for him. "Yet if hope has flown away, in a night or in a day—"

"In a vision or in none…"

"Is it therefore the less gone?" His smile broadened as he looked at her. "You're a fan?"

"Great," Tiff said. "Now we have *two* bookworms."

Laughing, Kayla broke away from Ty's glittering gaze and shoved the bassist toward the bus.

"How about we put the instrument cases toward the rear and the suitcases in front?" Seb asked as he inspected the cargo area.

There were already a few bags in there. His and Toni's, Kayla guessed. And Ty's, presumably.

Her gaze returned to him, and she was surprised to find him watching her.

Ty blinked and then sprung into motion. "Yep. Sounds good."

Kayla, Tiff, and Toni helped load the bay, and soon they were done.

"We have plenty of room for the rest of our gear," Seb said. "Not that we're taking much. The backlines are pretty intense at these festivals, as you saw at Dragonfly." He followed Toni up the steps into the bus. "This is the big league, ladies. I hope you're prepared."

"Holy shit," Tiff whispered as she reached the top of the steps. "This is such a vibe!"

Kayla followed her, and she had to agree. Holy. Shit.

It was a luxury home on wheels, complete with black leather sofas, gleaming granite countertops, and stainless-steel appliances. "Wow."

"Right?" Toni said, smiling wide. "There's a shower. A freaking shower! I don't know what I expected when Seb said we were getting a tour bus, but it sure wasn't this."

"There are four bunks and a bedroom in the back," Seb said.

"Can we afford this?" Kayla asked. This was an entire flight of steps up from the rented white vans they'd used on their mini-tours.

"Jordan and I pooled the label's budget with some resources we had," Seb said. "Don't worry about it. You guys are leveling up, and we want you to look the part."

"Rock on," Tiff said. "Who gets the bedroom?"

Seb and Toni shared a glance. "Well...I was thinking we'd take it," he said sheepishly.

Toni shoved her hands into the back pockets of her jeans. "It's just that we're the only couple, right? And we wouldn't want to subject you guys to, um...I mean, we..."

Tiff burst out laughing. "Oh my God! Yes, please take the room with the door. I do not want you banging on the bunk above my head."

Toni covered her face, her shoulders shaking with laughter.

Seb hugged her to him, laughing as well. "Subtle, Tiff."

"Oh, please. We're all adults here," she said, inspecting the contents of the fridge. "You *are* the only ones paired up, and it's only right that you get the room." Waving her hand in front of them as if offering a blessing, she spoke in a solemn tone. "Go forth and fuck in peace."

"You're such a heathen," Seb said, grinning.

"I have never claimed otherwise." Tiff spread out her arms and fell back onto one of the love seats that sat under the windows. "Just remember, if *my* bunk's a-rockin', don't come a-knockin'."

Kayla rolled her eyes. "Pick your bunk so I can choose the one farthest from you. I do not want to hear that."

Tiff ran the tip of her tongue across her top teeth. "Yeah you do."

"Excuse me," Ty said.

Kayla jumped at the sound of his voice. She stepped toward the others before turning to face him. Not everyone could handle their sense of humor. She hoped he would be cool about it.

"Sorry to interrupt, but they're asking us to move." Ty nodded toward the train station. Through the window, Kayla spied a scowling security guard. "Are we waiting for anyone else?"

"Nope." Seb threw himself onto one of the benches and propped his feet up on the table. "We're good."

Ty gave the group one last look before nodding and heading to the front of the bus. Kayla watched him go, curious about the new addition to their little crew.

"You're drooling," Tiff whispered in her ear.

Kayla waved her off. "I'm not."

She was intrigued, nothing more. Ty was attractive, but physical attraction had little to do with it. Kayla thought she saw something of herself in Tyrell and wondered if he'd seen something in her too. Considering the fact that they were all about to spend to the better part of a month rolling around in a metal box together, Kayla figured she had time to find out.

She picked up her oversized hobo bag, which contained most of her personal items, and headed back to check out the sleeping area.

"Can't say I blame you," Tiff said, following her. "He is yummy."

Kayla couldn't lie. "I didn't expect our driver to be so..."

"Hot?" Tiff provided.

"Young," Kayla finished, shaking her head. "I hope he can handle this monster."

"You mean you hope you can handle *his* monster." Tiff's smile was all teeth. She threw up her hands when Kayla glared at her. "Heathen. Remember?"

"Hands off the crew, *remember*?"

Tiff groaned. "Oh. Right. Like that's ever stopped anyone." She flicked a thumb toward Seb and Toni, cozied up at one of the banquettes, wholly engrossed in one another. It was sweet.

"Well, it's not happening again on my account."

"Sure, whatever you say," Tiff said. "I'll be sure to pick a top bunk." She winked at Kayla. "That way, I can enjoy the view."

CHAPTER 6.

"HOW'S IT GOING? HAVE YOU landed yourself a rock star yet?" When Ty agreed to take the Lillys on tour, Aaron's teasing had been relentless. The trend appeared to be continuing.

"You know, for a bunch of musicians, they're a pretty quiet group." Ty hadn't known what to expect from them, but their easy comradery was a pleasant surprise. He'd watched a couple of documentaries in preparation. Very few were about all-female bands, and almost all of them told tales of drug abuse, infighting, and general debauchery. "So far, so good. It's only been a couple of days."

"Are they a decent band? I'm more of a classic rock guy myself. Didn't get a chance to check them out," Aaron said.

"I haven't really heard them."

"Why not? Please tell me you're not being antisocial, Ty."

"I'm not antisocial. I just have things to do." He'd taken the job because of all the downtime, and he planned to make effective use of it.

"Sometimes I don't get you at all."

Their first stop had been an outdoor event in a small college town, and Ty had opted to stay on the bus rather than attend the concert. Seb and Toni had given Ty an odd look as he'd settled in the banquette with his book but hadn't said anything as they disembarked.

"I'll have plenty of opportunities to watch them play," Ty said. "It's a long trip."

"Yeah, yeah," Aaron grumbled. "How's the rig holding up?"

"She's fine, yeah. Drives like a dream."

"She should, for the amount of cash she cost me."

"Money well spent." Ty ran a finger along the leather trim of the dash. "The bunks are surprisingly roomy. The band and their manager seem pretty comfortable too."

"I'm glad." Aaron lowered his voice. "You're getting along with the client, though? No issues?"

"None at all, not that I know of anyway." Ty frowned. "Have they complained to you?"

"Nope, not a peep," Aaron assured him. "I was only asking."

Ty relaxed in the driver's seat. Growing up, he hadn't spent much time around women and hadn't made many friends at college of any gender. People tended to find Ty awkward. "Weird" was a descriptor that had followed him around for as long as he could remember. Too many piercings, too many books, too much jewelry, and too many people asking, *"Dude, is that a skirt?"*

"Hey, listen," Aaron said. "Thanks again for taking this job. I know you were reluctant, but you're actually doing me a solid."

"No, man. Thank *you*. I needed this." The money would make a nice foundation for the nest egg Ty needed to rebuild his life.

"Tours like these are tough to land," Aaron continued. "It's a new area for me, and the competition is tight. The reason why I wanted you for this is because I know you'll do an amazing job. You'll reflect positively on me, and that will get me on the radar for more gigs like this. So thank you."

Ty swallowed past the lump in his throat. He hadn't considered how much trust Aaron had placed in him. "I'll make sure nothing goes wrong."

"Also, you look like a damned rock star yourself," Aaron said, laughing. "I figured you'd fit right in."

Ty chuckled. "Don't hate me because I have more style than you."

None of the Lillys crew had batted an eye at Ty's unruly hair or the utility kilts he practically lived in, which were comfortable and convenient for long drives.

"Yeah, well, I hope you're getting along with everyone. I mean, you know, actually engaging in conversation."

"Everything is cordial and professional," Ty replied.

"Well, that sounds hella boring."

In fact, the person who'd engaged with Ty the most so far was Tiff, who flirted with him relentlessly. She was pretty cool but not his type. Ty could only handle Tiff's big personality in small doses.

Seb was pleasant enough, and Ty enjoyed chatting with him and Toni when they stopped for a meal. Their combined knowledge of music history impressed him.

Lilly herself was an enigma, and Kayla... Well, she was a different story altogether. Beautiful, funny, and wholly individual. Ty found his attention gravitating toward her more often than it should.

Unlike the others, there was a carefulness about her when he was around. Like she was trying to suss him out. He felt her eyes on him, and when he caught her staring, she would smile. But they hadn't talked as much as he would like. Ty found he wanted to know her, how she'd gotten into Poe and what else they might have in common besides their taste in footwear.

On the other end, Aaron yawned. "All right, dude, I'll let you be. Keep me posted."

"Will do."

"And try to have some fun out there," Aaron said, chuckling. "The band may be off-limits, but there are bound to be groupies. Live a little."

Ty disconnected the call. He wasn't in the market for a hookup. Even if he were, the contract he'd signed for this gig was enough of a deterrent.

He gripped the steering wheel tighter, cursing himself for the errant thought. He'd made that mistake with Meredith, and look at where it had gotten him.

The road stretched out in an endless ribbon of black, and they had hours to go before the next rest stop. Navigating to the app on his phone, Ty hit play on the audiobook he'd been listening to and settled in for the rest of the drive.

"*Chapter thirteen*," the narrator said in her mellifluous tone.

"What are you listening to?"

Ty snatched out his earbud and tossed it into the cupholder. "Sorry, I probably shouldn't do that while driving."

"You only had one of them in, right?" Kayla grabbed on to the pole next to the door and leaned forward into Ty's peripheral vision.

The urge to turn and look at her was almost overwhelming, but he kept his eyes forward and his hands at ten and two.

"Of course. I need to be able to hear any sirens or if one of you calls me on the intercom." He pointed at the dash. This bus had way more features than his granddad's ten-year-old Camry or even the red double-decker he'd driven the week before.

Kayla laughed softly. "No need to be such a stickler for the rules, Tyrell."

He liked the way she said his name, but… "Ty," he said. "You can call me Ty if you want."

"Okay, Ty." She moved forward and sat on the dash, her feet dangling over the stairwell.

Ty's heart jumped in his throat. "That's not the safest place to sit, and I'm pretty sure it's illegal."

"I won't tell if you don't," she said, bracing one foot against the half wall opposite her. She grabbed on to the handrail. "There. I'm secured."

"Better, but still."

Kayla glanced over her shoulder. "There's, like, nothing out there but asphalt and corn. I'll be fine. Warn me if you see a cow on the road."

Ty laughed. "Okay, will do." He kept his eyes forward, but her presence was palpable as she stared out the window alongside him.

"I couldn't live here," she said.

They were heading west, somewhere near the Ohio-Indiana border, and Ty had to agree. Though he might enjoy the peace and quiet and fresh air, Ty needed the amenities of a city, or at least those of a large town.

"Me neither," he said.

"Are you from Philly?"

"Born and raised," he answered. "You?"

"No, I'm from New…" She seemed to hesitate. "I was born in Atlanta."

"I thought I heard a touch of an accent," Ty said. He heard her shift.

"Yeah? And I've tried so hard to get rid of it," she said in an exaggerated southern drawl that had him smiling.

"It's barely detectable."

"There goes any hope of becoming an actress, I guess."

Ty loved this back-and-forth. He chanced a look at her. Took in the creamy, light brown skin of her exposed arms and the riot of red curls atop her head. In the shadows of the bus, he couldn't see the freckles that dotted her nose and cheeks, but he'd noticed them. He'd noticed a lot about her, not the least of which was the way she always had a pair of drumsticks in her hands. Like now.

Kayla twirled and tapped in graceful movements as if playing some unheard rhythm. The subtle click of wood against her denim-clad thigh created its own unique music, hands moving in synchronized harmony.

Ty turned back to the road. He could still see the white of her smile in his periphery.

"You never answered my question," she said.

"I'm listening to the second book in the Earthsinger Chronicles."

"L. Penelope?" She smiled. "I adore that series."

Ty wasn't surprised. "Are you a book person?"

"I am. Grew up reading the classics, of course—Langston, Morrison, Walker," she replied, and Ty wondered if it was possible to have a crush on someone's brain. "And Baldwin. Any relation?"

He smiled. "Not that I'm aware of, no."

"I also devoured all of Shakespeare," Kayla continued. "Poe, Anne Rice, L. A. Banks, Donna Tartt."

"That's a wide range."

"I was a precocious child."

"Same," he said, wishing he could pull over and give her his full attention. She was pushing every single one of his literary buttons. "The Vampire Huntress series changed my life."

"I have a signed copy of *Minion*," she said, blowing his fucking mind.

"Are you serious?" Ty glanced at her, his gaze caught in her sparkling eyes. Okay, not the greatest idea. He forced his eyes back to the road. "How?"

"It was a gift from my brother for my thirteenth birthday." There was a hint of melancholy in her voice.

"That's a good brother," Ty said.

"When we were kids, I wanted to open my own bookstore. He was so supportive. He even put together a business plan and everything."

"Wow," Ty said, genuinely impressed. "Was it a sound plan?"

"God no," Kayla replied, laughing. "He basically had me selling all of the books I owned. Which I would *never*."

"As if."

"It's nice to have another book nerd on this trip." Kayla clutched the drumsticks in both hands and laid them across her thighs.

Silence fell between them. This was officially the longest conversation they'd had, and Ty found he didn't want it to end. He
struggled for something to say before the silence could stretch on
too long, but Kayla beat him to it.

"Do you have siblings?"

"No." Ty shook his head. "It's just my grandpop and me."

"Oh."

She didn't want to pry, he could tell. But there was so much
wrapped up in that one syllable—pity, curiosity, regret for having
brought it up. Ty hated the tone people adopted when he talked
about his family. He could only imagine what she'd say, how she'd
sound, if she knew the whole story. Knew how much he'd lost. How
he'd spent the better part of the last year trying to clear his name
only to find himself blacklisted at every turn.

More pity. Probably some apprehension too, that niggling
doubt that maybe he'd gotten away with something and deserved
to be punished for it.

Better not to say anything more.

Ty nodded toward a sign at the side of the road as they
approached. "There's a service area coming up. Do we need to
stop?"

Kayla looked over her shoulder. "Yeah, we need provisions. Tiff
has already eaten through her stash."

He grinned. "All right."

Kayla stood. "How long until we get there?"

"About ten miles."

"I'll let them know," she said. "And I'll let you get back to your
book. It's a good one."

A short while later, Ty pulled the bus into a space inside the
rest area parking lot. He shut down the engine and stretched before
opening the door. Soon, voices moved in his direction as his passen-
gers all made their way to the front.

Lilly was the first to appear. She was definitely the most reserved of the bunch, and she only tilted her head at him before descending the steps. The singer was tall—as tall as him—pale and slim with hair so light blond it was almost white.

Toni and Seb followed. Seb was an inch or two taller than Ty with olive skin, dark, wavy hair, and remarkable hazel eyes. Toni was what his granddad would call a *brick house*. She was average height and all curves, with shoulder-length black hair—the ends dipped in purple. Her skin was medium brown, and her eyes a warm chocolate. They always seemed to seek out her boyfriend who, in turn, was always by her side when not attending to his duties. They made an attractive couple, and Ty wondered if they'd met on the job.

"I hope they have Peanut Chews," Tiff said as she exited the bus. "I'm kicking myself for not getting the party bag." Her long, black hair was tied up into a messy bun that was nearly the size of her head. She was the smallest of the bunch but had the biggest personality by far.

"How do you still have teeth?" Kayla asked, following her out. She turned and looked up at Ty. "Not coming?"

He blinked. "Uh, no, I have everything I need. I'll stay with the bus."

She shrugged. "Okay. If I see anything interesting, I'll let you know."

"You do that."

After they left, Ty did a quick sweep of the exterior, checking the air pressure on the tires and the latch on the cargo hold. Everything seemed in order, so he stepped back inside, taking the opportunity to use the restroom.

When he got back to his seat, he spotted Kayla walking toward the bus. He opened the door. "Forget your wallet?" She tossed a bag up at him, and he caught it in midair. "What's this?" Ty reached in and pulled out a slim, leatherbound notebook.

"For your collection," she said, grinning.

"What makes you think I have a collection?"

"If you don't, you can start one," she said, walking backward. "Consider it an upgrade from those yellow notepads I've seen you writing on."

Ty's jaw dropped. He hadn't known that she'd been watching him so closely. Before he could say anything, though, she was already walking back toward the rest station.

He watched her go for a moment before shaking his head and determinedly turning away. Kayla was a distraction. She looked at Ty as if she *got* him, got his whole vibe. And Ty thought he got hers. New people made him jumpy, but not Kayla. Ty closed the door and, despite himself, watched her cross the parking lot. Before she walked through the automatic doors, Kayla swung back to the bus, cocked her head with a half smile, and then turned and disappeared inside.

He reminded himself—hands curling around her unexpected gift—not to get too close, not to open himself up to new wounds when the old ones hadn't quite healed.

Cordial and professional. That's how it had to be.

CHAPTER 7.

THE CURSE OF FESTIVAL RAIN that started in upstate New York continued to follow the band, and Kayla was beginning to wonder if any of the dates left on the tour would afford them some sun. At least they had rocked the house. Again.

The press tent was larger this time around, more organized, and Kayla took a seat behind Tiff and Toni. The legs of her folding chair sank into the uneven grass, lilting her to one side. Kayla rested a foot against the back of Tiff's chair to steady herself.

Tiff turned, giving her a pointed look.

"What?"

The bassist nodded down at Kayla's knee, which shook. She hadn't even realized she'd been bouncing it and—in turn—shaking Tiff's chair.

"Sorry." Kayla dropped her foot to the grass and pulled her drumsticks out of her bag.

Tiff shook her head but grinned before turning back to face the rows of reporters.

Most barely paid them any attention, but a few were snapping pics and jotting down notes.

Kayla quietly tapped a rapid military beat against her shin. Her fear of being recognized grew with every junket they did. And it was ridiculous. The chance of a music journo knowing anything about

Little Miss Yolanda was miniscule. She was living in a completely different world from those children's books. Light years away from her mother's career.

Still, Kayla slipped on her sunglasses and said as little as possible. Or tried to.

"Every band has that one person who holds it all together," one of the reporters asked. "Who is it for you ladies?"

"It sure ain't me," Tiff replied, laughing.

"That would probably be Kayla," Toni said. Kayla involuntarily sat up. "She's got that...I dunno...that thing you hear about in rock documentaries. That special sauce that no one's ever been able to figure out that elevates bands to the next level."

"I think you all have that," the interviewer said.

"Maybe," Tiff replied. "But Toni's right. Lilly is the glue that keeps our shit together but Kayla... She's, like, the polish. The shine. It's magic, what she does with those sticks."

"Guys, c'mon." Kayla felt her face heat. "I bang on skins, that's all." She knew she was a valued part of the Lillys, but this was too much. And she didn't really want or need the attention.

"Kayla has the kind of musicality that only the best, the rarest of drummers possess," Lilly said, shocking her. Kayla turned to look at their leader. "When I'm singing, especially onstage, I can tell that Kayla is listening. Not only to my voice but to my words. She listens and she answers. It's, what do you call it?"

"Call-and-response," Tiff offered.

"Yes! That's it. Call-and-response between vocals and drums," Lilly said, nodding. "That's rare in my experience."

"Does that sound accurate, Kayla?" the reporter asked, craning his neck to try and see her behind Toni and Tiff.

Tiff shifted her chair a bit and practically pulled Kayla up beside her.

Great.

"Everything I play has been played before," Kayla finally answered. Praise made her uncomfortable, and she wasn't a fan of pedestals. Too far to fall. "There are no new rhythms; I just avoid the backbeat as much as possible, so it sounds new."

"Even if that were true," Toni cut in to say, "and I'm not convinced it is, it takes an enormous amount of talent and skill to find unique ways to use those rhythms, to reconfigure them into something new. Or even to work around them."

"And that's what you do, Kayla," Lilly finished for her.

Tiff nodded. "Don't sell yourself short."

An awkward laugh bubbled up from her throat. "Who knew I had all of that going on? I just try to give the band what they need," Kayla said, trying for a smile. "No pressure."

Tiff nudged her shoulder. "Don't be so shy."

Shyness had nothing to do with it.

"How's it been without Candi in the picture?" a woman asked, her voice carrying over the murmur of the crowd. The noise level dimmed as her question registered.

Lilly stiffened. To the side of the tent, Kayla saw Seb push to his feet.

"It was an adjustment at first," Tiff replied, choosing her words carefully. "But now it's like Toni's been here forever." Brushing her dark hair back from her forehead, she gave their guitarist a dimpled smile. "I can't imagine the Lillys without her."

Relief and gratitude filled Toni's expression. "Aww, thanks."

"It's funny, you said something similar about Candi last year," the reporter snarked. "What's the real truth?"

"When you're in any relationship, you find it hard to picture your life without the other person or people," Lilly replied, her voice steady and cool. "Even when things...aren't good. It's only when the circumstances change, when you're no longer bound, that you see the truth of it."

"So you don't have any hard feelings about Candi starting her own band?" This was from a guy in the back.

"Why would we?" Kayla heard herself reply.

Laughing lightly, Tiff said, "You guys are really trying to turn this into reality TV. I'm glad Candi has found a new gig. She's a fucking awesome guitarist, and I'm sure they'll do well."

Kayla had to admire the diplomacy. A few hours ago, Tiff had called Candi a string of names she blushed to remember.

"Rumor has it, Sugar Habit is going to do a few stadium dates with Noise Factory. Not worried about the competition?" the first reporter asked. Kayla detected a disturbing hint of glee in her voice, like she was ready to pounce on any hint of discord.

Kayla cursed internally. She hadn't heard that news and was sure the others hadn't either. Noise Factory had blown up over the last year, and any show with them would grow a band's audience exponentially. She seethed, wondering why YMI would hand an opportunity like that to an act with no proven record, though Kayla suspected she knew the answer to that.

Hinting at beef between the Lillys and Candi's new group could only help YMI's bottom line. Never mind how much it might hinder each group's success.

"There's no competition," Toni said. "I'm grateful to be here, and we all wish Candi well with Sugar Habit."

"End of story," Tiff added tightly.

Thankfully, the focus shifted to another act, and when they were finally done, Kayla led the group out of the tent.

"Fucking YMI," Tiff swore when they were clear of the reporter pool.

"Opening for Noise Factory would have really taken us to the next level," Seb agreed, falling in step as they walked along. "Don't sweat it. Jordan and I will come up with something even better."

"What did Jordan say about 'Hurt U'?"

"Let's talk about that somewhere else."

A guy from the local crew ran over and held a golf umbrella over their heads. "We can take you back to your bus unless you want to go to the hospitality tent."

"Bus, thank you," Lilly replied, joining them on the soggy grass. "I'd like to change." She sounded tired, and Kayla couldn't blame her. Just when they thought they'd put Candi and all of her drama behind them, it reared its ugly pink head again.

A few more roadies jogged over with umbrellas, and the four of them handed off their instruments before making their way to the Lillys' temporary home.

The door swung open as they arrived, and Kayla followed Lilly up the steps into the blessedly dry interior of the bus. She swept a hand over her damp forehead as the others filed in, and the door closed behind them. They continued toward the back of the coach, but Kayla lingered, her attention catching on Ty as he sat behind the wheel. His legs were folded under him, and he was reading, of course. But it was the presence of a pair of honest-to-goodness, wire-rimmed glasses perched on his nose that made a smile break out unbidden.

"Hey," she said, hopping up onto the dash. Ty didn't respond, but that was normal. She knew what it was like to be completely engrossed in a story. Kayla nudged his armrest with the tip of her Converse shoes.

Ty didn't look up from the book in his hands, but Kayla could see a grin tugging at the corner of his mouth. He held up his index finger in the universal sign for "wait a sec." After a moment, he finally pulled one of the earbuds from his ear. The faint sound of strings spilled into the air.

"Do any scribbling in your notebook today?" Kayla asked.

"A little. Thanks again for that." Ty picked up a bookmark he'd set on the dash and slipped it into the paperback.

It was so old-fashioned, it made Kayla smile. "That's so cute."

When he raised his quizzical eyes to meet hers, the warmth of kinship blossomed in her belly.

"Cute?" He squinted up at her before he seemed to remember he was wearing his glasses and removed them.

She nodded at his hands. "That you use bookmarks."

"Cute." Ty set the book down and leaned back in the driver's seat, folding his hands in his lap as if he were a parent or a teacher, and she was a child spouting nonsense he'd chosen to indulge. "That's an interesting choice of words. Do you not use them? Bookmarks?"

"Nope," Kayla replied. "Not since, maybe, grade school."

Ty crossed his arms. He had nice arms. He had nice...well, everything, but Kayla particularly enjoyed his arms, which were on full display in the black tank top he wore. "Don't tell me you're one of those heathens who dog-ears pages or, worse, folds them in half to keep your place."

Kayla held up a hand. "Guilty."

"Ugh." Ty shuddered, and Kayla laughed.

"Sorry to disappoint you."

He shook his head. "You should have more respect for the printed word than that."

She stretched her legs over the stairwell and rested her feet on the railing. "I have complete and utter respect for the written word, printed or otherwise, but books are made to be loved and enjoyed, not revered. Certainly not to be treated as precious commodities."

Something passed behind Ty's dark brown eyes before he looked away. "Not everyone gets such easy access to them."

Feeling like she'd said something wrong, Kayla straightened. "Yeah, of course. I know. I just meant..."

"I know what you mean." Ty looked up at her with a half smile. "And you're not wrong. Sorry."

"No sorry needed," Kayla said with a smile. "So, what are you reading, now?"

He picked up the book and handed it to her. "It's Octavia Butler—*Bloodchild*."

Kayla frowned, taking it from him. "I'm not familiar with that one."

Ty's eyes brightened. "It's incredible. If you like short stories, these are among my favorites. They're sci-fi, and she touches on everything from oppression to the female experience to caste systems. Racism, of course, but also...just...humanity and what it might look like in a universe with superior species."

Kayla turned the paperback over in her hands. "It looks interesting. Love the cover." She handed it back. "But the burning question is: Is it more interesting than catching our set?" she asked, pursing her lips. Kayla swore she could see a blush form on Ty's dark cheeks. He was kind of adorable.

"Shit..." he exhaled. "I... Sorry, I got caught up in..." He held up the book.

Kayla smiled at him. "I'm teasing you. You're not, like, obligated to watch us play."

"I like watching you play," he replied casually.

Kayla felt her cheeks heat. "You managed to catch a set?"

He shook his head. "No, but I watch you practice in the back sometimes. When we're not moving," he added. "And I've seen some of your stuff online. Amazing stage presence. Mesmerizing, really." Ty cut a look her way that made her a tad breathless.

Kayla didn't think Ty was flirting with her, not on purpose. But he was so freaking magnetic, she couldn't stand it.

Wait, was she flirting with *him*?

That needed to stop. It wasn't like her to be this chatty with someone she barely knew, but she couldn't seem to help herself around him. She liked their rapport. Conversation was harmless. Right? All they had done was chat about books.

"How was the crowd?" Ty asked, nodding toward the festival grounds.

"They were on fire." Kayla smiled at the memory of all those raised voices and arms. "I think we picked up some new fans."

Ty beamed with genuine pleasure. "Wow, I'm so glad for you. And you had fun?"

"The most fun."

"Even better," he said, the sentiment in his tone warming her. Ty had such a soothing voice. Like hot chocolate on a wintry night.

"Hey, Kayla?" Toni walked to the front of the bus, a towel wrapped around her shoulders. She handed one to Kayla. "We're gonna get our grub on in the hospitality tent, mingle with some of the other acts. You coming?"

Kayla wiped the rainwater from her arms, noticing the chill on her skin for the first time. "I need to shower before I'm presentable."

"Duh," Toni said. "Same. But after?"

"Sure, count me in." She turned to Ty. "You're welcome to tag along with us, you know."

"Yeah, no reason to stay cooped up in here," Toni added. "You have your own credentials, right?"

"Uh, yeah." Ty seemed reluctant to leave the bus, and Kayla wondered if he felt excluded. Or worse, unwelcome. "Thanks," he said. "I'm all right."

Toni shrugged and turned to go. "Lilly's in the shower, but she should be out soon," she said over her shoulder. "We better go claim our spot in line before Tiff, or we'll have to wait all night to eat."

Kayla turned toward the back of the bus. She glanced back at Ty, who had pulled a thermos from somewhere in his secret stash and was pouring himself a cup of brown liquid. Tea, if she had to guess. With his glasses, his quiet demeanor, and the ever-present book in his hand, the only thing missing from his English professor persona was a pipe and a smoking jacket. He reminded her of some of the lecturers at school in California.

"I hope you don't feel like you have to stay here," Kayla said to him. "Have to stay out of our way, I mean. You're part of the crew. Hell, you *are* the crew."

"I like to keep to myself," Ty replied as he screwed the top back onto his thermos and stuck it in a pocket on the door.

"Okay," Kayla said, feeling a little chastised. "I won't keep bugging you, then."

Ty's head whipped up. "You don't. Bug me, I mean." He looked at her, his expression caught somewhere between hope and panic. "I like talking to you."

Kayla exhaled, relief flooding her unexpectedly. "Cool."

"Cool," he echoed, a ghost of a smile on his lips.

CHAPTER 8.

KAYLA AND THE OTHERS HAD run back to the bus to dry off and change, only to get drenched all over again by the time they made it to hospitality. Fortunately, everyone there was equally wilted. Lilly led them to a low table in one corner of the tent, and the four women settled onto the poufs that surrounded it.

"I'm gonna see who's here." Seb kissed the top of Toni's head before wandering off.

"Ah, the glamourous life," Tiff said as she crouched down on the tiny cushion, nearly toppling over. She held out her arms for balance and righted herself, laughing. "Such luxury. There's mud everywhere."

"I've been in worse," a voice chimed in. Kayla turned to find a guy grinning at them.

Dressed in a seventies-style jumpsuit, with the feathered hair to match, he raised his bottle of Corona in salute. "Killer set, by the way. What's your band's name again?"

"We're the Lillys," Tiff supplied. "Hey, you're with Black Purple. Bassist, right?"

"Guilty as charged," he replied, twisting around on his own pouf to face them.

Tiff made room for him. "You guys were great. Really innovative."

"Thanks," he said. "I'm Ronan."

"Tiff." She accepted his outstretched hand and shook it.

"Bass too, right?" Ronan's eyes twinkled as his gaze roamed over Tiff. He was all Southern California tan, with sun-streaked blond hair and ocean-blue eyes. Totally Tiffany's type—or one of them.

Kayla caught Lilly's eye a little behind him, and she flicked her eyebrows in acknowledgment of what they were both evidently thinking.

"Yep!" Tiff's million-dollar smile was on full display, as was most of her dark-golden skin.

Kayla watched Ronan's wandering gaze take in Tiff's toned arms and thighs with subtle appreciation.

"That's Kayla, our drummer extraordinaire." Tiff pointed at her.

Kayla gave him a little salute. "Loved your set."

"Likewise."

"This is our guitar goddess, Toni," Tiff continued.

"Ah, yeah," Ronan said, narrowing his eyes. "I heard about you."

"Really?" Toni's brows rose. "Good things, I hope."

"Nothing terrible, not about you." He rubbed the back of his neck, squinting uncomfortably. "Sorry, but that drama surrounding your original guitarist made its way out west."

"Guess that means we've gone national," Tiff said. She raised her hand for a high five. "Come on, don't leave me hanging."

Toni obliged her. "Something for the history books, I guess."

"LA doesn't usually care about anything that happens outside LA," Tiff said. "They barely care what's happening *in* LA, so if we have their tongues wagging, we're about to break."

"As long as they wag for the right reasons," Lilly added.

"Is this your first time on the festival circuit?"

"Yeah," Kayla replied. "Any advice for some newbies?"

"Honestly, just enjoy it," he said. "Keep doing what you're

doing—tight, killer sets that leave them wanting more. How's your merch setup?"

"We don't have a lot yet, since they haven't released much," Seb said, walking up and extending his hand. "Sebastian Quick, manager."

"Ronan Paschal. Our manager's around here somewhere." They shook hands, and Seb took a seat next to Toni, handing her a can of seltzer.

"We have three shirt designs and some other gear with the logo," Seb continued. "We're waiting to see what sells, what the fans like, etc., before we commit to a bunch of product."

"You should check out our booth. Most of our merch is logo-based too, with variations in both light and dark colors." Ronan smiled. "I was a graphic designer before all of this."

"Neat story," Tiff said, leaning into Kayla. "This one designed our logo."

"Yeah?" Ronan turned his attention to Kayla, his gaze assessing. "You a designer too?"

"Kayla's good at everything," Tiff said in a mock-whine. "It's sooo annoying." She grinned and hugged Kayla to her. "Our resident genius."

Kayla squirmed, the word conjuring up memories of sitting at a dinner table full of publishers and educators, her mother discussing Kayla's academic progress as if she were a social experiment rather than her daughter. *Our own Little Miss Yolanda, in the flesh.*

"I'm not a genius."

"She's being modest," Tiff said, letting her go.

"I think I'll go mingle." Kayla stood and excused herself, needing to be elsewhere. Tiff always said stuff like that, and Kayla knew she'd meant it as a compliment, but it still grated. It didn't help that she hadn't told any of them about who she was, who her mother was. They knew her parents were both educators and that she'd grown up with some privilege, but she had wanted to keep her two worlds apart. She wondered, with the band's growing success, if that was even possible.

Kayla moved around bodies to get to the edge of the tent. It was crowded, probably because of the rain, and she considered heading back to the bus.

Ty was probably there, reading as usual, though he didn't seem to mind her interruptions.

"Kathy Larrington?"

Kayla's heart stopped.

Why did life always find a way to kick you when you least expected it? Backstage at a rock festival was *not* the place she thought her past and present would collide. Had some enterprising reporter put two and two together? Was this the moment Kayla had been dreading since the Lillys signed their deal with YMI?

She turned slowly and was stunned to find her prep school roommate staring back at her. Kayla's tension eased a notch, quickly replaced by confusion. "Siobhan? What are you doing here?" They hugged.

"I was about to ask you the same question. I thought I saw you onstage earlier, but I figured I was hallucinating or something. No way was Everton Academy's pride and joy up there playing in a rock band. Do your parents know what Little Miss Yolanda is up to these days?" She was laughing when she said it, but Kayla felt the ground crumbling out from underneath her.

Trying hard not to panic, she glanced around them before pulling Siobhan farther into the corner. "No, they don't," Kayla said, keeping her voice low. "And you can't tell anyone."

Siobhan's smile dipped into a frown. "Are you really anxious about your parents finding out about"—she gestured around the tent—"this? Seriously? Kathy, you're an adult. Why on earth do you still let your mother tie you up in knots? And don't try to tell me it's not Gisele you're worried about. I know your dad would be proud of you. You were incredible up there. For a second, I thought I was watching Za—" She caught herself before she could finish saying his name. "Sorry."

"It's fine." Kayla pushed down the wave of unexpected hurt. "I shouldn't care what my mom thinks. Anyway, I'm Kayla now."

"Aww, didn't Zach call you Kayla?" Smiling, Siobhan nodded once. "Got it. But tell me how this all happened. What's the deal with your band? Is it serious? It must be if you're playing places like this."

"Hang on. What are *you* doing back here with all the artists?" Kayla asked. "I never took you for the band groupie type. I thought you were more into models and athletes."

Siobhan grinned. "I'm friends with the lead singer of Broken Pilots."

"And by friends, you mean you're boning him."

Her grin widened. "You know me so well. Seriously, though, are you famous now? Because I have to say, you have the chops. We were all so impressed."

Kayla smiled. "Thanks. And no, we're not famous." The thought sent an unexpected chill down her spine. That should be the goal, after all. Shouldn't it? To get to the top?

"Not yet, you mean. That singer of yours had the crowd eating out of the palm of her hand. Everyone's talking about it."

"Really?" Kayla looked around at the other people in the room. She did catch a few people pointing at Lilly, awe on their faces. "We haven't been together that long, but things are moving pretty quickly. We signed a deal with YMI Records."

"Whoa," Siobhan said, her brows rising. "Kathy, babe... All kidding aside, does your family know about *any* of this?" She stepped closer. "And do these people know about your parents? Who your mom is? Who *you* are?"

"No and no, and I can't let them find out. Not yet." *Hopefully not ever.* Kayla sighed and reached back to massage her left shoulder. It ached, and all she wanted to do was crawl into her bunk and sleep.

Siobhan held up her hand. "No one will hear it from me, but you can't keep this a secret for long. Rumor has it, she has another bestseller on her hands."

"I know," Kayla agreed. She'd looked it up, relieved to find it wasn't another book in the Yolanda series only to have the blurb on the back cover nearly take her legs out from under her. "It's all about grief." She didn't miss how the light dimmed in Siobhan's eyes. Kayla's mother rarely spoke of him, but there was no doubt Zach would show up in the pages of the new book in one way or another.

"You know Zach was my schoolgirl crush?" Siobhan asked after a few moments of silence. She folded her arms around herself. "I never got to tell him that. It was the talent show that did it for me. When he was the one-man-band act? I knew he was your brother, but he was so damned cute."

"Ewww." Smiling, Kayla nudged her shoulder. "He knew. He told me the night he came out to our parents. He was worried it would break your fifteen-year-old heart."

"God, he was an amazing person," Siobhan said, and Kayla gave her a watery smile.

The night of Zach's accident, Siobhan had found Kayla sitting in the dark alone while her parents had gone to the police station. She'd stayed with her all night, something Kayla would never forget.

"He lived his truth," she said. "Now it's your turn."

"Not the same thing," Kayla argued.

"Of course it's not, but you do hide who you are from them. From your mom, at least." Siobhan took Kayla's shoulders in her hands and gently shook her. "You guys were seriously good up there, Kath...sorry, *Kayla.* I was as blown away as everyone else in the audience. You had us all buzzing. That's a gift. Don't let your mom make you feel ashamed or like it's not as meaningful as whatever she envisioned for your life. It's *your* life, cupcake. You're not a character in her books."

Kayla pulled Siobhan into a hug. It was strange to have the advice she'd once given to her brother echoed back to her. "When did you get so wise and all-knowing? Does it come with age?"

"Hardly," Siobhan replied, rocking them a little. She leaned back and released her. "I'm great with giving advice, not so great at taking it. Speaking of which…"

Kayla followed her gaze to where the lead singer of Broken Pilots made his way over to them, his eyes raking over every inch of Siobhan with a look that should have given Kayla a sunburn it was so hot.

Damn.

"Ladies," he said, his gaze locked with Siobhan's.

Color rose in her pale cheeks, and her green eyes sparkled. She took the singer's proffered arm and turned back to Kayla, practically glowing.

"Babe, this is Kayla, an old friend of mine. Kayla, this is Jamie."

"Cool to meet you," she said, shaking his hand. "Big fan. I'm looking forward to your set tonight."

"The Lillys, right? You're the drummer?" Jamie squinted at her. "Man, I gotta tell you, I'm pissed at you guys."

Kayla frowned, dropping her hand to her side. "Pissed? At us?"

"Yeah," he replied, though he was smiling. "You do know you stole the day, right? You're all anyone's talking about. Puts a lot of pressure on us tonight as the headliners."

"Oh." She exhaled. "Thanks, but I don't think anyone will even remember that we exist after you guys hit the stage."

"Don't sell yourself short."

"Listen to him, Kayla," Siobhan said. "Jamie doesn't joke around about this stuff."

"Not about business, no," he agreed. "Not about music."

"Broken Pilots is set to headline their first world tour," Siobhan said, beaming.

"I heard that. Congrats!"

"Have you guys toured yet?" Jamie asked Kayla. "Outside the festivals, I mean."

"We've played a lot in and around the mid-Atlantic. New York and Philly. A radio station concert in D.C.," Kayla replied. "Once our record is done, we'll do more. Maybe we could open for you guys," she said, only half joking.

Broken Pilots' sophomore album had achieved platinum, and the new one seemed poised to do the same. Bands like theirs were usually paired up with more established artists looking to reach wider audiences or acts their label wanted to push.

"Our people should talk," Jamie said, surprising her. "You guys might be a great fit to open our fall tour."

Kayla's jaw dropped. She couldn't have heard him right "*What?*"

"Oh my God! That would be amazing!" Siobhan exclaimed.

"Are you serious?"

"As a game of paintball with Jackson Pollock," Jamie replied. "At least for the U.S. dates. You'd need to be available for at least six weeks. We can see how it develops from there, assuming the suits agree."

"We could totally do that," Kayla hurried to confirm before he had a chance to change his mind.

"And your set would need to be twice as long as what you did today," Jamie told her as he searched her face. He frowned slightly. "Can you pull together a fifty-minute set?"

"Absolutely!" Kayla hated to sound eager to promise him any-thing but—hell!—she would promise him she could play blindfolded with one hand tied to a loaf of bread if it meant getting them this gig. "If you want, you can sit in on a rehearsal, or we can send a link so all of you can watch virtually," Kayla offered. "Your bandmates might want to kick the tires before buying the car."

Jamie eyed her thoughtfully before nodding. "You're hungry, and you're quick. I like it."

"She's the best." Siobhan preened.

"You have your phone on you? Take my digits."

Kayla's hands shook as she typed his number into her phone. She texted him so he'd have hers.

"Excellent," he said, turning his head to kiss Siobhan on the cheek. "I knew you were my lucky charm."

Siobhan smirked. "Is that a joke about me being Irish?"

"Just the truth," he said, pulling her to his side. "Glad to meet you, Kayla. Call me soon, all right? We'll set things up."

"You too," she stammered. "I mean, it was great meeting you too."

"You still have my number?" Siobhan asked. Kayla nodded. "Call me. I want to hear all about your new life."

"I will."

Kayla watched them go and then hustled back to the group. "Holy fuck!" she said when she reached them. "You're not going to believe what just happened."

CHAPTER 9.

"WE HAVE A SLIGHT CHANGE in itinerary." Seb stuck his head through the curtain that separated the cockpit from the rest of the bus.

Ty straightened in his seat. The band had piled back into the bus a couple of hours ago, and they were back on the road. "What's up?"

"Rather than drive straight through to Ann Arbor, we're stopping in Toledo," Seb said. "There's an awesome record shop there. We're hoping to do a last-minute in-store tomorrow. Jordan is going to put pressure on YMI to speed up the release of the album, and it wouldn't hurt to butter up to some indie music store owners."

"Sounds cool," Ty replied. "Will we be staying in Toledo overnight?"

"We've made reservations for a hotel there. And don't worry, your room is covered," Seb said. "It's better if we take breaks from the bus whenever we can. Once we start west, we'll have long stretches on the road and in those bunks."

"I don't mind the bunks." Except when they reminded him of the nights he'd spent in lockup. Ty shook his shoulders. That was all behind him. He needed to let it go. At least the nightmares had receded some since they left Philly.

"You good?" Seb asked. "You're a quiet one."

"I'm fine, thanks for asking. I'm trying to be unobtrusive," Ty added. He didn't say anything about Seb's assumption that Ty would be with them for the second leg of the tour.

Seb laughed. "You're not wallpaper, man. If this were a regular tour, we'd have half a dozen more crew members with us. Lucky you, you're the only one this time around. You're privy to all the inner chaos."

"I don't mind a bit of chaos."

"You say that like you didn't expect to." Seb lowered himself into the jump seat next to the door.

"To be honest," Ty said. "I didn't know what to expect, but it's all good."

"Glad to hear that. We tend to collect people."

"Collect them?"

"When we work with someone we like, we kinda adopt them," Seb explained. "And Lilly is comfortable around you."

Ty looked at him, surprised Seb had mentioned Lilly's comfort specifically. She'd barely said three words to Ty on the trip so far. What scant knowledge he had about her, Ty imagined Lilly would the last person in the group to find comfort around a stranger.

"I'm glad," Ty replied. "When you need a driver again, I hope my name will be on your short list." It didn't hurt to keep himself in the running.

Seb smiled. "Think you'd be up for the longer leg of the tour?"

Ty had a lot to consider. He did like driving the band so far, but could he leave his granddad for more than three weeks? He wasn't sure if *he* could handle it.

"Depends."

"We'd pay you well," Seb said. "And there are perks."

"Perks, eh?"

"If you got off the bus more, you'd find out," Seb answered, handing him a slip of paper. "Here's the name of the hotel in Toledo. We'll stop there for the night."

"Okay."

Chuckling, Seb retreated to the living area. "We'll lure you out of your cave somehow."

———————

After checking into his room, Ty called home. He usually reached out around dinnertime but had lost track. By the time he remembered, they'd been driving. It was against company policy to take personal calls while behind the wheel, and Ty didn't think it was safe or professional either way.

"Hey, son," Pop-Pop answered after the second ring.

"Did I catch you at a bad time?" He sounded out of breath. "What are you up to?"

"Up to my neck in sourdough."

Ty pinched the bridge of his nose. "Pop-Pop, it's almost eleven. I wasn't even sure you'd be up, much less baking."

"Is it?" He trailed off and murmured something Ty couldn't hear.

Ty pressed the phone closer to his ear. "Are you okay?"

"I'm fine, I'm fine, just cleaning my hands so I can talk to you," he said.

"Maybe hang up your apron for the night."

"Yeah, it's later than I thought," came the reply. "Time flies when you're waiting for dough to proof."

"Sourdough, you said?"

"I made my own starter too."

Ty could hear the pride in his voice. "That's awesome. Can't wait to try some when I get home."

"I'll freeze a loaf or two," he promised. "Where are you?"

"Toledo."

"Hmm, I don't see that on the calendar."

Ty had hung one on the wall in the kitchen so his granddad could keep track of his whereabouts. Since he returned home, he noticed how anxious Van got if he didn't have a clear sense of where Ty was at any given moment.

"They added a stop at the last minute," Ty told him, "and I wanted to update you. We're heading to Ann Arbor after that."

"Oh, I see. Good, good. I'll write it down now…" He trailed off again.

Worry prickled along Ty's spine. "Van? Are you sure you're all right? Should I call Ms. Peggy and ask her to check on you?"

"No, no. Don't bother her. Everything is fine. I just… Look, I don't want you to get mad, but that lawyer called, the one that contacted us right after you were released."

"Pop-Pop."

"No, I know. You said you didn't want to sue the university, but he thinks he can win you a big settlement."

Ty squeezed his eyes shut and pinched the bridge of his nose. "I don't want to put us through that."

"Don't worry about me, I—"

"Pop-Pop," Ty said, struggling to control his temper. His grand-dad meant well, but Ty needed him to drop it. "*I* don't want to go through all of that. Me. So please. Let it go."

Even if he could win a case like that, it would only thrust Ty back into the spotlight. He shuddered at the thought of seeing his face all over the local news. Again. All he wanted was some peace and quiet for them both.

"All right, son," his granddad said quietly. "I'm sorry, I only wanted… Consider the matter closed."

"Thank you," Ty replied, wishing he could hug his granddad and show him he wasn't angry. If the Wi-Fi in their house were better, he'd switch over to a video call. "Now, pack it up and get your butt to bed."

There was a chuckle on the other end. "Who are you talking to, little man?"

"You, old man," Ty replied, smiling. "I miss you."

"Miss you too."

"Good night."

"Drive safe."

Ty disconnected and flopped back onto the bed. It was queen-sized and larger than anything he'd ever slept in.

He was planning to sleep well tonight.

His nostrils stung from the bleach, and Ty tried to breathe through his mouth. The air in the jail tasted foul. Like hopelessness and defeat.

His cellmate told Ty, if he was lucky, they'd assign him to laundry duty.

"The shitheads in sanitation have it the worst," he said. "Get on the guards' good side, but don't let anyone see you sliding up to them."

A toothless grin and a wet laugh.

Ty rolled to his side as his cellmate rambled on about what he could expect once he was sentenced. He talked about being in the Hole, sent to solitary confinement for a week for hitting another man with a tray. This reality—this whole system—was violent and dehumanizing, and Ty couldn't believe he might be sent away. For two terrifying mornings, he'd woken up worried he'd be dragged down into an endless nightmare.

Surely, they would realize their mistake. Ty was innocent. It was so clear that Meredith Stanwick had lied, that Ty had never raised a hand to her. That she had stolen from him, not the other way around.

"Everyone in here is innocent," his cellmate said, laughing even harder when Ty told him he hadn't done anything.

Ty squirmed on the thin pad that served as his mattress, his body aware of every screw and bolt in the steel grate beneath it. He wished he'd been allowed to bring his e-reader to pass the time.

The sound of metal on metal made him open his eyes. It was hours past lights-out, and the only people walking the corridors should have been guards. The sound grew closer, and Ty lay perfectly still in the darkness. A sinking feeling in his gut said the sound was coming for him.

Ty bolted upright on the bed, sweaty and confused, his legs tangled in the damp sheets. For a moment, he didn't know where he was.

The bed was soft. And big. A clock with bright red letters floated in the darkness to his left. Light filtered through a crack under the door on his right.

Bus.

Band.

Hotel.

Right.

He reached out blindly to turn on the lamp, and light flooded the beige room. At home, he'd just turn over and stare into the darkness, waiting for the nightmare to come for him again. Without Van there to fuss, Ty decided to read instead.

After plucking his glasses from the nightstand, he picked up his book. Reading quieted his mind, or at least gave it something else to focus on. With any luck, he'd exhaust himself and catch another hour or two of sleep before dawn.

Bright laughter from the hallway broke the silence, and Ty nearly jumped out of his skin.

"Fuck," he muttered, angry with himself for being so

weak-minded. He was cleared of all charges. It was over. He'd moved on. *Was* moving on.

What other choice did he have?

Moving on to what, though?

"Fuck."

Ty slammed the book shut. His messenger bag lay open on the floor by the nightstand. Ty spied his new notebook poking out of the top. He grabbed it and a pen, and tried to put his feelings into words.

Darkness pervades
Rolls over my soul like night falling
Fear cracks the cold shell of my fury
Terror fills my lungs
I must breathe deep
And awaken

The words were nonsensical, but Ty felt better for having written something down. He thought of Kayla's smile as she handed him the unexpected gift, the budding acquaintanceship—friendship?— they were developing. It was nice having someone to talk to who didn't know about the baggage he carried and more than he'd hoped for on this trip.

Ty was on the road with a cool group of people; he had plenty of time to read and a few dollars in his pocket.

It would have to do.

CHAPTER 10.

"RISE AND SHINE!" TIFF THREW open the curtains, and daylight flooded their hotel room.

Kayla barely stopped herself from launching a pillow at her roommate's head. "Since when are you a morning person?"

"I'm turning over a new leaf. Blame the Norwegian," Tiff replied. "Do we have time to hit the hotel pool after breakfast? They have a pool, right? All hotels have pools."

"I doubt it." Under the covers, Kayla stretched. It had felt good to sleep in an actual bed. Across from her, Tiff hefted her bag onto her bed and started rifling through it. "What are you looking for?"

"My leopard print tank. Have you seen it?" Tiff stood at the foot of the bed, suitcase open, rummaging around the contents and throwing them about carelessly. Her clothes were strewn across the floor among other random items.

"You packed M&M's?"

"I can't be without my emms. You know that."

"I'm pretty sure they're available everywhere," Kayla said, chuckling.

After some time had passed, Tiff stood back and surveyed the chaotic mess with a dismayed look on her face.

Kayla shook her head. "Maybe it's back on the bus."

"Damn, it's probably in my laundry bag." Tiff sighed. "There goes my look for the day."

"You pack more clothes than the rest of us combined," Kayla teased, watching her toss garments back into her bag. "It's like you bring everything you own."

A look passed over Tiff's face, but it was gone before Kayla could decipher it. "You have to be prepared for anything."

"Then I'm sure you'll find something."

Tiff sat on the edge of the bed and snatched up her phone. "I need inspiration."

Sensing an hour of scrolling in Tiff's future, Kayla got out of bed. "While you do that, I'm going to grab a shower."

Tiff looked up, concerned. "Don't use all the hot water."

Raising a brow, Kayla realized Tiff was serious. "I'll be sure to save some for you."

Kayla plugged her phone into the bathroom outlet and set it on the vanity. She liked a little music to start the day, and this time she was in the mood for some old favorites. After navigating to a playlist, she hit start and grabbed her toothbrush out of her kit.

Kayla didn't know much about the record store they were slated to perform in later that afternoon, but she very much liked the idea of it. She pictured an old building and a store with a maze of rooms stuffed to the gills with stacks of vinyl. She thought of the vintage record player they might be using, of the funky smell of the place, and of the crowd who would fill it. All of it gave her chills of excitement as she rinsed and spit.

But her whole body froze when the song changed to Bloc Party's "The Prayer." *A Weekend in the City* had been one of Zach's favorite albums. Kayla's eyes filled, but she quickly blinked the tears away. It had been nearly ten years. Why did the pain still feel so fresh?

Because you never talk about him. No one ever talks about him. She forced herself to listen.

Just listen.

When it ended, Kayla put the song on repeat and started the shower, tying up her hair to keep it away from the water. As she stood under the warm spray, her muscles began to relax. She could still hear the music, but she was no longer focused on the lyrics. Memories of her brother came like a flood and for once, she welcomed them.

The hot water felt good, and Kayla took her time picking through each moment as it came.

Sitting on the swing at the playground while he pushed her.

Zach letting her win Trivial Pursuit night until he realized he couldn't actually beat her.

Lying on the floor of his bedroom and listening to old CDs, plastic cases strewn all over the floor like the world's biggest puzzle.

Kayla smiled to herself as she rinsed the soap from her skin and shut off the water. Grabbing a towel from the rack, she dried herself and threw on her bra and underwear. When she emerged from the bathroom, the cool air was a shock to her system.

"It's freezing in here!" Kayla tossed her toiletry kit on the bed and picked up the T-shirt she'd laid out for the day, shrugging into it. She reached for her jeans but stopped when she realized Tiff hadn't answered. Kayla looked up to find her perched on the corner of her bed staring down at her phone with a stricken expression.

Kayla tossed her jeans aside and went to her. "Hey. Everything okay?"

Tiff pulled her phone to her chest, hiding the screen. "Yeah, It's just...someone I hadn't heard from in a while."

"Someone you didn't want to hear from, or...?"

"I guess I wasn't expecting to ever again."

Despite being a ball of never-ending chatter, Tiff didn't talk about real shit. Kayla wasn't sure what to ask her. "Is it an ex?"

"No, my sister. Sort of." Her voice sounded distant.

"I didn't know you had a sister."

Shaking her head, Tiff looked down at her phone. "Peaches is... *fuck*. We grew up together. She's as close as it gets for me, I guess."

Kayla couldn't help but smile. "Your sister's name is Peaches?"

Turning to her, Tiff gave a soft laugh. "Yeah. It's on her birth certificate and everything."

"Oh God. Imagine having to explain that at the DMV."

Tiff's smile was brief, and Kayla began to worry something really was wrong.

"Did something happen?"

"Nothing that hasn't happened before." Tiff let the cryptic answer hang in the air and turned back to her bag. "Do you have a black tank top?"

"Uh, sure." Kayla took the hint and went back to her side of the room. "Here you go." She pulled the garment from her bag and tossed it over.

"Thanks."

An uncomfortable silence filled the room. She didn't like it. Tiff rarely spoke about her life before she met Seb and Lilly. Kayla was desperate to know more but didn't want to push.

"I need a shower." Tiff walked into the bathroom but left the door open.

Kayla packed her clothes, but she needed to do something with her hair. When she heard the shower running, she walked to the bathroom door.

"Is it all right if I do my hair while you're in there?"

"Yeah, sure," Tiff replied from behind the white curtain.

Kayla retrieved a brush, her favorite hair cream, and a scrunchy from her bag and went back to the mirror.

"I take it you and Peaches aren't close?"

Kayla thought Tiff might ignore the question but then she heard her soft reply.

"When we were kids, you couldn't pry us apart with the Jaws of Life."

Smiling, Kayla remembered being glued to her brother's side. "My brother and I were the same way."

The top of the curtain was yanked aside, and Tiff stuck her head out. "Since when do you have a brother?"

"Since when do you have a Peaches?" Kayla countered, scooping up a bit of the cream and rubbing it between her hands.

Rolling her eyes, Tiff disappeared back behind the curtain. "She's four years older. Kept me out of sticky situations when I was little."

"Sounds like a good sister." Kayla worked the product into her hair, pleased with the way her red curls responded.

"When I got older, I did the same for her. Or I tried," Tiff added.

"Is she in trouble?" Kayla stared at the closed curtain and hoped Tiff wouldn't stop talking. Kayla wanted to help if she could. The water shut off, plunging the room into silence. She took it as her cue to leave. "I'm putting a towel here on the sink for you."

A few minutes later, Tiff walked out of the bathroom. The tank top Kayla had loaned to Tiff fit more like a dress. Where Kayla had hills and valleys, Tiff had planes and angles. Kayla wasn't tall by any stretch of the imagination. Standing next to Tiff, though, she felt like a giant. It always amazed Kayla that such a tiny body could hold so much humanity.

"Do you want to talk about it?"

Tiff shoved some of her things into her bag with a little more force than usual. "Nothing to talk about."

Kayla tried to give her some space. She of all people understood how important privacy could be, especially when it came to family. Kayla finished dressing. Out of habit, she double-checked the drawers and the closet to make sure they weren't leaving anything behind.

They were silent again as they left the room and took the elevator down to the lobby, where they met the others.

"Everyone sleep good?" Seb asked.

"Passably." Lilly slipped an obscenely large pair of sunglasses on, looking every part the diva.

Seb grinned. "Glad to hear it." His gaze passed carefully over Tiff before he met Kayla's eyes. "You two all right?"

Kayla wasn't sure how to answer. She didn't want to put Tiff on the spot, so she nodded. "Yep, all good."

Seb looked at Tiff, who had her phone out again and was scowling down at the screen. "Tiff?"

"All good," she said before walking past him.

The group shared awkward glances as she left them and went through the front doors.

"Is she okay?" Toni asked.

"I think so." Kayla chose her words carefully. "I think she had some news from Cali that she didn't like. I'm not sure. She didn't say much."

A look of understanding passed over Seb's face. "Ah."

"I'm sure she'll tell us if she needs help with anything."

Seb cocked a brow at Kayla. "You think so?"

"She knows we're here for her."

He nodded. "She better."

"She does," Lilly agreed. "Where's Ty?"

"Here" came a voice from behind.

Kayla turned. "Good morning."

"Hey," he replied, his gaze darting from person to person. "Sorry if I kept you waiting. Are you all ready to go? Or did you want food first?"

"Food," Toni said. "But the buffet looks dire. Is there a diner or something nearby?"

Ty took his phone out of his pocket. "There's a place about ten minutes down the road with decent reviews." Today, he wore a pair of black cargo shorts and a Nothing But Thieves T-shirt.

Kayla wasn't surprised to find they shared the same taste in music as well.

She moved over to him. "Do they serve waffles?" Kayla knew most of Tiff's comfort foods.

Catching her eye, Seb smiled. "Good thinking."

"What did I miss?" Toni asked as Seb wrapped an arm around her shoulder and steered her toward the parking lot.

"If Tiff's in a mood, what better way to lift her out of it than an excuse to eat a gallon of maple syrup?"

She was standing by the bus when they reached her. "We ready to go?"

"All set," Ty replied, unlocking the door. He stood aside and let her enter. "First stop, waffles, apparently."

Tiff stopped and turned, her entire demeanor changing before Kayla's eyes. "Waffles?"

Grinning, Kayla pushed her up the steps and into the bus. "With real maple syrup."

Tiff practically floated up the steps. "So this is what love feels like?"

At breakfast, Tiff had returned to her usually chatty self, and Kayla figured everything was all right again. She was surprised when Tiff found her back at the bus and took a seat on the opposite bunk.

Facing her, Tiff spoke softly. "Sorry I zoned out on you before."

Kayla had been lounging on her bunk, practicing a new riff against her pillow. She sat up. "Hey, no need to apologize. I get it. Family can be…a lot."

Tiff snorted. "That's the fucking truth." Her gaze drifted to the ceiling. "Peaches is always hustling, trying to level up. She takes stupid risks. Always has. I mean, I've done my fair share of stupid shit, but I don't know when I became the one saving her ass all the time."

"You know," Kayla began carefully, "you don't have to always say yes. She's an adult, right?"

Tiff looked at her. "Technically." A soft grin curved her mouth. "Lately, I wonder. I don't think anyone would accuse me of being overly mature."

Kayla made a face of mock outrage. "What? You?"

"Fuck off," Tiff said, her laughter music to Kayla's ears. "You're right, though. I don't have to say yes, and I don't always. It's just... the guilt, you know? You said you have a brother, so you know the guilt is real."

"Had," Kayla heard herself say. She hadn't spoken about Zach to anyone in their group. It felt odd to do so now, like her two worlds were passing too close to each other and the repercussions might derail everything. But she'd opened the door to Tiff. "He died when I was fifteen."

Kayla expected Tiff to feel sorry for her, expected the usual pity and platitudes. Instead, Tiff looked at her with a curious mixture of fury and compassion.

"I'm so sorry," she said, her voice soft but firm. "That's terrible. No one should have to go through that."

"Thank you." It was a rote response, but she didn't know what else to say after so long.

"How?"

"There was a car accident. He was in a band... They were on the road at the time."

"Oh, shit" came Tiff's quiet reply. Her eyes were wide under her furrowed brow. "All this time... Why didn't you tell me?"

Kayla shrugged. "You said it yourself. The guilt is real."

CHAPTER 11.

TY CAREFULLY MANEUVERED THE forty-five-foot-long, twenty-eight-ton bus into the lot on North Michigan Street in downtown Toledo and parked it in the back corner, as instructed. Culture Clash Records occupied a two-story building and was much larger than he'd imagined. Ty liked the retro feel of the place. There appeared to be actual vinyl records decorating its walls, and some had been mounted inside the windows, giving it a real vibe.

Animated chatter floated toward him from the back, and Ty smiled at their excitement. He wasn't a part of the Lillys, but he was glad to be along for the ride. Seeing the business of being in a band from the inside was an opportunity Ty never imagined he'd get. It wasn't one he had been looking for, but Ty was glad he took the job when Aaron offered. If nothing else, it allowed him to meet Kayla, and she… Well, he could see them becoming friends.

"Hey, you." As if summoned by his thoughts, she appeared. "You have zero excuses for staying on the bus today. Live a little. Come inside. The book will wait, and you'll be able to keep an eye on this baby through those giant-ass windows."

He would have agreed to go just about anywhere with her. Despite technically being his employer, Kayla seemed genuinely interested in Ty enjoying himself on this trip. Her enthusiasm was infectious.

"Yeah, okay."

"Really?" Her brows lifted and she actually bounced on her toes.

"Of course," he replied, trying hard to tamp down his grin. He looked down at his shorts.

"No kilt today?"

"I thought I should change." His favorite kilt was simple and black but might still be too much for Toledo. He really wasn't sure.

Kayla's gaze slid over him before she seemed to catch herself.

It made Ty's thoughts go a touch hazy.

Maybe his interest in her wasn't purely platonic, which was an alarming thought. He took a step back.

"I think you look great but wear whatever makes you comfortable."

Ty turned and headed for the cargo bay, the compliment landing a bit too easily. "I'll help you all unload."

Kayla followed. "It's a pretty small stage area, from what I gathered, so I'm only taking a snare, the kick, a tom, and my hi-hat."

Swinging the bay door open, he paused. "Um, I have no idea what you just said."

"He's not a roadie, Kayla," Seb said, laughing as he joined them. He grabbed a bag of gear in each hand and pointed Ty toward the kick drum. "Can you handle that?"

"No problem."

They unloaded quickly, thanks to some help from a couple of the store's staff members who helped them bring the equipment inside. Ty stood by the counter while the band set up by the front windows. It was like a well-choreographed dance, everyone moving in sync to accomplish the task quickly and efficiently.

The store itself was wall-to-wall, floor-to-ceiling records. Ty didn't think he'd ever seen so much vinyl in one room. Flipping through the stacks, he spied an old George Clinton album he knew his granddad would covet and made a note to pick it up before he left.

"I had no idea vinyl was this popular," Ty said to Seb when he walked over.

"It's made a comeback of sorts." Seb thumbed through the stack next to him. "Really, it's still hardcore audiophiles that tend to buy it. Bands release limited quantities, some with special packaging or colored vinyl, etc. Like this." Seb picked up a double album from a band called Black Purple.

The name sounded vaguely familiar. It was printed in large, iridescent letters against a black background that looked blank until you turned it a certain way. Then, the rest of the artwork appeared, embossed into the thick paper. Even under the protective plastic, it was gorgeous packaging.

"It's cost-prohibitive for most artists," Seb continued. "But if you have a loyal following or a big budget like these guys, you can produce some nice stuff."

Ty nodded, looking around the store. They'd made use of every inch of space since it was at a premium. If he were into vinyl, it would be heaven. He pulled out his phone and snapped a photo of the store, making sure to include the bright red neon "records" sign that hung on the front wall, just above where the band would play.

The PA speakers crackled to life, and Seb excused himself to go help. One of the store employees adjusted the sound while the women tuned their instruments. Kayla sat in the back behind the scaled-down drum kit. From where he stood, she was almost entirely obscured by the speaker on its stand.

Since no one was paying him attention enough to call him on it, he moved to the other side to get a better view of her.

The shop had been relatively empty when they arrived, but now there were shoppers scattered here and there. No one seemed to notice or care about the group of instruments at the front of the store. Seb had said it was a last-minute stop, but Ty hoped they'd get a sizeable crowd.

He wandered down the aisles, stopping to scan some of the records.

"No idea," someone said. "Maybe they're local."

"I didn't see anything on the website," another person said.

Ty turned as nonchalantly as he could and thumbed through the records in the stacks behind him. He glanced up at the pair who had been talking.

"Are you guys here to see the Lillys?"

The one on the left, a petite blond with big, green eyes and a nose piercing, looked up at him. "Is that who's playing?"

Ty nodded.

Next to the blond, the redhead frowned. "What's the name?" The question came from a deep, baritone voice.

"The Lillys."

The pair looked at each other and then back at Ty.

"Never heard of them," the blond said. "How'd you hear about it? I follow the store on their socials, and I didn't see anything."

Ty didn't want to lie. He offered as little information as he could. "I think it was last-minute."

"Are they any good?" the redhead asked at the same time the blond asked "What kind of music?"

"They're incredible," Ty said truthfully, though he wasn't sure how to describe their sound. "I guess I'd say they're a mix of alt-rock and indie. Difficult to put in a box."

This seemed to please them.

"Sweet," the redhead said. "Thanks for the heads-up."

Nodding, Ty watched them move toward the front of the store and take up two places in front of the stage area.

He did this a few more times, casually strolling through the store and telling people about the awesome up-and-coming band in the front corner.

"They're about to hit it big," he said at one point, believing every word.

Eventually, there was a small crowd at the front of the store. Ty watched as, outside, people walked past the large windows and stopped, wondering what was happening. More than a few came inside.

Eventually, there were people lined up along every aisle, murmuring excitedly even though the show hadn't begun—the anticipation building.

A man walked to the front and took one of the microphones off its stand. He wore a black T-shirt with the store's logo. The patrons fell silent when he turned on the mic and a loud popping sound pierced the air.

"Hey, everyone. Sorry about that. Thanks for coming out on such short notice," he began. "The other day, we got a call from a friend back east about this hot, up-and-coming act, asking if they could swing by for an in-store while they were in the area. Luckily, we were able to invite them to be with us today. So, without further ado, please give a warm Culture Clash welcome to the Lillys."

There was polite applause as Kayla held her sticks in the air and clicked them together in a count-off. They were different than the ones Ty frequently saw her twirling between her fingers. Instead of wood, they appeared to be metal and plastic, with wire brushes on the ends.

It took a moment for him to recognize the song, "Shadowplay." He was familiar with the version performed by the Killers but knew it was initially recorded by someone else. Around him, people began to bop their heads and sway. They seemed to approve of the choice.

It was a repetitive groove. Hypnotizing, in a way, and even more so when Lilly began to sing. She stood in the middle of the make-shift stage, her eyes closed as she swayed left to right and back. Her movements were sinuous, almost snakelike, and her voice rode the frenetic energy of the song like a surfboard over a cresting wave.

Ty had seen live footage of the Lillys online. He'd looked them up when he accepted the job driving for them, and he'd caught a few impromptu rehearsals in the back of the bus. Seeing them up close was a different experience. Ty made a mental note to check out at least one of their festival performances while he had the opportunity.

The Lillys were terrific, the real deal, but it was Kayla he couldn't stop watching.

There was a graceful athleticism to her playing that made it seem effortless, like a well-oiled machine. It was mesmerizing. Even a little awe-inspiring, Ty realized, to watch someone with complete command over their instrument at the top of their game. Kayla moved almost like a dancer, and the drum set was her stage.

They launched into the next song, one Ty didn't recognize. It was more up-tempo, with a catchy guitar hook that Ty caught himself humming along with. People bounced along appreciatively, and he could see them warming up to the band more and more.

"Do you have any of their music in the store?" a voice behind him asked.

Ty frowned when the employee shook her head. Didn't the Lillys have a record out? If not, why not?

Polite-but-enthusiastic applause met the conclusion of the second song, and Lilly addressed the group.

"Thanks for being here. And thank you, Culture Clash, for having us. We hope we can come back again sometime when our debut record is released."

More applause.

Ty's focus drifted back to Kayla.

She smiled brightly, her skin flushed with exertion and pride. She knew they were kicking ass. The woman was gorgeous, especially when she played. A thought occurred to him. Maybe that's why he'd been avoiding seeing them onstage. Seeing *her*.

Ty had already developed a very unprofessional, borderline

inappropriate desire for her company. He didn't want to cross any lines.

Except...

Kayla kept her gaze on him as if she were performing for him alone. Each stroke was hard, fast, and precise, making the music come alive. Sweat beaded on her forehead, and she threw her head back as the band powered through a particularly tricky section.

The audience clapped feverishly along as if it were an invitation to join in, and a few started dancing where they stood crowded together. It was clear that each member of the Lillys was in their element, enjoying every moment of it despite the small venue. They genuinely loved to play.

Ty's gaze snagged on Kayla again.

She was looking right at him, her lips curved into a grin.

He tore his eyes away from her and watched the rest of the band as Toni slid into a guitar solo that blew the whole room away. She was frighteningly talented. And Lilly's vocals were on a level Ty couldn't fathom. Smoky, then sweet, and then growling with aggression. Tiff played bass like a demon possessed by another more rhythmically gifted demon.

It struck Ty what an idiot he had been. How had he not realized who he'd been driving around with all this time? These women were on the verge of major success.

By the time they finished the final song in their short set, Ty knew they were already well on their way. There were cell phones everywhere he looked, as people recorded the performance, no doubt intending to upload it somewhere online. Again, he wondered why the band hadn't released an album yet. This crowd would likely have cleaned out the store of every copy they had in stock.

Was it a problem with their label? Did it have anything to do with the dispute with their former bandmate? Not that it was any of his business, but Ty couldn't help his curiosity.

The patrons crowded the back of the store as the girls set down their instruments.

"The band brought some posters to sign, and we have some of their merch available at the counter if anyone's interested," the shop employee said as he retook the mic. "Give them some room to breathe," he added, laughing at the enthusiasm of the small crowd.

People did back up and let the band members move to the front of the store, where a line immediately formed at the small table setup.

"Where are you guys from?" a woman asked as the girls took their seats.

"We all live in the New York/Philadelphia corridor," Tiff answered. "Though not all of us are from the area."

"How long have you been together?" the blond from earlier asked. "And do you have anything I can stream?"

"We've been together for about a year and a half, except for Toni," Kayla said, putting her hand on Toni's shoulder. "This one is brand spanking new." She grinned.

Toni rolled her eyes but smiled. "I've only been with the band, officially, for a few months."

"Well, you guys sound like you were meant to play together." The employee that had introduced the band smiled at them. Others nodded.

"Thanks," Toni replied.

Ty got out of the way of patrons who approached the table for autographs. A few asked to take a selfie, quite a few of them with Lilly alone, but most with the entire band. Pride welled up in his chest. Which was absurd since he had nothing at all to do with the band. Still...

"Help me load?" Seb asked, appearing at Ty's side.

"Sure." Ty followed him to the stage. Together, they packed up the instruments and equipment and took them back to the bus. He used the remote to unlock the cargo hold. "Oh, by the way, there's a second remote key that I can give you," he said to Seb. "In case we get separated or, for some reason, I'm not on the bus when you need to get in."

"Yeah, that would be great. Thanks."

"No problem. I'll grab one for you," Ty said as they shut the cargo hold. He opened the front door, and Seb followed him inside. "It's kept in a lockbox in one of the cabinets here."

Ty crouched down to show him and used his code to unlock the box, retrieving a key. "Do you think you need more than one? I have two more."

"Nah." Seb took the key. "Greater chance of one getting lost. If we have to share, we'll probably keep better track of it."

"Smart thinking."

Seb went back inside the store, and Ty locked up the bus, walking around its perimeter to make sure everything was secure. When he came around to the sidewalk, a woman's startled gasp drew his attention.

Ty turned to find her frozen in place and staring at him, her eyes wide as she clutched a tote bag to her chest.

His first instinct was to offer a reassuring smile. "Sorry, I didn't mean to startle you." He gave her a wide berth, gesturing for her to continue past him.

She scowled, her gaze raking over him with a palpable distrust that made his skin crawl.

Ty wanted to say something, but he knew no words would convince this woman he was harmless. He could see the judgment in her eyes as she took in his appearance—his locs, his dark clothing with all of its straps and pins and holes. His skin color.

"Those buses have alarms," she said, pointing at the vehicle.

"Yes, ma'am. I know." He lifted the key and dangled it in front of her. "I'm the driver."

Confusion colored her expression and her eyes swept over him again. Then she looked at the record store and grunted with indignation before turning and walking away.

Ty sighed. He debated getting back on the bus, but he'd promised himself he wouldn't skulk away this time. Resigned and already on edge, he headed back inside.

The line had dwindled down to a few people. Seb was talking to one of the staff members, so Ty hung by the door. He wasn't in the mood to people *before* he'd been profiled by the woman outside, so he sure as hell wasn't in the mood now.

It felt like all eyes were on him, even though no one was really paying him any attention outside of a few curious glances. Everyone was too wrapped up in the Lillys, which should have put him at ease.

"Did anyone ever tell you that you look like the lead singer of Bloc Party?"

Ty startled. He hadn't even seen the guy walk up to stand next to him. "Uh..."

The man's eyes went wide. "Wait, *are* you the lead singer of Bloc Party? I love you guys so much. Are you broken up for good?"

"Sorry, I'm not," Ty told him, watching as the guy visibly deflated. He wanted to say *it's not that hard to tell one Black person from the next* but realized he did resemble the singer.

"Oh, of course not. Sorry," he added as if realizing he might have been insulting Ty.

"No problem." Ty tried for a smile. He probably should have said something, thanked the guy for the compliment...something.

"Are you with these guys?" The guy gestured toward the table.

"I'm just crew," Ty said, hoping the man would take the hint and go. Instead, he'd moved uncomfortably close.

"Lucky you." The fan's voice took on a wistful tone. "That was a great set. I hope they come through again sometime."

"I'm sure they will." Ty turned to watch Kayla as she chatted with one of the other patrons. Her smile was easy and genuine. She'd left her hair down, and it framed her face in fiery curls.

Kayla was a study in contradictions. Sweet but never fake. Compact but not delicate. And her mind was sharp, which was like catnip for him. Brains and beauty? Ty would be in so much trouble if he let his thoughts wander where they kept threatening to go. It had been a very long time since anyone had gotten under his skin like this.

Best to keep things professional. Friendly but professional.

Ty had roughly one more week on the road with the band. And he was more than content with the easy camaraderie he and Kayla had developed. He found he didn't want to risk that. Making friends had never come easily to him and, if nothing else, Ty wanted Kayla as that. The thought sparked a feeling of warmth inside.

When the store cleared out, Kayla rose from the table. She said something to the staff member, who nodded, and then made her way over to Ty.

"Did we suck?"

He laughed. "You know you didn't. And why ask me? I'm no expert."

Kayla's eyes twinkled. She had a gorgeous smile. "Your opinion is valuable. Besides, I know you'll be brutally honest."

"I will?" He arched an eyebrow.

"Yup. You have no reason to lie."

"I try never to lie," he said truthfully.

"I believe you."

Their gazes lingered, and Ty realized she could sense his discomfort. He shifted away from her. "Listen, do you know how long you plan to stay here?"

"Probably another twenty minutes or so. We promised to sign some of their merch for the store, and Seb wants to check their inventory for some old Caspian's Ghost album he's been looking for."

"If you don't mind, I'm going to get some air."

Her brow creased with concern. "You okay?"

"Fine," Ty replied, offering what he hoped was a decent smile. He hated that the woman on the sidewalk had gotten to him. "I'll be ready to leave when you are."

CHAPTER 12.

THE BOOKSTORE STOOD A BLOCK or two away from Culture Clash and had caught Kayla's eye when they were unloading the gear. Her first thought was to ask Ty if he wanted to come with her to check it out.

Kayla wasn't sure when their shy, reserved driver had become someone she wanted to make plans with, but it probably wasn't healthy. She did know that something was off with Ty when he left the record store.

She'd seen him in the crowd during their set, and he seemed to be enjoying himself. Ty had been all bright smiles and bouncing hair as he watched them.

The Ty who had just walked back to the bus was a different guy. Sullen, almost surly, and curt. He'd tried to hide it, but Kayla wasn't buying the smile he'd tried to force.

"Hey, Seb? I need to pop out to the bus. Do you have that extra key?"

"Sure." He tossed it to her.

"Any luck finding that record yet?"

"No, but they have some vintage Nirvana that might empty my bank account."

Kayla grinned when Toni grabbed his arm. "Yeah, no. That's not happening when we're saving for that *thing* we talked about."

Seb groaned but he was smiling when Toni pulled him away.

Kayla's hand hovered over the handle when she reached the door of the bus. She was tempted to go look for Ty, but what if all he wanted was to be alone? She could change out of her sweaty top and go check on him. What was the harm in that? Kayla was pretty adept at reading people. She'd let him be if that's what he wanted.

Opening the door, she stepped inside, turned toward the back of the bus and froze.

Shirtless, Ty stood in the middle of the living area with a towel over his head. Kayla was greeted by the sight of a broad back and flawless mahogany skin. Ty wasn't ripped like someone who worked out in a gym, but his lean muscles flexed as he buckled his belt.

He turned, startled to see her standing there. "Oh fuck!"

"Shit! I'm so sorry," Kayla sputtered as she turned away. If he had been anyone else in their group, it wouldn't have been a big deal. She and Ty did not have that kind of relationship.

Or *any* kind of relationship. Nor would they.

"It's fine. I wasn't expecting anyone yet," Ty said. "I grabbed a shower."

Kayla chanced a look at him. He was still shirtless, and she was treated to a view of his long, lean torso. She fought to keep her eyes above Ty's shoulders and not fixate on the way his kilt hung low on his hips.

"Did you need me?"

"What?" Kayla stared at him and knew full well her face was flaming red.

Blinking, Ty drew in a deep breath as he clutched the towel in his hands. "Are we, uh, ready to roll?"

"No, I..." *Jesus, get a grip.* Kayla scrambled to think of something to say. "There's a used bookstore down the street. I thought..."

"Really?" He dropped the towel on the table and tugged a shirt over his head.

"Yeah. Yep." Her voice still felt a tiny bit shaky. "Maybe you'd like to come, but if not I—"

"I would," he rushed to answer. Grabbing the wet towel, Ty walked to the cockpit and hung it on a hook behind his seat. Kayla hovered in the doorway while he pulled a pair of socks from his duffel.

Looking up, he grinned as he gestured to his feet. "I'm decent now."

"Ha. Ha. I feel like the indecent one. Anyway, I think I spied some L. A. Banks in the window, and I know you're a fan."

His smile was blinding. "Thanks for thinking of me."

The awkwardness of walking in on him when he was practically naked quickly dissipated. Having returned Seb's key, Kayla and Ty strolled to the bookstore together and fell back into comfortable banter.

Like Culture Clash, this place was stacked, floor to ceiling. They might have had every book ever published in stock. It was a maze of teetering columns, and Ty kept holding down the folds of his kilt like he was afraid he'd send one of them tumbling down.

"No way," he exclaimed quietly. Despite the classic rock pouring from the speakers outside the store, they'd both adopted their library voices once they stepped inside.

"What did you find?"

Ty pointed up at a glass case on the wall that held a copy of *Minion* by L. A. Banks. "Do you think it's a first edition?"

Kayla nodded. "It would have to be, right? Otherwise, why put it behind glass?"

"Ouch, or charge a mint for it," Ty said, wincing.

"How much?" She was too short to make out the numbers on the tiny price tag.

"Two-fifty," he said, deflating. "And, God, it's signed."

Kayla could afford that easily, but she knew enough not to

say anything. It was a lot of money but worth it and more, in her opinion.

"It's priceless, really," Ty said, echoing her thoughts. "She was a master storyteller."

"She was."

They wandered carefully through the store, drifting apart and coming together over and over. Kayla would find a title and show it to him. Ty would smile or comment and show her what he'd found. Eventually, the conversation was limited to smiles and nods.

She could have stayed under the spell for hours, books and Ty and the world at their fingertips on the pages that surrounded them.

At one point, she lost sight of his tall figure. Kayla carefully picked her way through the labyrinthine store until she spotted the bottom of his kilt. She allowed herself a moment to admire the curve of his calf muscles before giving herself a mental shake. Objectively, Ty was hot. She knew that even before she blundered onto the bus after his shower. This guy ticked all of her boxes, but Kayla hoped they could become friends. It was all she could offer him, given the circumstances.

"Hey," she said quietly, rounding the corner before she stopped in her tracks for the second time that day.

In his hands, Ty held a copy of her mother's newly published book. His brow furrowed as he scanned the pages.

Stepping back, Kayla took a moment to reorient herself. Her mother's face stared at her from the cover, her expression one of grace and compassion, wisdom and understanding. Gisele Larrington was capable of all those things to wildly varying degrees. However, she was an expert at writing exactly the type of thing other people needed, or wanted, to hear.

Ty seemed utterly engrossed in whatever he'd found on the pages. Emotions passed over his face like ripples in a pond.

"Find something interesting?"

Ty looked up at the sound of Kayla's voice, and the corner of his mouth tipped up into a grin. "I can't recall if I've read this author before. I saw the cover and thought she kind of reminded me of you."

"D-does she?" The air was suddenly very thin. Kayla leaned against one of the shelving units and hoped it was sturdy.

He flipped it over to read the back cover.

Kayla's stomach dropped as her mom's exquisitely photographed likeness stared back at her.

"This says she's written a series of children's books that's sold millions of copies. *Damn*. The Little Miss Yolanda series." He shrugged. "Never heard of it, but apparently she's president of..." His eyes widened. "Carradine University. Wow," he said softly as he looked at the front again.

It hadn't even occurred to her that a store this small would carry her mother's work, but of course it would.

When Ty held up the cover again, Kayla fought to control the tremor in her hands. "Looks just like you, doesn't she?" he asked, oblivious.

"It's...uncanny." Kayla congratulated herself for sounding so unaffected.

"She's even got your freckles."

"Yep," Kayla said dismissively. She didn't want to ruin their first time hanging out with her unresolved parental angst. Setting the book facedown on the nearest stack, she pointed to the shelf Ty had been scanning. "You read a lot of nonfiction?"

"Some," Ty replied with no hint of embarrassment. He cocked his head at her. "You don't?"

"To be honest, I haven't. Am I missing out?"

"Uh, *yeah*," he said, his eyes widening in surprise. "You can learn a lot through self-study."

"I hadn't thought about it that way." Kayla grabbed a book

from a different shelf, dismayed when Ty stopped to pick up her mom's book again.

Apparently, she'd earned another reader.

"Are you one of those perpetual students, always learning?"

Ty's jaw flexed, his smile hard to read this time. "Something like that. There's always something new to learn," he said. "It's a big world. The day we stop wanting to understand, the world will be lost."

"You're surprising," Kayla said as they turned down another aisle.

Ty peered down at her. "How so?"

She searched for words to explain. "I love that you love what you love, if that makes any sense. You're unapologetically *you*."

Stopping, he turned to her and frowned. "Is there something I need to apologize for?"

Without thinking, Kayla grasped his arm. "No, God, no. Not at all, I just meant..." She blew out a breath. What was she even trying to say? "I like you. That's all."

Ty's gaze softened before he ducked his head. He nodded. "Good to know 'cause I like you too."

"Cool." Kayla let her hand drop away as warmth ran, unbidden, up her arm and into her chest. This was straying into dangerous territory. She turned away.

And walked right into a stack of books.

Ty's arm shot out above her head, steadying the precarious pile.

Kayla couldn't stop herself from following the line of his arm down to his shoulder as she turned to face him.

He met her eyes, his going dark. "Kayla, I—"

For a moment, time stood still.

She could do it. Just once. Lean up and...

The sound of someone clearing their throat brought Kayla back to her senses just as Ty dropped his arm and stepped back.

They stared at each other for a long minute. In a moment of startling clarity, Kayla realized how much she actually liked this guy. Like, *really* liked him. She couldn't remember the last time she felt the giddy anticipation of being in a room with someone. It wasn't about sex—if he was even interested in sex, that is—but about companionship. The easy banter. Their shared interests.

As if he could read her thoughts, Ty gave her a sheepish grin. "We should get back before the others think I've kidnapped you." There was a little more edge to the joke than she would have expected.

"Oh," Kayla said. "We don't want that." She moved to leave, but Ty took her hand and gave it a squeeze.

"I don't know if I should even say this, but...I meant it when I said I like you," he said, his voice low. His gaze dipped from her eyes to her mouth and back, faster than a blink. "I do. A lot. You're a very cool chick."

"I'm a cool chick, eh?"

Ty pushed her hand away and laughed. "Too corny?"

"Just corny enough," she said, holding out her thumb and index finger to demonstrate. "Only just." Kayla looked at him. "This was fun. You're fun. We should hang out more often. No pressure," she added.

"No pressure," he echoed. "Are we allowed to hang out? I wouldn't want to get fired for breaking my contract."

Kayla couldn't tell if he was joking or not, but she rushed to reassure him. "Socializing with me isn't part of your job, Ty. I don't want you to feel obligated."

"Obligated?" He arched an eyebrow. "Not at all. I was making a joke, a bad one, about the clause that says I can't *fraternize* with my boss."

This brought her up short. "Does it actually say that?"

"Essentially." Ty walked toward the register to pay.

"Really?" Kayla scoffed, following him. "Whose dumb idea

was that?" And then she remembered. *Ugh, Candi.* Ruining things even when she wasn't around anymore.

Laughing to himself, Ty paid for his books, and they walked back to the bus.

The others were boarding as they approached, and Kayla tried not to feel any particular way when Ty put some space between them.

She understood the logic, even agreed with it. Whatever was happening between them, friendship or anything that friendship might possibly lead to, it didn't need an audience.

Ty stopped and turned to her, his gaze lingering on hers for a moment before he looked away. Smiling, he walked backward. "Okay, well...that was fun. You know where to find me if you wanna hang again."

Kayla wanted to keep that smile on his face for as long as she could. "With your nose buried in a book. Where else?"

CHAPTER 13.

THE FESTIVAL IN ANN ARBOR was small, and the crowd was less enthusiastic than the other shows they'd played thus far on the trip. As a result, the band's energy flagged in the middle of their twenty-five-minute set. It was a letdown, but Kayla figured not every show was going to be a resounding success.

She had things on her mind, and by *things* she meant Ty.

And her parents.

Her mother's latest text sat unanswered on her phone.

MOM: You haven't RSVPed for the banquet? Please tell me you plan to be there for your father's special night.

Kayla hadn't even opened the text, just read the preview. Her mother wouldn't know that she'd seen it. Kayla hadn't RSVPed because, if she did, it would mean her first trip home in almost five years was actually happening. Plans meant dealing with her mother in person. It meant Kayla telling her about her life and the band and dealing with the fallout. It meant becoming Katherine Larrington again, for her parents' friends and colleagues.

Kayla wasn't sure she had enough spoons saved up for that just yet. But the date of the banquet was set in stone, so Kayla was only delaying the inevitable.

Without thinking, she kicked her legs over the side of her bunk and wandered to the living area.

Toni and Seb were huddled over an acoustic guitar, various notebooks and scraps of paper on the table in front of them along with a digital recorder. Lilly lounged with her long legs stretched out along one of the benches, her head against the window. Tiff lay curled on her side, her head resting on Lilly's bent knee, sound asleep. No one looked up at Kayla as she passed by.

She slipped through the curtain into the cockpit, drawn inexorably to the presence of the person on the other side.

Ty was as he had been throughout the trip, his eyes focused on the road and an ever-present audiobook pulled up on his phone.

Kayla sat in the jump seat, content to observe him for a while. She didn't understand the calm that came over her when Ty was close by. They were strangers, but she couldn't deny they had a connection. Or at least, the spark of one.

"What's wrong?" Ty asked after a few minutes. He flicked on the turn signal and moved to the right lane, handling the bus with ease.

"I didn't mean to disturb you." She hadn't realized he'd heard her come in.

"You're not" came his quiet reply. He removed his earbud. "What's up?"

Kayla hesitated. The spine of her mother's book, tucked inside the mesh on the door behind him, was lit up by the strobe of passing streetlamps. "Family stuff."

"Ah," Ty said. "Well, I'm a good listener if you need to vent."

Kayla moved from the jump seat to the dash, turning to face him.

"It makes me nervous when you sit there." His eyes moved back and forth between her and the dark road ahead.

She braced her foot against the opposite wall and held on to the railing.

Ty visibly exhaled. "Still not a fan, but...okay. I'm listening."

"What were you listening to?"

He cut her a sideways glance before answering, probably recognizing the delay tactic for what it was.

"I just finished *Bloodchild*. I'll probably take a break before I move on to more audio," he said. "Let it marinate."

"It was that good?"

Ty nodded. His gaze flicked over to her. "I think you'd enjoy the different stories. I can lend you my paper copy if you want."

"Sure."

"You'll have to wait 'til we get back to Philly," he said, his words slowing.

Kayla studied his face, the slight curve of his full mouth. "Does that mean you want to hang out in Philly?"

"Maybe," he said, drawing out the word. His smile was slow. "If that's what you want."

She did. Very much. "I don't know much about indie bookstores in Philly. You could show me your favorites."

"I could."

They were silent for a few heartbeats, and Kayla let the possibility of more time with Ty sink in. It eased some of the tension in her belly, and she raised her other leg to rest her foot against the driver's seat, next to Ty's thigh. She'd needed to feel close to him but didn't know where the boundaries lay. It was an overture. A bold one, and very much unlike her.

After a moment, Ty reached down and grasped her ankle, giving it a light squeeze before returning his hand to the wheel.

"So? Family drama," he said. "Lay it on me."

Kayla groaned. "You know when your family does that thing where they refuse to accept that you're an adult, no matter how old you get, and insist on dictating every aspect of your life?"

Ty's brows lifted. "Uh...no, can't say I do. Sounds fucking annoying, though."

"You mean your granddad doesn't try to guilt you into doing what he wants?"

A shadow passed over his face and his brows drew tight.

"Did I say something wrong?"

"No, I..." He exhaled slowly. "Sorry, I don't mean to pry."

"I know."

"But if you *ever* need to talk, I'm here," she said.

Ty briefly lifted his eyes to hers. Even in the low light of the cabin, she could see his pain. Had an inkling what he would say before he said it and her heart was already breaking for him.

"My parents died when I was young."

Kayla's blood turned cold. "Oh my God," she breathed. "Ty...I'm...I'm so sorry, I didn't mean to..."

"It's okay," he said, but his hands tightened on the steering wheel. "It was a long time ago."

"How...?"

He shrugged. "My mother died when I was six months old. Freak accident. A car hit some debris on the Schuylkill—that's the interstate that runs through Philly. The guy flipped his Beemer over the guardrail and landed on her car."

"Jesus..."

"Yeah." He chewed on his bottom lip. The light glinted off the flat, gold hoop that lay against the bridge of his nose. Kayla didn't remember seeing it there before. "They say she died on impact. So that's something, I guess."

"Fuck... I'm so sorry."

"Me too."

"And your dad? Was he in the car too?"

Ty grimaced. "No, he…"

Even from an angle, Kayla could see sorrow filling his eyes. "Hey, you don't have to tell me."

"It's okay," he said, clearing his throat. "My dad died when I was eleven. He was great, though, a great father to me. By all accounts, he had been a wonderful, supportive partner to my mom. A loving son to my grandfather. That's who raised me, really. I wouldn't be who I am without him, so I can't really imagine my life going any differently. If that makes any sense."

"Yeah, I think so. But, God, I can't even imagine living through something like that at such a young age," Kayla said, her heart aching. "Your parents sound like lovely people. I'm sorry they were taken from you so soon."

"Thank you," Ty said, swallowing hard. "My mother was a teacher. Elementary school."

"And your dad?"

"He was a contractor, but I think he would have done something else with his life if he'd had the money for college," Ty replied, pride and sorrow warring in his voice. "He was always reading. He read to me, taught me to read."

"It's like he lives on through your love of books," Kayla said without thinking.

Ty glanced over at her and smiled softly. "Yeah. I never thought of it that way, but yeah."

"And your grandfather? Is he a big reader too?"

"Not as much. We lived with him, and he and Dad sort of co-fathered me. I still live with him," he finished, a note of bitterness in his words. "Dad hadn't really prepared for the future—my future—college and stuff. I guess he thought he still had time."

"I'm so sorry," Kayla said, feeling like a broken record. "He sounds like a wonderful man. They both do."

Ty smiled softly. "Yeah, Pop-Pop's the best man I know."

"Pop-Pop?"

He chuckled. "I've called him that all my life. His name is Van, which I also call him when he's acting up."

Kayla grinned. "It sounds like you have an extraordinary relationship with him."

"I do," he said, nodding. "I don't know where I'd be without him." Ty's voice cracked, but he coughed to cover it up.

Kayla's heart swelled with affection. Ty was too sweet for words.

"So, your family," he said. "Tell me more. If you want to, that is."

"I feel like an asshole complaining about them after what you just told me," she confessed.

"Don't." Ty's voice was gentle. "Talk to me."

Where should she begin? Kayla needed to find a way to explain without revealing all of her carefully held secrets.

"Well, my mother, she's made a career out of teaching others how to be perfect parents with perfect kids. Being her actual children felt like living in a pressure cooker. For me, especially. I was always ready to blow."

"You have siblings?"

"I did," she replied. "A brother but..." She met Ty's sad gaze.

"Ah, man. I'm so sorry."

"Thanks. It was a long time ago." Kayla echoed his words. "That doesn't seem to matter to the pain, though."

Ty nodded. "Did you guys get along?"

Kayla smiled. "We did. He was the best."

"Okay, Mom's demanding. And Dad?"

"Dad is brilliant. Kind. And completely under my mother's spell. He's been head over heels for her since the day they met. In our family, what she says goes."

"She sounds...like a lot of work," Ty hedged.

She laughed. "That's putting it mildly. Don't get me wrong, I love my mother—both of my parents—but she made living there impossible at times."

"Gotcha. What do they do?"

Here is where things got tricky, and she took a moment. "They're both teachers."

"Really?" His tone brightened. "What do they teach?"

"Him, literature. Her, education with an emphasis on early development."

"No shit," he said, sounding thoroughly impressed.

It made her smile. Of all the people she could talk to about her parents' areas of expertise, Ty would be the one to really appreciate it.

"I thought about teaching," he said, his tone wistful.

"Why don't you?"

"Life." The weight of that one word told Kayla there was way more to the story, but they were only twenty minutes from their Detroit hotel. She filed away a reminder to ask him about it again later.

"Anyway, my mother's standards are high, and I don't measure up to them."

"Well, that's bullshit," he said, scowling.

"What is?" Seb asked as he made his way toward the front.

Ty's hands tightened on the wheel.

"We were discussing a frustrating ending in a book," she lied smoothly.

Ty glanced up at her briefly but did not say anything.

"Two nerds in a pod," Seb said, grinning. "Kay, you up for doing an interview when we get into Detroit? YMI's PR guy called. A reporter finagled a sit-down with the band for twenty minutes."

Kayla loathed interviews but supposed she'd have to get used to them. "Sure, I'm game if the others are."

"Sweet, I'll confirm the time." He turned to Ty. "Hey, man, thanks again for doubling as a roadie on this trip. It's not part of your job description, but I really appreciate it."

"We all do," Kayla added.

"Happy to help," Ty said. "It's been interesting seeing this whole thing from the other side."

"I keep meaning to ask. Has anyone ever mistaken you for a musician?" Seb gestured to Ty's outfit, which consisted of another one of his utility kilts and a Black Panther tee. He'd rolled up the sleeves to reveal the lean, long arms that were quickly becoming an obsession for Kayla. "You've got the look."

"Do I?" Ty glanced down at himself. "No, no one has ever assumed that about me, personally. But I was mistaken for Kele Okereke back at the record store."

"From Bloc Party?" Kayla asked, incredulous. "Um, isn't he in his forties?"

Ty snorted. "Yep."

"I don't know if that's a compliment or an insult."

"Both?" Ty asked, laughing.

Seb leaned against the half wall and folded his arms. "You play at all?"

"Not really," Ty said. "Well, I guess I sing a little. And I write."

"A budding songwriter." Seb nodded appreciatively. "I knew it had to be something."

Kayla knew Seb was sizing Ty up, however subtle he thought he was. Her thoughts went back to the conversation about Ty's troubled past, and she wondered if it had anything to do with his father's death or his mother's accident.

"Maybe Kayla can talk you into laying down some backing tracks with me," Seb said. "I pitch in on the low notes."

Ty met her gaze. "She could probably talk me into it."

Kayla pressed her lips together to hide her grin.

"Cool, cool," Seb said, straightening. "How much farther do we have?"

Ty checked the navigation app. "We're about twenty minutes out. Thirty, if we hit traffic on Michigan Avenue, but I don't see anything but green on the traffic maps."

"Perfect." Seb's thumbs tapped furiously on his phone as he walked away.

"I should probably gather my shit," Kayla said.

"Okay," Ty murmured. His eyes were on the road.

Kayla stood to go and paused. Even though being around him did wicked things to her pulse, Ty also inspired a stillness in her that was rare. Kayla wanted more of it.

"I was thinking about taking a walk by the river tonight if you aren't too tired after the drive."

"Hmmm. I don't know."

Surprised, Kayla frowned, but Ty kept his eyes on the road. "No problem. Just thought I'd ask."

"It's not that I don't want to go, Kayla. I'm just worried."

"About?"

Ty looked up at her, his eyes dark with something she hadn't seen in them before. "Whether I can resist kissing you before my contract ends."

CHAPTER 14.

THE HOTEL LOBBY WAS A collage of gleaming marble, wide pillars, and twinkling glass, shades more luxurious than anything Ty had ever stepped foot in before. It wasn't that he'd never had the opportunity. He just didn't understand the need for the trappings of wealth—even someone's mass-produced, mid-budget ideal of it.

But Ty was grateful for the experience, and the king-size bed in his room was like a cloud when he tested it out.

After they checked in, the members of the band retired to their respective rooms to freshen up before their interview. It seemed like quite a bit of their activities were last minute—from the in-store in Toledo to this—but Ty figured that's how it was in their business. What they did resembled trying to capture lightning in a bottle.

After a quick shower, Ty stacked the pillows against the head-board and propped himself against them, resisting the urge to sink down and sleep. He was curious about the interview, loving all the behind-the-scenes glimpses into this world he was only visiting for a short time.

He plugged in his phone and decided to check on Van, putting the phone on speaker as it rang. He closed his eyes.

"Hello, Tyrell?"

Ty's eyes popped back open as the woman's voice on the other end startled him. He sat up. "Hello?"

"Hi, it's Peggy."

A wave of panic stole Ty's next breath. He grabbed the phone from the nightstand. "What's wrong? Where's Van?"

"Hey, hey. Everything is all right," she said soothingly. "I didn't mean to scare you. I'm here with him now."

In the background, between Peggy's assurance and the thudding of his own rabbiting heart, Ty could hear his granddad fussing up a storm.

"I told you not to bother Ty," Pop-Pop said in the distance.

"I didn't, Van. He called you." To Ty she said, "I heard the smoke detector beeping when I passed by on my way to the store. I knocked on the door and used the extra key you gave me when I didn't get an answer."

"I didn't answer because I was busy putting out the fire," Pop-Pop argued behind her.

"Fire?" Ty jumped up, searching the room for…what, he didn't know. "Is he hurt?"

"No, not at all. It was only a splatter of grease that caught in the pan," Peggy replied. "He's not hurt, only embarrassed."

"Could you put him on?" Ty closed his eyes and tried to control his breathing. *This* was why he didn't want to leave for so long. "Pop-Pop?"

"I'm here," he grumbled. "I told this nosy woman I didn't need her to call you. All panicking over nothing. My grandbaby is out of town for work. You shouldn't have bothered him," Pop-Pop groused to Peggy.

"For the eleventieth time, I didn't!" Peggy spat back.

"Van!" Ty snapped, needing to get his granddad's attention. "What happened, exactly?"

There was a long-suffering sigh on the other end of the call that did more to settle Ty's nerves than anything yet. "I was frying up some pancetta for this potato dish I saw on Stanley Tucci's show. I turned my head for one second, to get a spoon, and the damned stuff burned to a crisp. Grease everywhere, and nothing but charred bits in the pan. I swear, bacon would do just as good. I know bacon."

Ty ran a hand down his face and sank down onto the bed. "Pop-Pop."

"I'm really fine," he replied, sounding at least a tad contrite. "I know what you're thinking, and I'm fine. Could have happened to anyone."

"I should come home tonight."

"You're starting back tomorrow, aren't you? I see it here on the calendar."

"Yes, but—"

"And what do you think will happen in the next twenty-four hours?"

Ty was torn. Being away had been good for him. Had gotten him out of his head for a while and cut into the debt he'd accrued, but maybe it had been a mistake.

"Don't you dare say it," Pop-Pop warned him.

"I shouldn't have taken this job."

There was a moment of silence before Ty heard Van say something muffled to Peggy. When his granddad returned to the call, his voice was quiet but sober.

"Tyrell," he began, and Ty's back stiffened. "I am fine. These things happen. I won't let you use it as an excuse to stop living your life. From what you've told me, this trip has been good for you. You made a little money and you got to see more of the country. Tell me something. How have you been sleeping?"

"Better," Ty replied with reluctance. The guilt was too much. "But I'd never sleep again if something happened to you and I wasn't there to do anything."

"What, so, you're planning to stay home with me all day, every day, for the rest of my life?" his granddad asked, irritation creeping into his voice. "That's not a way for a man in his prime to live, son. Besides, you act like I'm some old man who needs tending. I have a lot of life left in me too, you know."

Ty couldn't help the shaky laugh that escaped. "Don't I know it."

"What time do you get in?"

"We're leaving after breakfast," Ty replied, doing the mental calculations. "It's about a nine-hour drive, but I don't know if they plan to stop for lunch or for any other detours."

"Either way, sounds like you'll be home late," Pop-Pop said. "You'll probably be hungry. I'll have something waiting for you."

"Don't wait up."

"I'll do what I please," he replied, but there was humor in his voice. "Or at least as my eyelids please. I may be snoring when you get in, I may not. We'll see. Either way, I can't wait to hear how it went."

"I promise to tell you every detail if you promise to stick to baking when I'm not home." Ty expected him to argue.

"Deal," Pop-Pop grumbled. "Let me get back before Peggy throws away good food. I swear, that woman will be the death of me."

Ty grinned. "She's sweet on you. Go easy on her."

"Stop talking nonsense," his granddad replied.

"Funny thing is," Ty added, "I'm pretty sure you're sweet on her too."

The call ended with more grumbling from Van and a request to pick up some real maple syrup, since he was "so close to Canada, he could skip there."

Despite its expansive size, Ty felt cooped up in the room after he hung up. He decided to head back down to the lobby in search of a snack, resisting the urge to seek out Kayla and steal another minute of her company.

Ty was in real danger of losing his head over her. He couldn't believe he'd been so bold with her earlier, though the idea of kissing her sent heat coursing through him.

"Calm down," he muttered to himself as he stepped onto the elevator. "You'd think you'd never kissed anyone before."

To be fair, it had been a while. The last time Ty had spent any significant time with anyone other than Pop-Pop was before the whole ordeal with Meredith. Ty's ex, Shawn, hadn't even bothered to check in with him before, during, or after everything went down.

So, yeah. It had been quite some time since Ty had felt this kind of connection. Had *allowed* himself to connect. He'd been writing more too. Not about the isolation and humiliation of what he suffered through, but about hope. Potential.

The elevator arrived in the lobby in time for Ty to catch the girls and Seb walking toward the far end. A short woman in an ill-fitting sundress walked briskly alongside them. Curious and, let's face it, eager to cement his plans with Kayla, Ty followed.

There were several others seated in the area as they arrived, and he hung back. The band took seats on one side of the bank of chairs, and the group of a dozen strangers occupied the other, with Seb hovering in between. Ty guessed they were reporters, judging by how they held out their cell phones to record and vigorously took notes on their notepads. Old school versus new, he thought.

"I didn't expect this to turn into a press conference," Seb said. He laughed, but Ty could see the tension around his eyes.

Lilly sat with her arms folded, watching the people across from her with open suspicion.

"When my colleagues found out I was meeting with you, they followed me from the festival in Ann Arbor," the woman in the sundress said. "I hope you don't mind."

"It's fine," Seb replied, though it clearly wasn't. Even Kayla looked tense. "We can give you twenty minutes, then they need to get some rest."

"Sure," the woman replied. She turned to Lilly. "How are things without your former guitarist, Candi?"

"Candi moved on several months ago, and we wish her all the best," Lilly replied smoothly. "Toni's with us now, and it's like a breath of fresh air. I couldn't imagine us without her."

The answer sounded rote, and Ty wondered how many times Lilly had been asked the same question.

"You said something similar about Candi when I asked you about her in New York last fall," another reporter said.

What an original question.

He looked like a throwback to the Seattle grunge scene circa 1992, complete with a flannel shirt tied around his waist. Considering the high that day was over 90 degrees Fahrenheit, Ty assumed he wore it ironically. His question, however, was meant to make the girls uncomfortable, and Ty disliked him immediately.

"A band is like a marriage," Lilly said, evidently unbothered by the need to repeat herself. "Sometimes, it leads to happily ever after, and sometimes it ends in divorce."

"Working with Candi was awesome, and she really brought something unique to the table," Tiff added, pulling from the script they'd all mentally constructed. "But like Lilly said, it didn't work out."

"Toni, have you found your place in the Lillys?" another woman asked. She was petite, with medium-brown skin and short, glossy curls.

"Yeah," Toni said, looking at the others. "I think so. I feel like a part of the family."

"Not worried they're going to kick you out too?" the grunge guy asked.

"Dude, no one kicked Candi out," Kayla snapped. Her eyes flashed with anger, and Ty wanted to smack the guy for baiting her.

"I thought you wanted to talk to the band about this festival tour," Seb spoke loudly, and all of the reporters looked at him. "It's their first time out, and I think they're killing it."

"Hi." Another reporter raised his hand. "Seth Chin from *Swerve* magazine. I caught your set at Dragonfly completely by accident, and I was totally blown away. How has it been for you, transitioning from the smaller clubs to these, like, huge festival audiences?"

"The crowd they pulled in Ann Arbor wasn't *that* big," grungy muttered, and, geez. What an asshole.

Wisely ignoring him, Kayla responded. "It's been an adjustment but also just so incredible. I have a bird's-eye view from behind my kit, and it's wild to see so many people grooving to what we do."

"It's, like, a literal sea of faces," Toni added, smiling at Kayla. "And most of the time, they're hanging on every note."

"You think you'll be able to win back New York audiences?" This was from the woman in the sundress.

"I wasn't aware we'd lost them," Lilly replied coolly.

"I was at the showcase," the woman said. "I think that was the last time Candi was onstage with you, right? It was...memorable, but not for the reasons I think you hoped it would be."

An uncomfortable silence filled the room as Lilly stared the reporter down.

Tiff leaned over to whisper something to Toni, and Toni nodded before taking a deep breath.

"You all realize Candi's not with the Lillys anymore, right?" Tiff asked, grasping Toni's hand as she addressed the entire pool of reporters. "Does anyone actually care about the music, or are you all looking for a catfight?"

The woman gestured around the pool of reporters. "I think we're all here for the same reason, to get the full story about a group of women who are being touted as the next big thing. This, despite having a tumultuous start and no release date for their debut album. Could it be true that this is all a stunt to prop up Candi's ambition to be taken seriously?"

"What an outrageous—" Kayla began.

"I think we're done for tonight," Seb said as he moved to stand between the girls and the reporters.

"She has a point," a man said from the back of the group. "There does seem to be a lot more going on behind the scenes than onstage. Did losing Candi take the wind out of your sails as a band?"

Seb opened his mouth to say something, but Lilly held up her hand. She turned to face the reporter, her expression terrifyingly stark.

"The Lillys are a family with one goal in mind, to make music. We depend on each other and lift each other up. And when one of us no longer believed in that ideal, there was a mutual decision to part ways. We were fortunate to find someone, in Toni, who not only had the talent but the willingness to forgo ego for the greater good."

"The *greater good* being this band?" the guy asked, scribbling in a notepad. "So the rumors of your demise are premature?"

"We've only just begun," Lilly replied, and the reporter nodded, smiling to himself. It was a great quote.

"I think we'll leave it at that," Seb said. "Thanks for coming."

"Just one more question," said a woman who had been quiet the whole time. "This one is for Tiff."

After a moment, Tiff nodded. "Sure."

"I was wondering if your new *family* was aware of your old occupation."

"My...what?" Tiff seemed genuinely confused.

"What are you talking about?" Seb asked, his eyes narrowing.

"Is it true that you worked as a prostitute in Los Angeles before coming to the band?"

"I..." Tiff's mouth opened and closed.

"Where are you getting that from?" Seb asked the woman.

The reporter scrolled to something on her phone. "Your sister lives in LA, doesn't she? Is she in the *family* business too? All four of you have interesting histories. For instance, Ms...er...*Whitman*, I'd almost say you lead a double life."

Ty looked at Kayla.

Panic. Pure panic filled her eyes before she seemed to shutter it away.

"Let me answer your first question," Tiff cut in, her voice calm and even. "No, I've never been a sex worker. Even if I had been, I wouldn't be ashamed about it. It's an occupation, not an identity. People do what they have to get by in this world."

"Including sell their bodies for money?"

Toni let out a sharp laugh. "Are you serious, lady? What do you think actors do? Dancers? Musicians? We all work with our bodies, many of us for money. For some people it's *only* about the money. A worker in a cubicle isn't selling their body and mind to their employer? The construction worker? The miner? God, people like you are such hypocrites."

Lilly, Toni, and Kayla's heads all turned sharply toward her, each bearing differing expressions—from surprise to pride to admiration.

"So, you deny the allegation?" grunge guy asked Tiff.

"I think she gave you the only answer you deserve," Seb said through gritted teeth.

"And you, Kayla?" the woman said suddenly. "Aren't you worried about your family's reputation?"

All the color drained from her face, and Ty's hands fisted at his side. What the actual fuck was wrong with these *reporters*?

"We're done here," Seb said and gestured for the girls to stand. Through shouted questions, Seb tried to get the group out of there. They were outnumbered.

Without thinking, Ty grabbed a passing bellman. "Hey, could you get security?"

Taking in the scene, the bellman pulled out his radio. "We need a team in the conference area lobby ASAP."

Ty was already moving. He reached the crowd and pushed through, putting himself between the more aggressive reporters and the girls. Cameras flashed, and Ty ignored the sense of déjà vu that came over him.

With the help of two security guards, Seb and the bellman managed to maneuver the band over to the elevators.

Ty wanted to go to Kayla. He could tell she was upset. They all were. When the elevator arrived, the group piled in with security, but there wasn't enough room for Ty. He held back, trying in vain to catch Kayla's eye before the doors closed.

CHAPTER 15.

KAYLA WAS SO ANGRY SHE wanted to pummel someone. She pulled a pair of sticks out of her bag and began pacing the room, tapping out a paradiddle against her thigh.

"What the fuck was that?" Tiff asked. "Can they ask those kinds of questions?"

Seb was scrubbing furiously at his forehead with one hand. In the other, he held his phone up to his ear. "Jory. We just got ambushed. Hang on." He set the phone down on the coffee table.

They were in his and Toni's room, perched on a high floor overlooking the Detroit river.

"You're on speaker," Seb said.

"What happened?" Jordan's voice came through the phone.

"YMI messaged about a reporter that wanted to interview the girls," Seb replied. "Only, *one* reporter turned into more than a dozen, and they were armed to the teeth."

"Armed?"

Seb glanced at Tiff, who was biting her nails as she paced in a small circle.

Kayla walked over and put her arms around Tiff's shoulders, pulling her in tight. Tiff trembled, antsy, in her arms.

"They asked me if I've ever worked the streets in LA," Tiff said. "I think it's about Peaches."

Seb frowned at her. "Who?"

"Fuck," Jordan said.

Kayla let go of Tiff, who paced a few steps away. Tension lined her body as she clasped her hands above her head.

"That fucking girl. She did something, I know it," Tiff said.

"Does someone want to tell me what's going on?" Lilly asked. She looked at Seb, but he shook his head.

"Tiff?" he asked.

"It's probably going to come out anyway, Tiff." Jordan told her.

"I have a sister. Peaches," Tiff began.

"I thought—"

"She's not my *blood* sister," Tiff cut off Seb's question.

Kayla hadn't realized that no one else knew about Tiff's sister. It made her wary of whatever Tiff was about to say.

"We came up together. In the system. She's older, though she sure as shit doesn't act like it." Tiff dropped her arms to her side. "Anyway, we had different…goals for our lives. Peaches isn't much of a big-picture person. She does what she can to get from day to day, moment to moment. Beyond that…" She sighed. "She doesn't think about the consequences."

"And she's… She works…on the street?" Toni asked carefully.

Tiff moved to the sofa and plopped down. "She was on her own for a while, did okay. Then she hooked up with some lady who promised her, what did she call it? *Protection.* Something about safety in numbers."

"Like a madam?" Seb asked, his brow furrowed. He crouched down in front of Tiff. "Why didn't you tell any of us?"

Tiff looked at the phone, and Seb followed her gaze.

"Jory, you knew about this?"

"I knew some of it," he answered. "Tiff filled me in on the rest last week. Peaches has gotten herself into some hot water."

"She called me," Tiff said. "Apparently, she got tired of the arrangement with the woman and skipped out. Now, she's been chased out of the business entirely. She can't work."

"She could get a...different job," Lilly said.

Tiff laughed to herself. "I love my sister, but I wouldn't hire her to brush my teeth. She isn't the most reliable person."

"My immediate concern is the reporter who brought her up," Jordan said. "Did you catch which outlet she was from?"

"No," Seb said, cursing under his breath. "I snapped a few photos before we started. I'll send them over and point her out."

"I'll track her down." There was a pause. "Do we think this was YMI?"

Seb shot to his feet. "You think they planted her?"

"It was their idea to hold it last minute," Kayla said, unable to wrap her head around it all.

"They're trying to discredit us," Lilly said flatly. "Make us look like a joke band."

"Is this really all about Candi?" Toni sat down next to Tiff and put her arm around her shoulders.

Kayla was glad to see Tiff curl into her.

"First, they sign her new band, then she gets the choice opener slot, and now these random questions? I thought once we were done with her, we were done. She won't go away," Kayla said.

"She's not going to go away." Lilly sat down next to Tiff and took her hand. "But neither are we. What do you want to do about your sister? She needs money?"

"If we give her money now, she'll only ask for more later."

"We'll deal with that later," Jordan said. "If she's vulnerable, and needs to hustle—as you said, Tiff—anyone showing up on her doorstep with a check might get information out of her that you don't want publicized."

Tiff shook her head. "She wouldn't sell me out," she hurried to say, though she didn't sound certain of that.

"Maybe not voluntarily," Jordan said, sounding every inch the Ivy League educated attorney he was. "But even fragments of truth can be twisted by the right pen. I'll reach out and see what her immediate needs are."

"You don't have to do that." Tiff sounded weary.

"Yes, I do."

There was a long silence as they all looked around at each other, each eye landing on Tiff.

"Seb, a moment in private?"

Seb picked up the phone and walked to the bathroom, closing the door behind him.

"I don't know about you guys, but I'm starving," Toni said, meeting Kayla's gaze before turning her eyes to Lilly. She squeezed Tiff's stiff shoulders. "How about you, kiddo? Wanna find out what's good in Detroit?"

Tiff shook her head. "I'm not hungry."

Lilly's sharp intake of breath was subtle, but Kayla understood her alarm.

Tiff looked up at Lilly, her eyes rapidly filling with tears. "I'm sorry."

"For?" Lilly knelt in front her. Tiff shrugged. "Then don't apologize until you have something to apologize for. Come on. Let's get some food for you."

Tiff didn't argue when Lilly stood and pulled her up.

"Are you coming?"

"Seb and I will meet you there," Toni replied.

Lilly turned to Kayla, her brow raised in question.

"I'll join you there. I need to take care of something first."

The hotel stood at the western edge of downtown Detroit, the sky-line lit up against the black sky. A few puffs of cloud hovered above, reflecting the light from the taller buildings down the way. People walked lazily along the paved nature path as Kayla crossed it.

She found Ty looking out over the river. His kilt flapped gently around his calves as they flexed.

"We should probably exchange digits," she said coming up beside him. "Thought I might find you here."

"I needed some air." Ty was leaning against the railing, his long fingers knit together as he stared down at the water.

"Thanks for your help back there." Kayla had felt a wave of relief when she saw Ty running over with hotel staff hot on his heels. "It got ugly."

"Is it always like that?"

"Not lately."

He turned his head to her. They were shoulder to shoulder, and she could almost feel the heat from his body seeping into her skin.

"Is Tiff okay?"

Mirroring his pose, Kayla folded her fingers. "She will be."

"Was it true? About her sister?"

"That's not my story to tell."

Ty drew back. "Shit. Sorry. Of course. Forget I asked."

"It's okay," Kayla said. "Relax."

Ty snorted. "Relax. Yeah, okay."

They said nothing for a while. Kayla was grateful for the moment of peace. She listened to the sounds of the city and the water. She tried to pick out Ty's breathing, but he was too quiet.

"Family," he said after a while.

"Family," Kayla repeated. "They can really do a number on you."

Ty nodded. "True. But it's easy to take them for granted. Take for granted that they'll be there." He turned back to the river.

"What Lilly said, I get that. I see that, with the five of you," Ty said. "You guys really are a family unit or whatever you want to call it. It's as strong as anything created by blood."

She smiled. "You should see us when Jordan is around." At his raised eyebrows, she added, "He's our attorney. And Seb's BFF."

Something shifted behind Ty's eyes. "He's a lawyer?"

"Yeah, and he's terrifying when he wants to be. I'm glad he's on our side."

Ty seemed to contemplate that. "I'm glad too, then."

Inside her pocket, Kayla's phone vibrated. She considered ignoring it but remembered the others were probably ready to eat.

LILLY: We found a spot. Will you come?
KAYLA: Yep. Send me the address.

Lilly texted her a place on Congress, not far away.

"You hungry? I'm meeting the others for dinner."

Ty straightened and turned to her. "Thanks, but I think I'm going to head to my room. Get some sleep."

Kayla tried to tamp down her disappointment. "No problem. Probably a good idea. Long day tomorrow and...yeah."

Ty looked different. Sad. She hadn't noticed when he faced the water, but under the path lights it was clear.

"Are *you* all right?"

He ran a hand over his hair. "I'm fine. Tired."

She didn't push. "Okay, well..."

They stood there awkwardly for a long moment, Ty studying her face.

"Family can be frustrating. They can be...demanding and unfair and…sometimes you just want to…" He broke off and stared over her head.

Kayla's skin prickled and her fingers itched to touch him.

"But I'll tell you something, I'd give fucking *anything*…" Ty choked up and Kayla did reach out then. A light touch on his arm. He swayed a little at the contact, lowering his gaze to hers. "I would do anything to have my dad back." He gave a helpless shrug.

"I know."

Ty cleared his throat. "Sorry, I'm in my head tonight. I'm gonna go crash."

"See you in the morning."

He managed a small smile before he walked away, and she was glad to see it.

What he said about family had struck a chord. As much as her mother vexed her and refused to view her as a whole-ass adult woman, Kayla didn't know what she would do without her. She loved her parents more than anything, and more than anything, she didn't want to cause any strife for them.

That reporter…the way she'd looked at Kayla, like she'd uncovered a juicy secret, had sent a chill through her veins.

What if she'd discovered who Kayla was?

What if she was planning to write about it?

Her parents might learn about Kayla's life, the band, Candi, Peaches…all of it…in a newspaper article. No. She couldn't allow that to happen.

She had to tell them the truth.

In the time it took to walk to the restaurant, Kayla RSVPed to her father's dinner and responded to her mom.

KAYLA: I'll be home on Friday.

CHAPTER 16.

"HAPPY BIRTHDAY!"

Ty stood in the doorway to the kitchen, not knowing where to look. The cake on the table was stunning, three layers covered in what appeared to be buttercream frosting decorated with tiny candy books. Some were closed, others open with black faux lettering on their glossy pages. On top, the cake read "Happy 25th Birthday Tyrell" in dark green piping.

Pop-Pop had hung a few balloons from the ceiling fan. How he'd gotten up there, Ty didn't know, and he vowed to have a chat with him about later, but...wow. This was an incredibly sweet thing to wake up to. He'd gotten in late the night before, the house dark and silent when he arrived. He'd collapsed into the bed and slept for twelve hours straight.

"You didn't need to do all of this." Ty pulled his granddad into a hug, kissing his cheeks loudly like he used to do to him when he was little.

"Who else is going to celebrate you?" His grandfather pulled out a chair and pushed Ty into it. "Knowing you, you'd pretend it was just another day."

"It is just another day," Ty argued for the fourteenth year in a row. After the death of his father, he hadn't felt much like celebrating any holiday, much less his own birthday. Pop-Pop's, sure—he'd go all out for his granddad—but not his own.

"I know you don't like to make a fuss, but twenty-five is a big deal. You're a quarter-century old."

"That reminds me," Ty said, squirming under the attention. "Don't you have a big one coming up this year?"

Pop-Pop opened the freezer and pulled out a quart of ice cream. "Don't remind me."

"Seventy-five, by my calculations," Ty continued, pretending to do the math. "Isn't that a diamond jubilee or something like that?"

"I believe that's more for anniversaries."

"Well, it'll be the anniversary of your birth," Ty said. "Same thing. And it's worth making a big deal."

"No need for anything big," his granddad said, predictably. "All I need is you and maybe a few friends. We can go out to dinner or something."

"Sure." In truth, Ty had been organizing the celebration for months. His granddad's birthday wasn't until November, but the plans were already set. "Whatever you want."

His grandfather set two bowls down next to the spoons and handed Ty a knife. "I couldn't find any candles, so you'll have to make your wish without them."

"All right, I wish…"

"No, no. You have to close your eyes and imagine there are twenty-five candles on the cake, then blow them out."

"I do, do I?" Ty grinned.

"That's the rule," his granddad said, his expression playfully stern.

"Gotta follow the rules, then." Ty did as he was told.

He thought of the last several months and how lucky he'd been to have a home to come to after everything that happened. He thought about Pop-Pop—the love he had for him and the camaraderie they shared. He wished the old man could be around forever.

"Done." Ty opened his eyes.

"Now, cut your cake," Van said. "But be careful, those little books are hard as rock candy. They'll pop right off."

"They're amazing," Ty said, carefully cutting around a few of them. "When did you learn to do all of this?"

"Oh, you know me. I always work it out in the end."

Smiling, Ty concentrated on lifting the slice he'd cut without dropping it. "Well, it's incredible. You missed your calling, I think."

"Never too late to start something new," Van replied. He held out a plate, and Ty laid the slice of cake gently on its side.

He cut a piece for himself while his granddad served the ice cream.

"Butter pecan!"

"Your favorite."

"You're too good to me," Ty said around a bite of cake. It was perfect, light and fluffy with a delicate vanilla flavor. The buttercream dissolved on his tongue, and he hummed with satisfaction. "This is incredible. Truly."

"Thank you." His granddad smiled. He wiped his mouth and reached behind him, pulling a cookbook from the counter, and handed Ty an envelope that had been stuck inside.

"What's this?"

"A little gift, that's all." His granddad slid his fork into his slice, but Ty could feel his attention on him.

"You didn't need to get me anything." Ty opened the envelope, nearly choking on the bite he'd just taken. He held up the check and fixed his grandfather with a stern gaze. "Van…" he began, keeping his voice even. "Where did you get this money?"

There were far too many zeroes on the check, and a sickly unease settled in the pit of Ty's stomach.

His grandfather carefully wiped his mouth and then rested both hands on the table, taking a deep breath before he met Ty's gaze. "I love you, you know that. Right?"

"Love you too." Ty waited.

His grandfather took another deep breath as if steeling himself. "I want you to go back to school."

Ty closed his eyes. "Van."

"I sold some of the stock in my retirement fund."

"What?" Ty stared at his grandfather in disbelief. "Why would you do that?"

"It's my money," Van huffed. "I can do whatever I want with it."

"Yes," Ty conceded. "Of course, you can, but..." He blew out an exasperated breath. "This is a lot of money."

Ty had yet to find a school willing to admit him without prejudice. He didn't have the heart to tell his grandfather that. And there was no way he planned to keep the money anyway.

"You're worth it."

"I don't even know if I want to try and go back," Ty hedged.

"Well, what do you want to do?" his granddad asked. Picking up his fork, he cut into his slice of cake. "Whatever it is, I'm sure that money will help."

"You know I can't accept this."

"I know no such thing," the old man replied. "I know you're still hurting. I know you're a little lost, and you have nothing to hold on to—except for me." He raised his eyes to meet Ty's. There was sadness there and a fierce determination. "You're twenty-five, Tyrell. It may not seem like a big deal right now, but thirty will come soon enough. Where will you be then?"

Ty sagged into his chair. "I honestly don't know. I haven't had time to figure it out."

"I know, but I also know you're putting off thinking about it." There was a long silence while he ate his cake.

Ty only picked at his with his fork. His granddad was right, but Ty didn't know where to start. He had so few options at the moment. He supposed he could audit a few classes a week, but he'd pay for those himself.

"One other thing I want to talk to you about," his grandfather said. "I'm...I'm selling the house."

Ty's head snapped up. "What? When? Why?" He knew his panic showed on his face, but he was about to freak out. They'd lived in this house for as long as Ty could remember. Where would they go?

"I know what you're thinking," Van said. "I've thought it through. Been thinking about it for years, actually, and I believe it's time."

"Time for what?"

"They built that new senior living complex down on the Delaware."

"Senior...living?" Ty frowned. "What are you talking about?"

"It's nice, actually." His Pop-Pop's expression brightened. He pulled a pamphlet out of the cookbook and handed it to Ty. "Take a look."

His hand shook when he reached for it, but Ty flipped through the glossy images and read over the marketing text. It did seem like a nice place, but he couldn't picture his grandfather living there. Ty couldn't imagine Van Baldwin living anywhere but here, in this house, with him. Which, when he thought about it, was probably his granddad's point.

"It's a community, with lots of group activities and conveniences." He sounded excited. Eager, even. "You're always telling me I need to get out of the house."

"Yeah, but I didn't mean permanently," Ty replied, trying for a smile.

His Pop-Pop chuckled. "It has a commercial kitchen they use for classes. I've already asked, and I'd be able to use it for my cooking experiments."

"It does sound nice," Ty reluctantly conceded. "But..." *What about me?* It was on the tip of his tongue, but his granddad was right. Ty was twenty-five years old. It was time to find his own path, whatever it was.

"I'm not moving right away," Van said. "And it will be a while before I can sell this place. This neighborhood has changed in the last fifty years. Not many people looking to buy around here."

"Would it be enough to cover the cost of living at"—he checked the name—"River Willows?"

"Between the sale of the house and the rest of my retirement fund, I'll be set for, oh...ten, fifteen years," Pop-Pop replied. "More, if I'm frugal with my baking ingredients."

Ty put the check back into the envelope, along with the pamphlet. "No need to be frugal because I can't take this money."

Van sighed. "Tyrell...son..."

"No." He shook his head. "I'll make my own way, I mean it." Ty held out the envelope.

After a brief standoff, his granddad took it. "I'm not kicking you out, you know. You take these next few months to figure out what you want to do."

Ty nodded. "Thanks."

"Now, eat your ice cream before it melts completely."

It suddenly tasted like sawdust, but Ty obeyed.

There was a package waiting for him at the front desk when he went by the Sumney Coaches office.

"What's this?" he asked their receptionist, Bram.

"Dunno," they answered. "Aaron said to give it to you when I saw you. I see you, so here it is."

"Er...okay. Thanks." Ty tucked it under his arm as he walked to the assignment board. Despite it being a couple of decades into the twentieth century, Aaron hadn't updated the internal operations of the business when he'd bought it a few years ago. Assignments were still posted to a giant board in the hall outside the employee locker room. Payroll was still managed via paper checks. It was all very old school, and Ty kind of liked it.

The smell of diesel greeted him when someone pushed through the double doors that led to the service bay. Ty looked over in time to catch a glimpse of the bus he'd driven for the Lillys. The longing he felt for the time he'd spent on the road with them, with Kayla, was a dull ache in his chest. It sat alongside the growing uncertainty that was the rest of his life.

He'd been witness to a group of people who knew who they were and what they wanted to be, to do. He envied them.

On the ride home the band had been huddled in the living area fielding various phone calls. They hadn't stopped for lunch, and Kayla had only come to the cockpit for a few minutes before being called back. When Ty dropped them off at 30th Street Station, she rushed off saying she would be in touch, but he hadn't heard from her.

Why would he? When she'd come to him by the river, he'd been too caught up in his own shit to be there for her. It was for the best that they didn't go for that walk. He had no doubt in his mind he wouldn't have been able to stop himself from kissing her, if she had been willing. And with everything going on in her world, she didn't need him invading it with his own drama.

Friends was easier. No, not easier, *safer*.

He hoped they could still be friends because there was likely zero chance he was going on the road with her again.

Shaking himself, Ty scanned the board for an assignment that looked interesting. Something to take his mind off of devilish grins and fiery red hair.

"Interesting doesn't matter," Ty muttered to himself. "Find something that pays well." *So you aren't tempted to take Van's money.* It was a sizeable sum.

"What you got there?" Leo was one of the other drivers that had started around the same time as Ty. He stopped next to him and pointed at the package under Ty's arm.

He'd completely forgotten about it. "I'm not sure."

Leo arched a brow. "Uh, it's got your name on it."

Ty refrained from rolling his eyes. "Indeed. Hold this?"

He handed Leo his thermos and turned the parcel over in his hand. It wasn't big and felt a lot like a book. Peeling back the brown paper wrapping, Ty's eyes went wide.

"Holy shit," he whispered.

"You order a book?" Leo asked, craning his neck to see.

"No, I... It's..."

Someone had sent him a first edition copy of *Minion*. For a second, Ty couldn't imagine who would know what the book meant to him. Then realization dawned. He flipped carefully through the pages until a note fluttered to the ground.

Leo snatched it up. "You got a secret admirer, Ty? One of those ladies from the senior center in Lancaster, perhaps? Did you get yourself a sugar mama?"

Ty swiped the note out of Leo's hand. "Dude, c'mon."

"Though if you did, I hope she can afford more than an old paperback."

Turning away from him, Ty unfolded the note.

Ty,

Sorry I haven't been in touch. I heard it was your birthday. I hope you don't mind, but I saw this and had to get it.

Would love a rain check on our walk. Call me sometime.

~K

973.555.3802

Ty read the note twice before folding it in his palm. He stared down at the cover of the book, at the faint signs of aging around its edges. It was a thoughtful gift, and Ty wasn't sure if he should even keep it. When he opened the cover and read the inscription, his jaw dropped.

Dear reader,

The sky is your only limit.

LA Banks

He ran a finger over the author's signature.

"There's something you don't see every day."

Blinking, Ty shut the book and turned to find out what Leo was talking about.

He pointed at the board. "Didn't you go on the road with a band?"

Ty's gaze snapped up to the listings. He half expected to find the Lillys' West Coast tour posted there, but it was a high school marching band.

"Different kind of band," Ty replied, his chest loosening as hope bloomed. "Totally different."

CHAPTER 17.

WHEN SHE'D DONE THE CALCULATIONS, Kayla realized she hadn't spent the night at home—in her parents' house—for over five years. It was a wonder her mother hadn't sent a private investigator to track down her whereabouts. Of course, as far as she knew, Kayla was still living in California.

Kayla wondered if she should feel bad about the deceit, but if her mother had known she was on the East Coast, she would have insisted upon her coming up to visit them every weekend, if not more.

She didn't look forward to telling her parents any of her truths. But if Kayla was serious about being her own person at the ripe old age of twenty-five, she needed to grow a pair of brass ovaries and come clean before someone else did it for her.

Kayla pulled her rental into the circular drive and killed the engine. The house hadn't changed much since the last time she'd been there and still stood—grand and imposing—at the end of the tree-lined lane. She got out of the car and peered up at the third window from the left, on the second floor, remembering all the times she sat there and dreamed of being back in Georgia.

Zach used to take her up to the roof when their parents were sleeping and point out the stars.

It was odd, being back here. Already, Kayla didn't feel like herself. The car she'd rented was exactly the type of car you'd expect to see in their neighborhood—sleek, sophisticated, and boring.

The front door opened. Geoffrey Larrington stood tall and proud, shielding his eyes from the sun to see her. In his canary-yellow polo shirt and dark gray trousers—no doubt handpicked by her mother—he looked like a stock photo from a real estate ad. But he beamed when he recognized her.

"Is that my little girl?" he asked, smiling wide as he jogged down the few steps that led to the gravel path. "Kathy, look at you!"

She'd dressed in a pale blue sleeveless sundress and a pair of white canvas wedges that she'd picked up just for the occasion. She didn't want to rehash old arguments over her usual attire and how it wasn't ladylike.

"Hi, Daddy!"

Her father took her by the shoulders. His gaze swept from the top of her head down to her toes. "You're as beautiful as ever," he said, his voice filled with admiration and pride. "It's been too long."

"I know, I'm sorry."

"Hush, you're here now." He folded her in a warm, gentle hug, and her eyes began to sting.

Kayla loved her dad. He was a wonderful man, with a big heart and a keen mind. His only fault was loving her mother too much to go against her wishes, no matter what they were.

He kissed the top of her head and released her, his smile so wide it reflected the sunlight. "I didn't know you were coming. Are you here for my dinner?" he asked. "How did you even find out about it?"

"Mom texted me."

His smile dipped a little before he seemed to catch it. "Oh. Well, she must have wanted to surprise me."

"Sure," Kayla said. It was more likely her mother didn't think she'd show, which—to be fair—would have fit Kayla's MO. She'd never been one for lavish dinner parties, while her mother seemed to place at least part of her success on the number of invitations she received or the titles of the guests she hosted.

"Where is Mom?" she asked, grabbing her purse from the passenger seat before she closed the car door.

"On campus," he replied as he walked to the house. "She had a lecture this morning and a conference call this afternoon. Something else too, I think, but you know your mother. It's difficult to keep up with her schedule. But let's talk about you!"

The house was calm and quiet, and Kayla followed her dad through to the kitchen. It had always been her favorite room in the house, aside from Zach's room. Lydia, their housekeeper, had always made the best snickerdoodles. She'd retired in the years since Kayla had moved away. She didn't even know what staff her parents employed now.

Her dad went to the fridge and opened it. "Water? Juice? A glass of wine?"

She smiled. "It's still weird when you offer me alcohol."

He turned to look at her over his shoulder. "You're an adult, aren't you?"

"Not sure Mom would agree," Kayla muttered, though not low enough.

"Katherine Yolanda Larrington," he said in a familiar tone. "Could I request that you not get into it with your mother this weekend? I know...I know you two don't always see eye to eye."

Kayla snorted. "You have such a gift for understatement, Daddy."

He grinned. "Still so cheeky." He turned back to the fridge and brought out a pitcher of what looked like freshly squeezed lemonade. "I can see I have my work cut out for me, keeping you and your mother on good terms."

Keeping? "Daddy, it's not your responsibility to smooth things over between Mom and me. We just...see things differently."

Her dad pulled two glasses down from the cabinet and poured lemonade in each. "Ice?"

She shook her head. "Who's helping you around the house now?"

"We have a service come in twice a week to clean and straighten, but I've recently discovered an interest in cooking."

"Really?" Kayla smiled. "Daddy, that's awesome! What's your specialty?"

"Right now, it's eggs à la scrambled," he joked. "But I tinker. Just last Friday, I made bouillabaisse."

She whistled. "Wow. Impressive. Isn't that one of Mom's favorite dishes? What did she think?"

He averted his eyes and took a sip from his glass. "She got stuck at a book event in Boston and ended up staying overnight. The new title is doing well."

Kayla briefly closed her eyes because she could see the disappointment in his face as clear as day. "Well, I bet it was delicious."

His smile returned. "It wasn't bad."

"It's funny," she mused.

"What is? The idea of me cooking? I wasn't completely useless in the kitchen when you and Zach were growing up," he said. "Remember pancake Saturdays?"

Kayla's chest warmed at the memory. Pancake Saturdays had been her favorite when she was small. Her father and Zach would make two or three different kinds of pancakes, once or twice a month—when time permitted. As she'd gotten older, they'd happened less frequently as her mother signed her and her brother up for more and more after-school and weekend activities. Debate club. Chess club. Violin lessons. Greek and Latin.

Kayla shoved the ancient hurt away. "You make the best pancakes in the whole world."

"I do," he agreed, winking. "Maybe we can make some tomorrow. I have some interesting ingredients we can try."

"I'd love that, Dad. I really would."

Kayla's mother called to say she was running late and would meet her father at the dinner. He ordered a car service, and he and Kayla rode over together. She'd offered to drive, but he wouldn't hear of it.

"I didn't tell her you were here," he said when they pulled up in front of Filbert Hall.

The grand old building sat on the northwestern corner of the Carradine campus. Kayla had vivid memories of being there as a teen, prowling its marble halls and reading the inscriptions on art installations and medal cases, imagining she'd created or won them herself.

"I'm sure she'll be surprised," Kayla answered, accepting his hand as he helped her out of the back of the black luxury SUV.

There were a few photographers out front taking pictures of guests as they arrived. Kayla checked her gown, a simple black sheath that her mother couldn't possibly find fault with that she'd accessorized with a pair of Louboutins and delicate gold jewelry. The entire outfit was exactly the type of costume her mother always begged her to wear for these functions. Kayla had thought about leaving her hair down, just to feel more like herself than a prop, but opted for a chignon. She certainly didn't need to give her mom any more ammunition. There would be plenty of that when Kayla broke the news about the Lillys.

"Are you all right, sweetheart?" her father asked. "You seem a little preoccupied."

Kayla smoothed her hands over the satin lapels of his tux and smiled. "I am perfectly fine. Happy to be on your arm tonight, handsome man."

As expected, her dad blushed. "No more than I am to escort my lovely daughter. Oh! There's Derren Bergman. You remember him? You went to school with his sister, I think."

Kayla turned to follow his gaze. "Siobhan, yes."

Her brother's best friend waved as he headed their way. Kayla hadn't seen Derren since her and his sister's high school graduation.

"Looking very smart," her father said, clapping Derren on the shoulder. He smiled as his gaze bounced back and forth between the two of them. "I'm so glad you both could be here tonight."

Derren had always been a favorite of her dad's. Kayla wondered if he had secret hopes the two of them might end up together one day. There was zero chance of that. Derren was a self-absorbed narcissist. She never understood what Zach saw in him. Derren was a legacy Theta and had been homecoming king at their university. Zach had hated frat culture, but Derren had thrived within it.

"Wouldn't have missed it," Derren said, his smile too wide and bright. "You look fabulous, Kath. It's good to see you."

"Thank you. And you," Kayla replied as she fixed the point on her Dad's pocket square. She slipped her arm through his. "Let's go get you honored, Daddy." Derren followed behind.

They made a pretty picture, the three of them, but it was incomplete. Kayla wondered where her mom could be.

Ten minutes later, Gisele Larrington arrived in a flurry of apologies.

"I'm so sorry I'm late. My publisher put me on a call with a reporter from the *Bulletin*. Well, you know how these things go." To her credit, her eyes widened only slightly when she saw Kayla.

"Hi, Mom."

"Katherine." It was a long, drawn-out word. "I'm *so* pleased you could make it." It was a performance, but there was a hint of genuine warmth. Probably the best Kayla could hope for given the circumstances. Seeing her mother again wasn't yet the lightning storm Kayla had expected, but the forecast between them was definitely chilly with the threat of freezing rain. "You look lovely, dear." Her mother's gaze traveled over Kayla from head to toe. "I always did love that silhouette on your frame." High praise indeed. She picked a piece of invisible lint from Kayla's shoulder.

"Thanks, Mom. You look beautiful." She did. She wore a soft, shimmering gown of deep claret that skimmed over her figure and swept to the floor. The gown's neckline dipped modestly, revealing a hint of collarbone. Her auburn hair was swept up in an elegant updo, and her makeup accentuated her features with subtle grace. Diamond studs sparkled from her ears, glinting in the light of the chandeliers.

"Oh, you flatter me." Her gaze scanned the crowd. Kayla had to admit, her mother was good. She somehow managed to sound civil, even congenial.

"If anything, Kathy is conservative in her flattery," Derren said. He took her mother's hand and raised it to his lips. "You're stunning tonight, Mrs. Larrington."

To Kayla's surprise, her mom gave Derren a cool look and deliberately withdrew her hand.

"I didn't realize you would be here tonight. How is your family?"

"Everyone is well," Derren replied, recovering quickly from the rebuff. He plastered on his usual toothy smile. "My mother wanted me to tell you she thoroughly enjoyed your latest book and wants to have lunch with you soon."

"I'm sure we'll arrange something." Her tone was dismissive. Apparently Kayla wasn't the only one in her mother's crosshairs tonight.

They found their way to their table, close to the center of the room. Kayla was seated next to her father, with her mother to the left of him. Surprisingly, Derren was also at their table, though luckily a few seats away. Kayla recognized one or two of her father's colleagues.

"I must have a word with someone about the guest list for these events," her mother said to no one before she seemed to catch herself. "Surely, the governor should be in attendance. Geoffrey was, after all, the first African American recipient of the Folcroft grant, which brought notoriety to the state. Not to mention a substantial amount of money to Carradine," she added.

"Gisele," Kayla's father chided, though he tried to cover his discomfort with a festive air. "I'm sure the governor has better things to do than attend a stuffy, academic event."

"Geoffrey, I heard a rumor you're thinking of releasing a book?" Dr. Isaac Morris, an old colleague of her father's, cut into his lobster tail and looked at her dad expectantly. "Are you finally going to finish that personal project you've been hinting at?" he asked.

"Dad, are you writing again?" Kayla smiled, exchanging a look with her mother.

Her father lowered his chin, but he couldn't hide the soft grin. "I've been tinkering. And there's some interest from an independent press."

"That's wonderful!" Kayla exclaimed. "When can I read the new poems?"

"Katherine." A warning. "Don't indulge him." Her mother lifted her glass, holding it out as a server appeared with a bottle of merlot.

"Poetry? Really?" Dr. Morris asked, his brows rising. "Why is this the first I've heard of this? Gisele, we might have a poet laureate on our hands."

"Geoffrey's been working on his *volume of poetry* for nearly twenty years," her mother replied with an uncharacteristically nervous laugh. "It's merely a pet project. A trifle compared to all the important work he's done and will do."

"Mom," Kayla said more sharply than she'd intended. "Dad's poems are incredible, and I, for one, am glad he's finally going to publish them."

Derren watched the exchange over the rim of his highball glass, his eyes full of amusement. Kayla hated that he was there to witness it.

"Thank you, sweetheart." Her father patted her hand. "But perhaps your mother is right. I do have another project in the works. An examination of Octavia Butler's world building and its connection to social justice."

His lips curved up as he spoke, but there was an unmistakable dullness to the shine from moments ago.

"Yes." Her mother pounced on the change in topic. "It's quite a rich tapestry to explore. I've touched on her words in my lectures, and the university library has—"

"But, Mom," Kayla said, loud enough to cut her off. "Those two projects aren't mutually exclusive. There's no reason Daddy can't do both, is there?"

"Really, Katherine," her mother began in a chiding tone.

Around the table, it grew quiet. Derren's eyes widened with unmistakable glee. Of course he would enjoy this. There had always been a one-sided rivalry between their two families. Siobhan had never bought into it, but Derren and his parents played a perpetual game of Keeping Up with the Larringtons.

"I would never hold your father back from his leisurely pursuits," her mother continued. "It would simply be a much better use of his time to work on—"

"He's *retiring*, Mom." Kayla tried hard to control her volume. Beneath the ivory linen of the tablecloth, her hand had curled into a fist. She eyed the cup of breadsticks near the center of the table like drumsticks.

Her dad patted her leg. "It's all right, honey."

But Kayla wasn't about to let her mother belittle him at a dinner thrown in his own fucking honor. What was *wrong* with her?

"I vote for the poetry," Kayla said, "because the world needs more beauty."

Gratitude poured off of her father in waves. He gave her a warm smile.

"If he doesn't publish his Butler study, someone else will," her mother countered coolly. "There's a renewed interest in her work. Besides, I love you, Geoffrey, but you're no Hayden."

"Oh, for fuck's sake," Kayla muttered. Not quietly enough, apparently. Shit.

This time, their entire table went quiet, but Kayla didn't care. She wouldn't stand for this.

"Darling," her mother said, her voice deceptively serene even behind her tight smile, "would you mind coming to get some air with me? Now?"

Kayla's face burned. She rose with as much dignity as she could muster and followed her mom out of the ballroom. They walked in silence until they reached the end of the long hall.

Her mother turned into an alcove and gave Kayla a pointed look.

Kayla glared at her but stepped inside the small space.

"That was unacceptable behavior, even for you," her mother began, her voice low and her eyes flashing with anger. "What has gotten into you?"

"I'm sorry if I found it extremely distasteful to mock Daddy in front of his peers."

Her mother stopped just short of rolling her eyes. "I see you haven't outgrown your flair for the dramatic. No one is mocking your father."

"Are you kidding me right now? You just stomped all over his passion project. You know what his poetry means to him."

Her mother waved a hand dismissively. "It's a hobby. Nothing more."

"So, what? It's not important because it's not important to *you*?" Kayla pinched the bridge of her nose. "God, you haven't changed one bit."

"It seems you haven't either," her mother retorted. "How dare you show up here after all this time and pretend to understand anything that is happening here? I invited you because I thought you would want to be here for his big moment. I expected you to support him and manage to behave with some small modicum of decorum."

Kayla's jaw dropped. She hated that her mother still had the ability to sting her, especially because she wasn't entirely wrong. Kayla could have handled that a lot better.

She blew out a breath and tried a different approach. "Mom... Dad's poetry has always been close to his heart."

She raised her chin. "I know that. But—"

"And you know he's wanted to publish a volume for years. Ever since I can remember," Kayla finished.

"But there's so much more he could be doing with his energy and time," her mother said. "Don't you understand that? Tonight could be the beginning of a distinguished period in his career."

"Or maybe you could just support Dad's passions, even if they don't tick a box on the Gisele Larrington checklist for Black Family Excellence."

Her mother's lips tightened, and Kayla cursed under her breath.

"Sorry," she said, wishing she had the language to get through to her mom. "I shouldn't have said that."

"No, no. Please go on. My daughter, whom we haven't seen in more than a year, clearly has something on her mind." Her tone couldn't have been more condescending if she'd tried, but there was a layer of hurt underneath, and Kayla did regret being the cause.

She studied her mother and saw a note of something else behind the anger and the outrage. Disappointment. All at once she was thirteen years old again, desperate for her mother's approval and praise. She had to find common ground or tonight would be yet another black mark on her record. She sighed.

"You really do look beautiful," Kayla said genuinely. "I've always loved you in that color."

Her mother blinked. "I... Thank you. You, too, look very nice. Your hair..." She trailed off. It had always been a point of contention between them, and Kayla had made an effort with the chignon. She knew her mother appreciated that, at least.

"Look, Mom, I..." Under the weight of the moment, Kayla's confidence faltered. "I know I can be hotheaded. It's just that you can be...so..."

"What?" her mother asked.

Controlling. Unreasonable. Oblivious. "Exacting."

Her mother snorted softly. It was such an uncharacteristic display of...normalcy...that Kayla sputtered. "I don't mean to say... that...demanding the best from the people around you is wrong, per se..."

"Thank you so much for your permission. Do go on." She sounded almost...*amused,* rather than irritated. Progress! Her mother smoothed her hands down the front of her gown. The deep claret of the material was striking against her dark olive skin tone. "Did it ever occur to you that I am...exacting for a reason other than my own ego?"

"I never said—"

"You didn't have to say it," her mother cut in, sounding almost defeated. "You've made it abundantly clear how...how selfish and controlling you think I am. How unreasonable and..." She exhaled an uncharacteristic sigh, and Kayla was surprised to see her posture ease even the tiniest bit.

"I love your father with all of my heart and soul—and my children." The unexpected mention of Zach's existence nearly stole Kayla's breath. Her mother never spoke about him. Ever.

"I am...hard on you because, whether you choose to acknowledge it or not, we—as a Black family in this corner of the world—we

GIRLS WITH BAD REPUTATIONS   163

live under a microscope," she continued, forcing out the words. "And yes, I realize I'm largely the one who put us here."

"Some of us more than others," Kayla heard herself say.

A flash of hurt passed through her mother's expression before she schooled it. "I don't know how many times I can apologize for making you feel like, how did you put it when you left home?"

"A trophy kid? A prototype for Little Miss Yolanda?"

"Very...colorful," her mother replied. "I wanted the best for you. I always wanted the best for you and for..." She hesitated as she always did before saying her brother's name. "For Zachary... and for your father. I've worked so hard, pushed so hard, because anything less would be a failure. Those books are about securing your future."

Kayla was still reeling from hearing her mother say Zach's name, the occasion was so rare. The parting dig didn't land with its usual sting. "Nice, Mom," she muttered.

"You misunderstand me." Her mother shook her head. "*My* failure. Our privilege is hard-won, Katherine. It had always been a battle to keep it."

Frowning, Kayla didn't know what to say to that.

"Oh, hey. There you are," Derren said as he rounded the corner. "Everything all right? They're clearing the table for dessert."

"We're fine," her mother replied. She turned to a mirror that hung on the wall and made a show of fixing her hair. To Kayla, "Unless there more bits of wisdom you wish to impart before you return to California tomorrow? To...whatever it is you do out there."

And wow.

Wow.

Kayla could feel herself shrinking, mowed down by her mother's expertly sharpened tongue. She fought hard not to slink away. She gave a quick shake of her head.

"You finally told them about your band?" Derren asked.

Kayla spun to look at him. Panic. Pure, unfiltered panic stole over her.

"Band?" Her mother turned her narrowed eyes on her.

"Why is everyone here in the hall?" her father asked as he walked toward them. "Should I have them serve dessert out here?"

"What *band*?" Kayla's mother asked.

"Was I not supposed to mention it?" Derren said. He looked at Kayla and mouthed the word *oops*.

Now she'd have to kill Siobhan for not keeping her mouth shut.

"Sweetheart?" Her father cupped her shoulder. "Is there something you need to tell us?"

Kayla's gaze darted between her parents.

"Tell them," Derren said.

Kayla shook her head. Apparently, her tongue had shriveled up and fallen out, no doubt the result of her mother's withering stare.

"She's a drummer," Derren oh so helpfully provided, "and—"

Kayla grabbed his arm. Hard.

"Is that what you've been up to? Playing the drums?" her mother asked, her lips twisting as if the words had a sour taste.

"I dabble," she croaked and then cleared her throat. "It's nothing serious."

"But—"

Kayla gave Derren a look that made him finally snap his jaw shut.

"I...think it's cool that you're still *dabbling*," he said, narrowing his eyes.

"Indeed," her father said, but his smile was sympathetic.

Her mother briefly closed her eyes.

When she opened them, she didn't look at Kayla. "Well, as you're fond of reminding me, it's your life. You're capable of making your own decisions."

Kayla was nearly too stunned to speak. It wasn't much, but it was something other than an outright dismissal of her autonomy. "Thanks, Mom," she managed eventually.

She turned to her husband. "We should go back. The ceremony will start soon."

After a beat, Kayla's father nodded. "Yes, let's all return to our seats."

Her mother didn't wait for them as she made her way back to the ballroom.

Grinning, Derren gave Kayla a thumbs-up as he jogged to catch up, as if he hadn't almost eroded what little ground she may have gained with her mother tonight.

When they were seated, Kayla's father leaned to whisper into her ear. "I'm proud of you, sweetheart." He kissed her temple. "So very proud of you. We both are."

The lights flashed, signaling the beginning of the program.

Kayla leaned up and kissed her father's cheek. "I'm proud of you too, Daddy." She was, though she didn't share his confidence when it came to her mother. She had to accept that they would never see eye to eye. Not ever.

CHAPTER 18.

TY WANTED TO HATE THE place but, he had to admit, River Willows was pretty nice.

"Through here, you'll find our art studio, where residents are encouraged to pursue artistic endeavors they've been putting off because of work or familial obligations. We provide oils, water-colors, and canvases, as well as clay for pottery—the kiln is just through those doors."

Anya Lemorsk, the director of the River Willows Senior Community, was a tall woman in her early to mid-fifties with fair skin, kind eyes, and the poise of a beauty pageant contestant. Her dark brown hair was tucked neatly into a chignon that sat at the base of her slender neck. She was every bit the salesperson, but Ty found her to be warm and genuine.

She led Ty and his granddad on a tour of the River Willows complex, revealing a place that was so well suited to Van that even Ty couldn't deny it, as much as he wanted to do so.

"And here is our pièce de résistance." Anya pushed through a wide stainless-steel door and gestured them into the largest kitchen Ty had ever seen.

He thought he heard Van gasp.

"Mr. Baldwin, I understand you're an aspiring chef," she said, smiling at his reaction.

Ty's grandfather hurried toward the two commercial, built-in refrigerators that sat in the corner. Sighing loudly, he ran his fingers over the gleaming metal as if they were made of silk.

"These are Traulsens," he said reverently.

"I don't know much about them, I admit," Anya said. "But they're supposed to be the best."

"They cost a fortune," Pop-Pop said, looking over at Ty. There were honest-to-goodness tears in his eyes. "And these ranges…"

"We hold cooking classes every Sunday afternoon, but the kitchen is available for individuals any other time. By appointment," she added. "You'd be able to experiment all you like. Basic ingredients are always on hand, and we can special order anything you might need at cost."

It was his granddad's version of heaven, Ty was sure. He sighed inwardly. This was definitely happening, and he'd need to sort his own self out sooner rather than later.

"We like to think of ourselves as a family here at River Willows, not a facility," Anya said to Ty as they watched his granddad *ohh* and *ahh* over the double sink in the granite island. The thing was bigger than their bathtub at home. "We'll even help with the sale of your property if assistance is needed."

Ty raised an eyebrow. "And how, exactly, does that work?"

Anya smiled. "We merely put you in touch with some Realtors we trust, ones we know will take your home to market in the best shape and price it to sell. We don't take a commission, if that's your concern. It's merely a courtesy."

She was good, Ty had to give her that. He nodded.

"Tyrell, come check out this view." His granddad beckoned, and Ty walked over to join him by the french doors. They led out to a patio with a view of the Ben Franklin Bridge spanning the Delaware River, Jersey just on the other side.

"I'll leave you two to discuss," Anya said, stepping back through the kitchen door.

"Okay," Ty said. "This place is ridiculous." He smiled at his granddad. "I can see why you'd want to live here. Hell, *I* want to live here."

"If I could bring you with me, I would, but they don't allow anyone under fifty-five. Besides," his granddad continued. "That would defeat the purpose."

"Of me landing on my feet and finding my independence?" Ty asked, not bothering to hide the sarcasm.

"You joke, but I think it will be just the fresh start you need." Van turned back to the water. "I'd be happy here, but only if I know I've done right by you."

"Old man," Ty said. "If you never did another thing for me ever again, you would still have done right by me."

Pop-Pop nudged him with his shoulder. He was several inches shorter, so he brushed against Ty's arm. They watched as a boat sailed past, its white sails reflecting in the water.

"You deserve a place like this," Ty said softly, even as a lump formed in his throat. "There aren't any openings until fall?"

"Well," Van said, rubbing his cheek. He briefly glanced up at Ty. "There's a unit available now, but I..."

"Really?" Ty turned to him. "Why didn't you say?"

His granddad shrugged. "I don't want to leave you on your own in that house."

"Van..." Ty said. He hugged his granddad to him. "I'll be fine. It's not like you're moving to Mars. C'mon."

Laughing, Pop-Pop pulled back and looked up at him. "The apartment does have a view of the Ben Franklin Bridge."

"Seriously? You mean I could come down and watch the fireworks with you on New Year's Eve?" Ty said. "Sold."

He turned and strode toward the kitchen door, stopping to look back at his granddad. "Well?" Ty grinned at him. "I guess we better get you packed."

———————

"I'm glad you called," Kayla said as they walked down Market Street.

"I'm glad you're back in town," Ty admitted. He had been nervous to do more with her number than thank her for the book. So he jumped at the chance to join her when she invited him to meet her in Old City.

They strolled past Independence Mall, where tourists lined up to view the Liberty Bell. Red, double-decker buses slinked by, while cars weaved around them and the horse-drawn carriages that carried even more tourists around the historic area. They were lovely to look at but left little presents behind.

"Watch your step," Ty said, guiding Kayla around a pile of droppings as they crossed 5th Street.

"Thanks. I guess New York doesn't have the market cornered on horseshit," she said, laughing.

The impulse to take her hand was strong, but Ty refrained. It hadn't been lip service when he said he'd wanted to kiss her, but he wasn't sure where the time apart had left them. It wasn't as simple as picking things up where they'd left off now that it wasn't expressly forbidden. Now, they were simply two people enjoying each other's company.

His attraction to her hadn't waned, and he thought he felt the same interest from her from time to time. Their hands brushed together, off and on, as they walked. Ty resigned himself to let nature take its course.

"The listing is on Strawberry Street," Kayla said, checking her phone.

"Listing?"

Kayla kept her eyes forward, but Ty didn't miss the smile tugging at the corner of her mouth. "Didn't I mention it? I'm looking at an apartment."

"Are you moving here?" Ty's heart literally skipped a fucking beat. He needed to get ahold of himself.

"Not sure yet," Kala replied carefully. "Waiting to see which way the wind blows."

"I see. Well, we have a few blocks to go, then," Ty informed her, grinning like a fool and not even caring.

"Are you familiar with this area? It seems a pretty dope spot."

"It is," he agreed. "Full of tourists and locals. I drive those red buses from time to time when they need extra staff." He pointed one out.

"Oh! Do you get to do the whole history lesson thing?" Kayla flashed him an exuberant smile.

"Nah, they have regular tour guides for that," Ty replied. "Some of the other tour lines have staff that do both, but the red line contracts out most of their drivers."

She nodded, deflating a little. "Must get repetitive, driving around a loop day after day, listening to the same historical jokes." She adopted a gruff but cheerful voice. "*What did Betsy Ross say when they asked if she enjoyed sewing? 'Oh, sew-sew.'*"

"Yikes. Yeah, probably," he replied, laughing. "I haven't done it enough to get bored. I love history, especially local history. Minus the bad puns."

"Somehow that doesn't surprise me." She grinned.

They made a right onto Strawberry Street and searched the building for the address of the listing. It was closer to an alley than a street, and Ty wondered how safe it was at night, especially for a woman walking alone. They were in an area of town known for its restaurants, galleries, and bars. The building wasn't far from the main drag, which made Ty feel marginally better.

"Good thing I don't own a car," Kayla said as she pushed the buzzer on the front door. "There doesn't seem to be any parking around here."

"Welcome to Philly," Ty said.

"New York is worse," Kayla replied. "Trust me. It's why I live across the river."

A man appeared in the glass door and showed them inside. "Katherine?"

Kayla seemed to think twice before nodding. "Yes."

Ty raised an eyebrow at the name. It didn't suit her. He made a mental note to ask about it sometime.

The man smiled, but it was wooden. He gave Ty a once-over, his gaze lingering on his cropped locs and the piercings in his nose.

"I'm only here to lend my opinion on the property," Ty said, feeling compelled to explain his presence.

The man visibly relaxed. "Right this way." He led them down a short hall to the elevator. "There's a freight elevator in the back that can accommodate a fair amount of furniture. On weekdays, we have strict move-in hours—ten a.m. to four p.m., and eight to eight on weekends. Are you new to the city?"

"I would be, if I decide to move."

"From?" He raised his brows expectantly.

"All over," she replied, turning to watch the numbers climb.

The doors opened on the top floor of the four-story building. The architecture was industrial, with exposed brick walls and wide aluminum pipes above. The narrow hall had no windows to provide natural light, but the fluorescent lamps hanging from the ceiling were bright.

The man, who hadn't bothered to introduce himself, unlocked a white door to the right. "This unit is one of two on this floor and sits on the north side of the building, so it gets some light from midmorning to midafternoon in spring and summer."

Since it was late afternoon, golden light bathed the white walls of the space, which was open if not a little sterile.

Kayla walked over to the windows. "Is that the street we walked down?"

Ty joined her there. "Market Street, yeah."

"What's that spire over there?" She pointed.

"That's Christ Church," Ty informed her. "Founded in 1695, though that part of the structure wasn't built until the eighteenth century. It was once the tallest building in the United States," he added, pulling the factoid from some pocket in his brain where he stored random information he picked up driving tourists around the city sights.

"Really?" Kayla asked.

"That's right," the man said, giving Ty an assessing look as if reevaluating his estimation of him.

Ty didn't give a shit what this dude—in his too-tight jeans with his over gelled hair—thought of him, as long as it didn't affect Kayla's application.

"This area is steeped in history," the guy said. "I'm sure you passed the mall on the way here?"

"Yeah," Ty replied. "I'm a local, so we went the scenic route."

"I see," the man said. "Let me show you the apartment."

He led them to the galley kitchen, which was spacious enough with a large island that reminded Ty of the one at River Willows. He realized they weren't far from Van's new home and imagined what it would be like to live so close to him and in a place like this.

A pipe dream. There was no way he could ever afford such a place.

"You have the usual trappings—stainless-steel appliances, granite countertops," the Realtor rattled off, sounding almost bored. "Everything is state-of-the-art."

They followed him down a hallway, where he pointed out a surprisingly large bathroom with a skylight, a small den, and eventually the main bedroom.

It was enormous, probably the size of Ty's and his granddad's rooms combined, if not larger.

"Since there are no windows on this side of the building, they added a couple of skylights." The Realtor pointed them out.

"Nice touch," Kayla said.

"Where are you living now?" he asked.

"North Jersey."

"Moving for work?"

Kayla nodded. "I suppose so, yeah."

"And...what is it that you do?"

"I'm a musician," she said, inspecting the walk-in closet.

Kayla had her back turned to them, so she missed the look of disdain that crossed the man's face, but Ty didn't.

The man's gaze traveled over Kayla, from head to toe, before zeroing in on Ty. "What sort of music do you perform? This is a quiet building. The residents expect a degree of...courtesy when it comes to parties, etc. And there's an expectation of...safety."

Kayla turned to look at him, apparently picking up on the implications. "I don't spend a lot of time at home," she said. "And I don't really throw a lot of parties, but I'll be sure to keep that in mind."

The man pursed his lips. "From what I understand, the music business can be unpredictable. You'll need to have a steady income to—"

"Would I be able to take a six-month lease?"

The man smirked at Kayla. "The owner doesn't normally do that, but if the money is a problem, perhaps this isn't the place for you."

"The money isn't a problem," Kayla said smoothly, her tone dismissive. "I prefer shorter terms because I never know when I'll need to move for work. And, of course, I prefer to pay for my lease in advance."

Ty bit back a grin. This woman was so fucking badass.

The guy visibly swallowed. "That would be eighteen thousand dollars, not including the security deposit."

"Three thousand dollars a month?" Ty exclaimed, stunned. "For a white box with high ceilings?"

"This is a highly coveted area of the city to live in," the guy said. "You'd be hard-pressed to find so many amenities at your doorstep in the neighborhoods you're probably accustomed to."

"It's less than half the price of anything this size in New York," Kayla said, disregarding the man's ignorance. "That's what attracted me to this property. It's so...cheap."

Her barb landed perfectly, and the Realtor cleared his throat. "Well...if you're interested in taking this unit, I'll call the owner and see if they'll accept your terms."

"I don't know," Kayla said, drawing out the words. She scrunched up her nose and looked around as if the apartment weren't the perfect industrial loft in a fantastic part of the city. "I think I'll keep looking. Ty, what do you think?"

Ty thought he might be in serious danger of kissing her right in front of this pompous asshole. Kayla was phenomenal.

"I definitely think you can do better," he replied. He looked straight at the Realtor as he said it, unable to contain the smug grin he knew was on his face.

Kayla sighed dramatically. "The search continues." She turned to the man. "Thanks for your time, but I'm gonna pass. This place just doesn't live up to my...expectations."

CHAPTER 19.

TY TOOK KAYLA TO THE Franklin Fountain, an old-fashioned ice cream parlor around the corner from the apartment they'd viewed. Both were still laughing at the look on the Realtor's face when she walked away with his twenty-seven-hundred-dollar commission. Asshole.

The staff at the malt shop wore white shirts and black pants, with a long white apron over the top. It was all very retro, down to the black bow ties and the little white paper hats on their heads. The menu's offerings included ice cream flavors like Hydrox Cookie, Grape, and Pistachio, as well as some beverages Kayla had never heard of—phosphates with names like Japanese Thirst Killer and Hemingway Dream.

"What's a Lime Rickey?" she asked the server.

"Lime juice, simple syrup, and seltzer water," they replied. "It's nice and refreshing, especially on a sticky day like today."

"It reminds me of fizzy lemonade," Ty said.

Kayla and Ty sampled some of the ice cream, which was encouraged. They tried the shop's signature vanilla bean—creamy and full of flavor—and some of the more exotic choices like Teaberry Gum and Cotton Candy. In the end, Kayla settled on a single scoop of Rum Raisin in a cup.

Ty ordered Butter Pecan in a waffle cone. He'd asked for a single, but it looked huge.

"That's an entire meal," she said as they exited the shop. They grabbed one of the bistro tables on the sidewalk, in the shade of a young tree.

"I usually get a double, but I'm trying to be good." Ty licked at a bit of melted ice cream that trickled down the side of his cone.

Kayla turned her attention to her own ice cream, which was safely in her cup. Taking her first taste, she hummed around a spoonful with genuine pleasure, her eyes almost rolling into the back of her head as the flavor exploded on her tongue.

"Is there actual rum in this?" she asked as she scooped up another spoonful. When Ty didn't answer, she looked up, only to find him staring at her with a dazed look.

She grinned. "Didn't your mother ever tell you it was impolite to stare?"

As soon as the words were out of her mouth, she realized her mistake.

Ty blinked rapidly and dropped his gaze to his hands. He picked up his spoon, absently sweeping it back and forth inside his cone.

"Ty, I..."

He shook his head, a rueful smile tugging one corner of his mouth. "It's fine." He lifted his gaze to hers, and his smile broadened, though it was sad. "Really, don't worry about it."

Kayla wanted to reach across the table and take his hand, but his body language didn't scream touch me, and she wasn't sure they were back at that place yet. Or if they ever would be.

"How is your grandpop?" she asked.

Ty's expression brightened, then dimmed. "He's good. Great, actually. He's...uh. He's decided to move into a place not far from here, down on the river."

She frowned. "Don't you live with him?"

He nodded. "I do. I did. I guess I'll need to find a place."

"You're not moving with him, then?"

Ty stabbed his spoon into his cone. "It's for seniors, so...no."

"Oh. Well, if you need someone to go apartment hunting with you, I'm happy to return the favor," Kayla said, hoping to earn another smile.

"Thanks," he muttered, apparently lost in his thoughts.

Kayla mentally kicked herself for misspeaking. She'd been so caught up in just being with him, basking in his quiet presence, his quick wit, and his focused attention that she'd forgotten. She'd actually forgotten all the pain he carried, which said a lot about the both of them.

Given all the shit life had piled on him, the fact that Ty was able to smile at all was a fucking miracle. And that he carried it so gracefully made Kayla realize that she wanted to dig a little deeper. Needed to.

"Where did you study?" she asked, ready to retract the question after a long silence ensued.

"What makes you think I did?" His tone was off.

"You're one of the smartest people I've ever met," she said honestly. "I just assumed. And I shouldn't have, I'm sorry."

After a few anguished moments, Ty nodded. "You're kind to say that. I did go to school for a while. I was three years into my bachelor's when I left."

"What made you leave?"

Ty exhaled and sat back as she stabbed at the ice cream. "I was accused of cheating—plagiarizing another student's paper." He looked up at her. "I didn't."

"Of course you didn't," Kayla rushed to say. The idea was absurd, and she let that show in her face. "You weren't able to clear your name?"

"I tried. The girl who accused me, we were...friends or, I *thought* we were friends. She'd stolen my draft and changed bits of it to make it look like her original work and turned it in before I handed in mine."

"Fuck that chick."

"Oh, it gets better," Ty said wearily. "When I confronted her, at first, she denied it. Then she accused me of stealing *my* paper from *her*. And when I was able to show the professor the time stamp of my first draft, which predated hers, she..." He shuddered.

Kayla sat up. Leaning forward, tempted to take his hand. "What?"

"She said I *hit* her." His eyes on her were dark. "The professor called campus police. They arrested me. I was charged with simple assault."

"Oh my God...Ty..."

"I didn't touch her."

"I don't believe for one second that you did!"

Ty dropped his gaze as if his shame made his eyelids heavy. "No one believed me. I spent two nights in lockup awaiting arraignment...the longest two nights of my fucking life to that point. I thought the judge would see that I wasn't a threat to anyone, but he decided to make an example of me."

"What happened?" She had to remind herself to breathe.

"I spent three weeks in jail."

"Oh my *God*. Ty..." The shock of it made her blood run cold. "Why weren't you granted bail?"

"Oh, I was. We couldn't afford it. Eventually, though, Pop-Pop found a lawyer who helped. I was granted supervised release. So, yeah...that's my sob story."

He had nothing to feel ashamed of, and it made Kayla's heart ache for him that he clearly thought he did.

"Did it go to trial?"

"No, the charges were dropped," Ty said, finally looking up. "The school knew Merry was lying, but she was a legacy kid. Meredith Stanwick of the Main Line Stanwicks. I lost my scholarships and my place in my class. Merry... She, uh, she got into some bad shit. Drugs. She ended up dropping out. About three months ago, they, uh... She was found dead."

"Oh no." The swing of emotion from rage to sympathy left Kayla breathless.

"Yeah, it's awful. I mean, she was a horrible person, but no one deserves to go out like that. Naturally, her family thinks it's *my* fault. Like I was a bad influence on her or something." He took a deep breath. "And *now* it's like...I'm on a list somewhere. No other decent school will have me. Not that I can afford it anyway."

"I can't imagine...what it's been like for you," she said, keeping her voice low. They were in the middle of a cluster of tables next to the curb, each one hosting a group of people—families and friends all enjoying cool treats on a hot day.

"I expect that's true," Ty said, a hint of bitterness in his voice. "I don't think I could have written anything as convoluted as my life story, not without some critic somewhere saying how preposterous it was."

"What's the saying? Truth is stranger than fiction?"

"Truth is truth, but fiction is all some people need to ruin the lives of others," Ty said.

Kayla couldn't stop herself from reaching for him this time. She covered the hand he had fisted on the table, his rings cool against her palm.

Ty looked down at their hands, then lifted his eyes to hers with a slow blink.

She gave his hand a squeeze before retracting hers and picked up her spoon, toying with the rapidly melting ice cream in her cup. She fished out a raisin and ate it, wishing the rum were more potent. Or maybe just wishing for some rum.

"I used books—education—as an escape as a kid," Ty said. "Still do, I guess."

"Funny, I used music to escape from books," Kayla admitted.

"My life was planned out for me almost from birth. My mother... She has very particular ideas about the role each member of her family should play."

"What's your role?"

"Dutiful daughter. Academic prodigy. Someone she can use to demonstrate her intellectual superiority," Kayla replied. "I was supposed to be an example."

"Of...?"

"Her perfection as a mother. An educator. Girls and women in general. Black girls and women specifically."

Ty whistled low. "That's a lot of pressure to put on a kid."

"Didn't your dad or your granddad ever give you the talk?" Kayla asked. "The one where they tell you *you have to be better*? That you have to be the best so that no one can question your place in the world?"

A passing police car turned on its siren, and Ty flinched. He shook his head with a wry grin. "I got a different talk."

Kayla's stomach clenched. Of course he had.

Ty nibbled at the edge of his cone and then sighed. He stretched his arm toward a nearby trash can and tossed the cone away. "How did you get started with the drums?" Ty asked. "It doesn't seem like the..."

"Most likely instrument for a girl?"

Ty gave her a look. "I was going to say the easiest instrument to get your hands on. The sets are big and loud and expensive, aren't they?"

"Yeah," Kayla conceded. "My first kit wasn't mine. It belonged to my brother."

"Tell me you had a garage band when you were sixteen." He grinned, leaning forward.

"Fifteen. Sort of. I used to hang with Zach's band." Kayla laughed when he applauded. "Is that too clichéd?"

"No, no. I love it." He had such a wonderful smile, Kayla thought she might get lost in it. "What songs did you play? Tell me everything."

"Everything, huh?" Her lips pulled into a smirk.

"Absolutely everything." Ty drew one knee up to his chest and wrapped his arms around it, watching her with an open, eager expression. God, he was fucking adorable.

"Well, in the beginning, I sucked," Kayla said, remembering those first few months hacking away at Zach's practice pads. "I'd go into my brother's room, throw on a local radio station, and try to play whatever came on."

"What was the first song you ever played?"

"Geez." She ran a hand down her throat, trying to think back to that moment when everything clicked. "If we're talking complete songs, it was probably something by Nirvana or Soundgarden. Nineties songs were in heavy rotation in my brother's band."

"Did you guys write anything?"

"Not really. Unless you count jamming. Zach was determined to learn from the masters—John Bonham, Steve Gadd, Sheila E., Dave Grohl. He listened to everything. Played everything, or at least he tried."

"Do you have a favorite drummer?"

"I feel like I'm being interviewed." Kayla rested an elbow on the table between them.

"You are." Ty mirrored her position, which brought them closer. "I was serious when I said I wanted to know it all."

"Favorite drummer. Hmmm…" Kayla pretended the answer wasn't right on the tip of her tongue. "Zach's favorite was Taylor Hawkins, but mine is Stewart Copeland."

"The Police, right?"

"I'm impressed! Yeah, he's just…his hands, the dexterity he has. His musicality." Kayla tried to find the words. She lifted a hand in the air and played an imaginary drum with her spoon, hoping she could show him what she meant. "The way he hears rhythm, it's magic."

"I'll have to listen to them more," Ty said, sounding in awe himself. "If I had to guess, your academic parents aren't too fond of your career choice?"

"My dad is." She smiled, knowing he would be if he knew everything that had happened for her. "I think he'd be content with me doing just about anything, as long as it was legal and I was happy doing it. My mom? Her reaction would be a different story."

Ty's brows rose. "Oh, to be a fly on that wall. But don't sweat it, your mom will come around once she realizes what a badass, multi-talented, superwoman she's raised. She should be proud."

"I don't suppose you'd like to come home with me and explain that to her?" Kayla asked, only half joking.

He snorted. "In theory, I'd probably go anywhere with you." Ty's eyes went wide as if he hadn't meant to make such a confession.

Kayla wanted to pounce on it, but she let it hang in the air, giving him the out if he needed one. When he didn't add anything more, she said, "Right now, I'd like to go walk off some of these calories."

"Have you been down to the Delaware yet?" he asked.

"Does driving down I-95 count?"

"Hardly." Ty jumped to his feet. "What time do you have to be back at the studio?"

She glanced at her phone. "I have another hour or so."

He smiled. "Come with me."

They made a right on Front Street, walked to Dock, crossed over, and made their way along the cobblestone street to Columbus Boulevard. There was a mid-rise hotel on the bank, and Kayla caught a glimpse of the water just beyond.

"Is that Jersey on the other side?"

"Yeah," Ty said. "Camden."

"Looks like you could swim across," Kayla noted.

"Yeah, no. I wouldn't recommend jumping into *that* water," Ty said, laughing.

He led her to a small park that sat on the bank of the river. Colorful hammocks had been strung up between the trees, while a rainbow of patio sets, complete with umbrellas, lined the pavement a level below.

"Okay," Kayla said. "This is pretty fucking cool."

"Right?" Ty smiled with pride and held his hands out wide. "Welcome to Spruce Street Harbor Park. This is the south end of it, and it stretches north. That way." He pointed toward the hotel and gestured beyond it. "We have a love-lock gate and everything, 'cause we fancy like that."

Ty held one of the empty two-person hammocks steady, and Kayla climbed into it. He joined her, and their bodies pressed together from torso to knee. Despite the heat, Kayla found she didn't mind one bit.

"At night, the lights in the trees come on, and it looks like... well...it's pretty magical." Ty's voice was low, almost reverent, as he pointed above them.

"I can imagine." Kayla matched his voice.

"We'll have to come back one evening."

A light breeze came off the water, and the area was quiet, despite the number of people. They spoke in hushed tones as if they too didn't want to spoil the atmosphere.

"I'd like that."

Ty turned to her, and she did the same, bringing their faces closer. At that moment, it was hard for her to accept that they'd only known each other for a short time. That they weren't already well on the path to something.

So, when his gaze dropped to her lips, she was more than ready to start.

"You make my head spin," he whispered into the space between them. "I envy you your sense of self. And the way you know exactly what you want out of life."

"Come back out on the road with us," she blurted before she could stop herself. Ty's gaze narrowed, and he searched her eyes. "You said it yourself, your grandpa is moving into his new place. You'd be in the house alone. Plus, the money's good. Right? And it'll give you time to think. Read." *Spend time with me.*

He gave a slow nod. "Yeah, but—"

"Don't decide right now," she rushed to say, unwillingly to hear the word no come out of his mouth just yet. "Think about it and text me. Or call me. I'll tell Jordan to request you specifically. If you want."

His eyes darkened when she said the word. *Want.*

"Do you...think that's something you might want?" she asked, suddenly nervous to hear his reply. When he leaned in closer and pressed their foreheads together, her pulse quickened into the rapid sixteenths she often played on the hi-hat.

"Honestly, the only thing I've wanted in a long time is this."

For a moment, time seemed to freeze, and Kayla held her breath, reveling in the energy sparking between them.

A sigh escaped the back of Ty's throat. He tipped his head to the side and pressed his lips more firmly into hers, his exhale ghosting across her cheek.

Internally, Kayla jumped for joy. She let him direct the kiss, which was little more than the coming together of their lips, over and over. Ty never tried for more, and Kayla was content to ease into whatever was forming between them.

When they broke apart, his hand came up to cradle her head. Rolling into him, Kayla pressed her palm against his chest, his T-shirt soft under her fingers, hard muscle underneath. She needed to get back to the studio, but this was good. Really good.

"Um...any idea how we're supposed to get out of this thing?"

Ty's chuckle was as soft and sweet as the ice cream had been. "Not a clue."

CHAPTER 20.

KAYLA: What r u up to today?
TY: Driving a high school swim team to Silver Springs
KAYLA: Is that in NY?
TY: MD
TY: You?
KAYLA: Studio
TY: Shouldn't you have your hands wrapped around a pair of sticks?

KAYLA HID HER GRIN BEHIND her sip of coffee. There were so many ways she could answer Ty's text but she didn't know if they were at the sexual innuendo stage of their...friendship? Whatever it was, she wasn't about to do or say anything to scare him away.

"Okay, Kayla." Richie's voice was suddenly in her ear, and Kayla almost dropped her phone.

"Yep. Yeah. Are you ready for me?"

A slight pause. "I...want to test the new microphone I put on your kick. Could you give me a steady beat?"

"On it." Kayla adjusted her position and rhythmically tapped the toe of her right shoe against the pedal. The sound of the kick drum filled the air like a heartbeat, and she made sure to apply consistent pressure and a tempo of around sixty-eight beats per minute. Her hands, however, were still free and she tapped the sticks against her thigh in 9/8 for a while, loving the feel and swing of the time signature.

"Got it," Richie said after a while. "Hold on a sec."

KAYLA: Sorry, we're in the middle of mic-ing my drums.
TY: I don't know what that means but I won't bother you anymore.
KAYLA: You're not a bother
TY: Good to know

"Okay, I'm good," Richie said. "Whenever you guys are ready."

KAYLA: Gotta get back to work
TY: Play well.
KAYLA: Drive safe.

She hesitated and then added a winking kiss emoji to her text before sending it and silencing her phone.

"Tiff, play that riff you were jamming on last night," Toni said in the headphones.

From her seat behind the drums, Kayla could only see the back of Toni's head, but she had a clear view of Tiff and Lilly through the glass door.

Kayla had a love-hate relationship with the isolation booth Richie had set her up in. While she understood the need for it, technically, she often felt cut off from the energy the four of them could generate when they were in the same room. Energy she could almost see through the glass as the others chatted away from the microphones.

She was tempted to open the door between takes, just to feel more like a part of the process.

Tiff began playing a low, growling bass line. Kayla remembered her playing it the other night and the rhythm that had popped into her head. She tapped it out against her thigh, perfecting the hitches and changes before she took it to the kit.

Toni struck a chord. An F-minor, Kayla thought. She didn't have anything close to the perfect pitch Toni had been blessed with, but the chord was somewhere in that vicinity. Toni let the chord ring before dropping into a series of arpeggiated chords that built in intensity with each measure that passed.

Kayla lightly tapped on the pedals at her feet, wanting to jump in so badly but not wanting to disturb the foundation Toni and Tiff were building. Both of them were still at half volume, something they often did when they were working something out. As if playing it any louder somehow cemented it before it was ready. It wasn't uncommon for the three of them—Toni, Tiff, and Kayla—to jam on the same riff for hours while Lilly hummed along, and she and Seb jotted notes in their songbook.

So far, only a few of those had given birth to full-fledged songs. But with the label breathing down their necks for a finished album, they needed to come up with more new material. Fast.

"You feeling anything, Kayla?" Tiff asked in the headset.

"Yep," Kayla replied. When they reached the top of the next measure, she shook off her restraints and played at full volume. The guitar and bass immediately followed suit and, soon, they were jamming in earnest.

After another thirty minutes, the session came to a natural conclusion. Kayla wiped the sweat from her brow with the hem of her T-shirt. She was glad she'd decided to tie her hair up into a high ponytail. The booth had become a sauna.

"I need some air," she said into the overhead mic before she took off her headphones and climbed from behind the kit, careful not to trip over any of the cables and stands.

As soon as she opened the door to the live room, cooler air hit her overheated skin and she sighed with relief.

"You're all...moist," Tiff said, wrinkling her nose.

Kayla gave her the finger. "You wanna switch places?"

Tiff held up her hands. "Nope." She lifted her bass strap over her head before setting the instrument in its stand.

"Is it too warm in there?" Lilly asked as they all walked to the control room.

"I'll manage," Kayla replied.

"Did you close the door to the booth?" Richie asked.

"Yeah."

"I'll turn the air back on in there," he said. "It'll cool it down quick. Sorry, but I have to turn it off when we're recording. That room is small, and the mics would pick up the sound from the HVAC."

Kayla nodded, already feeling less heated.

"There's water in that little fridge." Richie pointed to the corner. "I think Seb went to get the door. Jordan's here."

Lilly sank into one of the leather armchairs under the window. "He said he'd have news about the Broken Pilots tour, among other things."

"Ooo!" Tiff exclaimed. "I'm so excited for that tour."

"We have to get through the second set of festivals first," Lilly reminded her.

"And finish the new songs," Toni added as she hopped up onto the end of the console desk.

"And record the album," Kayla said.

"Yeah, yeah, I know." Tiff circled her hand in the air and grabbed four bottles of water from the fridge. She handed one to Toni. "Lots of work to do, I get it. Why are you guys always trying to kill my buzz?"

"Not kill it, *kjære*, just temper it a bit." Lilly smiled fondly at

Tiff and ran a hand down her arm when Tiff perched on the armrest of her chair. Kayla was coming to understand Lilly more, and knew she often used that particular Norwegian term of endearment when she was in mama-bear mode.

Tiff gave Lilly a bottle of water and tossed another to Kayla, who caught it one-handed.

It was deliciously icy in her hands and went down her throat like an Alaskan dream. Okay, maybe she was warmer than she thought. Feeling a little light-headed, Kayla leaned forward to put her elbows on her knees, letting her head hang down between them.

"You all right, K?" Seb asked as he entered the room. He put a hand on the back of her neck, his palm nice and cool against her skin. "Christ, you're burning up. Are you coming down with something?"

Kayla shook her head. "Nah, just got a little overheated in the booth."

"Shit." Richie sounded alarmed. "You should have taken a break sooner." He got up and left the room.

"I'm fine, I'm fine," Kayla said. "Really." Five concerned expressions were directed at her. She loved these people so fucking much.

"Hey, kitten," Jordan said, his voice close to her ear. Kayla turned to find him sitting next to her.

"Hey yourself."

"I know you hate to stop once you get going, but remember to take care of yourself. Yeah?"

She smiled. "I'm fine—really—but yes. I will."

Richie returned with a few bottles of Gatorade. He handed one to Kayla. "Drink this. It'll help."

"Thanks," she said, taking it gratefully. Kayla opened it and drank deeply.

"I got a few if anyone else needs one, and there's more in the vending machine." Richie sat the other bottles on the window ledge. He was particular about liquids on or around the console.

Kayla could understand why. The thing had probably cost a fortune.

"I had a meeting with Andre this morning," Jordan said, slipping into business mode. There was a collective groan. "My sentiments exactly, and he isn't going to be your favorite person after I tell you what I learned."

"What now?" Tiff asked.

"It seems YMI has positioned their weight behind Candi's new act," Jordan said.

Lilly sat forward in her seat. "Positioned it how?"

"They've been together for five fucking minutes."

"It's ridiculous," Jordan agreed.

"YMI suggested sending Sugar Habit out on tour with Broken Pilots instead of the Lillys."

"Like hell," Toni snapped, her eyes flashing with anger.

Tiff jumped to her feet. "They can't do that!"

Jordan held out his hand. "Calm down, luv. You're right. They can't."

"Andre is such a goddamned asshole," Tiff growled, walking in tight circles in the middle of the room. "I wish he'd fuck off back to Silicon Valley or wherever and let Daniel handle the label stuff."

"Agreed," Toni said. "I like him. He's definitely the *good* twin."

"Me too," Seb said. "And Daniel actually knows a little bit about music. Unfortunately, Andre thinks of YMI as his own personal soap opera. I'm more convinced than ever he deliberately set up that ambush at the hotel in Detroit."

"I'm inclined to agree," Jordan said. "Anyway, he can't force Broken Pilots to take Sugar Habit on tour with them, so him telling me he wanted to send them instead of you was purely a power play. I think he plans to set the two groups up as label rivals. Generate some drama and publicity."

"Jesus H. Christ," Seb swore. "Maybe we should have taken the deal with Sonic Records instead."

"I'm handling it," Jordan said. "I just need you lot to be aware. And ready. How are the new songs coming along?"

"We'll have four, possibly five ready to record by the time we come back from the West Coast," Lilly said. She had that look of determination on her face that told Kayla she wasn't going to let YMI or anyone else derail their plans, and Kayla loved it.

"Excellent," Jordan said, smiling for the first time since he arrived. "Can't wait to hear them. I'm still working Andre for permission to release 'Hurt U' early. After that video you sent of Sugar Habit performing the song, the sooner we can get it out the better."

"I'll pull it up." Richie sat in his office chair and rolled up to the control board. "If I recall, you only have a few things to clean up in overdubs and then we can move on to mixing."

"Don't we have that string quartet booked for the A room for the next week?" Toni asked, switching seamlessly into her role as co-owner of Phactory Sound.

"It won't be a problem," he replied.

"Good. We don't want to get on the wrong side of those college ensembles," Toni replied. "They have deep pockets."

Kayla took a moment to admire her ability to juggle both careers, but she had such mixed emotions about releasing the song. As their first original, "Hurt U" was bound to get attention. It was what they all wanted, to be recognized for their work. But recognition meant more press, less privacy.

"Why is Andre giving us pushback?" Tiff narrowed her eyes at Seb. "Is it because they want Sugar Harlot or whatever to get the jump on us?"

"It's more likely because we don't have a producer yet."

"Do we need one?" Toni asked.

"It's rare for a band, especially a new one, to produce their own records," Seb replied.

"Can't you do it?"

Every head swung to Toni, and Kayla wondered why they hadn't thought of that before.

"I don't think I can." Seb sounded uncharacteristically hesitant.

"Why not, babe?"

He looked at Toni. "Well, I mean...I'm your manager."

"It would be unusual." Jordan narrowed his eyes in thought. "But...for the single...we might be able to get away with it."

"You *are* a Grammy-nominated songwriter, after all." When Seb looked at her, Kayla winked and was happy to see him smile.

"She's right, Seb." Lilly met his gaze and something silent passed between them.

"Works for me," he said with a grin.

"Speaking of which, we should get back to it." Kayla got to her feet. The electrolytes were working their magic, and she felt better already.

"Could I borrow you for a tick?" Jordan asked her.

"Uh...sure."

While the rest of the band filed back into the live room, Jordan opened the door to the hall and followed Kayla through it.

"What's up?" she asked, fighter jets firing up their engines in her stomach.

"I heard you and the driver, Tyrell, were getting friendly," he said.

Kayla shifted on her feet. "Tiff?" she asked. He nodded. "She's such a blabbermouth. We're friends, yeah. Sorta. I think."

"I got the impression it was...a bit more," Jordan hedged.

"I honestly don't know," Kayla confessed. "We got...close...on the road, and we hung out a bit after. I took him apartment hunting with me."

"I'm aware," Jordan said, looking at her in that scrutinizing, lawyerly way of his that made Kayla feel like she'd been called to the dean's office. He lowered his voice. "Did he... Has he told you anything about...what happened?"

Kayla nodded, her stomach clenching. "Ty told me about the accusations of plagiarism and about being arrested for something he didn't do. Why?"

"After Tiff mentioned you two were close, I looked into him," Jordan said. "His employer already divulged his arrest and that he'd been completely exonerated, but—as you said—no details."

Kayla's skin prickled. She wondered if there was more to the story than Ty had told her, but it felt...wrong, somehow, to hear the details from someone other than Ty. On the other hand, there was clearly something Jordan felt she needed to know.

"And...you found the details?"

"They weren't hard to find," Jordan said. There was a sadness in his eyes she'd never seen before. "What happened to him, it was a gross injustice. The case against him was entirely circumstantial. Tyrell had a rock-solid alibi and shouldn't have been arrested at all."

"Then why was he?"

Jordan shook his head ruefully. "I could bend your ear about the level of judicial prejudice in the American court system, not that it's much better in the UK. The long and the short of it is, they were under pressure from the girl's family. Tyrell's life was easy to pick apart. He lives in an area known for violent crime, has no real family other than his grandpa..."

"And he's Black."

Jordan nodded. "He fit the narrative."

"Jesus," Kayla whispered.

"If it weren't for an enterprising public defender, he'd probably still be languishing in jail or worse," Jordan said. "Because of his relatively clean background, the fact that his alibi hadn't been looked into, and the alleged victim's inconsistent story, the criminal charges were dropped."

"Thank goodness." Kayla's heart was in her throat. "Was the girl expelled?"

Jordan's jaw tightened. "Of course not. Her family has too much influence. I suspect Ty found it impossible to return to campus. Even with the criminal charges dropped, plagiarism is a difficult stain to wash clean and it was a rather highly publicized case."

"But *she* was the one who copied *him*," Kayla said, incensed.

"Again, it's all about influence."

Kayla shook her head. She hadn't known Ty long, but she couldn't picture him cheating to get ahead, much less of being capable of something so heinous as assault. Poor guy.

"I can tell by the look on your face that you care for him," Jordan said. His voice was tender. "I hesitated telling you any of this, but I had a feeling you two had grown closer than you were letting on. This is where the whole mixing business with pleasure thing gets messy."

"Right."

"I know you probably prefer to leave this between the two of you," he added, "but I don't work for Ty, I work for you. And I needed to make sure you knew the facts."

Kayla nodded. "I get it. Thanks."

"This was only the technical details," Jordan said. "I'm sure he'll share, over time…if you guys, uh…"

She bit her lip, wishing she could still feel his soft kiss. "Got it."

"There's one other thing," Jordan said. "Tyrell was in a degree program when everything went to hell. He lost his funding, and I get the impression money is tight, but I don't think he's sought any compensation from the school."

"You think he should sue?"

"He shouldn't have to," Jordan said. "All he would really need to do is engage an attorney and ask the trustees to settle out of court. In a case as clear-cut as his, he'd probably get a sizeable amount. Enough to finish his degree and then some. They ruined his life."

Kayla frowned. "He hasn't pursued *any* legal recourse?"

"Not that I'm aware," Jordan said. "It's not my area of expertise, but I have contacts. I could put him in touch with someone who would work pro bono, or at least for a nominal fee. If he's interested. I thought the offer might sound better coming from a friend, or a... you know," he finished with a wink.

Kayla looked away but nodded again. "I'll try to bring it up to him."

"Do what you can," Jordan said. "I hate to think of someone's life being ruined over something like this."

Kayla leaned up and wrapped Jordan in a hug, and he returned it, humming.

"Thank you," she said as they separated. "You're good people."

"Takes one to know one," he replied. "And like I said, it's obvious to the others that there's something brewing between you two, but Ty was technically an employee. I need to make sure your bases are covered if he were to ever work for us again."

"I get it."

"Good. Honestly, I don't know why we bother with the no-fraternization clause anymore," he muttered to himself and then paused. "There's something else."

Kayla's nerves were suddenly on edge. "About Ty?"

"About you." He cupped her elbow and pulled her farther away from the others. Lowering his voice he said, "I went over what happened in Detroit. The one who asked you how your family would react to you being in the Lillys..."

"You think she knows who I am, who my mother is."

Jordan nodded toward the control room. "I don't understand why you haven't told the others yet."

"My parents don't know about the band. I wanted to tell them when we got back from the first leg, but I—"

"Not your parents." He glanced back at the group before meeting her eyes again. "Though you might want to take care of *that* soon. They're going to find out sooner or later."

Kayla didn't have the words to make him understand. She barely understood herself why she kept who she was from the rest of the band. From Seb.

"I don't want drama" was all she could manage.

Jordan gave her a long, assessing look.

After a quick glance over her shoulder, she lowered her voice. "If people knew…about me and Little Miss Yolanda, my mom… it… You don't go from being, like, America's favorite little brainiac to…" She gestured to herself. "I don't want every damn interview, every write-up, to be about how little Yolanda ditched school to join a rock band. It wouldn't be about the music anymore."

"You're not Candi."

"I know." When his gaze didn't falter, she repeated it. "I *know*."

"Good," he said, taking a deep breath. "I understand your concerns. And I maintain that the best way for you to manage them is to *talk* to them. Talk to your parents. Keeping everyone in the dark is only going to cause more harm in the end. You want everyone to stand beside you, Kayla, my love, not to feel left behind."

"I get it, and you're right." He was, though Kayla wasn't sure when or how to make things right. The band would be upset, but they'd get over it. Her mother…? She sighed. "I'll fill in the blanks for everyone. Promise."

His trademark smirk returned. "Now, go in there and beat the hell out of those drums, you little beastie."

CHAPTER 21.

KAYLA STARED DOWN AT HER phone, at the links Jordan had sent out. Press coverage from the first leg of the tour.

They were gathered in his Manhattan office for a band meeting. Jordan had news. After learning about YMI's decision to position the group against Sugar Habit in the media, Kayla wasn't sure she needed to hear more *news*.

Her phone pinged with an incoming message.

DAD: It was lovely to see you, sweetheart. So happy to hear you're still playing. I know how much you and your brother loved to play together.

Kayla smiled.

KAYLA: I'm so proud of you, Daddy. And I can't wait to read your first volume of poetry. Don't let Mom talk you out of it. Promise me.
DAD: We'll see.
DAD: By the way, I love this photo of you.

Kayla studied the image. The person standing between her mother and father looked rigid but confident. Like a mannequin in a tableau depicting proper society etiquette. Hair, neat. Clothing, impeccable. Smile, modest. Katherine Yolanda Larrington was the very picture of feminine academic excellence. Not even her mom could take issue.

For Kayla, it was like looking at a Stepford clone of herself.

"Holy shit, did you see the article from *Swerve*?" Tiff bounded across the room toward her.

Kayla closed her messages and looked up. "No."

"We look badass." Tiff thrust her phone under Kayla's nose.

"Slow down, speedy." She laughed, taking the phone.

Tiff squeezed down next to her on the love seat. "Tell me we don't look like one of those groups from the eighties."

"I don't think our hair is big enough." Kayla zoomed in for a better look. "You actually have a kind of Furiosa thing going on."

Tiff had gone for postapocalyptic chic the day the photo was taken, black leather and nylon mesh that wrapped her nut-brown skin as if she were a confection. She'd wrestled her mane of jet-black hair into a long, thick braid that hung around her neck like a whip.

"Wait until you see what I'm doing for the second leg."

"Can't wait," she replied studying her own outfit. The stylist for the shoot had put her in tight black jeans with ripped knees, a sparkly silver tank top with a deep V neckline, and a cropped motorcycle jacket. It wasn't...*awful*. In fact, the whole look was much better in the photo than it had been in person. This girl—wearing minimal makeup, her hair in a riot of red coils—was a world away from the person in the photo her father had sent. Kayla actually *recognized* herself standing with her bandmates and didn't hate what she saw.

She wondered what Zach would say. Could almost hear his voice.

You ready to take over the world, little genius?

"Earth to Kayla."

She looked up to find Tiff staring at her. "What? Sorry."

"I asked if you're amped to get back out there."

"Yeah, I am. How many of these festivals are we doing?" Kayla was already losing track of their schedule.

"Four or five more, I think."

"Five," Jordan replied walking by them. He continued over to his desk and sat down behind it. "I'm glad we're settled on bringing Carlos into the team."

Carlos had been instrumental in bringing the Lillys to YMI, and had been let go when the label was sold. YMI barely had an A&R team anymore, which sucked. Carlos was a good guy, though. Kayla was glad they'd be working with him again.

"We have a YMI problem," Jordan added.

Lilly narrowed her eyes. "When don't we?" She was leaning against the wall by the window.

"They undercut us with Candi and her group," Jordan agreed. "And now they seem to be feeding certain news outlets with information."

His gaze landed pointedly on Kayla before breaking away.

A trickle of unease slid down her spine. "What's going on?"

Seb pushed out of his chair. "The label wants more creative control over the band's image."

"Meaning?" Lilly crossed her arms, her cool gaze dropping a few degrees.

"A label-approved stylist will be putting together a wardrobe for you for the next leg."

"The fuck?" Tiff shoved to the edge of the chair. "We can't wear our own clothes?"

"It's not unusual for a label to want to cultivate a certain image for an act," Jordan said. "And normally, you would work together to create something everyone was comfortable with."

"YMI wants complete control," Seb added.

"We can say no, though. Right?" Toni glared at Seb before

turning to Jordan. "We have the right to refuse or whatever, don't we?"

Jordan's sigh was a deep one. He leaned his elbows on the desk and rubbed a hand over his face. "Your original contract had some...stipulations that I wasn't able to carve out of the revisions. I didn't think... I had no idea Andre would be..."

"Such a dickhead?" Tiff asked. "Doesn't he have Sugar Habit to play with now?"

"That's a good question. Why is he so hot for us?" Kayla looked from Jordan to Seb.

"He likes attention," Seb said flatly. "All the shit that went down with Candi turned a lot of eyes on you, on the label. When it died down, people stopped talking about YMI."

"He signed Candi's band to get the spotlight back on YMI?" Saying it out loud, Kayla could hear the twisted logic.

"There's no such thing as bad press," Tiff said, shaking her head.

"Perpetuating the idea of a beef between our two bands, digging into our pasts, all of that is to sell records?" Toni asked.

"That's fucked up." Tiff rose to her feet. "But not surprising, I guess."

"None of this really matters." Lilly's tone was measured, her control firmly in place, but Kayla could see fatigue at her edges. She ran a hand through her hair, which had been shaved the sides with the rest left long, the ends trailing along her waist. Sunlight from the window glinting in the near-white strands. "We're musicians, not dolls. But if we have to play the part for a while, that's what we have to do. As for the press..." She leveled her gaze on Jordan. "Is there anything we can do, legally, to stop them from invading our privacy?"

"Truthfully, no." Jordan replied. "They have to right to anything in the public record, and we can't stop them from contacting people. Short of harassment or defamation, I'm afraid you're fair game."

Tiff cursed under her breath and turned her back to the room.

Kayla stomach dropped to the floor.

"The best we can do," Jordan added, "is not volunteer any information they don't already have."

"Like?" Toni asked.

"Full names, place of birth, etcetera." Jordan didn't look at Kayla, but she knew his words were meant for her.

"If they don't have our names, they can't dig too far back," Toni said.

"Not as easily." Jordan pulled his keyboard forward and started typing. "Your previous attorney did one thing right when it came to your contract with YMI." He clicked a few times and nodded to himself. "The label contract is with the band's anonymous LLC and not with you as individuals. It's why YMI wasn't able to force you to keep Candi as a member."

"How does the LLC help us in this case?"

Jordan turned to Kayla, his focus so intense her shoulders tensed. "It means that YMI probably has a note somewhere in their system of your legal names but, contractually, they only deal with the band as an entity. *That* is what's on file."

"My name isn't a secret, thanks to my mom telling everyone who will listen about the band," Toni said.

Seb put a warm hand on her shoulder and she reached up to clasp it. "So we have a buffer."

"Of sorts," Jordan said. "A good reporter can find out just about anything, though. Especially if they're pointed in the right direction. I can't prove Andre didn't seed the questions in Detroit, but it seems likely."

"Then we prepare ourselves. Next time, we'll know what to expect," Lilly said.

The room was silent as everyone processed the news. Kayla, for one, wasn't reassured. The woman in Detroit had rattled her with those questions about her and about Tiff.

Seb and Jordan walked the group through the details for the next leg of the tour.

"You'll have more people with you, including a couple of roadies."

"One needs to be a backup driver," Seb said.

"Already noted." Jordan drummed his fingers against the desk. With his close-cropped curls, smooth chin, and modern rectangular glasses, he looked like an overworked accountant. "The label noticed your traffic spike during the last festival. Remember, they'll be keeping a closer eye on you."

"And our clothes," Tiff muttered.

Kayla snorted quietly. She knew Tiff too well. If the label thought they were going to take control of the band's image, they were in for a surprise. Hopefully one that wouldn't make a mess of things.

"Oh, before I forget…" Jordan opened the large bottom drawer on his desk and pulled out a large manila envelope. Opening the metal clasp as he rose and walked to the center of the room, he dumped the contents on the coffee table. "You've got mail."

"Is that…" Toni stared down at the spill of envelopes, her dark eyes wide with disbelief. "Actual fan mail?"

"I didn't think people did that anymore." Kayla picked an envelope out of the pile. All of the envelopes had been opened. She looked up at Jordan.

"I had someone go through them, just in case."

"In case of what?"

Jordan arched a brow. "Any threats."

"This is an awesome photo!" Toni held up a glossy eight-by-ten of her onstage with her guitar, Minx. The background was a velvety night sky speckled with stars and the silhouette of the crowd below, many of them holding up their cell phones. Toni's face was partially obscured by shadow, but Kayla could make out the electric purple tips of her hair. It was a striking effect. The photo had captured Toni in full performance, her eyes half-closed, mouth slightly open as she played.

"Look, there are two copies," Tiff said, picking up the second one. It has a sticky note attached to it. "One is for you to keep and the other they want you to sign and send back."

"It'll end up on eBay," Seb said, nudging Toni's hip. "You've officially made it."

Lilly picked up a package addressed to her. It was about the size of a shoebox, and her brows furrowed when she pulled out the contents.

"Wow," Tiff said, turning to her. "That's gorgeous."

"It is." Lilly held the delicate lace shawl up, spreading it out to inspect the design, a mix of ivory and gray, with swirling patterns and a subtle snowflake accent.

There were a few more requests for signed photos, a love letter to Tiff—"Oh, my God. I am framing this."—and a vintage Caspian's Ghost T-shirt for Toni.

"This is so cool!" She held up the shirt.

"That's too big for you." Seb tried to take it, but Toni snatched it back.

"Hey, get your own. I'll sleep in it."

"Make sure you wash any garments before you wear them," Jordan said. "I had someone check for anything that could prick or cut you, so you don't have to worry about that."

"Geez," Kayla said. "You really think someone would send us stuff to hurt us?"

"He's not being paranoid." Seb eased the T-shirt away from Toni. "There are all kinds of people in the world."

"You'll start to get gifts from fans on the road too. Be careful what you accept," Jordan added. "And if you feel like saying no might lead to an uncomfortable situation, say yes and hand the gift off to a member of the crew. Festivals, the larger ones anyway, have staff trained to deal with overzealous fans."

"And like Jory said, we'll have an entourage this time out."

"Are we on the bus again? I don't think there's room for anyone else." Kayla couldn't help but think of Ty, his earbud in his ear and his arms draped over the steering wheel. She suppressed a smile.

"In addition to a larger bus, there will be an SUV with a trailer," Jordan replied. "It will be comfortable, as far as these things go."

"It's getting late," Lilly said. "Is there anything else? I want to go by the brownstone and grab some clothes. At this rate, I should just buy a place in Philadelphia."

"And sell our home? You just finished the studio in the basement with that little area for my basses." Tiff signed her contract and absently handed it to Jordan. "I'd really miss that house."

"You don't want a new one? Maybe with a separate apartment?" Lilly's brows rose slightly, which meant she was worried about Tiff's reaction.

"Hmm...I hadn't thought about that." Tiff walked over and slipped an arm around Lilly's waist. She barely came up to the Norwegian's shoulder, and it made Kayla grin. "I love your house, but a separate apartment would be nice."

"Unless you'd be happy with the guest room again?"

Tiff looked at Lilly like she'd lost the plot. "Hell no. You've put ideas in my head now. Mama needs her privacy."

Lilly ran a hand over Tiff's hair the way a mother might a child's. "There's nothing stopping you from finding a place of your own."

Turning to grab both of Lilly's arms, Tiff gasped. "And leave you all by yourself? Who would eat the mounds of food you can't stop cooking?"

"Uh, I volunteer as tribute," Toni said, sending a ripple of laughter through the group.

Finally, Lilly hugged Tiff to her and rested her chin atop her head. "Watching you eat is too much fun."

Standing together, Tiff and Lilly were quite a sight—tall and slim, short and curvy, dawn and dusk, ice and fire.

"Toni and I are heading back to Philly," Seb said. "Tiff, you need a lift?"

"I'll go with Lil. I want to pick up the pink bass anyway. I think he's feeling neglected."

Kayla signed her contract and handed it back to Jordan. "I need to head over to Springfield and pick up more sticks."

"I guess we'll see everyone at the studio." Toni handed over her paperwork and grabbed Seb's hand.

Kayla lingered behind, turning to Jordan after Lilly and Tiff departed.

"What's up?" Jordan picked up his leather messenger bag and started packing to go.

"I just... Before, when you said I'm not Candi... I know that. I'm allergic to drama," Kayla said, and Jordan smiled. "But there's a lot at stake. When I joined this band, I never expected it to get this far. I never expected the attention or the label interest or any of it."

Jordan stopped what he was doing. "What are you saying?"

What was she saying? Kayla could hardly tell him that she never thought the Lillys would get this far, let alone be on the verge of breaking into the mainstream.

"You know who my mom is." Jordan nodded. "If it gets out that her daughter dropped out of college and is playing drums in a band, it could affect her credibility."

Frowning, Jordan laid the bag down. "Why, because it might affect book sales?"

Kayla shook her head. "You don't know how uptight her... our...community is."

"I'm not sure I follow."

"Rock music isn't *respectable*," she said, quoting her mother. "Which is bullshit, but what if paparazzi start following us around again? What if they keep digging into Tiff?" *Or me?* she thought.

She thought about Zach, about the hollow look in her parents' eyes after his death.

Their mother had blamed herself. As if Zach's choice to go on the road with his band was somehow hers to veto. He'd been an adult, fully capable of making his own decisions. And that decision had nothing to do with what happened. But speculation about the role of alcohol and drugs in the accident had only cemented her mother's feelings about it, not to mention her attitude toward rock music in general.

"Most of the media will tune into the music and the fact that you're four kick-ass women."

"But they don't have Candi to focus on anymore. What if—"

Jordan placed his hand gently on Kayla's shoulder. She spun to look up at him, her fears spilling out like water out of a broken pipe. She hadn't even realized she'd been pacing.

"I'll do everything in my power to protect the privacy of the band, but like I said before, you need to talk to everyone. Soon."

"Fuck me," Kayla muttered to herself.

Jordan's smile was sympathetic. "If you're that concerned, your other option would be...well...to leave the band."

Kayla heard herself gasp. "*What?*"

He shrugged. "If you're determined to keep your two worlds completely separate, that might be your only choice. Of course, *I* think that would be a horrible solution. You're a member of the Lillys for a reason. I mean, no one twisted your arm to join, did they?"

"No."

"No one's forcing you to stay?"

"Of course not." She frowned up at him. "I love these guys, the music, I love being…" *Me.* "This is what I want to do with my life. I just don't know how to have it without everything blowing up in my face."

Jordan squeezed her shoulders lightly before dropping his hands to his sides. "Well, love, you'd better figure it out soon. Your star is rising, and it'll be hard to hide when you're at the center of the night sky."

CHAPTER 22.

TY BRUSHED HIS FINGERTIPS ACROSS the bottom of the gilded frame, acutely aware that he was touching music history. According to the inscription, the platinum-dipped LP had been presented to Phactory Sound Studios for their part in the recording of one of his granddad's favorite songs.

He pulled out his phone and snapped a photo, shooting off a quick text to Van before strolling farther down the hall. The walls on either side were covered with gold and platinum records, CDs, and even plated cassette tapes. He spied an 8-track hanging on the wall in one of the offices. It was only the second one he'd ever seen in person.

"This is surreal," he murmured.

"I know." Seb stepped up beside him. "Kayla mentioned you were stopping by. It's good to see you again. How's it going?"

They shook hands. "All right, thanks."

It was deceptively quiet in the hall, and Ty wondered if the band was on a break. But when Seb opened one of the doors and stepped inside, music filled the air. To say it was loud was an understatement. Ty felt as he'd been swallowed by an ocean of sound.

"Richie, this is Tyrell," Seb said, addressing a guy who sat in front of an enormous console. It was covered with hundreds of buttons and knobs and looked like it belonged in a seventies-era NASA control room. "Richie's dad founded this place way back when."

"Nice to meet you," Richie said, spinning the black leather chair to face Ty. "Welcome to the Phactory."

"Good to meet you." Ty shook his hand. "This place is amazing."

"Thanks." Richie smiled before turning back to the board of buttons and dials. Three large flat-screen monitors sat above the desk on what looked like a curved shelf. There were two giant speakers mounted to the wall above them.

"Hey, come over here," Seb called over to Ty, who joined him at an expansive window that looked into another room.

Toni and Tiffany stood on the other side, each with instruments in hand and headphones over their ears. It was mesmerizing, the way they coaxed such fantastic music from slabs of painted wood and bits of metal wire.

To the side of them, Lilly stood with her hands over her earpieces, eyes closed as she listened intently.

Ty scanned the room for Kayla and noticed another, smaller room off to the side where she sat, arms flailing. The drum kit itself practically filled the room.

"Why are the drums in a separate room?" he asked no one in particular.

"Bleed," Richie said. His hands were in constant motion, darting out to twist a knob or move a slider as he kept a close eye on the monitors in front of him. They displayed what appeared to be bars of sound waves, in what had to be more than a dozen rows, and Ty watched—fascinated—as the rows filled with more waves.

"Is this your first time in a studio?" Seb asked.

Ty nodded. "Yeah."

"Pretty cool, eh?"

"It is," he agreed, turning to peer into the other room.

Toni and Tiff had locked eyes and seemed to be communicating in some silent language, bobbing their heads in time.

Lilly lifted her arm, and they both looked at her and nodded. Ty saw Kayla lift her chin. Then the song shifted as Lilly began to sing.

Over and over, the tide will turn
Over and over, the lessons learned
Over and over, the mighty fall
Over and over, we paint the walls

"This is one of the new songs we're working on," Seb said over the crescendo of the music. "What do you think?"

"It's good!" Ty said, and it was. He wanted to hear it from the beginning.

Seb smiled, his shoulders moving back and forth to the rhythm. "Let's hope the label agrees. By the way, I hear you might have some lyrics we should check out. You've been holding out on us, eh?"

"I don't know if I'd call them lyrics."

"Kayla seems to think so." Seb gave him a knowing grin.

"We'll see." Ty didn't know how it worked with record labels, but he'd heard some horror stories. He hoped the Lillys had a good relationship with theirs.

The song ended, and there was a muffled chorus of *whoop!* from the other side of the glass.

"I think we have it," Richie said, still twisting and sliding pieces of the console.

"Where'd you learn to do all of this?" Ty asked him, stepping closer to inspect the board.

"Right here—my dad built this place when I was little," Richie replied.

"You're standing next to music royalty," Seb said.

Richie chuckled. "Hardly."

There were pieces of masking tape at the bottom of each slider's column, and Ty tried to discern the scribbles that someone—presumably Richie—had jotted down. A few were clear—bass, guitar, lead. Others weren't.

"Who or what is *Tom 1*?"

Richie pointed to the monitor. "That's the mic on Kayla's left tom drum, that's the right, this is the kick, the snare, etc.," he continued, pointing them out.

Ty realized the notes on the tape were mirrored on the monitors. It was all very...precise. He'd always thought of recording as a more haphazard affair.

"Impressive," he said. "I guess you'd need a lifetime to learn."

"Not really," Richie replied. "Toni's picking it up pretty fast."

"Toni?"

"She's a partner here," Seb said, no small amount of pride in his voice.

Toni wasn't much older than Ty, if at all. "Wow. Did she grow up in the business too?"

Seb made a gesture with his hand that said *kinda*. "She's been around music most of her life but not in studios. No, she was just determined to own one."

"And I talked her into becoming my partner here," Richie finished.

Ty was equal parts impressed and envious. It sounded like Toni had set a goal for herself and achieved it. Meanwhile, he was still trying to figure out what to do with his life.

"I need food." Tiff burst into the room with that pronouncement. Her eyes went wide when she noticed Ty. "Oh, hells yeah! Bookworm!"

Tiff launched herself at him, and Ty barely had enough time to brace himself to catch her. Laughing, he returned her enthusiastic hug. "Good to see you again," he said as he released her.

Tiff held on to his arms. "It's so good to see you."

She glanced over her shoulder, and Ty followed her gaze to Kayla, who made her way through the other room toward them.

"Make her squirm a little," Tiff said, winking.

Ty's gaze locked on Kayla's, his throat suddenly dry as she walked into the room.

"Hey, Ty," Toni said. She gave his shoulder a quick squeeze as she passed him.

"Hi."

Lilly nodded, and he returned it. Then Kayla was there.

"Glad you could come." Her voice was soft.

Ty could feel everyone's attention on them. Everyone except for Richie, who seemed oblivious to the electricity sparking between them. Ty cleared his throat. "I've, uh, never seen a recording session in person before."

"What did you think? Maybe you'll stick around to see how the song ends?" Kayla's expression was curious. Hopeful. Ty knew what she meant, so he answered the question she was really asking.

"I haven't decided yet, about your tour."

She dropped her gaze, nodding. Looking back up at Ty, she searched his eyes. "Can we talk?"

"That would be good," Ty replied, because he needed them to be on the same page. He didn't know what to make of her, of any of this. A more significant part of him than was wise wanted to push her up against the ornate soundproofing and kiss her until neither of them could breathe.

"Guys, I'll be back." Kayla walked toward the door he'd first entered through, and he followed her. She led him down the hall, through another door—the place was a maze—and into a sort of common room.

Two leather sofas sat in an L shape in one corner, three vending machines in the other. A large flat-screen TV was mounted to one wall, and various framed magazine and newspaper articles lined the other.

Kayla closed the door behind them and took a seat on one of the sofas.

Ty sat on the other, facing her.

"I'm delighted you're here," she began.

He couldn't even suppress his grin. "You're kinda making it impossible to refuse, considering your gift...the other day... You're too good at this."

"At what?"

"Persuasion."

Kayla frowned. "I don't want to pressure you. I just wanted—"

"I know." It had come out a little bit louder than he'd meant it, and Kayla flinched.

Ty took a breath and nodded toward the hall they'd just come down. "I wasn't sure if the offer to drive was still good."

"Why wouldn't it be?" Kayla looked confused.

"I have baggage."

"You mean you're not perfect?"

He smiled because he knew what she was doing. "No, I am. I'm utter perfection, didn't you know?"

Kayla's smile didn't quite meet her eyes. Her gaze fell to her hands, which were twisted into a pretzel where they rested on her knees. "Ty, I know we talked about it before, but if you take the gig I need you to understand that you are in no way required to spend time with me, outside of your job description."

It was his turn to frown. "If I thought you were the type of person to abuse your power that way, I wouldn't work for you, much less..." He stopped, unsure how to finish that sentence.

Kayla's expression warmed. "I only wanted to make it clear. In case it wasn't. I really hate when people are vague."

"Me too!" Ty offered her a smile and could see the tension drain from her shoulders. "It's cool. All right?"

"Yeah," Kayla said exhaling. "So...you're coming with us?" After a beat, she ducked her head, color rising in her cheeks. "I'd miss having you around."

"I'd miss being around," he confessed. "But I need to think about it. With Pop-Pop and everything."

"Oh, of course," Kayla rushed to say.

They stared at each other for a long moment, and Ty could feel the familiar pull returning. His heart thudded against his rib cage, demanding that he say yes. That he'd follow this girl wherever she went for as long as he could and see where they landed.

His head made him take a step back from where they'd drifted closer. "You guys sounded good."

She flushed, and it was fucking adorable.

"Thanks. Can you stick around for a while?" Kayla asked as she stood. "We have another hour or two here, and then we were thinking of heading over to this place called the Electric Unicorn when we finish. You been there?"

"No, but I've heard about it."

"Another first," Kayla said, grinning.

"I get the feeling I'll experience a lot of firsts if I keep hanging out with you."

The Electric Unicorn was exactly the kind of place Ty liked— eclectic, inviting, and unpretentious. He couldn't believe he'd never been there before. Then again, the only time Ty spent downtown was for work. That, and when he was in and out of court.

Shaking off the sense of dread that often followed him to this part of the city, Ty settled in a stool at the bar next to Kayla.

Lilly parked at a high-top table next to the window and pulled out her phone.

Seb and Toni walked to the front of the venue. There was a small but well-appointed stage, velvet curtains framing the portico in deep burgundy.

An older man emerged from a door at the side of the stage. He made a beeline for Toni, sweeping her into a hug before doing the same to Seb.

"That's Elton," Kayla said, drawing Ty's attention to her. "He's the owner. Nice guy. Very British."

"Like *very* British," Tiff added, sidling up to the bar. "Wait, you haven't met Jordan. Has he met Jordan?" she asked Kayla.

"Not yet," Kayla said.

Ty looked back and forth between them, waiting for one of them to explain who Jordan was. "Who?"

"Oh, he's our attorney-slash-business-manager, slash-big-brother, slash-mother-hen," Tiff supplied. "Basically, don't fuck with us, or he'll fuck with you. Legally speaking, that is. Though, I'm sure he could hold his own in a fight. The guy is ripped."

Ty wondered if Tiff was even capable of giving short, succinct answers.

"He's in New York, but he comes down to Philly often since we're recording here, and he likes to feel like a part of it," Kayla supplied.

"We're not his only clients," Tiff added, "but we're his favorites."

"I don't doubt it," Ty said.

A bartender took their drink orders and handed them the bar menu. After placing an order for tater tots and wings, Ty took in the rest of the bar area.

"Those aren't American license plates," he observed.

"I think those are English, though I know Elton has some from different states and from places in Europe," Kayla said as she accepted her bottle of lager from the bartender.

"All the places I want to visit," Ty admitted.

"You will," Kayla said.

Ty had ordered the same lager as hers, and they clinked bottlenecks before he took a sip. The liquid was cold and refreshing as it went down. He was relaxed, he realized.

Ty couldn't remember the last time he'd gone out like this, much less when he had felt so at ease.

Laughter rang out behind him, and Ty marveled at the smile on Lilly's face as Elton gestured wildly, clearly in the middle of what must have been an epic tale.

"That's a sight you don't see every day," Seb said as he and Toni approached the bar. He nodded at Lilly. "We should record this moment for posterity." Fishing out his phone, he took a photo of the smiling blond.

"We should put that up on our website," Toni said.

"She would murder us all in our sleep," Kayla replied, and the three of them laughed.

A streak of envy shot through Ty. This was a group of friends, a makeshift family, complete with inside jokes and easy rapport. It was something Ty had never been a part of, and he wanted it. Badly. His grandfather had been right. Even before the arrest and everything that happened, Ty hadn't really found his place in the world.

"We, uh…" Seb began, glancing at Toni. She nodded, and he took a deep breath. "We have some news."

He gestured for everyone to follow him over to Lilly's table. Dragging along a couple of the barstools, the six of them squeezed around a table meant for four.

"You're pregnant!" Tiff exclaimed.

"Ugh, Tiff, really?" Seb groaned and reached into his pocket.

Beside him, Toni danced in her chair. "I told you, I told you."

Rolling his eyes, Seb handed Toni a twenty-dollar-bill. "Yeah, yeah."

"For the record, no," Toni said. "I am not with child." She slapped the twenty down on the table. "Next round's on Seb."

Seb graciously accepted some good-natured ribbing and then raised his hands in a settle-down gesture. "Children, the lot of you."

"So what's the big news?" Kayla asked, picking up Toni's left hand in search of a ring.

"It's not that either," Toni said, laughing.

"Not yet, anyway," Seb stage-whispered.

A collective "oooooo" filled the air, and Toni's brows rose. She looked at Seb.

He winked at her. "Okay, we do actually have some news, if you'll let us share it."

"We're listening," Lilly said.

Leaning back in her seat, Lilly wrapped her hands around her biceps in a way that spoke volumes to Ty. It was protective, apprehensive, and he knew the feeling all too well. Something was about to change, and Lilly wasn't comfortable with it, even before knowing what it was.

Seb and Toni exchanged another quick look before he spoke again. "Nia and I have decided to get a place together."

"Nia?" Ty frowned, confused.

"Oh, right! You don't know the epic love saga between Seb and *Nia*. It's his pet name for Toni," Tiff said as an aside. "They were childhood sweethearts, Seb skipped town before they could elope, then they reunited after Toni joined our merry little band, and now they plan to live happily ever after in..." She paused, giving the couple a questioning look.

"Philly," Toni said.

"Really?" Tiff's smiled wavered. "But what will that mean for the band?"

"We're always down here these days anyway," Kayla said.

"True," Tiff replied, tapping her chin with her index finger. She turned back to Ty. "So they'll live happily ever after in Philly, where they will eventually get married and raise talented little offspring, thus creating a musical dynasty that lasts for generations."

"You've given this a disturbing amount of thought, Tiff," Toni said, laughing.

"Am I wrong, though?"

Toni ducked her chin, a smile plumping her cheeks.

Seb wrapped an arm around her. "Calm down, Tiff. Let's start with the moving in part first." He grinned.

Tiff sighed and slumped in her seat. "Fine, but I call first dibs on the guest room. It would beat staying in a hotel."

"Have you found a place?" Kayla asked. "And when did you have time to look?"

"We searched online while we were on the road and did a couple of open houses when we got back," Toni replied. "We have a few more to look at this weekend when we're not at the Phactory."

"We have a lot of work to do," Lilly said, her tone flat.

Seb looked at her, a frown creasing his brow. "And we'll work around it. Worst-case scenario, Nia and I can do a virtual tour." He turned to Toni. "There's one place we really like."

"It's not far from here, and it has great views of the Delaware River," Toni said, clearly excited.

"Excuse me," Lilly said, standing. "Lavatory."

The group fell silent as she walked away.

"Uh-oh," Tiff said.

"I'll talk to her." Seb kissed the side of Toni's head and followed Lilly to the back of the bar.

Ty felt for Lilly, but he wondered why the news would hit her so hard. Not that it was any of his business. Yet somehow, he felt like he was a member of this little group. Part of him wished he could be, somehow.

"It sucks that we won't all be in the same area, but Lilly is such a drama queen sometimes," Tiff huffed. She took a sip from the bright green concoction in her glass. "I wonder if it's a Scandinavian thing."

"She not a big fan of change, that's all," Toni said, though she kept glancing toward the back of the bar, concern etched in her features.

"Well, I, for one, think it's awesome news," Kayla said.

"Me too. I'm happy for you guys." Tiff lifted her glass. "To the start of your musical dynasty."

The four of them toasted, and Ty eyed Kayla over the length of his bottle. She held his gaze as they both drank.

"Well, since we're going to be recording down here for the fore-seeable future," she said, dropping her gaze to the table, "I've sorta been looking for something in Philly too."

"Really?" Toni asked.

Ty cocked his head. "You're *seriously* thinking of moving to Philly?"

Kayla bit her bottom lip, pulling it into her mouth, and Ty's gaze got stuck there before he forced himself to look away. "Why not? It's not like it wasn't already on the table," she said. "My lease is up soon anyway."

"Well, hell," Tiff said. "Philly sounds like the place to be. I'd better start packing."

"You'd leave Lilly all alone in Brooklyn?" Toni asked.

"Oh, please." Tiff rolled her eyes. "As soon as you and Seb said you were moving here, I knew there was no way Lilly wouldn't follow."

Toni frowned. "What? Why would she?"

"We're about to find out." Tiff nodded toward Lilly and Seb as they made their way back to the table. "Twenty bucks says I'm right."

"All right, then," Seb said, pulling Lilly in close with an arm around her waist. "More news. Lilly has decided to move down here too."

Her eyes on Toni—and one brow arched to the heavens—Tiff

reached into the center of the table and snatched up the twenty-dollar bill.

"Guess the Lillys are relocating," Kayla said.

"Sweet!" Tiff exclaimed. She turned to Ty. "You're from here, right?"

"Born and raised."

"Good. Maybe you can teach me how to properly use 'jawn' in a sentence."

CHAPTER 23.

TY OPENED HIS EYES. THE streetlamps outside cast shadows through the blinds that looked like bars on the ceiling. He flinched.

"*Fuck.*"

The house was empty, and he felt his granddad's absence like a physical presence. It pressed down on his lungs, making it hard to breathe.

It had only been a few days since he'd moved Van into his new apartment at River Willows. Being alone in the house felt odd without the hum of the radio or the TV—or the constant smell of baked goods on the air.

Every tick of the AC unit in his window, every car horn on the street, every single fucking noise was like nails scraping against a chalkboard to Ty's ears.

He couldn't live like this.

Ty checked the time. It was just past eleven. Eleven wasn't late for a working musician, was it?

Taking a chance that he wasn't acting like a creep, he opened up his text messages.

TY: Still need a driver?
KAYLA: Yes!

TY: I'm in.
KAYLA: Awesome!! Wait, are you sure?

He listened to a car drive by—heard laughter and shouting as some friends greeted each other, music blaring from the speakers.

TY: I'm sure. I need someplace quiet to read.

This was a different setup than the last leg of the tour, and Ty felt like he'd finally stepped through the looking glass. While he drove the forty-five-footer that would transport the members of the band and some staff, they were caravanning with two custom vans full of merchandise, one of which hauled a trailer carrying extra equipment.

"Welcome to the big leagues," Tiff said, yanking Ty into a hug. "Shit's getting serious now. We're bringing our own roadies!"

"Two," Toni said. "Two roadies and a one-person merch crew, but yeah. It's definitely a step up."

"Now you don't have to pull double duty," Kayla added, smiling at Ty.

"I really don't mind," he said.

She was glad that Jordan had essentially given his blessing for the two of them to pursue…whatever this was. Still, Ty was there in a professional capacity, and she wasn't going to take advantage of that. If anything developed between them, it would happen in its own time.

Ty helped them load their luggage into the cargo hold. They'd brought considerably more than the first trip. Most of the other gear would ride in the vans or the trailer, but the guitars and basses would stay with them. The bus had a state-of-the-art alarm system and was a veritable vault when it was locked up tightly.

As they boarded, Seb clasped Ty on the shoulder. "Good to have you back."

"Thanks for having me."

"Are you kidding? I should be thanking you for putting up with our bullshit."

Ty smiled. "I'm looking forward to it. It'll keep me on my toes."

"Careful what you wish for," Lilly said as she passed them both on her way up the steps.

Seb followed her, chuckling.

"Did you bring enough books for five weeks?" Kayla stopped next to Ty, her hands shoved into the back pockets of her jeans.

His gaze snagged on a flash of midriff as her tank top rode up, and Ty blinked before meeting her eyes.

"I'll have plenty to occupy me."

She grinned. "Oh, of that I have no doubt."

Ty was fairly certain she put a little extra swing in her hips as she climbed the steps. She needn't have bothered. He was already hooked. Five weeks on the road with her might be his undoing, but he'd go down with a smile.

"All right, folks, listen up." Seb addressed the group after everyone was seated. "These next five appearances have the potential to make or break us, in terms of what people come to know us for. Right now, we're building a good little buzz, but we're still fighting against all the bad press and speculation that Candi's...departure... generated."

"Not to mention the fact that YMI is trying to stir up shit," Tiff said.

"Where are we on that?" Kayla asked, as he leaned against the counter next to where she sat. He took satisfaction in the way she shifted her body ever so slightly, moving closer to him.

"Richie and I finished most of the mix for 'Hurt U' before we left. I trust him to clean it up on his own. A buddy in Wales, Dolan, will master it. And since we're on track to finish the album when we get back, YMI's nonsense is a nonstarter," Seb said. "Also, Broken Pilots has made it clear it's either you guys opening for them or no one from YMI's roster."

"Wow," Toni said. "They can do that?"

"It's their tour," Seb replied.

"Perks of owning your own label," Tiff said.

"They're indie?" Kayla asked.

"They bought out their contract and launched their own imprint, yeah." Seb cast a glance at Lilly.

"One day," she said, and he nodded.

"Agreed. All right, a little logistics," Seb continued, gesturing for Toni to scoot over before he sat next to her.

She put her hand on his thigh. It was a simple, intimate gesture, but Ty had to wrench his gaze away. He'd never had that kind of connection with anyone. Couldn't even imagine it.

Actually, he could.

Kayla's curls were loose and soft against his upper arm, and he imagined them elsewhere—pressed against his lips, sifting through his fingers.

"...and Ty," Seb said.

Ty's head snapped up. "Yeah?"

Seb's eyes did a quick circuit of his face, a small frown on his brow before it disappeared. "I was saying, we have a relief driver for you."

"Oh? That's all right, I don't need one."

"You do, it's policy," Seb said. "We're going to be pulling several overdrives, where we'll be going more than four hundred and fifty miles in one go. And after ten p.m., you're not allowed to go for more than eight hours straight."

Ty had known that. "Right, of course." He shook his head. *Focus, dude.*

"We've got you covered." Seb addressed the room again. "The bus is base. The vans will be labeled A and B." He held up a headset. "There are four of these around, so we'll stay in constant contact even when there's no decent cell signal."

"You're so organized," Toni said. "It's kinda turning me on."

"Speaking of which, you two take the bedroom again," Tiff said.

"If no one minds?" Seb asked. Everyone shook their heads. "All right, cool. Jana and Fizz are on merch and provisions duty. They're driving van A. David will..."

"Fizz?" Toni asked.

Seb nodded. "That's what they prefer to be called."

"Just making sure," Toni said.

"They'll be in van B. Ty..." Seb turned to him. "David has a class B CDL. When you need a break from the wheel, let him know, and he'll take over."

"Thanks."

"I'll introduce you before we roll out." Seb checked his phone. "Which should be in about ten minutes, so make sure you have everything stowed that needs stowing. Okay, gang?"

"Yes, boss," Tiff said, giving him a salute.

"Please," Seb said, laughing. "I'm not the boss. I'm just a minion."

Tiff's grin was wicked. "Does that make Lilly our Gru?"

The first few hours of the drive passed quietly. After a long, full-body hug from Kayla that had left him a little light-headed, the band huddled in the living area to talk. From what he could glean, there was a lot of tension between the Lillys and their label.

Ty didn't understand much about the music business, but he'd read some of the stories. Artists hamstrung by label demands, their creativity stifled by commercialism. It was a wonder anything new and different ever made it through official channels.

He'd just finished listening to a chapter of a book when Seb walked onto the deck. Ty popped out his earbud.

"Hey."

"How is she handling?" Seb braced his hands against the overhang and peered through the front window.

"Like a dream." Ty ran his fingers around the leather-wrapped steering wheel. "This is the most luxurious thing I'll ever drive, I swear."

Grinning, Seb dropped into the jump seat. "I hear that. I don't even want to think about what this would cost to buy."

"Dare I ask what it cost to rent?"

Chuckling, Seb ran a hand through his dark, thick waves, the black cotton of his Lillys crew T-shirt straining around his biceps. Everything about the guy screamed *musician*.

"Man, you don't want to know."

CHAPTER 24.

"CAN YOU REPEAT THAT B section?" Kayla watched Toni's fingers closely as she strummed the chords again, her brain working on latching on to the drum pattern she could almost hear under the music. Her thigh was numb from tapping the sticks against it, and her palms were a little clammy.

Next to her, Tiff fingered her acoustic bass, the strings making more of a buzzing sound than actual notes. Her doll-like face was scrunched in concentration.

"I like it," Tiff proclaimed when Toni finished for the third time. "I can already feel the bass line coming together. Something dark and funky."

"Me too," Lilly said. She sat curled up in the corner of the banquette, her face turned toward the window. "It's good."

If Kayla didn't know better, she would have thought Lilly wasn't even listening. But Lilly was always listening. Always thinking. Always...Lilly.

"You think so?" Toni asked, still so shy around them. Kayla wondered how long it would take for her to feel like a full-fledged member of the group.

"It has potential," Lilly said, turning to look at her. "I love the chorus, or what I think is the chorus."

"I pictured that as the section that moves from the B-flat power chord into the dyads and then..." Toni's picking hand was so efficient, Kayla loved to watch her play. There was no wasted energy. Her acoustic guitar was a gorgeous Martin Grand Concert with a sleek carbon fiber body.

"That's a vibe. And back to the F? Or...?" Tiff asked, hiking up the sleeves of her oversized Mars Volta tee.

"Maybe, yeah. Or a sus G7." Toni played the progression. "Or we could do something unexpected, like an arpeggiated F-sharp minor flat five."

"But with lots of space left for Lilly to do her thing."

Tiff's brow scrunched in with concentration as she plucked at her bass, evidently hearing far more than Kayla could. She and Toni spoke the language of audiation, something Kayla barely understood.

"I'll leave you two to tinker." Kayla got up and stretched.

They'd been on the road for six hours, and it had been an exercise in restraint. With Tyrell only a few feet away down the aisle, on the other side of the privacy curtain, Kayla's thoughts kept drifting.

Over the last week, she'd only seen him once. He'd come by the studio during their last rehearsal and hung out for a few hours. It had been a long night, though, and he'd had to leave before she was finished. The near miss had left her irritable.

Now, he was right there, and she wanted nothing more than to sit in the dark of the cockpit and listen to him talk as the road stretched out before them. Listen to his thoughts unfold and really get to know him. It felt like they'd been stuck on pause since the kiss they shared in the hammock.

"I'm going to go find out how far we are from the next rest area," Kayla said.

Glancing over her shoulder, Tiff smirked. "Good idea, Kayla. You should totally do that."

Kayla walked away, tossing a middle finger over her shoulder.

Behind her, Tiff made kissing noises, and Kayla wondered if she and Ty were at the stage where he would help her hide a body.

She pushed the curtain aside and closed it quickly behind her, not wanting the glare from the lights in the common area to disturb Ty's concentration.

"Hey," he said softly, pulling the bud out of his ear. "I was wondering when you'd come for a visit."

"I didn't want to seem too eager," Kayla confessed.

"To them or to me?" he asked. "Because if it's for me, I'd rather you were eager as fuck."

Kayla grinned. "Oh, really? Eager as fuck, huh?"

"As fuck," Ty said, the white of his smile incandescent in the dark.

"Well, I'm here now." Kayla assumed her perch on the dash, bracing her leg against the wall and grabbing the handrail before he could protest.

Ty gave her a sidelong glance and then fixed his eyes back on the road. It was late, nearly dinnertime, and they seemed to be in the middle of nowhere—not a single streetlamp to be seen.

"How are you holding up?"

Ty straightened in the seat, twisting back and forth a little. "Fair to middlin'."

"You need a break?"

He squinted. "I'm all right. There's a rest area coming up. I'll just grab some Starbucks."

"Don't forget you have David back there."

"I haven't forgotten," Ty said. "We haven't been on the road all that long. I'm good."

"Okay, then." Kayla bent one knee to sit sideways on the dash, the windshield on her right. She watched the road for a while, the broken yellow line that kept disappearing under the bus. It was so quiet.

"You can listen to your book, I don't mind," she said, turning her head to watch Ty.

He flicked his gaze to hers. "You really expect me to listen to Benedict Cumberbatch while you're sitting right there?"

"What's he narrating?" Kayla asked, bypassing the compliment his question implied.

"Kelly's *Casanova*."

"Oh, wow," Kayla said. "Great book."

Ty hummed. "You should check out the audio. It's an experience."

"Okay," Kayla said, holding out her hand.

Ty frowned. "I didn't mean right now."

"Why not? We can listen together."

Ty's gaze bounced back and forth between her face and the road. He inhaled deeply. "All right," he said, his voice a little gruff. He handed her one of his earbuds and put the other in his left ear.

Kayla put the bud in. A moment later, Benedict was in her ear. A moment after that, heat stole over her skin as the actor's rich, velvety voice poured from the tiny speaker. But it wasn't Ben's admittedly dulcet tones warming her blood.

Ty kept sneaking glances at her, and Kayla loved that she could steal his focus away from his beloved books. She also adored the way he bit his lip every time she caught him watching her.

Having Ty's attention was addictive, and being this close to him was almost unbearable. Every time her knee bumped his, sparks jolted through her veins. She wanted to be closer still.

The only thing keeping Kayla from grabbing his gorgeous face and kissing him senseless was the fact that he was driving. Self-preservation for the win.

"Are you a fan of his Sherlock?" she asked to pull her thoughts back from the precipice.

"Very much," Ty replied. "Though I'm a fan of Sherlock in general."

"Who's your favorite?"

"That's a tough one."

Ty squinted in thought. He had long, thick lashes—the kind women always said they envied. She was no exception.

"Robert Downey Jr.'s portrayal surprised me," he said at last.

"In a good or bad way?"

Ty stopped the audiobook, which was probably wise since Kayla couldn't seem to keep her mouth shut long enough to listen to it.

"Good." He glanced at her.

"Cool."

"I mean...he's hot." Something in Ty's voice made Kayla feel like maybe he was testing her.

"He is, for an older guy," she agreed. "Is...he your type?" This was tiptoe territory and Kayla caught herself holding her breath for his answer.

Ty made a *so-so* nod. "I mean, I wouldn't say no to Iron Man, but I don't think I have a type."

Kayla nodded. Her knee brushed the hem of his kilt as she shifted to put her hip against the dash. Little shivers ran up and down behind her kneecaps as Ty turned to watch her from the corner of his eye.

"I have to say, lately I've been a little preoccupied with redheads."

Her heart did something funny in her chest. "Oh?"

Ty made a hum of agreement. "Specifically redheaded drummers."

"Drummers, eh?" she asked, drawn to press her knee against his leg.

"To be honest, I haven't been able to stop thinking about this one...that...I kissed a while back," he said almost shyly.

Kayla released a breath that had been trapped in her lungs far too long. "I haven't been able to stop thinking about it either."

He smiled the bright, sunshiny smile that had quickly become one of her favorite sights. "Yeah?"

"Definitely."

"Think we might do it again sometime?"

Kayla shivered. "Yes. Definitely."

"That's good," Ty said, grinning. "Really good."

———

As it turned out, the rest stop was actually a large commercial area off the interstate. Several strip malls lined either side of the local highway, but when Ty pointed out the large mall down the road, they all decided to stop there.

"The clothes the stylist sent along are okay, but I need some pieces to make them more my style," Tiff declared.

Kayla could see her point. She'd bristled at the idea of someone choosing her wardrobe, even though she understood this was part of the whole "being signed to a label" experience. Still, she couldn't help but cringe as flashbacks of the run-ins she had with her mother came to mind.

KATHY: 16 YEARS OLD

"Young ladies do not wear tuxedos to school functions," her mother declared.

"Gisele," her dad chided softly, "that's a rather anti-feminist view, isn't it? Young people should feel free to wear whatever they want to the spring dance."

"If she were any other child, I might agree," her mother countered. "But she isn't just any child."

"So this is about you," Kathy said.

"Kit-Kat." Her dad gave a slight shake of his head.

"Do not indulge her with that infantile nickname, Geoffrey," her mother snapped before turning to Kathy. "And no, this is not only about me and my place in this community. Or your father's. Whether you like it or not, you have a spotlight on you that has nothing to do with either of us. You are a young, Black woman in a predominantly white school."

"And?" That had been the case for as long as Kathy could remember. "No one cares."

Her mother gave her a pitying look. "Never, for one instant, allow yourself to believe that. No matter where you go, no matter who you're with. Someone will always care."

Kathy plopped into an armchair. "No one's ever said anything to me about being Black. And even if they did, I don't know why I can't wear what I want to wear. Hang out with who I want to hang out with. Zach does."

Her mother took a seat next to her father, who reached over and laced his hand through hers. It was the kind of united front Kathy was used to seeing from her parents.

"We've done our best to shield you and your brother," her mom said. "Perhaps we've done too good a job, but you will learn when and where to pick your battles."

"And what I wear to a dance isn't a battle I should fight?" Kathy asked. "The clothes I wear, the friends I have... Which battles are worth it, Mom?"

———————

They browsed a few clothing stores, and Kayla found a couple of pieces she could use to personalize the outfits that had been chosen for her. Tiff walked out of the mall with three large shopping bags swinging from her arms. The huge smile on her face was the result of having indulged in a comically large chunk of pecan fudge that she had practically inhaled on the spot.

"Is that a Music Warehouse across the street?" Her arm linked through Seb's, Toni pointed.

"Looking to buy another guitar?" Lilly asked her.

"Not really, but I always check out what's available," Toni replied pulling Seb in that direction. "Just in case."

"I do need some strings," Tiff said, walking backward.

Kayla looked at Ty, who was smiling. "I guess we're going to one more store."

After darting across the road in an impromptu game of Frogger, Kayla and Ty straggled behind the group as they entered the enormous store.

It was busier than she'd expected. The sound of competing instruments slammed into her ears and it took a moment to orientate herself to the environment.

"Is it always like this?" Ty asked, his eyes wide as he took in the store and its patrons.

Everywhere she looked, Kayla saw musicians decked out in quintessential rocker gear.

"Kind of, though this seems...a bit much for a weekday."

Many of the customers, mostly male-presenting, were dressed head to toe in black T-shirts and ripped jeans with combat boots. Most had long, straight hair. A few wore it pulled back in ponytails. It was like being at an eighties metal revival.

Kayla giggled when she saw that Toni was testing out a guitar on a small stage set up for such demonstrations. "Toni may have found a new toy." Guitars and stacks of amps were everywhere around her.

"Where are the drums?" Ty asked.

"They're usually in a separate area. We tend to get loud, you know." She winked at him.

He smiled and Kayla led him toward the back of the store where she instinctively knew the drum section would be, and it was.

What she hadn't predicted was the drum clinic taking place. "Ah, that explains why there are so many people here."

"What's going on?"

Kayla glanced behind them, noting several people with lanyards identifying them as instructors. "Looks like we came on a good day. There are music teachers and other pros here doing demos."

"How cool!"

Kayla strained to see who was running the drum clinic, but no one was on the dais. Without thinking, she grabbed Ty's hand and pulled him along the outer edge of the drum room until they came to an area with kits set up for sale. It wasn't until he squeezed her fingers that she stopped and looked down, confused.

When she met his eyes, Kayla was greeted by a soft smile and a lip bite that had her mesmerized.

She didn't know how long they gazed at each other before a voice interrupted.

"In the market for a new kit?"

They both turned to the store employee, a middle-aged white man in his mid to late forties whose name tag read "Bruce." The tag also noted that he'd been working at Music Warehouse for ten years. Bruce was smiling at Ty.

Ty smiled back. There was an awkward silence as the two men stared at each other until Ty realized Bruce's question had been for him.

"Oh, me? No, I'm—"

"Just looking?" Bruce said smoothly. "Let me show you something that just came in. I think it might tempt you."

Bruce turned away.

Brows raised, Ty looked down at Kayla and she grinned. "Come on, let's go see if you can be tempted."

They followed Bruce to the back corner, where a gorgeous tortoiseshell drum kit sat gleaming under the fluorescent lights.

"Now, *that* is hot," Kayla said, mostly to herself.

Bruce laughed. "You said it, not me." He lowered his voice conspiratorially. "These days, I'd get in trouble for saying it was sex on chrome legs." Waggling his eyebrows, Bruce nudged Ty as if he were in on the joke.

Kayla felt Ty shift beside her uneasily. She offered Bruce a bright, bubbly laugh. "I know what you mean! People are actually expected to treat others with respect nowadays. Imagine that."

Bruce's grin crumpled and he took a step back. Clearing his throat, he returned his attention to Ty. "As you can see, this is set up for double bass, and we've kitted it out with a few extras."

The set did indeed include two bass drums, mounted on stands, and four toms arranged in a semicircle around the kicks. Above them sat a snare drum and, next to that, the hi-hat. Several more cymbal stands, holding two crashes and a ride, had been added.

"They have the resonance of oak, but the new hybrid shell makes them ultra-durable," Bruce said. Pulling a pair of sticks from a pouch on his half-apron, he offered them to Ty. "Go on. Give them a spin."

Ty held up his palms. "No, man. I don't play."

Bruce's hand dropped a little. "Oh, sorry." He glanced between Kayla and Ty. "Are you looking for a starter kit for the little one?"

Ty opened his mouth to respond, but Kayla grabbed his hand. "We're thinking about it. Do you think this would be too much for a thirteen-year-old?"

It totally was.

Bruce blinked before his salesman's smile reasserted itself. "Not at all!" he replied with dollar signs in his eyes. "He can grow into it."

For some reason, the fact that Bruce assumed their imaginary drum student child was a boy irked Kayla more than anything else.

Owl-eyed, she smiled at him. "Would it be all right if I tried them out? We're about the same height."

She could tell Ty itched to say something. His cheek trembled with the grin he was clearly fighting.

"Go for it." Amused, Bruce handed Kayla the sticks and folded his arms as he moved next to Ty.

"Do I sit in the chair?" Kayla had to avoid Ty's gaze or else she'd break and start laughing.

"Yep," Bruce replied. "Settle yourself on the throne, little queen."

Ugh. Kayla made a show of climbing behind the drums. "Wow, these are so big." She grasped the wrong end of the sticks and scrunched her brow. "Do I just smack them?"

Ty snorted.

Bruce, to his credit, only smiled as he walked around to her and held out his hands for the sticks, which she gave to him. "See this little contoured tip? That's what needs to make contact."

"Ohhhh," Kayla said, wide-eyed. She took the sticks back, gripping them firmly.

"Good, now, go ahead and hit this one here," he said, indicating the snare drum between her thighs. "Give it a good, hard smack with the tip."

In front of her, Ty rolled his eyes. The innuendo was a lot, but Kayla did as she was told, bringing the tip of the stick down on the taut skin of the drum. It made a satisfying sound. She giggled. "Oh!"

"Fun, right?" Bruce asked. "Try one of the cymb...er...brass plates."

Jesus on a stick, Kayla thought to herself. Almost anyone would know what a cymbal was, wouldn't they? Maybe not.

She gingerly tapped on the end of the ride until it rang out softly. "This is so loud," she said, frowning. "Maybe we should rethink bringing this into the house, babe. We'd never get any sleep."

She'd delivered the statement as she looked Ty in the eye, daring him not to crack.

He did, covering his mouth as he fought to control his laughter. He cleared his throat. "But think of how much fun Edgar would have," he said.

Kayla raised a brow as if to ask *Edgar?*

Ty shrugged one shoulder and started laughing again.

Bruce's gaze danced between them, his smile flagging as he tried to catch the gist of the joke. "I have a son about your boy's age, and let me tell you, if he didn't have a set of drums in the garage to play, I don't know where he'd spend all of that energy. Especially in the winter when I can't ship him off to camp." His laugh was practiced, as was the story.

Kayla questioned whether or not the guy even had a son. Not that she had any room to talk.

"Besides," he continued, "drums teach discipline and focus. Why don't you try playing the full set? See if you can hold a rhythm for a while. It's not easy. You'll see."

As much as Kayla hated to admit it, Bruce wasn't wrong. The drums were a very disciplined instrument that required incredible concentration and coordination. It was an argument she'd tried to use with her mother, once upon a time, to no avail.

Any instrument that requires you to spread your legs isn't suitable.

Like the cello didn't exist.

Kayla shook out her shoulders and gripped the sticks the way she normally would, with one palm down and the other up. It was traditional, which gave her more control. The pair Bruce had given her had evidently been used for demos before, judging by the nicks near the tip, but they were hardwood—hickory, she guessed—and she could produce a lot of sound with them.

Kayla started with the bass drum, tapping her foot on the pedal in a four-count before playing consecutive eights on the snare.

"Very good," Bruce praised. "You're a natural."

Kayla smiled and added a four-count on the hi-hats to match the kick drum, adding grace notes of syncopation for emphasis on certain beats.

The result was a high-energy backbone filled with fast-paced triplets, and Kayla got lost in the pocket as she grooved. She hadn't realized she'd closed her eyes until someone to her left said, "Goddamn!"

Opening her eyes, Kayla realized she'd drawn a small crowd. A few people had gathered to watch her play, nodding along to the beat encouragingly. One young teen had his phone out and was recording.

In front of her, Ty stood with his arms wrapped around his midsection. His smile was blinding, but it was the look of...pride... on his face that made her breath catch. She faltered, finishing the demonstration with a limp *ba-doom-crash*.

"Wow," Bruce said quietly. When Kayla looked at him, his expression was contrite. "Clearly, I need to apologize. It never occurred to me..." He broke off, shaking his head. "Are you in a band?"

"Yeah," Kayla said, handing him the sticks as she stood. She was acutely aware of the people staring at her. "Something like that. Thanks for letting me take the kit for a spin. And I'm sorry if I... *we*...deceived you."

Bruce's brows rose. "God, no. I'm sorry. At the risk of sounding... We don't get too many drummers in here who look, well, like you. No offense."

"None taken," Kayla replied honestly. "Hopefully, you'll see more and more of us."

Bruce's smile was genuine. "How amazing would that be?"

CHAPTER 25.

TY KNEW THEY'D LEVELED UP as soon as he pulled into the parking area for Neon Fest. For one thing, the grounds covered acres. There were more semis and buses than there had been at the other festivals, and far fewer vans and cars. Many of the tour buses bore custom wraps with the artist's name or logo emblazoned on them. Ty recognized quite a few. He wasn't usually the kind of person to get starstruck, but he planned to put his backstage credentials to excellent use this time.

Of course, the biggest reason for that was his desire to spend as much time around Kayla as he could. After hanging out most of the day and her riding shotgun again last night, Ty had chosen the bunk across from hers as his own, not ready to be away from her.

She'd been so close and yet so far. Their growing closeness had only stoked Ty's growing appetite for all things Kayla. He craved her company and realized he'd been holding himself back from the one thing he knew would tip him over the edge from mild flirting into full-on pursuit. Kissing her again would change everything, at least for him, because he had come to feel so much more for her.

Ty had always known he was wired differently than probably most. Knew that he needed an emotional connection to someone to feel the physical pull that seemed to come so easily to others. The kiss he'd shared with Kayla in the hammock had been nice. Warm and comforting. But if—when—they kissed again, his heart would likely be in danger. He wasn't sure how he felt about that.

After the bus emptied, Ty took a quick shower, dressed in a gray Lillys tee the band had given him and one of his black kilts, shoved his feet into his Docs, and slipped his lanyard over his head. He'd made sure to give spare remotes to David and to Seb before they left, so he locked down the bus and set the alarm.

The Lillys were on in a few hours, but Ty wanted to soak up every bit of the atmosphere that drove who Kayla was as a person. The music, the crowds, the synergy she had with her bandmates. He'd never experienced anything like it—likely never would—but maybe he could absorb a little of it by proxy.

On his way toward the festival grounds, Ty called to check in on his grandfather. Pop-Pop answered after the third ring, sounding out of breath.

"Hey, son! Are you packing to leave?"

"I've already left," Ty reminded him. "We're in Savannah now."

"Oh, that's right," Van said. "Georgia. I remember now. I used to talk to a girl from Georgia, back when I was in the air force. Pretty little thing. Her name was…" he trailed off. "Hmm, hang on, it'll come to me. Anyway, her people were from Marietta. Worked as a receptionist at one of the hotels downtown."

Ty listened as he walked, working hard to ignore the niggle in the back of his mind. He worried that his granddad's forgetfulness was more than the natural result of his advancing age. Van was having more of what he called his "senior moments" of late, and Ty wondered if that was the real impetus behind his sudden desire to move to River Willows.

"Vernice," Ty reminded him. "You told me about her last week. You feeling okay today, Pop-Pop?"

"That's it! Vernice," he said, rolling her name in a long, appreciative drawl. "That girl had a pair of legs that just would not quit."

He laughed. "And yeah, I'm fine. Better than fine. You'll never guess who they've got coming to teach this Sunday's cooking class."

"Should I try, or are you going to tell me?"

"None other than Miss Patti LaBelle," his granddad announced.

"Wow, really?" Ty lifted his lanyard to flash his credentials at the gate and stepped through. The area was bustling, with people milling about or rushing from A to B. He stopped by the medical tent to get his bearings. "That's really awesome," he said, looking for the sign that would direct him to Artists Alley.

"I told you this place was great," his granddad said. "She's going to give us the secrets to her famous sweet potato pie."

"That sounds cool." Ty spotted a performer he recognized heading down one of the rows and decided to follow, hoping they were headed in the same direction. "I can't wait to try your version. I know you'll doctor it up."

"I don't know," Van said. "Sometimes, there's no need to mess with perfection."

As he'd hoped, Ty saw Toni duck into one of the tents. He headed that way while his granddad told him all about an art class he'd taken that morning.

"And…you're happy there?" he asked, for probably the hundredth time.

"I told you to stop worrying about me so much," Van replied after a soft sigh. "I'm fine—more than fine. You worry about your own happiness. And when you find it, you hold on with both hands."

As providence would have it, Ty ducked inside the tent to the sound of Kayla's laughter, like bells, traveling toward him on the air. He spotted her in the corner, talking to Tiff and Seb, her smile as bright as the sun.

Kayla was beautiful, unconventional, and glowed like an ember at the edge of the group where she stood.

What if he could belong there? Ty could almost picture it, being a part of her world. Being surrounded by music and friends and all the new experiences they could have together. Being their driver wasn't a bad thing. Maybe this was what he was meant to do, at least for now.

"Tyrell?"

His granddad's voice snapped him back to reality. "I'm here, sorry."

"Sounds busy there. Let me let you go," Van offered. "I need to clean up before my match."

Ty frowned. "Match?"

"One of these old dudes had the nerve to challenge me to a round of pool."

"Van," Ty said in a warning tone, though he was grinning. "Please don't take too much of the man's money." His granddad was a shark.

"I only plan to teach him a little lesson about judging a book by its cover," Van said. "Call me tomorrow after five. I have bridge in the afternoon."

"So much to do, so little time."

Kayla's gaze landed on him, and she smiled. Ty watched as she said something to the others and then crossed the tent toward him.

Van chuckled. "As it should be. Love you, son."

"Love you too."

Kayla stuck her hand on her hip and narrowed her eyes at him. "I hope that was your granddad."

"It was," he replied, pocketing his phone.

"Good, I don't want to have to hurt anyone." She dropped her arm to her side and grinned.

Ty stepped closer but didn't touch her.

"I can't see you breaking out the Vaseline to whoop someone's ass, but rest assured"—he let his gaze reveal a little of his thoughts, pleased when her eyes sparkled with understanding—"you have nothing to worry about."

Kayla sucked in a quick breath which she exhaled shakily. "Good to know."

Ty wasn't sure how long they stood that way, inches apart with their gazes locked, but he could have stared at her for days.

"I really want to kiss you," he confessed as his pulse doubled. There was no use fighting this anymore. He was stupid over this woman.

"What's stopping you?" There was a challenge in her eyes.

Ty accepted it and leaned forward to meet her lips. She tasted of coffee, with a hint of cream and sugar. Under it all was Kayla, spicy and sweet.

"About damn time," Tiff said.

They startled, breaking the kiss, and Kayla turned away, laughing under her breath.

"Don't let me stop you," Tiff said, holding up a cup of honest-to-goodness popcorn. "I was enjoying the show."

Kayla rolled her eyes. "We are not here for your amusement."

"Says you."

Ty wanted to pump his fist when Kayla slipped her arm around his waist and tucked herself into his side. It was a possessive move, and he loved the fact that she was claiming him for all to see. He draped an arm across her shoulders and felt like he belonged there. With her.

"The crowd's a good one from what I hear," Seb said when he walked up to them with Toni by his side. "This is a relatively new festival, only the third year for it, but it's already the biggest in the region."

"That explains the lineup," Kayla said. "I was surprised when I saw how late in the day our slot was."

"Daniel owns a stake in one of the sponsors," Seb informed them. "He pulled some strings to get us a later time slot. Wanted to give you a chance to play a longer set in front of a full crowd."

"I like Daniel," Tiff said. "He's definitely the good twin."

"He's a good guy," Seb agreed.

"The twins own the label," Kayla explained to Ty, and he nodded.

Seb looked at Toni and then down at the arm around Ty's waist.

"So…" Toni said. "Do we ever enforce the no-fraternization clause in the contracts, or is it just for show?" She grinned up at Kayla, who stuck out her tongue.

Seb laughed. "At this point, it's decorative."

Ty squeezed Kayla against him.

"Is this a thing now?" Seb asked.

Kayla looked up and gave Ty a soft smile. "We're figuring it out."

By the time she left his side to prepare for their set, he felt like that half of him was standing around naked and exposed.

Ty had never stood in the wings for a concert before, but that's where he found himself when the Lillys took the stage, and he was instantly addicted. Not only did his spot by the soundboard afford him a perfect view of Kayla and her kit, he could see the crowd as well. And what a crowd it was.

Tens of thousands of people screaming at the tops of their lungs at every swivel of Tiff's hips, every flourish from Toni's guitar, and every note from Lilly's mouth. And when they broke down one of the songs for Kayla's extended drum solo, they clapped along with the bass drum, whistling and cheering her on. It was electric.

And Kayla, she was a revelation.

Ty knew firsthand how powerful she was, but watching her play—her curls unleashed and floating around her head like a halo, sweat glistening on her face, neck, and arms—he realized she was a fucking goddess. He was floored by the fact that she'd allowed him into her orbit and that she seemed to want even more from him. Time with him. It was exhilarating to be seen by her.

"They're really good," the guy next to him said. He stood with his arms crossed, bobbing his head to the beat. "I've never heard of them before."

Ty nodded and glanced around him. Everywhere he looked, there were people in crew shirts gathered at the edge of the stage, each one completely engrossed in what Kayla and the others were doing. A few people danced in place, while others had pulled out their phones and were recording.

Though he had absolutely nothing to do with their music, Ty felt a kernel of pride blossom in his chest. He knew how hard the women worked to be this good, how hard they worked to perfect their craft. They deserved every bit of success that was coming their way. He wondered how long he could hang on for the ride. Wondered how he could be a part of their journey. A part of Kayla's. If his own path could somehow exist alongside theirs. Hers.

"Sing with me, Georgia!" Lilly cried out. "*And when you say go, you mean go, not baby come baaack.*"

As one, the crowd joined in. "*And when you say stay, you mean play, and maybe go away again, again, again.*"

Ty didn't know the song, but he bounced on his toes, the energy flowing through him, making him feel electrified.

"Shit!" someone exclaimed behind him.

Ty spun in time to see two of the stagehands scrambling to pull a cord toward them. He followed the line to the middle of the stage. The microphone in front of Tiff's amp had been unplugged by another member of the crew.

"Dude, can you run this out there?"

A woman shoved a coil of cable into Ty's chest. Instinctively, he took it and dashed out onto the stage, keeping his head low. He caught Kayla's eye, and she gave him a quizzical look until he stretched out his arm and tossed the cable to the techie.

The guy nodded and gave Ty a thumbs-up, which he took as his cue to hustle back toward the wings. On his way, he gave Kayla a wink, and she smiled.

Ty's heart pounded in his chest.

There were thousands of pairs of eyes on him. He could feel them against his skin. It was a rush unlike anything he'd ever experienced. And though he wasn't the one creating the music that made them scream, he still felt like part of the moment. There was a problem, and he was there to help fix it. To keep the crowd's euphoria going, to keep the band's energy from ebbing. It was a bit role, but Ty ate it up, waving to the people who cheered for him as he left the stage. He almost wished something else would break so he could feel that again.

"Thanks!" the woman said in his ear. "Sorry, I thought you were crew, but good looking out."

"No problem," Ty shouted over the music as Tiff's bass rejoined the mix.

He'd just done that, been out there.

For one thrilling moment, he'd been a part of what they had created, and he wanted more of that.

CHAPTER 26.

KAYLA HAD SAT BACK AND watched, proud and amused, as Tiff, Seb, and Toni praised Ty for his quick thinking. She'd been surprised to see him onstage and grateful she hadn't lost track of the song they'd been playing. Her brain did funny things when he was around, not to mention her heart.

They were on the road again. After the success of Neon Fest, Kayla was flying high on more than the beer in her hand. Or the shots of tequila Tiff had poured when they got back on the bus. The bottle sat empty next to the sink, along with at least a dozen other empties.

Kayla sat in the banquette across from Lilly, who smiled up at Tiff while she reenacted the interpretive dance one member of the crowd had done after they'd scrambled up onto the stage.

The expression was such a rarity that Kayla leaned her head against the window and just stared at her as the bus swayed gently back and forth.

Ty was at the wheel, and Kayla longed to go up and talk to him, but Seb was there. And she figured it was good for Ty to get to know her little family since she was pretty sure she wanted him to be a part of it. And just how had that happened?

There was something about Ty that resonated with her on a level she hadn't experienced before. They seem to be cut from the same cloth, one woven together by a weird combo of anxiety and a bone-deep need for independence. Kayla didn't know where things were heading, but she was enjoying the ride.

Toni slid into the booth beside her. "Hey, girl."

"Hey," Kayla replied, rolling her head to look at her.

"You killed it again tonight."

"Thanks." She squirmed, never great at taking compliments. "I was just trying to match the energy you guys were putting out."

Toni nudged Kayla's shoulder with her own. "What? You're the power source. How do you not know that? You're a monster on the skins."

Kayla nodded. It was an exaggeration but still nice to hear.

Lilly sat forward and leaned against the table. "Toni is right," she said, surprising Kayla.

"About what?" Tiff pushed in next to Lilly and placed four cold bottles of beer in the center of the table. "Toni's never right about anything."

Toni flipped her the bird. "I was just telling Kayla we're never letting her go, no matter how much Broken Pilots begs her to be their new drummer."

"What?" Tiff's eyes went wide. "She's ours, and we ain't letting her go."

Laughing, Kayla shook her head. "What are you even talking about? No one's trying to scoop me, especially not Broken Pilots. Besides, I'd never leave you guys."

"Good." Toni locked elbows with her. "'Cause I'm stuck on you like glue, baby."

"I heard you put on a clinic at that music store," Tiff said.

"I barely played."

"You were signing autographs," Toni countered. "Ty said you were amazing."

Well, he would say that.

Lilly eyed her closely. "What's going on in that bright red head of yours?"

"Nothing," Kayla said. "Everything's fine." Lilly waited. They were all waiting.

"Guys," she finally said, blushing. "Intellectually, I know who I am and what I'm doing, what we're doing. It's just that... Sometimes, there are these moments when I can't believe this is my life and I wonder..." She broke off, afraid that giving voice to her concerns might somehow manifest them.

"Do you regret your choice to join us?" Lilly asked, her gaze sharp and focused.

"No, of course not," Kayla replied quickly. "It's... I..."

"Feels like a dream?" Toni asked. "Like you're going to wake up back where you started?"

Kayla nodded, deciding it was as close to the truth as she was willing to get. "Between you guys, and the studio, and the road..." She rubbed the center of her chest. "It's a lot."

She hadn't had anything like Toni's childhood drama, but Kayla knew Toni got it. The sense of belonging somewhere, to someone, was foreign to her too.

Tiff sniffed. "Aww, honey." She got up and wrapped Kayla in a hug. "I love you."

Tiff wasn't one to drop the L-word often.

"I love you too," she replied, half laughing and half crying. "Jesus, I'm sappy tonight."

"It's the adrenaline," Lilly said. "And the copious amounts of alcohol," she added. Lilly reached for one of the bottles and held it up. "To us."

Tiff released Kayla and sat back down, picking up a beer and handing it over before taking one herself.

Kayla took the remaining bottle, and the three of them raised theirs to join Lilly's in the center of the table.

"To the motherfucking Lillys," Tiff said.

Toni giggled, and they all shouted "To the motherfucking Lillys!" before they clinked bottlenecks and drank.

"I feel left out," Seb said, grinning as he approached. "Any Hoegaarden left?"

"There had better be." Lilly narrowed her eyes at Tiff. "Why are you looking at me?"

Seb crouched down and pulled a twelve-pack out of the storage area. "I'll restock, don't worry."

"Are we driving straight through to Nashville?" Toni asked when Seb leaned against the wall beside her.

Seb looked down at her. "I thought we'd stop in Atlanta for the night. Maybe tomorrow night too, since we don't need to be in Nashville until Thursday."

"I've never been to Atlanta," Toni said excitedly. "Have you, K?"

Kayla had, many times, when she was little. "Yeah, I..." She took a fortifying breath. "I was actually born outside the city." She forced a smile, glancing up at the others when the group went quiet.

"Oh. I thought you were from somewhere in New England," Toni said.

"I am. Sort of. I mean, my family moved there when I was young."

"Wow, a Southern girl." Tiff gave her an appraising look. "I never would have guessed. You, like, don't even have an accent. Did you before? Were you a little Southern belle?" she asked, adopting a laughable drawl.

Laughing, Kayla shook her head. "No, my mother would never have allowed it."

"She's a teacher, right?" Toni asked.

"Yeah, she is. Actually...I wanted to talk to you guys about that." As soon as the words were out of her mouth, Kayla's heart thumped hard against her rib cage. Her fear was irrational. She knew that. They wouldn't care about the books or her role in them. They'd probably laugh and endlessly tease her about them. It would all be fine. And yet it didn't stop her from breaking into a cold sweat.

"Is your mom okay?" Seb tilted his head, his brows drawn together with concern.

"She's fine. It's not that."

He nodded, clearly relieved.

"You're trembling." Lilly moved toward her, her brow furrowed. "What's wrong?"

"Sorry, I…" When she stuttered to a stop, all eyes turned to her, and the space fell silent as if they were all preparing for the worst.

Tiff sank into one of the side seats, while Toni and Seb drifted close together, subconsciously seeking comfort. That almost made her smile.

When her gaze found Lilly's, Lilly gave her a small nod and a soft smile. *You can do this*, she seemed to say.

"I'm Little Miss Yolanda," she blurted.

Four pairs of eyes blinked at her in confusion.

"I mean…" Tiff began. "I get it. The red hair and all. And you're a total nerd."

"Who is Little Miss Yolanda?" Lilly asked.

"I remember reading a few of those as a kid, the books," Toni said. "But what do you mean *you're* her?"

Kayla gave a little shrug. "I'm her. I'm the inspiration for her."

"They're popular?" Lilly asked, sliding onto the banquette so that only Kayla remained standing.

"Super popular," Tiff replied. "They're about this impossibly fucking perfect little girl who always listened to her parents, and always worked hard in school, and always, *always*, did everything right. I fucking hated those books."

Cringing, Kayla nodded. "Me too."

"And you're a pain in my ass, but you're not *that* bad," Tiff said, teasing.

"I'm confused, what does this have to do with your mom?" Seb asked.

"She wrote them. *Writes* them," Kayla said, waiting for the boulder in her chest to ease up so she could *breathe. Just breathe.*

"No fucking way!" Tiff was on her feet. "Holy shit, your mom must be *loaded*. Those books are freaking everywhere!"

"Your mom writes the Little Miss Yolanda series?" Toni's mouth hung open, her eyes wide with shock. "Wow...that's... Wow, Kayla. And *you're* her? You're Yolanda."

Kayla felt herself nod but she was waiting for the penny to drop.

"Hang on." Of course, it would be Seb to figure it out first. "This is why you use a stage name."

"Your name isn't Kayla?" Tiff's voice was loud in the small face, and her tone not exactly friendly. "Is your last name even Whitman?"

"No. It's Larrington."

There was a collective gasp from Seb and Toni.

"Your mom is Gisele Larrington," Toni said.

Tiff stared at Kayla, owl-eyed. "The scales are falling from my eyes. Seriously. This explains *so* much about you."

"I'm sorry," Kayla replied as she waited for them to render their judgment. "I should have told you before." She dropped heavily onto the nearest seat. "It's only...I've been running away from Yolanda for so long, I liked having something completely separate from the books. From..." *My mother's expectations and disappointment.*

"I totally get it," Tiff said, recovering faster than Kayla had expected.

In fact, no one looked particularly peeved. Of the group, only Lilly wore a frown.

"You have not told your family about us, have you?" she asked quietly. There was a note of hurt in her voice that Kayla hadn't anticipated.

"Not yet, but I plan to." Kayla sighed. "My mom...won't be thrilled. But it's my life, so..."

"She's a professor or something, isn't she?" Toni shifted to face Kayla. "What's the big deal about her daughter being a musician?"

Kayla gnawed on her lip. "It's about the *type* of musician. If I were a classical pianist, or an opera singer, or—hell—even if I played jazz, it would be way more acceptable in her world than her daughter being a drummer in a rock band. Plus..." Kayla took a fortifying breath. "I...didn't finish college. I didn't live up to the standard Yolanda set. The one that sold millions of copies in twenty languages. My mother views me as her biggest failure."

There was a beat of silence.

"But..." Tiff started. "How could that be? You're a brainiac."

"Education isn't always formal," Toni said.

"Being a dropout's nothing to be ashamed of," Tiff said. "School wasn't really my thing either."

"I'm not ashamed," Kayla replied, a little more defensive than she'd meant to be.

"It kind of sounds like you are," Toni countered.

Kayla groaned. "No, I... Imagine you're a renowned expert on education in the United States, revered as the architect of every parent's dream child, and it comes out that your only daughter is not only a drummer in a rock band but also failed to finish college," Kayla finished breathlessly.

"Do people really care about that shit?" Lilly asked.

"In her world, it would land like a nuclear bomb," Kayla replied. "She'd be a laughingstock and so would Yolanda. Across the line, her book sales would likely plummet. Her speaking engagements would probably dry up, but it's not only that."

"What, then?" Lilly asked.

Kayla shut her eyes for a moment. She needed to tell them about Zach but inviting the pain she carried to blossom from a dull ache into an open wound wasn't something she looked forward to.

"When I was fifteen, I lost my brother." She opened her eyes when she felt a hand close over hers and found Tiff clasping it. It loosened something in her chest. "He was seven years older than me, and I...I *worshipped* him." To her surprise, a laugh bubble up from her chest. It was better than tears.

"K...I'm so sorry," Seb said. "I had no idea."

Lilly put a firm hand on her shoulder and gently squeezed. Between her touch and Tiff's hand, Kayla pushed through the clog in her throat.

"Zach was a drummer in a band for as long as I can remember. He started in the school band when he was eleven or so and took to it like a fish to water."

"You two had a lot in common, then," Lilly said.

"We did." She smiled up at her. "But he was... He burned *so* damned bright. Everyone in his orbit fell in love with him. And talented, he was a freaking genius behind a kit. Even from a young age. A natural, his teacher said. Mom, of course, hated it."

"Really?" Toni asked. "You'd think she'd love having a child prodigy in the family. Well, two of them."

Kayla smiled. "She did. Zach was also a math genius, but the drums were his world. My mom tried to stop it, tried to quash his involvement with his band. My dad stepped in, though, and Zach and his bandmates went to college together. Kept playing. During the fall and spring breaks, they'd book shows. They even had a little following." She smiled, remembering.

"That's so cool. It's like you're following in his footsteps," Tiff said.

"He'd be proud of you," Toni added.

Kayla knew he would. She nodded. "The summer of his junior

year, he had an opportunity to go to Germany. There's a prestigious math laboratory there. My mother was over the moon about it, but Zach said no. They argued, and it was…" She took a shaky breath. Tiff hand tightened almost painfully, but Kayla welcomed it. "That night, he had a gig in Syracuse…" The words shut off abruptly, refusing to leave her lips. When she looked up, she realized she didn't have to say more about it.

They were all staring at her with various expressions of pity and understanding. No anger. No disappointment. Only the compassion of people who cared deeply for her and hated to see her hurting. Hated that she had lost so much, even if they couldn't understand the depth of her loss.

"Zach was the heir, and I was the spare. When he diverged from the path my mom laid out for him, she turned her efforts toward me, and Yolanda was born," she said, her voice scratchy. "But Zach *got* me. He was the only one who seemed to understand how much I hated the role she'd cast me in. The-the-the *dresses* and the shoes and the hair, all the trappings of a proper young lady, blah fucking pink frilly blah."

Seb choked out a laugh. "Sorry, I…can't even imagine you in pink."

Some of the tension in her shoulders released, and she smiled. "I wear it sometimes."

"With your studded leather jacket and assless chaps," Tiff said, snorting.

They shared a muted laugh that died down quickly, the room filling with awkward silence.

"So, anyway, sorry if I've been cagey and secretive. And I know it's a lot to dump on you guys, but I'm fucking terrified of what will happen. The reporter in Detroit acted like she knew all about me. It would be too salacious a story for the wider press to ignore."

"See? *Salacious*," Tiff said. "Total brainiac word."

Kayla patted her arm in appreciation. "That reporter must know something. Why else would she be sniffing around?"

"Don't forget, she's sniffing around me too," Tiff groused.

"Have you spoken to your sister?" Lilly asked.

"She's not returning my calls." Dropping Kayla's hand, Tiff pulled her knees up to her chest and wrapped her arms around her legs, making her look ten years younger. "I'll probably split from you guys after that last show in Ontario and head to LA to straighten her ass out."

"We all seem to be dragging our histories along behind us," Toni said. "My mom is making waves too."

"Add to that all of the shit with Candi, and I guess it does reinforce the whole wild child, sex, drugs, and rock-n-roll cliché," Tiff added.

Kayla nodded. "I may not get along with my mom, but I respect everything she has achieved. She's sacrificed a lot—including, I guess, her relationship with me. But she's done so much good. She's introduced things into the curricula at schools nationwide that have been ignored for a hundred years. Normalized things that the academic world, in general, had relegated to specialized study. Thousands of kids learned to read with the Yolanda series. But her and I, we…"

"Sounds like a complicated relationship between two badass women," Toni said.

"The relationships between parents and their children can be the most challenging there are," Lilly said, her tone softening. She took a deep breath. "All right. I think I understand now."

"Okay." Seb put a hand on Kayla's shoulder and squeezed. "You telling your parents will take the sting out of whatever the reporter thought she had on you, at least as far as they are concerned. That's good. After that, when we're with the press, tell the story *you* want to tell."

"Take control of the narrative," Toni said. "And honestly, don't let your mom's success overshadow your own achievements. You're on the cusp of big things, girl."

"Hellz yeah," Tiff said. "We're the motherfucking Lillys."

She loved these people, truly she did, but Kayla knew it wasn't that simple. Even if her mother stood behind her decision to play with them, to be in this band, it wouldn't negate the fallout. The very real impact on her parents' livelihood.

Kayla loved the Lillys. But if it meant sparing her family more pain and embarrassment, she might just have to walk away.

CHAPTER 27.

THE RELIEF DRIVER, DAVID, WAS a veteran of touring, and he seemed to take everything in stride. Aaron had sent him along in lieu of some of the younger drivers because of his experience. He was also married with grandchildren and could be trusted to remain professional around the women in the band.

Ty eased the bus into the rest area and opened the door so David could take over the next shift.

"Do you need to use the facilities or anything?" Ty asked the white-haired man as he climbed the steps. David was pale and portly, with a jovial disposition.

"Nah, I'm good." He set a thermos into the larger cupholder. "Got my mint tea and my Werther's candy. I can go for hours."

Smiling, Ty relinquished the driver's seat. "I saved my settings under profile number one. Feel free to make adjustments and then save them under number two," he said. "That way, we only have to push a button to get things back to the way we want them when we're driving."

"Fancy," David said, settling into the seat. He took only a minute to orient himself before giving a thumbs-up. "I'm all set. Are you riding in the SUV?"

"No, I think I'm going to use the spare bunk and try to get a couple of hours of sleep."

"I've never been able to sleep in those," David said.

"Really?"

"It's my back. I can't ever get comfortable."

"Bummer," Ty replied as he gathered his belongings. "If you need me to take over, let me know."

"I'll be fine." David closed the door and adjusted the mirror on that side. "Sweet dreams."

"Happy driving."

Being a passenger on the bus was an odd sensation, and Ty crept into the sleeping compartment as quietly as he could. He removed his shoes, drew back the curtain on his bunk, and was about to climb in when he heard, "Psst."

He turned to find Kayla peering up at him from her bunk opposite his. Ty smiled down at her.

"Didn't mean to wake you," he whispered.

"You didn't."

They were gazing at each other, something that was happening more and more, and Ty's pulse ticked inside his chest like a countdown to something great.

"Are you planning to read?" Kayla asked and then shook her head. "Wait, you need sleep. Of course you need sleep. I'm an idiot."

Ty couldn't help his grin. He'd never seen her ramble like that before. "I'm not particularly sleepy, but I'm not allowed to drive again until morning. Contractually."

"Oh." Her eyes were huge, blinking up at him.

Ty crouched down so that they were eye level. "Hey," he said softly, something gentle unfurling in his chest.

"Hi there." Her grin was so freaking adorable.

"If you weren't sleeping, what were you doing?"

"Thinking," Kayla replied.

"Oh, yeah?"

"About peeing."

Ty coughed, almost choking on laughter as he tried to stay quiet. "I'm sorry, what?"

Kayla grinned. "You know when you're comfortable and you don't want to move, but you have to pee? And when you have to pee, and you actually do it, it's such a *relief*. But to do that, you'd have to move and—"

"And you're already comfortable," Ty said between gasps. This person.

"See? You get it," Kayla said, all smiles.

"Well, don't let me keep you."

Kayla frowned and then said, "Oh! No, I don't actually need to go. I was just thinking about it."

"Oh my God. Really?"

"Really," she said, smiling. "I was thinking how lucky it was I didn't have to pee because then I'd have to get up when I've only just gotten comfortable."

Ty shook his head. She was doing this on purpose.

They fell into a pregnant silence, their gazes locked.

"Would it be outrageously forward of me to invite you inside?" Kayla asked. "We can talk, or…"

Suddenly Ty's pulse was racing for a different reason. "I love talking to you."

"Same." Kayla scooted farther into the cubby and pushed the curtain wider. "Come hang out with me."

Ty didn't need to be asked twice. He stretched out along his side, facing her.

Kayla reached over him and pulled the curtain shut, enclosing Ty between the fabric behind him and the warmth and softness of her in front. He had to close his eyes, grateful he'd worn shorts that day and not a kilt.

"There," she said. "Now we're cozy."

The reading light over their heads was bright enough for Ty to see her glittering eyes and the red of her pouty lips. He was staring.

He knew it, but he couldn't stop.

"What are you thinking right now?" Kayla asked, sounding almost as breathless as Ty felt.

He met her gaze. "I was thinking this is the second time I've laid down next to you. I was thinking about the first time, and…and about how amazing it was to kiss you but how brief it had been. I think about that a lot, actually."

"I do too," Kayla replied, her voice barely above a whisper.

"I also realized how jealous I am of you," he admitted.

"Jealous, why?"

Ty fixed his gaze on the crimson ringlets of her hair, following the serpentine loop of one coil from where it sprang from her head to where it curled against her shoulder.

"You know who you are and what you want."

"Oh, wow. You think so?" She laughed softly. "I'm not so sure."

"Granted, I haven't known you long. But from what I've seen, you aren't afraid to be *you* or to go for what you want. Even when people don't behave toward you the way they should, with respect, like that Bruce guy at the store or the Realtor in Philly."

"That's the way we were raised. My parents never wanted us to feel like interlopers in spaces that weren't necessarily designed for us, if that makes sense."

"It does." Ty nodded. "I see that in you. When we were at the store, you let that guy's assumptions roll right off your back. You turned it into a game and made him look like an idiot but not in a mean way. You taught him a lesson but it was out of…love."

"Love?" She was laughing in earnest now. "I wouldn't call it that."

"But that's what it is," Ty insisted. "It takes a lot of love and patience to deal with people who constantly dismiss you without chopping their heads off."

"I envy your view of the world."

Ty frowned. "No, don't do that. To me, everyone has an agenda. Not you," he hastened to add. "I didn't mean you, or any of your friends, just"—he made a vague gesture—"the world in general. It's why I envy you and this life you've carved out for yourself. You and Toni and Tiff, navigating this very white, very male space and holding court like queens. God, watching you onstage was..." Ty ran out of breath. Now, *he* was the one rambling. "Stop me, please, before I embarrass myself."

She reached a hand toward his face. "Is this okay?"

"More than." He shuddered at the feeling of her warm palm against his cheek.

"I love how responsive you are to touch."

Ty hadn't ever realized it before. It was entirely possible he'd never been this responsive before. That it was all her doing, his response to her.

She traced the line of his brow with a fingertip, and Ty's eyes fluttered shut.

"You like this."

"Mmmm." He groaned wordlessly and dropped his head down onto his bicep.

Kayla's hand slid gently downward, over his cheekbone, around the sensitive curve of his jaw, and down his neck. Her breath was warm in the space between them. "Yeah," he groaned as she dragged her fingers along the line of his arm. "Mmmm," he said again, letting out a shaky breath.

She repeated her exploration, dragging her nails lightly up to his throat and repeating the slow journey back down again. Ty's heart was jackhammering in his chest, every cell in his body on fire. He wanted nothing more than for her to stop. And for her never ever to stop.

Her hand found his and Kayla laced their fingers together. They lay so close, only an inch or two between them, but she didn't try to draw him closer. Just clutched his hand tightly, as though he might try to escape.

Shifting, she put one leg between both of his and pressed her body up against his side.

Breathe, he told himself.

"This is nice," she said quietly.

He nodded, too tongue-tied to say anything remotely intelligent or eloquent about it. Ty was unable to move away if he'd wanted to—which he absofuckinglutely did not want to.

He felt her breathe in deep against his shoulder, then hum contentedly as she exhaled. It was such a tiny sound and felt so warm against him that Ty had to work hard to suppress another shiver.

It isn't enough. Ty pressed his forehead against hers. "I wish I could hold you properly."

"I can fix that." She rolled over onto her stomach and scooted down the bunk, facing him. Lifting a hand, she beckoned him. "Come here."

Kayla tugged on his arm and eased him down toward her until his face was mere centimeters from hers. She trailed her fingers down his arm before threading them together.

This close, Ty could feel nearly all of her pressed against nearly all of him. Could feel the rabbiting of her pulse beneath her skin, matching his own.

Her eyes, which had been lowered, raised to meet his and they just...caught there. Gaze in gaze, breaths intermingling.

"I want to kiss you so badly," she said. "I want to kiss you again and again, but this is more than enough if this is all you want."

Ty made a choked sound. "No, I need to kiss you."

"Oh, thank God."

CHAPTER 28.

KAYLA WANTED TO SEND A letter of complaint to every film, article, and book that had ever made sex in the bunk of a tour bus out to be anything other than ludicrous. She was sure it was only feasible for members of Cirque du Soleil, but whatever.

It wasn't like she and Ty would do more than make out, or so she thought.

Ty's hands were everywhere—in her hair, on her thigh, his palm splayed just under her breast—and he explored her mouth with an expert tongue. She loved kissing him. He was greedy but gentle and kept checking in to make sure she was still on board.

Consent was so goddamned sexy.

"Jesus," Ty groaned softly as they came up for air after another breath-stealing kiss. "You are so…"

They moved quietly and spoke in hushed tones. Something about them having to restrain themselves was a huge fucking turn-on for her. Who knew?

Ty moved his mouth to her neck, his fingers skimming across her waist. He toyed with the hem of her T-shirt, and Kayla arched her back to give him better access.

Taking the hint, he slid his hand underneath and splayed his palm across her side. The warmth of his skin was heavenly, and Kayla took a moment to appreciate it.

His thumb brushed back and forth across her skin, making her shiver.

Ty lifted his gaze to hers, his eyes wide. "Too much?"

Unable to trust her own voice, she quickly shook her head.

The sweetest smile stretched his full lips before he dipped his head and nosed gently along her jawline.

Without thinking, Kayla rolled against the thigh he had between her legs, knowing he could probably feel the heat of her despite the two layers of denim that separated them. She wanted—needed—skin-on-skin contact.

"Take off your shirt," she whispered in the cocoon of the bunk.

Without skipping a beat, Ty deftly whipped his Henley over his head and tossed it into the corner. Hovering over her, he let Kayla look her fill.

She'd expected him to demand the same of her. When he didn't, she lifted herself off the mattress enough to reach down and grab the hem of her T-shirt.

"Wait," he whispered, covering her hand with his. "You don't have to... I mean, we don't have to rush anything, if you—"

"I know," Kayla assured him. "I don't feel rushed. Do you? Because if you do, we can slow down. If not...I...I want to feel you," she finished quietly.

This seemed to spur him into action. Soon, Kayla's shirt and bra joined his shirt in the corner. Ty stared at her with eyes so hot she thought she might combust on the spot. He skimmed his palms up her rib cage and covered her breasts, his hands warm and a little rough. Kayla arched into him, spreading her legs, as far as her jeans would allow, to wrap them around his hips.

"Of all the days not to wear a kilt," Ty said, dipping his head to nuzzle her neck.

Kayla slipped her hand into his locs and gave them a gentle pull.

He lifted up enough to meet her eyes, his dancing with mirth and swimming in lust.

"I have had dreams about you and those kilts of yours," she said.

His gaze dropped to her mouth. "Yeah? What kind of dreams?"

"You behind the wheel and me on your lap, facing you while we made out like teenagers."

"That sounds dangerous," he said, chuckling. "Hot but dangerous."

Soft lips grazed her skin as Ty made his way down her neck to her chest. Space in the bunk was at a premium, especially with the curtain drawn shut, but he was nimble. He managed to plant wet, open-mouthed kisses on her breasts, her stomach, stopping when he reached her waist.

He rested his forehead against her belly. "You're so beautiful. I wish..."

Kayla cupped his head between her hands. "You wish what?"

Ty met her eyes. "Wish we could be alone. As...fun as this is, I don't want my first time with you to be like this." He gestured around them. "Assuming you want a first time."

Kayla bit her bottom lip. He was too adorable for words. "If you don't know what I want by now, I've really got to work on my signal game."

"Yeah?"

"Same book, same page."

"I like it," he said, giving her a devilish grin. "Think we can get some alone time?"

Kayla hummed, smiling. "That can be arranged. We have a few hotel stays on the itinerary."

Ty grinned. He reached down to adjust himself, wincing, and Kayla realized he was in agony.

"Poor thing."

Arching an eyebrow, Ty straightened and lay down beside her. "Worth the wait."

But she didn't want him to wait.

Kayla pressed her hand against his flat stomach and ran her fingertips down his torso. She made quick work of the button and zipper of his shorts and worked them over his hips.

"What are you doing?" he whispered, watching her hands with wide eyes.

She hesitated. "Should I stop?"

"I...er...no?"

"Want to feel you," she replied, pushing down his boxer-briefs until his arousal sprang free, hard and happy, and slapped up against his belly.

When she wrapped her hand around him, Ty's whole body jerked. "I'll make a mess," he rasped.

"I don't care," Kayla said. She wanted to feel him unravel. Needed to. She stroked him, loving the way pleasure looked on his striking features. It softened his sharp angles.

"Oh, fuck, fuck, fuck," Ty rasped when she skimmed a thumb across the head of his cock. "Shit, I can't...I—"

"Rock into my fist," Kayla said, tightening her grip and loving the groan it elicited from his throat.

Ty nodded frantically, his hips rocking against her in slow, undulating waves. His breath was hot in her ear, broken words of pleasure escaping.

"This won't take long," he said, groaning when Kayla bit the side of his neck. "Jesus."

"Let go," Kayla demanded, smiling when Ty began to shudder in her arms. He buried his face in her hair.

"Coming," he whispered. "Coming now."

Warm liquid landed on Kayla's hand and stomach as he continued to rock and shudder and moan softly in her ear. She held him, stroking her hand up and down his back when he collapsed on his side next to her.

After a few minutes, his breath evened out. Ty shifted his weight, resting most of it on an elbow. He stared down at her. His eyes on hers, he flattened his palm against her belly, his pinky toying with the hem of her joggers.

Kayla nodded. "I'm so close already."

"Fuck." Ty slid his hand into her pants, down into her underwear, his nostrils flaring when he found her wet and wanting.

As promised, it only took a few clever strokes of his fingers before she clamped a hand over her mouth, screwing her eyes shut as she shattered.

When Kayla opened her eyes, Ty was smiling at her with wonder.

"Well," he said, his hand cupping her gently now. "That was a first."

"Dry-humping?"

He glanced down at the mess they'd made. "Not really dry, though, is it?" He laughed, withdrawing his fingers. "I meant sex on a tour bus."

His eyes drank her in as if mapping each inch of her exposed skin.

"It's a first for me too," Kayla said, smiling when his gaze returned to hers. "Can't say I'm a fan of the venue, but..." She ran her hand up his back and cupped his head.

Ty dipped his head to kiss her, and she smiled into it.

He shifted his weight, and Kayla grimaced as chilly air hit her wet, sticky skin. "Uh, mistakes were made."

He looked down between them, his shoulders shaking with silent laughter. "How are we going to take care of this without traumatizing the others?"

"Clearly, we did not think this through," she said, unable to stop smiling.

Ty's eyes went soft as he gazed down at her. "Thinking isn't something I excel at when you're around."

Kayla couldn't even manage a reply because the feeling was more than mutual.

CHAPTER 29.

APPARENTLY, THEY'D BEEN LUCKY SO far during their first festival season. The light rain and minor inconveniences they'd suffered through were nothing compared to what they were experiencing now.

With things progressing in her love life, the universe had apparently decided things were running a little too smoothly for Kayla on this leg of the tour.

One of the vans had blown a tire on the highway, nearly taking out a passing car. Luckily, Jana, one-half of their merch team, was an excellent driver. But the accident set them back several hours. They'd barely made it to Shreveport in time for their set. And to top it off, the grounds were so muddy, when it was time to roll out, they discovered the bus was stuck.

Festivals meant soggy fields, unruly crowds, funky port-a-potties, equipment failure, and zero sound checks. They meant playing for people who couldn't care less who you were or what label you were on. They were there to see their favorites and made sure you knew you didn't rank among them.

The Lillys had been spoiled before, and now shit was getting real.

As they rolled past Dallas on their way to Austin, Seb tried his best to put a positive spin on the situation. Bless him.

"I know these last few dates have been rough, but it's like that sometimes," he said, holding on while the bus rumbled down I-20. "Think of this as paying your dues."

"I want a refund," Tiff said, rubbing her thigh. She bore a nasty bruise from a tumble she'd taken on the slippery stage in Memphis.

"It'll be worth it, I promise," Seb said, rubbing her back. Such a nurturer, he was. "The good news is the buzz has been positive. YMI is happy."

"Yippee for them." Tiff stretched, grimacing from her obvious pain. "Just tell me Austin is dry. I'm tired of being waterlogged."

"Dry, sunny, and hot," Seb said. "No rain in the forecast for days."

"Well, thank God for that," Toni said, twisting her hair up into a knot. "Any chance we'll check into another hotel soon? I'd love a proper shower."

"Not until we reach Arizona," Seb said, shrugging. "Sorry."

"We'll manage." Lilly ran a hand through her hair. The long blond strands fell in a curtain over her shoulder. "While we're in Austin, we should have the bus serviced. I grabbed the last clean towel this morning."

"Ty's already scheduled it," Seb said.

At the mention of his name, heat crept up Kayla's neck. The two nights they spent in Atlanta, holed up in Ty's room, they hadn't progressed beyond kissing and heavy petting, but it was more than enough to make her an addict. She was experiencing some serious withdrawal symptoms.

"How many days will we be in Arizona?" she heard herself ask, already plotting a way to steal time away with Ty.

Rubbing his hands together, Seb grinned. "I was going to wait and surprise you guys, but you all look so fucking miserable." He laughed when Tiff gave him the finger, grabbing it and kissing the tip. "Hold off on that until you hear what I have to say."

The four of them held their collective breath while they waited, but Seb dragged it out like the drama queen he was.

Kayla wondered what could be so big that Seb felt the need to tease them about it. Had they picked up some radio rotation? Scored a spot on *SNL*?

"Seb, spill it," Kayla pressed.

"Bloody fucking hell, just tell us!" Tiff exclaimed. Poor cranky thing.

"Fine, fine," he said, relenting as he let her go, tousling her hair in the process.

Kayla thought she might have heard her growl.

"After Pheonix Fest, I booked us four days at a spa in Sedona."

Tiff jumped out of her seat and into Seb's arms. "Oh, my God! Seb! You cruel and magnificent bastard!"

Laughing, Seb hugged her until she winced and pulled away. Concern replaced the humor as he cupped her shoulder and tried to turn her around. "Shit, Tiffany, you're really hurt. Why didn't you say anything?"

"It's nothing." Tiff squirmed out of his reach. "I'm fine." Her smile was artificial, but he let her go.

Kayla exchanged a look with Lilly as the room fell quiet.

"Really," Tiff said, attempting a laugh. "It's nothing that four days in a goddamned *spa* won't fix." She plopped down in her seat. "I've never been to a spa, unless you count the nail salon near Santee Alley. I'm going to get a twenty-four-hour massage. Is that a thing? That should be a thing."

"I hate massages," Toni said with a shudder.

Seb frowned. "Since when?"

"Since forever," she replied, looking up at him. "Except when you give them, babe. You're the only one allowed to bend and shape me."

His mouth twisted into a wicked grin. "I should hope so."

Kayla groaned, if only to cover up for the fact that she was imagining Ty's hands bending and shaping her. "On that note..."

She slipped past Seb and made her way to the front of the bus.

Ty had both hands on the wheel, his fingers drumming to the music on the radio as he hummed. His kilt was chocolate brown today, and he wore round sunglasses and a gray and black fedora that made him look like an emo bookworm from the early aughts.

Kayla slid her hands onto his shoulder, loving how he relaxed under her touch. "Hey," she said, giving him a squeeze.

"Hi." Ty reached one hand back to rub his thumb across the back of her hand before returning to the wheel. "I was just thinking about you."

"Were you?" She moved to her favorite place on the dash. "That's convenient since I was just thinking about you too."

"Yeah?" He glanced at her and flashed one of his brilliant, white smiles.

"Oh yeah," she assured him, resting her bare foot against his thigh. As expected, he dropped his hand to her ankle and caressed her skin, sending shimmers of pleasure up her nerve endings.

God.

"I just got the best news," she said, flexing her toes against the hard muscle of his thighs.

"Care to share?"

"How does two days at an Arizona spa sound?"

Ty's brows dipped. "Sounds expensive. Seb told us we had a two-day stopover in Sedona, but as far as I know, my room is at the Days Inn."

Kayla arched a brow, even though he wasn't looking at her. "Ty..." she said. "Do you really think you're going to even glimpse the inside of the Days Inn when I'll be alone in a room at a spa? Like, really?"

He bit his lip but failed to hide his grin. "I would never presume."

Kayla leaned forward and covered his hand with hers. "I appreciate that, and I shouldn't presume either. But you? Presume all you fucking want. I want to hang out."

His smile returned. "Yeah?" She nodded. "You think you can just wine and dine me in a fancy spa, and I'll put out?"

"A girl can dream," Kayla replied, loving the way they could be sexy and playful at the same time. "But it doesn't have to be about *that*. You know that, right?"

"I do."

Kayla had never known anyone like Tyrell Baldwin, and she wondered how far it could go. She was way too into him already and found it way too easy to imagine him on the road with them on their first world tour, in the studio hanging out while they finished the album, waking up next to him in her bed...

"I love that I'm in your thoughts even when I'm not around," he said softly, his gaze flicking briefly to hers.

Kayla thought she saw the same hopeful longing in it that she'd been feeling for him, so she decided to honor his truth with a bit of her own.

"Lately, most of my thoughts have been about you."

Austin brought back the high the band had experienced at Neon Fest in Savannah. The setup was clean, dry, and professional, and it had freed them to concentrate on delivering their best set of the tour so far.

High above the crowd of over thirty thousand people, Kayla bathed in the energy surrounding the four of them onstage.

Tiff's injury didn't seem to bother her as she played, and she was her usual, flamboyant self. She'd woven pink extensions into her waist-length black braids, and they swung around her like blades as she whipped her head back and forth, playing the absolute fuck out of her bass.

Kayla had never heard the Lillys sound this good.

Maybe it was Austin—the atmosphere and the crowd. Perhaps it was the feeling that they'd been waterlogged and had dealt with hostile crowds and washed-out sets and emerged undeterred. Stronger. Maybe the promise of king-size beds and mud baths had kept them going. Whatever it was, they were on fire.

Toni's solos were inspired. She'd clearly gained confidence on the road, and Kayla could hear it. Could see it.

And Lilly was a fucking Svengali, directing the crowd's response like a conductor. Her voice had grown more potent as well over these last few dates, something Kayla hadn't thought possible.

During the breakdown of the current song, she tracked Lilly as the singer prowled the front of the stage, watching for the smallest cue. When the blond swiveled her hips, Kayla rolled along the toms. When Lilly flipped her hair to one side, Kayla answered with a cymbal crash.

It was the kind of call-and-response Kayla had never experienced with Lilly before.

Lilly turned her blue eyes on Kayla, her lips curved into a smile as she danced over toward her. Kayla watched—rapt—as Lilly climbed up onto the bass drum.

One of the stagehands darted over and grabbed her arm to steady her as she stood upright, hovering near her hip in case she lost her footing.

But Lilly stood rock solid, like the fucking goddess she was, while Kayla stomped down on the pedal, beating out the steady undercurrent of the tune. At that moment, it was as if they shared a heartbeat.

Lilly held Kayla's gaze, her own blazing with a light Kayla had rarely seen in her, and lifted the microphone to her lips.

"*I will fight for you,*" she sang. Behind her, the crowd cheered and repeated the line. "*I'll do right by you,*" Lilly continued, keeping her eyes in Kayla's. "*And if the world turns dark...I'll hold up a light for you.*"

Again, the crowd repeated the line, despite the song being completely new to them. It was one of the ones they'd written for the album. Lilly had asked to add it to the set for the second leg of the tour.

Kayla had questioned whether it was ready. But now, at this moment, she recognized what she hadn't before. Heard what Lilly had heard. The song was destined to be a hit.

"*And if the world turns dark...*" Lilly sang, holding out the last note as she threw her head back, her back arching dangerously.

Below her, the stagehand looked up nervously, his arms raised as if to catch her.

Lilly popped upright, grinning wildly. "*I'll hold up a fucking light for you!*"

She spun and jumped over the man's head, landing on her feet like a cat.

Lilly danced, her hair wild around her, as the three of them—Toni, Tiff, and Kayla—rocked through the outro.

The four of them had dipped into some untapped ley line of magic, and Kayla was electrified.

"Holy shit, holy shit. Did you feel that? Holy shit!" Tiff kept repeating as they clambered down the metal stairs.

"That was..." Toni seemed at a loss for words, but her face showed everything. Joy. Disbelief. Pride.

Kayla felt all of those things.

Beside her, Lilly was breathing hard and smiling. Smiling. Lilly!

"You guys were on fire!" Seb exclaimed as he ran toward them.

He scooped Toni up into a hug, spinning her around as she laughed in his arms. When he stopped, they kissed deeply before he pulled back and lowered her to the ground. For a moment, they only had eyes for each other. Then Seb seemed to remember where they were.

"Seriously," he said. "I don't know if you could tell, but the crowd went absolutely wild for the two new songs."

"I'll never question your judgment again," Kayla said to Lilly, who grinned back.

"I had a hunch, that's all." Lilly pushed the damp tendrils of her hair out of her eyes.

"Keep having them," Tiff replied.

Kayla scanned the area, wondering if Ty had caught their set. She spied him a few feet away, his eyes hot on her. She frowned, wondering why he hadn't come over.

"Excuse me," she said, but no one was listening. When she reached Ty, he looked like he was about to burst. "What're you doing over here?"

"I didn't want to intrude," he said, breathing hard. His nostrils flared. Something had him vibrating out of his skin.

Concerned, she stepped into him. "You wouldn't be intruding."

Ty dropped his gaze and nodded. "Okay. Okay." He let out a harsh breath and met her eyes. "You…You were fucking incredible up there. All of you. God, Kayla…"

Kayla smiled so wide, her cheeks hurt. "Yeah?"

He sputtered out a laugh, and then his arms were around her and he was lifting her off her feet.

Laughing, Kayla wound her arms around his neck. "I didn't know you were planning to watch us today."

Ty leaned back to look down at her. "I couldn't keep my eyes off of you," he said, getting more excited with every word. "But what else is new? All I could think was, look at her. *Look at her up there*, on top of the world. I wanted to scream to everyone around me, that's Kayla Whitman, that's my—" He stopped short of finishing that sentence, his eyes wide.

"Your what?" Kayla ran her nose along his throat, and his arms tightened around her. She knew she was sweaty and gross, but Ty didn't seem to care.

"You're mine," he said quietly.

Kayla met his gaze.

"If you want to be. If you want…me."

Kayla kissed him, answering him in the only way she felt capable of at that moment. She kissed him because she'd liked him from the moment they'd met. She kissed him because he had quickly become an integral part of her life, and she longed to keep him in it, somehow. Some way.

She was falling. It was too soon, but it was also way too late.

CHAPTER 30.

"YOU TWO ARE SWEET," A voice said behind them.

Breaking the kiss, Kayla's smile faded quickly when they turned to find one of the reporters from Detroit standing a few feet away. It was the woman who had asked Kayla and Tiff the really intrusive questions.

Clearly on edge, Kayla straightened and slipped her arm around Ty's waist.

He threw a protective arm across her shoulder and took immense satisfaction that he could be by her side when she needed someone.

"Hi," the reporter said, giving Ty a once-over that felt somehow intrusive. "Sara Marsh. I'm doing a story on the Lillys. Well, more specifically, on you, *Miss Larrington.*" She turned her eerie green eyes on Kayla. "Sorry, I meant to schedule an interview, but I got a lead on something, and I needed to chase it down."

"Now isn't a good time," Kayla said, stiffening beside him. Ty frowned at the name the reporter called her. It seemed familiar, and he assumed it was Kayla's real name. Larrington. She didn't seem like a Larrington, it was too...formal sounding.

"I just need to clarify something," Sara said, blocking their path. She pulled a notepad from the back pocket of her shorts and made a show of flipping the pages. "You've had an interesting life."

Holding up her hand, Kayla leveled the woman with a look that would have made his blood run cold had it been turned on him. "I'm sweaty and tired, *Ms. Marsh*. You'll have to wait until the presser or schedule something with my label."

"Are you sure you want me to ask my questions in front of the press pool?" The reporter arched a brow. She wore the smug expression of someone who felt they had the upper hand.

"What are you playing at?" Kayla asked, her temper flaring.

Without thinking, Ty positioned Kayla slightly behind him.

"I'm just doing my job."

"I believe she told you, twice now, that this isn't a good time," Ty said, glad his voice sounded calm and firm. He remembered having to deal with people like Sara Marsh.

When her flinty gaze zeroed in on him, he didn't flinch. "You're Tyrell Baldwin, right?"

"That's my name, yeah," Ty said. His voice sounded hollow to his own ears. He dropped his arms to his side and straightened his shoulders.

A slow smile spread across Sara's mouth.

"Your band," Sara said, chuckling as she closed her notepad. "You people are like a walking reality show. I could make my whole career writing about the four of you..." She paused and gave Ty a disdainful look. "And the company you keep."

"Get the fuck out of here," Kayla spat, seething.

Sara held up her press pass. "I'm on the job. I have every right to be here."

Before he could stop her, Kayla lunged.

Ty held her to him, speaking low into her ear. "Calm down, it's not worth all this."

He could tell she wanted to argue, but all of her attention was on the piece-of-shit reporter. "Get. Out!"

"Whoa, whoa, whoa. What's going on here?" Seb stepped

between them and Sara, giving the reporter his back. "Hey, are you all right?" He spun around, glancing down at her credentials. "You're from the *Bulletin*, right? What are you doing? You asked to set up a formal interview with the band. You can't just show up and ambush us like this."

Sara held up her hands. "I'm here to cover the festival."

"I asked around about you," Seb said, crossing his arms as he looked down at her. "Music isn't your 'beat.'" He tossed up air quotes around the words.

"That's true. I'm more of an investigative journalist," Sara said. "And right now, I'm investigating the link between crime syndicates and the music industry."

"What?" Seb and Kayla asked simultaneously. "Lady, I don't know where you're getting your information, but someone sold you a bridge in Brooklyn. There's no story here."

"Perhaps you're not aware of your driver, Mr. Baldwin's, past."

Seb narrowed his eyes. "You think we don't vet our people? You think I would let anyone fucking near the band I thought posed any hint of a threat against them?"

"So, you're saying you knew that he was accused of assault? And that the woman who accused him disappeared, only to be found later dead from an alleged drug overdose?" Sara started scribbling.

"What I know," Seb said, "is that you're done here." He raised an arm and waved over a member of the festival staff.

Ty watched it all unfold as if he were underwater. Only Kayla's hand in his kept him in the moment.

"Hey," Seb said as the staff member approached. She was a tall woman with sharp features and a no-nonsense air about her. "This member of the press is harassing my artist."

"I'm only doing my job," Sara protested, her voice dripping with fake innocence.

The other woman rolled her eyes and held out her hand. "Well, you can do your job somewhere else. I'm going to have to ask for your pass."

"But—"

"Now, please," the woman said. "Or I can call for security and have them escort you out. Your choice."

Scowling, Sara ripped the lanyard over her head and dropped it on the ground. "Not smart to piss off the press," she spat as she glared at the woman. She turned to Seb and finally to Kayla and Ty. "Not fucking smart at all."

After she left, Kayla bent over and put her hands on her knees.

Cursing under his breath, Ty rubbed circles on her back. He met Seb's worried gaze. "I'm so sorry."

"Dude, don't even sweat that," Seb said. "Jordan and I will take care of it."

"I'm sorry about that," the other woman said. She pulled out a card and handed it to Seb. "I'm Bettina. If anything like this happens again while you're here, my number is on there. Or you can flag down any of the festival staff, and they'll find me." Her gaze roamed over the three of them, regret etched all over her face.

"Shit happens." Seb gave her a reassuring smile. "Thanks for helping out."

"It's my job," Bettina said, smiling.

Kayla finally managed to straighten up. "Thanks, we appreciate it."

"No problem. Killer set, by the way—I'm pretty sure it's already up on YouTube." Bettina gave Kayla a salute before she jogged off.

The euphoria their performance seemed like a distant memory. All Ty could think about was Kayla. She turned to him.

"I'm serious, guys," Seb said. "Don't let that rattle you."

Ty gave the tiniest shrug of his shoulders, his eyes downcast. Kayla took his biceps into her hands and shook him gently. "We've got your back," she said as if willing him to understand and accept it. "*I've* got your back."

He lifted his gaze to hers. Slowly, doubt turned to belief, and he gave her a sharp nod. "And I've got yours."

The bus was quiet. When anyone did speak, it was in the kind of hushed tones people used around mourners. Ty remembered it well from when his father had died.

If his pop could only see him now.

Seb had insisted that David drive the first leg of the sixteen-hour-long trek from Austin to Sedona, and Ty hadn't had it in him to argue. He'd accepted Seb and Toni's offer to let him use their room to make a private call to his granddad, having gone back and forth about bothering Van. In the end, Kayla had convinced him.

Still, he hesitated.

Pop-Pop was happy in his new home, making new friends. He'd finally gotten out from under the shadow that Ty's nightmare had cast over both their lives. Despite what Van might think, it had never been his cross to bear.

But Van Baldwin was a stubborn old man. Ty knew his granddad would walk through fire to do anything for him, and he loved him for it. It's also the reason why his thumb hovered over the call button on his phone.

If he told his granddad about the reporter, he'd want to do something. And, really, there was nothing he could do. But if he didn't call, and Van found out some other way, there would be hell to pay.

He pulled up his granddad's contact and pulled the trigger.

"Your ears must have been burning," he said, picking up on the first ring.

Ty smiled. "I wondered why. Are you talking about me again?"

"Always," Pop-Pop said. "Always. Gotta brag about my genius grandson and his bright future as a university professor."

Ty cringed. "Oh, yeah? Who are you telling these tall tales to, Miss Peggy?"

"The one and only," his granddad replied. There was a smile in his voice. "She's been to visit me a couple of times. Said she misses having me around next door, baking up a storm and making her house smell like Willy Wonka's chocolate factory."

"Oh, yeah? I bet that's not all she misses, you old dog." Ty grinned and sat on the edge of the bed. "Don't think I didn't catch all those googly eyes you two made at each other."

"First I've heard of it," Pop-Pop said. "I asked her out a few times, and she always turned me down. But since I've been here, she can't seem to stay away."

"Maybe it's the venue," Ty teased. His granddad started singing the theme from *The Jeffersons*, and Ty laughed. "Exactly."

"Maybe." His voice trailed off. "Anyway, she's always asking about you—where you are and what you're doing these days. I guess she misses having someone next door to keep an eye on the block."

"I'll be sure to check on her when I get back," Ty said. He liked Miss Peggy and figured she was the closest thing to a mother figure he'd had growing up, albeit a distant one. He'd always kept to himself.

"Good, good. I told her you were on the road with a rock star. Or is it a band?" his granddad asked. "I forget."

"It's a band, and they aren't big yet, but they will be." Ty was sure of it. "That's actually what I'm calling about."

"Have I heard anything of theirs on the radio?"

"No, Pop-Pop, I don't think so. They're set to release their single pretty soon, though, I think," Ty replied. "I'll let you know. Look, I... There's..." He paused and took a breath. First things first.

"Everything all right, son?"

"Yeah, well…" No. "I have some news. I met someone." He heard rustling in the background, and then the noises on the other end of the call faded.

"What's… What's their name?"

Ty's heart swelled to three times its size. He'd never hidden his sexuality from his granddad, but neither had he discussed it with him. When he dated Shawn, he never explicitly mentioned their relationship to Van. As far as he knew, Ty and Shawn were just friends. Or so Ty thought.

"And are they good to you?" his granddad continued. "'Cause, in the end, that's all that matters to me."

"Her name is Kayla, and she's really good to me," Ty said, hearing how gone he was for her in his own voice.

His granddad must have heard it too because he sighed and cleared his throat. "Is she one of the musicians you work with?"

"Yeah. She's the drummer."

"What?" Van laughed. "Leave it to you to find a woman who plays the drums in a rock band."

"It's more and more common these days, though not common enough," Ty said. "Anyway, she's cool. You'll like her."

"Does she mind that you always have your nose buried in your books?"

"Believe it or not, she loves to read," Ty said. "I can't say we're alike, per se, but we…we complement each other."

"That's the best—when you can find someone like that," Pop-Pop mused. "I had that with your grandmother."

"I know," Ty said.

"Well, I can't wait to meet your little drummer girl."

Ty laughed. "Uh, you will. Just, please, don't call her that to her face."

He heard his granddad snicker. "Duly noted."

"There's…something else," Ty said, sobering. "A reporter's been sniffing around."

"Sniffing around about what?" Van said, his tone suddenly hard. He'd always been fiercely protective of Ty, which he both loved and hated.

"She's on some kind of mission to make the band look bad. Digging up stuff on everyone's past, their families," Ty said. "I'm not quite sure why, but she's been relentless. They seem to think their label is looking for a scandal to exploit and are using the press to drum up interest. This woman is all over it."

"That's not like any decent journalist I've ever met," his grand-dad said. "And I've known quite a few. Sounds more like a tabloid reporter looking for some dirt. And anyway, why should anyone care about it?"

"Pop-Pop…" Ty began, wishing he could skip this part. "She knew who I was. And she seemed to know about Merry." There was a long silence. "Van?"

"I heard you," his grandfather said. "Do you know what this reporter looks like?"

"She's a short white woman, late thirties to early forties, with orange-ish hair and green eyes. Oh, and she always wears this vest with, like, a billion pockets on it."

His granddad made a disgusted sound. "I've seen her."

"Where? When?"

"This morning," he ground out. "Dropping off Peggy."

A dozen thoughts hit Ty at once. Anger first, because if that vile woman had gone anywhere near his grandfather, Ty wasn't sure what he might do when he saw her again. Then a sense of betrayal that blindsided him. Peggy? He'd known her since he was a gangly tween, with spindly arms and legs that he hadn't yet grown into.

Was she using his grandfather to get information on Ty? To feed to Sara fucking Marsh? For money, maybe?

"Van," Ty said, guessing that his Pop-Pop's thoughts might be traveling the same paths. "Don't confront her."

"Oh, I'm gonna confront her, all right."

"No, don't. Please," Ty begged. "Let me handle it. I'm asking you."

"How dare she come up in here, smiling with those false teeth, asking about you like she cares," Pop-Pop said. Ty had rarely heard him so angry.

"I know, I know, but please. Let me take care of this. I might know someone who can help." Ty said.

"What kind of help?"

"Kayla's band has a great attorney. Since this involves them, maybe he'll have some advice." It felt strange to say it out loud. Ty never liked to ask for anything from anyone, let alone people who were practically strangers.

He'd rejected the idea of a fundraiser for his legal fees until he realized Van was tapping into his retirement. Even then, he used the money to pay his granddad back. Ty didn't like the idea of owing anyone anything. And if it weren't for Kayla's reputation on the line, not to mention her relationship with her family, Ty would probably handle this on his own.

"You trust these people?" his granddad asked, sounding incredulous. "You don't even know them."

"I trust her, and *she* trusts this guy," Ty replied. It was as simple as that.

His grandfather exhaled. "All right, then. That's good enough for me, but don't think I'm going to let Peggy's skinny little behind back through these doors until she can explain herself."

"You can tell the staff that she is an unwelcome visitor for now," Ty said. "Let them deal with it. You never even have to see her again if it turns out she's feeding the press information."

Van grunted.

"Okay?" Ty asked. "I'm going to need a verbal confirmation that you hear the words I am saying."

"Yes, yes," Pop-Pop huffed. "I hear you. Bossy."

Exhaling, Ty smiled. "Thank you. And I'm sorry."

"Child, what are you sorry for?" He sounded exasperated.

Despite the fact his granddad couldn't see him, Ty shrugged. He'd always felt like he'd been a burden to his grandfather. Ty knew, in his heart, Pop-Pop didn't feel that way—not even a little bit. Still, it didn't stop Ty from wishing he hadn't made the man's life all about him. Even when he'd grown up and thought he was well on his way toward finding his own way, the world kicked his legs out from under him. And Van had been right there to pick him up. Just as he had for his dad before him.

It was time for Ty to figure things out on his own, time to protect his granddad and not rely on him to swoop in and save the day.

"Tyrell," Pop-Pop said softly. "In case you forgot, and in case I haven't said it lately, I'm proud of you. Of the person you've become. I know you don't think you've achieved as much as other people your age, but you had a difficult path. I tried to smooth it for you, but I'm not perfect."

"Don't say that." Ty's throat tightened, and he fought to swallow around the lump in his throat. "You were more than any kid could ever hope for. I was so lucky to have you. I am so, so lucky."

Ty heard a sniffle on the other end, and he wiped at his own eyes.

"Well, now that you've got me crying like a baby, I'm going to go chop some onions," he pronounced.

"What are you making?"

"Don't know yet, but at least I'll have an excuse for all this blubbering."

CHAPTER 31.

FOR THE ENTIRE EIGHT HOURS of Ty's shift behind the wheel, Kayla barely left his side. She was so grateful he hadn't run screaming after the debacle with Sara Marsh that she didn't want to let him out of her sight.

He didn't seem to mind, not even when she sat on the floor in the cockpit and leaned her head against his leg. Ty ran his fingers through her hair, occasionally detangling a curl. His touch was gentle, reassuring.

Kayla decided to take it as proof that whatever was happening between them hadn't been derailed by the band's drama.

"We're close," Ty said.

Kayla climbed to her feet and looked out the window in time to see the road sign for Slide Rock State Park. She wished it weren't dark out. Kayla had never been to this part of the country, and she'd heard it was known for its stunning red vistas.

The hotel itself sat nestled in Boynton Canyon, and Kayla loved its iconic Southwestern style. Judging by its size, it was more of a resort than a hotel, with low-slung buildings sprawled along its grounds.

"This place must be gorgeous in daylight," Ty said as he pulled the bus up to the front of the main building.

"I was thinking the same," Kayla said. "I can't wait to explore it."

"Mind if I tag along?" He grinned at her.

"I'd be pissed if you didn't." She pecked him on the lips. It was meant to be a quick kiss, but Ty slipped a hand behind her neck and held her to him, deepening the kiss and making her head spin.

Kayla blinked dazedly when he released her, and he smiled. "I know better than to piss you off."

Voices from the back reached them just before someone shoved the curtain aside.

"Can you believe the size of this place?" Tiff asked, clutching her pillow under her arm. She was dressed in an adult onesie covered in cartoon donuts.

"Uh, Tiff?" Kayla stifled a laugh. "Are you sure you're awake, honey?"

Tiff frowned at her. "I'm awake, but I'm going straight to bed as soon as we check in. I'm fucking tired."

Chuckling, Seb hugged Tiff to him. "I'll get us sorted, don't worry. Ty, after we unload, follow the signs for bus parking. I think they said it's around to the right."

"No problem," Ty replied, unbuckling his seat belt.

Since they only needed their clothes, unloading took no time at all. They'd also brought their acoustic instruments inside, in case inspiration struck. Kayla and Lilly guarded the gear while Seb and Toni checked them in. Tiff sank into one of the chairs in the lobby and was asleep in seconds.

"I don't know how she does that," Lilly said.

"It's a skill set I don't possess."

One corner of Lilly's mouth curved into something close to a grin. She cut her eyes to Kayla. "You and Ty seem…fortified."

"Fortified?"

"Strong," Lilly said. "I wondered if what happened with the reporter would unsettle you, but you seem to have come together even more. I'm glad."

"Me too," Kayla admitted.

The automatic door chimed.

Ty walked in and headed straight to her side. "Bus is parked and secure," he told Lilly.

"Thank you." Lilly inclined her head ever so slightly. "I'm glad you're with us."

His brows rose. He glanced down at Kayla and then back at Lilly. "I'm glad too."

"I hope you'll stick around for a while. And I want to see some of your writing," Lilly added, turning to Seb when he and Toni walked over.

Ty seemed dazed.

"Okay," Seb said as he started passing out envelopes. "I got one of the larger casitas. It should accommodate all of us but still give everyone their privacy."

He handed Kayla an envelope.

"This contains your room key—try not to lose it—as well as a map of the grounds. There's a shuttle that will take you into Sedona anytime between eight a.m. and eleven p.m. If for some reason you need to go before or after that, they'll arrange a car to take you." He looked around. "Where's Tiff?"

Kayla pointed over her shoulder.

"Jesus, how does she do that?" Seb asked, laughing to himself.

After rousing Tiff, the group was whisked away in a golf cart. Gary, the driver, explained the history of the resort, asked where they were from, and generally earned the ten-dollar tip Seb pressed into his hand when he dropped them off.

"Casita means little house, doesn't it?" Tiff asked, looking up at the two-story, adobe-style building. "This ain't little."

Seb grinned. "Surprise! There are six bedrooms, three on each floor, a full kitchen and dining room, a gas fireplace—not that we need it in this heat—a hot tub on the viewing deck upstairs, and a private pool by the patio."

"How can we afford this?" Lilly asked.

"Don't worry, we didn't break the bank," Seb said. "Jordan called in a favor. We're paying a fraction of what anyone else would pay." He jogged up the two steps that led to the front door and unlocked it before turning around. "Besides," he said, smiling, "we're celebrating."

Seb gestured everyone to come in, and they filed inside behind him.

Kayla couldn't believe this place. Seb hadn't been kidding when he mentioned the full-sized kitchen and dining room. The latter was as large as the one in her parents' home.

The decor brought the Southwestern style of the exterior inside, with smooth, beige walls, exposed-beam ceilings, and regional accents in the soft furnishings.

"Um, does this mean we've made it?" Tiff asked, her eyes wide as she looked around, fully awake now.

"What are we celebrating?" Lilly asked.

Seb took out his cell phone, punched at the screen for a moment, and looked back up at the group. "This."

Music poured over them. Kayla looked around, but she couldn't locate the speakers. It was as if the air itself was producing the sound. It took a moment for the song to register.

"Is that...?"

"Holy fucking shit," Tiff exclaimed. "It's us!"

Kayla reached out blindly for Ty's hand and squeezed when he notched their fingers together.

The group stood in the middle of the room as the song played. "Hurt U" had been vital to them as a unit. It was the song that bonded them together. It was the song that had seen them through the transition from Candi to Toni. And it was to be their first national single.

"Has it gone live yet?" Lilly asked.

Seb checked his phone. "In three minutes, it'll be live on the East Coast."

"Where?" Toni asked before biting her bottom lip.

Seb pulled her to his side and draped his arm around her shoulders. "Spotify, Apple Music, Amazon, you name it."

"Oh, it's real now, bitches," Tiff said, grinning so wide her smile was half-gums, half-teeth.

"We need champagne," Kayla said.

"Already on it." Seb released Toni and ran toward the kitchen, the five of them hot on his heels.

"Hurry up," Toni said. "We've got less than sixty seconds."

Seb pulled a bottle of champagne from the fridge. "Can someone look for the glasses?"

Ty released Kayla's hand as they both went for the cabinets. "Got 'em!" Kayla said. Ty helped her set a half dozen flutes on the stone countertop.

"Twenty-eight seconds," Toni said.

Seb popped the cork, laughing when it ricocheted across the room. "Glad that didn't break anything."

"Pour," Toni demanded, pointing at his phone when she set it down. The analog clock showed twelve seconds remaining.

As Seb filled each glass with bubbly, Lilly handed them out. He had just enough time to grab one himself as the clock ticked down to midnight Eastern.

"Five," Tiff said.

Lilly lifted her glass. "Four."

"Three." Toni grabbed Seb's hand.

"Two," Kayla said, raising her flute in the air.

One.

"Again," Ty begged. He was sprawled on his back across the colorful area rug.

Kayla made a mental note to photograph him like this, loose-limbed, natural, and smiling. And tipsy. He smiled, flashing his ridiculously perfect white teeth, and Kayla had the irrational desire to lick them.

She hit play, and the Lillys' first single streamed out of the Bose Soundbar beneath the TV. It was three in the morning, but the room was soundproofed. And Kayla was pretty sure they weren't the only ones still up.

"I'm so proud of you guys," Ty said.

Kayla believed him. His eyes shone with it, and she wondered how they'd gotten here so fast, in this comfortable, unfettered place of nurturing support. She'd barely known him six weeks.

"I'm proud of us too," she said. Ty lifted his hand and held it up to lace his fingers through hers. It was quickly becoming their thing, and Kayla loved it.

Whatever the Sara Marshes of the world tried to pull, they couldn't stop this from happening. Couldn't stop them. Or the Lillys.

The single sounded really fucking good.

"We sound really fucking good," she repeated aloud.

"Yeah, you really fucking do," Ty said, pulling gently on her hand until she moved forward to lean against him.

"I keep meaning to tell you," Kayla said, folding her arms across his chest to rest her chin there. "Swear words sound really sexy coming out of your mouth but also kinda foreign too."

Ty's brow creased. "Foreign?"

Kayla nodded as much as her position would allow. "Like... they don't really belong. Like you're not used to them."

Ty seemed to think about it. "I guess I use them sparingly. At least," he added, rolling over her until she was on her back, him hovering above, "I did. I'll use them more if you think they sound sexy."

"You mean you don't curse like a sailor around anyone else?" she teased.

Ty's gaze narrowed. "I'm not like this at all with anyone else, Kayla. Only you. Except…"

"Except what?"

"Larrington?"

Shifting, Kayla took a deep breath. "Remember that book you picked up in Toledo?"

Ty dropped his head to his chest. "Y-yeah," he replied as his shoulders began to shake.

"What?" she asked, pushing his shoulder when the soft chuckle turned into cackling.

Ty flopped onto his back, breathless with laughter. "I knew it."

"Knew what?" Grinning, she looked down at him.

"It *is* you on the cover of the Little Miss Yolanda books."

She could feel her face twist up into a grimace, though she was still fighting a smile. "Yeah, it's me."

"Fuck," he said, his laughter dying down. "Leave it to me to be falling for Little Miss Yolanda. Pop-Pop's never gonna let me live it down."

Kayla's breath caught. "Falling for?"

He turned his head, his eyes alight with warmth. "Feeling rushed?"

"I feel privileged," she said, grinning to cover up the fact that velociraptors had taken off in her stomach.

"Do you?" he asked, his voice soft.

Kayla averted her eyes. She didn't know what to do or say when Ty got all intense like this. It thrilled her, while at the same time, it sent her thoughts into a tizzy. Was he really tumbling down the rabbit hole right alongside her? Was it possible?

"Hey," he said, rolling to his side and lowering his face to hers to press a quick kiss to her lips. "Don't freak out."

Her gaze shot to his. "I'm not freaking out." Ty arched a brow. "Okay, maybe I'm freaking out a little. This is fast, isn't it? You and me?"

Please say no.

Ty shrugged. "I don't think there's a countdown calendar when it comes to stuff like this," he said. He touched a finger to her temple. "You just know. Here." He brushed his fingers over her breastbone, right over her pounding heart. "I've loved getting to learn your rhythms, Ms. Larrington. What's your full name?"

"Katherine Yolanda." When he snorted, she tickled his side. "Katherine Yolanda Larrington. And you are?"

"Tyrell Asani Baldwin, at your service." He pecked her on the nose, and Kayla began to tilt her head for a kiss when his name registered.

"Wait." She leaned back to look at him. "Tab? Your initials spell *tab*?" For some reason, she found this hilarious and couldn't contain her snort of laughter.

Ty tried to look affronted and failed. He smiled at her. "Go ahead, I've heard all of the jokes."

"Nope, I'm not going to tease anyone over their name. I learned that lesson long ago."

His mouth softened as he curved a hand over her hip. "You would never be deliberately cruel. I know that much about you, *Kayla*. I want to know everything about you."

Jesus. This man...

Kayla wrapped him in a tight full-body hug that Ty returned.

He was everything she never knew she wanted, and Kayla hoped like hell she could keep him.

CHAPTER 32.

TY SENT SO MANY PHOTOS of the resort and its surroundings to his grandfather that Pop-Pop asked him to stop, but he couldn't stop taking them. The place was like a movie set—surrounded by the otherworldly red rocks Sedona was known for and stacked with every amenity known to humankind. Nearly eighty acres of tennis courts, basketball courts, restaurants and shops, pools, and the spa.

It went a long way toward keeping him from dwelling on everything swirling around him. The reporter. Selling the house. Even being with Kayla, building whatever they were building, brought with it a kind of pressure.

Maybe she understood him better than he realized because she kept looking after him. Centering him in a way no one ever had.

"Of course Jordan will help. You don't even need to ask," Kayla assured him.

She kept him from staring at her laptop for hours trying to figure out if there was anything that Sara Marsh knew that they didn't.

"Your problem is our problem now," she'd said. "Let Jordan figure it out."

Rather than argue, he'd let her drag him out for a walk and it had been just what he'd needed.

"Explain to me again what a vibrational massage is?" he

asked as they followed the road back toward the main building. They were meeting the others for lunch at one of the resort's seven restaurants.

"The description said they use these oils that vibrate at certain frequencies," Kayla said as if that were perfectly apparent. "And they use them to manipulate your chakras."

"And...I...want my chakras manipulated?"

Kayla stopped in the middle of the path and turned to him. "I guess? It sounded less intense than some of their other offerings, but we don't have to do it."

"I didn't say I didn't want to. I merely wanted to get a better idea of what to expect."

Kayla squinted up at him. "Are you sure?"

Her face was clean of any makeup, and the sunlight brought out the freckles splashed across her nose and cheeks. She was so present in her own body and so goddamned beautiful. Sometimes it hurt to look at her.

"I'm very sure," he replied, not even remotely talking about the massage.

Ty had never been in love before and had always feared he wouldn't recognize it, if and when it ever happened. Staring down into Kayla's soulful brown eyes, he understood how irrational that fear had been.

There was no other name for the emotion she roused in him, no other word that could encompass everything he'd come to feel for her. He thought maybe love wouldn't even quite cover it. It kept growing exponentially with every minute he spent with her.

And when Kayla looked at him the way she was right now, Ty thought maybe she'd agree with him. They were at the beginning of something that had the potential to go all the way.

"Look," she said, pointing over his shoulder.

A paraglider floated in the distance, skirting around the base of the monoliths like a curious butterfly. They looked so free, with nothing but blue sky behind them and red earth below.

"Can you imagine the rush?"

"Yeah," Ty said, watching her. "Totally."

After a quick pit stop at their casita, they joined the gang at the Adobe Café. Ty was surprised to see someone else sitting with Seb, Toni, Lilly, and Tiff.

"Jordan!" Kayla exclaimed.

Surprise shot through him. Jordan wasn't anything like the lawyers he'd dealt with before. The guy was attractive, with rich, henna-brown skin and bright eyes.

"Hello, darling." Jordan stood and accepted Kayla's crushing hug.

She leaned back, smiling brightly. "I didn't know you were coming."

"I finished the contract negotiations for Redbird early and thought I'd drive out and surprise you lot."

Jordan's accent caught him off guard. British, if he had to guess.

He turned to Ty. "You must be Tyrell." Jordan extended his hand.

Shaking it, Ty smiled. "Ty is fine."

"Ty, it is." Jordan gave him a slow once-over.

Ty knew that look—curiosity mixed with mild interest. He stepped closer to Kayla. "Nice to meet you."

Jordan's smile sharpened. "Nice to meet you too, Ty." He returned his attention to Kayla. "I approve."

She rolled her eyes, laughing as she patted his cheek. "The Jordan Igwe seal of approval. We can all sleep soundly now."

Lunch was handmade tamales, served with fresh guacamole and pico de gallo. Ty hadn't realized how hungry he was until he finished his third serving.

Kayla gave him an amused look. "Favorite food or just starving?"

"A little of both," he confessed.

"Now that our bellies are nice and full, we need to talk a little business," Jordan said. The transformation from trusted friend to trusted attorney was subtle, but Ty hadn't missed the way Jordan sat a little straighter in his chair or the way the others shifted to face him.

Ty wondered how much about him Jordan knew, how much Kayla had told him.

This group clearly respected him. Including Kayla, judging by how she wiped her mouth and sat back to give him her undivided attention. Mostly undivided. She still rested her hand on Ty's thigh, her thumb sweeping back and forth.

"First, congratulations on the single," Jordan said. "I'm not sure if any of you have been on Spotify, but you've already hit a couple of the curated lists."

"Really?" Tiff asked. "Rock on."

"It's a good sign. It means you'll get exposure alongside some of the other, more established artists with new releases," Jordan explained.

"It also gives Indio Fest attendees something to check out before you go onstage there next week," Seb added.

Jordan nodded, but his mouth grew tight around the edges. "True. Since we're on the subject of Indio, I have some news you're not going to like."

"Let me guess," Kayla said. "Candi's band has been added to the lineup?"

Jordan's eye widened, and he looked around the table. "Have you been on the Indio website already?"

"No," Lilly replied, picking up her phone.

Jordan watched her hands as she unlocked it and swept her fingers across the screen. "Sugar Habit is playing, yes," he confirmed.

"So?" Tiff said, tossing a tortilla chip onto her plate. "Who gives a shit? They can't slow our roll."

"Damn right they can't," Toni agreed. They exchanged a high five.

"Why are they above us in the lineup?" Lilly asked, her eyes sliding up to Jordan's face.

"What?" Kayla twisted to try and see Lilly's phone. "How? No one knows who they even are."

Jordan held up his hand in a calming gesture. "It's Andre. He pulled some strings to get them added to the lineup Sunday night."

"I thought we were playing closing night," Lilly said.

"Not anymore," Jordan ground out.

"Then, when are we on?" Toni asked.

Jordan sighed. "Friday."

"Friday...night?" Seb asked carefully.

"Late afternoon," Jordan clarified.

Ty expected another outburst from Tiff or even Kayla, but the group went silent. He didn't know much about festivals or how they worked, but he didn't think playing on the opening afternoon was the best spot for a band with the amount of buzz they'd generated.

"Fuck that guy," Tiff muttered.

"Tiffany," Jordan warned.

"No, seriously," she said, her voice getting louder. "Screw him. Andre knows fuck all about music. He's doing this to get off."

"No, he's doing this to generate press," Toni said. "He probably figures if he has two rival bands on the same label, he may as well profit from the rivalry at these events as well."

"Since when are we rivals with fucking Sugar Habit?" Kayla asked. "They didn't even exist five minutes ago."

Her fingers twitched against his thigh, and Ty pulled the straw out of his glass of water. He dried it and pressed it into her hand, where she immediately began tapping it against him.

It took a moment for her to realize it but, when she did, she turned and gave him a grateful smile before pressing a kiss to his cheek.

"Andre is becoming a real problem," Lilly said.

"No shit," Toni agreed.

"I'm trying to figure out the best way to deal with him. Legally," Jordan said. "In the meantime, you can't let him think he's pulling your strings."

"Isn't he, though?" Seb asked. "He's behind that shit in Detroit and that reporter, Sara, sniffing around Kayla, Tiff, and now Ty."

"She's trying to get to my grandfather," Ty said.

Kayla jerked upright and turned to him, eyes wide. "What?"

"What do you mean?" Jordan asked.

All eyes were on him, and Ty squirmed a little under the attention.

Kayla leaned into him. "What did she do?"

Ty explained about Peggy and Van but assured them that Sara Marsh wouldn't be allowed to get in to see his granddad at River Willows. "They have great security there, and they're aware of the situation." Ty hadn't told the staff at the facility why the reporter had been snooping. The last thing he wanted to do was bring undue attention to his granddad or jeopardize his place in his new home.

"That's good to know," Jordan said.

The conversation turned back to their record label and the Indio festival, but Ty couldn't shake the feeling that he'd stepped into the center of a spotlight he didn't belong in.

These were good people working together toward their dream. And he was their driver. He had nothing to contribute except unwanted attention from the media. What good could really come from his being with them?

When he was alone with Kayla, things were perfect. Amazing. But this—the nosy reporters, the inevitable media coverage, the speculation... He'd just crawled out from under his own microscope. If he and Kayla hadn't gotten together, he and Pop-Pop would be settling back into their quiet life in Philly.

Driving mall charters and high school bands?

Kayla sighed next to him. "Fuck all of this noise, we'll deal. Right?"

There was a chorus of "right" from the group, and then she turned her gorgeous brown eyes on Ty. Kayla's gaze made a quick circuit of his face, the tiniest frown creasing her otherwise smooth brow. After their walk on the trail, the sun had left a golden kiss on her skin and brought out the blond highlights in her copper hair.

"Right?" she asked, only loud enough for him to hear as the others chattered around them.

Ty drew her close and kissed her forehead, breathed her into his lungs, and was immediately settled. There was no point in questioning it anymore. It just was. And leaving her wasn't even an option. Ty was falling in love, and it felt so... "Right."

CHAPTER 33.

THE MOOD ON THE BUS was subdued. Kayla told herself it was because everyone was still blissed out from their time at the resort, though that had been cut short. They needed to be in California a day earlier than scheduled, thanks to YMI's Machiavellian bullshit, and Kayla added that to the long list of things she hated about being signed to a record label.

She lay in her bunk, thinking about Ty, the bus rocking gently around her. He was on her mind most of the time these days and had been for at least the last month. Kayla marveled at how quickly that had happened. She'd gone from single, with no thought toward finding anyone—it hadn't even been a blip on her radar—to finding Tyrell Baldwin. Someone she couldn't imagine her life without now.

It was just like it had been with this band. Somehow, Kayla had found her people. She knew she'd do pretty much anything to protect them, even if that meant giving them up. Because being who she was might be a liability that YMI could exploit for years to come. Every interview, every feature, would be about *the surprising fate of Little Miss Yolanda*. She could see the storyline unfold, from the tragic death of her brother, "a young talent," to scrutiny of her mother's "questionable advice" for other parents. Would her publisher drop her?

Kayla's real fear ran deeper than that. She worried she was

walking someone else's path. Zach's path. This—getting signed, touring, all of it—had been *his* goal. Had Kayla merely traded in her mother's dreams for that of her brother? She was even using the name *he'd* given her.

God.

Her brain was on fire.

Ty was driving, and she wanted to go to him and just...sit. Even if they didn't talk, she loved being in his presence, surrounded by his quiet energy. But even Ty had been more subdued than usual over the last day or so, and she thought she'd give him some space.

Kayla was restless, though, so she pulled her pair of Vic Firth sticks out of her back pocket and began to drum against the ceiling of her bunk. Playing was the only thing that settled her mind until she met Ty. And if she couldn't be with him, she had this.

She was startled when music filled the air, blasting from the speakers embedded in the walls of their house on wheels. It took a moment for her to recognize the band, Broken Pilots. Kayla smiled when she remembered the band would be on tour with them later in the year. She wondered if Ty might be able to come along then too. If he'd even want to. If she was still a part of all this.

"You're listening to KRCK 94.2, Los Angeles, and that was the latest from Broken Pilots," the announcer said. "Good news, kids, the band will hit the road this fall on their first world tour in over three years. Rumor has it, lead singer Jamie Bamber has fallen in love with a new band out of NYC and plans are underway to put them on the bill. The group is called the Lillys, and as promised, I have their debut single. Let's check it out. Here's 'Hurt U' by the Lillys."

There was an ear-crunching scream—which could only have come from Tiffany freaking Kim—followed by a chorus of shouts.

Kayla lay frozen as the song, *their* song, poured out of the speakers.

"Oh my God."

She got to her feet and went to the curtain that separated the common area from the sleeping area, taking a breath before she opened it, expecting a tangle of arms and bodies engulfed in a bouncing group hug. Kayla laughed at the sight before her.

Tiff had jumped up onto one of the love seats, a bottle of champagne in her hand.

Toni and Seb were making out like teenagers over by the sink.

Lilly sat in her usual spot, tucked against the window in the banquette, but a smile lit up her face in a way Kayla had never seen. She slid into the seat next to her.

Side by side, they watched as Tiff pulled Toni away from Seb and the pair began to sing along.

"No you never mean to hurt the one you loooooooove!" they belted. Badly.

"Good thing you're the lead singer."

Beside her, Lilly pressed against her shoulder and laughed. "Good thing."

"Are you playing air guitar, Seb?"

"You bet your ass." He grinned, his eyes bright and wild.

Tiff picked up a plastic spoon and held it up to her mouth like a microphone. "Who am I?"

She pulled a clip out of her hair, the dark strands spilling around her as she lip-synched through—Kayla was guessing here—an imitation of their leader.

As impressions went, it wasn't bad. She'd managed to approximate Lilly's penetrating gaze that seemed to hypnotize crowds wherever they went.

"Do I really look like that?" Lilly asked, grinning as she covered her eyes.

Kayla pulled her hand away. "No, you look like a goddess onstage. This one." She raised her voice so Tiff could hear her. "She doesn't have your natural grace."

"Fuck off," Tiff said, grinning wide. "You can't talk to me like that. I'm on the radio!"

"Yes you fucking are!" Seb replied and the three of them continued their dance-a-thon.

"It's real now," Lilly said, turning to meet Kayla's eyes.

She nodded. "Yep, it's real."

Lilly surprised her by leaning in and pressing a soft kiss to her lips.

Dazed, Kayla smiled when Lilly pulled back. "Wow."

Shrugging, the blond grinned, winking. It was so unlike her, and it spoke volumes. She sobered. "Sorry."

"Don't be." Kayla touched her mouth. "Ty, who?"

Lilly rolled her eyes, laughing. "You aren't fooling anyone. You're crazy about him."

No point in denying it. "I am."

"You'll have to thank him for this," Lilly said, pointing at the speakers. "We needed a boost."

"Rolling into Cali with a hit single," Tiff said as she hopped into the seat across from them. "Take that, Sugar Habit from Hell."

"Uh, did they change their name?" Kayla asked, smirking at her.

"I changed it for them." She took a swig from the bottle of champagne and offered it to Kayla.

The bubbles felt good going down. Kayla handed the bottle to Lilly.

"That was 'Hurt U' by the Lillys," the DJ said as the song ended. "Great tune if you ask me, but tell me what you think. At me on the bird app, drop a comment on our site, or request the song on our hotline. Next up is…"

The speakers went silent, and Kayla's gaze flicked toward the front of the bus.

"Good looking out, Tyrell!" Seb shouted.

"Congrats, guys," Ty replied via the intercom. "That was pretty fucking cool."

"I can't believe we have an original song on the radio," Toni said, breathless and clinging to Seb's side. Her smile was wide. "I never thought anything like that would happen to me."

"It didn't happen *to you*," Tiff said. "You *made* that shit happen. We all did."

"The motherfucking Lillys," Lilly said, the profanity sounding somehow elegant in her soft accent.

"Damn right," Seb said. "Now you'll have the crowd singing along with you."

"I can't wait for that," Kayla said, already imagining it.

"It doesn't matter what day we play on. We're going to rock the house," Toni said.

Tiff slapped her palm against the table. "Hell yeah."

And, God...Kayla loved these people.

Compared to the size of Indio Fest, all of the other festivals they'd played were miniscule. A few of them could have fit in the parking lot twice over. Kayla never really got nervous before a gig, but jet fighters fueled up in her stomach, readying for takeoff.

"Holy mother of grass," Tiff said, her face pressed to the window as they followed the long line of cars, buses, and vans to the area designated performers only.

"You're from this area, aren't you, Tiff?" Kayla asked. "You've never been to Indio Fest before?"

Tiff shook her head. "Couldn't afford it."

"It's outrageously expensive," Seb added. "It's why so many of the tickets are snatched up by the millionaire crowd. They come here and glamp."

"And raid other cultures for their festival wardrobes," Toni said.

"Appropriation for the win," Tiff said with a fake cheer. "Ugh. Asswipes."

"Not everyone who attends has money like that," Kayla said. "Some people save up all year to go to these huge festivals. Those are the people we'll play for, right?"

"Rock on," Tiff said. "Way to put it in perspective, Emily Dickinson."

"I told you not to call me that," Kayla huffed. "If you're going to give me a literary nickname, at least be creative about it."

Tiff's eyes flashed with amusement. "Oh, it's game on, then."

When the bus pulled into its designated spot, the group sprang into action. Kayla was used to them lugging their own gear from their vehicles to the backstage area, but Indio staff met them with a couple of large golf carts, ready to whisk them and their equipment away to where they needed to be.

Sunny California was living up to its name. It had to be well over ninety degrees, and it was still morning. Next to her on the cart, Ty's utility kilt fluttered in the breeze. Kayla's brain supplied the image of him wearing it with nothing underneath.

The crew dropped them off in front of a row of white tents.

"You don't have your own tent, but since it's early on, you can probably commandeer one as your own and not have to share for a while," their driver said. His thick Southern Cali drawl made the words sound like a second language.

The tent itself was huge and comfortably appointed, with throw rugs on the floor and poufs scattered around low tables. A long table along the back held aluminum buckets of ice, bottles of water, and bottles of beer. One had the airbrushed logo of a vodka company on the front and a bottle of the product chilled inside, nestled in ice along with a set of shot glasses. Upon closer inspection, Kayla realized the shot glasses were made of ice too.

"Fancy," Tiff said, grabbing a bottle of water that probably retailed for ten dollars. It made a snapping sound as she twisted the cap.

"Anyone up to exploring?" Seb linked his hand with Toni's. "We're gonna take a look around and see who's here."

"I'm in," Tiff said, gobbling up a slice of pizza.

Lilly joined them, leaving Kayla alone with the rest of their entourage, including Ty.

She found him chatting with Jordan.

"K, I was just telling Ty that I have a friend in Philly who might be able to help him get a little money out of the school," Jordan said.

"And I was telling Jordan I'm not interested in the money. I just want to protect my granddad," Ty replied. Kayla could tell he was a little agitated but still trying to be polite.

"Jory, take off your barrister wig for a minute and listen to what Ty's telling you."

Jordan sighed. "Yeah, okay. I'll drop it. But if you change your mind…"

"You know a guy." Ty smiled. "Thanks, man, I really do appreciate it."

"Any friend of Kayla's…" Jordan said as he backed toward the front flap of the tent. "Catch you two lovebirds later."

"He said you told him I wasn't interested in suing anyone," Ty said.

"I knew you were eager to put everything behind you. I never heard you once mention anything about getting retribution. It's always been about moving on and keeping your grandpa safe."

Ty stepped closer. He raised a hand and ran it over her hair, which she'd tied up into a ponytail—a futile attempt to deal with the heat.

"How is it that we've known each other for no time at all, and yet you understand me so well?"

"Karma?" she asked, slipping her arms around his neck and drawing him down.

"Kismet," he whispered against her lips.

CHAPTER 34.

TY WAS SO AMPED UP for the Lillys' set, he was ready to bounce out of his skin. His crew credentials gave him the option of watching from the wings—as had become his habit—or hanging out with the pit crew right in front of the stage. This time, he opted for the pit.

Behind him, thousands of festivalgoers had poured onto the vast field and claimed their spot. Ty knew most of them would be there the entire weekend, unwilling to give up their coveted position on the field. Many would draw blood to be where he was now.

He didn't know the band currently onstage, but they weren't bad. They played a mix of hard rock and dark wave that seemed to wash over the slowly filling audience.

The Lillys were up next, and Ty kept checking behind him to see what kind of crowd they'd have. The field wasn't even half-full. It was totally unfair. They'd worked their asses off only to get sidelined by some label politics.

"Who are you here with?" A big, beefy security guard pointed at the credentials hanging from Ty's belt loop.

He lifted the festival-branded pass and showed him the one beneath containing the Lillys' logo.

"Don't know 'em," the guy said, his voice booming over the music coming from the speakers right behind him.

"They're on next," Ty replied, shouting.

"Ohhh, I see," the guy said. "They got one of the load-in slots." At Ty's confused look, he pointed at the field. "They're the bands that play while people are still loading in."

"Oh."

"Tough gig, but you gotta get your foot in the door somehow, right?" The man slapped Ty's shoulder with one of his enormous paws. "Smart thinking, wearing that kilt—it's hot as Hades out here. Wish I'd thought of it. Looks good on ya."

"Uh, thanks." Ty grit his teeth. He wanted to tell him that the Lillys were more than background music. That they had been slated to play on Sunday—the biggest day of the festival. And that their single was going to dominate the charts.

Of course, he wasn't sure about that last part. He didn't even know why he felt so defensive of the band. It's not like he was actually *in* it. Ty only knew it was important to Kayla, so it was important to him. And he'd come to think of the others, of Seb and Toni, Tiff, Lilly, and even Jordan, as friends. They'd treated him as such.

"The Lillys are going to blow these people's minds," Ty said to the guy, who had returned his attention to the crowd.

"Sure, kid. I hope they do."

Twenty minutes later, the Lillys took the stage.

Kayla came out first. She wore a tiny handkerchief shirt he'd never seen her in before and had paired it with the black leather pants she favored. Ty loved the way they hugged her ample curves, but wondered if she'd overheat in this weather.

Ty called out to her, but she didn't hear him. He watched her climb behind her kit and check it, tightening the screws and adjusting the pedals. She looked so professional, so focused. And absolutely stunning.

Tiff and Toni took the stage next, each dressed in black jeans the stylist had sent them, which Kayla said had cost more than his entire wardrobe. Toni had paired hers with a purple crop top, and Tiff with a distressed Blondie tee. Both wore determined expressions as they picked up their instruments and settled them on their hips.

Toni turned up her guitar amp and hit a few notes.

Behind him, Ty heard some of the crowd cheer. He turned to look, noting that it had filled in a bit more in the last half hour. It was still only a fraction of the size of the audience the Lillys deserved.

Kayla raised her sticks over her head and tapped them together in a steady rhythm.

Ty expected the bass and guitar to kick in. When they didn't, he realized she was trying to get the crowd to clap along. He raised his hands above his head and clapped with her.

Kayla glanced down, smiling when she realized it was him. She shifted, and the sound of the bass drum joined in.

Slowly, people began to clap.

Toni sauntered to the front of the stage and plucked a single note that rang out over the rhythm. It seemed to go on forever as she stomped on a pedal and did something to the string that made the note bend and shimmy.

There were noises of approval from the crowd, people shouting "yeah!" and cheering her on.

She stomped on the pedal again, or maybe it was a different one—Ty didn't know how this shit worked—and began to strum over the chords.

Suddenly, the song coalesced for him. It was their viral hit cover of "I Burn." He let out a cheer, and a few people behind him echoed it. And by the time Tiff's bass kicked in, the clapping and whistling had grown louder.

Then Lilly stepped onto the stage, and Ty's jaw dropped.

He'd seen her live a couple of times now and knew she had a knack for showmanship, despite her stoic nature. But the woman who took the stage was someone else entirely.

Lilly didn't just walk. She prowled. She wore a skintight black catsuit that appeared gossamer thin, though he couldn't actually see through it. There was a long cape, made of the same material, attached at the shoulders that floated behind her. She was regal, godlike, and she looked down at the audience as if they were her subjects, her worshippers, and she was blessing them with her presence.

A roar rolled across the field. It started with the people suddenly pushed up against the barrier behind him and spread back toward the fenced-in border.

Ty watched, amazed, as the girls casually repeated the same chord progression, over and over, until they had the crowd under their spell. It was a master class in performance, and he lamented that there weren't more people there to witness it.

Lilly sang the opening line, making eye contact with most of the front rows, including Ty. He thought there might be a glimmer of recognition when she saw him, but her gaze only met his for a split second before she was on to the next person. He wondered if she saw any one individual at all.

The song kicked into another level when the chorus came around for the second time. During the bridge, Ty's eyes went to Kayla as she hit the drums with a ferocity that made his skin tighten.

She was fierce. A machine. Despite being nearly dwarfed by the kit she played, she wielded so much power over it.

By the time the song ended, the audience on the field had doubled in size. He had to step out of reach of the arms straining over the barrier as security personnel came over to warn people to stay back.

"Okay," Ty's new friend, the security guard, said to him. His smile was huge. Appreciative. He nodded, clearly impressed. "*Okay.* These girls are fire."

"Duuuuuuuuude!" Tiff screamed when they were all back in their designated tent. "My dudes, we fucking killed that shit! Did you hear that crowd out there?"

Kayla was laughing. "We were there too, Tiff, so yeah. We heard them."

"Yeah, babes." Tiff threw her arms around Kayla, who stumbled back a bit before righting them both. "That was awesome. We are awesome. I can't believe we did that."

"You guys sounded better than ever," Seb said, smiling from ear to ear.

"It was Lilly," Toni said, wiping her forehead with a hand towel. "Girl, where were you hiding all of that?"

"No shit," Kayla agreed. "I mean, we all know you're sexy AF, but that? That was some next level, the goddess Aphrodite shit."

"Freyja," Lilly said, smiling as she peeled the top of her catsuit down. She wore nothing underneath, and her small breasts were high, with rosy nipples at their peaks.

Only Toni averted her eyes, busying herself with her guitar.

"What's a fraya?" Tiff asked, grabbing a bottle of water from one of the buckets.

"Freyja is the Norse goddess of love," Lilly replied. She pulled a black tank top over her head and smoothed it down before rolling the rest of the catsuit off her long legs. At least she was wearing underwear. "If you're going to call me a god," Lilly continued, "at least make me a Norse god. The Greeks and Romans aren't the only pantheons. They aren't even the oldest."

"Goddess of love, eh?" Toni said, her tone teasing.

"Love, beauty..." Lilly stepped into a pair of capris and yanked them up. "Sex," she added with a toss of her damp hair. "And war."

"I like it," Tiff proclaimed, handing out bottles of water.

"Speaking of war," Jordan said as he entered the tent. "Ty, could I talk to you for a moment?"

"Sure." Ty looked at Kayla, who had changed into a pair of leggings and a Lillys tee. He held out his hand to her.

She shook her head. "I don't want to intrude."

Ty smiled at her. "You never could."

Jordan led them to a quiet area behind the tent. His expression was pinched, guilt warring with something else.

"What's up?" Kayla asked him.

Jordan looked back and forth between them and took a deep breath. "Right, so...I did a thing. In my defense, I sort of started the thing before I actually met you, Ty, and I didn't think much of it, but now..." He held up his hands in supplication. "So, I'm sorry in advance."

"Slow down," Kayla said.

"What did you do?" Ty asked.

Jordan seemed to collect himself, and suddenly the attorney in him took over. "I passed your name along to that friend in Philly I told you about. I know, I know," he said, holding up his hands. "You don't want money, but it came up when we were talking. He was actually my flatmate at uni, but anyway. He's good, and he specializes in cases like yours."

Ty's gut clenched. "And?"

"There's a lot you don't seem to know about how your case was handled."

"What do you mean?"

"You were released after evidence came to light that cleared you. Is that your understanding?"

"No," Ty replied slowly. "There was no evidence, so the charges were dropped. To be honest, I didn't care. I barely remember any-thing from the meeting with the judge, other than him telling me I was free to get back to my life. I just wanted out of the whole mess. I wanted...I wanted it to be over."

"And I bet they were counting on that," Jordan said. "The thing is, as I understand it, you were essentially cleared. But your arrest is still a matter of record."

"What's the difference?" Kayla asked.

"I'm not an expert, but a dismissal usually means the police failed to build a case. They don't always come right out and say that a suspect is innocent. In Ty's case, the whole thing should have been expunged from his record. Like it never happened," Jordan explained.

"That's what they told me, that my record had been cleared," Ty said.

"Only it wasn't," Jordan told him.

"But...I was free to go wherever I wanted, without supervision," Ty argued, his head spinning. "Merry recanted her story."

"They lied," Jordan said. "For whatever reason, you still have a record. And I don't doubt that's why you've had such trouble with other schools, finding work before Aaron brought you on. Didn't you ever follow up with the precinct? Your attorney should have at least done that much."

"My lawyer was...not great. All I cared about was getting back to my life," Ty said, shaking his head. *And I buried my fucking head in the sand.* "Fuck."

Ty hadn't realized he'd let go of Kayla's hand until she sandwiched his between hers. She squeezed, and he exhaled the breath that had been trapped inside his lungs.

"Not to sound selfish," Jordan said, "but clearing this up would also help us, help Kayla. So my motivations weren't entirely altruistic when I reached out to Rami. Full disclosure."

"No, I get it," Ty said. He was still trying to process all of the information. He looked at Kayla. "What do I do?"

"Don't worry about me or the band. Do what's right for you," she said, looking up at him with such trust and belief. It floored him.

"I'm so fucking in love with you," he said, unable to stop the words from spilling out into the world.

Kayla's eyelashes fluttered a few times as she held his gaze. She swallowed before pulling her bottom lip between her teeth.

Ty didn't need her to respond. He could see his own heart reflected in her eyes. Not for the first time, Ty got a little lost in them. They shined with hope, respect, and—yeah—love. For him. He was so fucking grateful to have her in his life.

"I, uh, feel like I shouldn't be here for this part," Jordan said.

Ty somehow managed to tear his gaze away from Kayla's, even though he wanted to kiss her soundly. He turned to Jordan.

"You really think your friend Rami would help me sort this out? I mean, I don't have much cash."

Waving a hand as if to dismiss Ty's concerns, Jordan smiled wide. He pulled out his phone. "He's set aside tomorrow afternoon to meet with you."

"Tomorrow?"

"I know it's a Friday, but city hall will be open. I just texted him that you're onboard, and don't worry about the money right now," Jordan said, his fingers flying across the touchscreen on his phone. "I am putting you on the red-eye from LAX. It leaves at ten fifty, so you have plenty of time to get there. David will cover you behind the wheel, and we'll contract a local driver for his relief."

Ty was speechless.

"Are you sure you want to do this, Ty?" Kayla asked. "It might mean more press coverage and more people like Sara Marsh poking around."

"It should shut her up actually," Jordan said. "But Kayla's got a point. Don't do it for anyone but you. But if I were you, I'd want the slate wiped clean."

Ty thought about what he had gone through—the sneers and the public scrutiny, the court of public opinion that had him tried and convicted before any evidence had even been presented. He thought about his granddad and how hard he'd fought for him. Ty thought about the hundreds—probably thousands—of others in his position who didn't have the resources being offered to him. He thought about the support he'd turned down—all the help that could have cleared this up months ago.

But if he had, he never would have met Kayla. And doing this, sorting out his own mess, would help her situation too.

"Book the flight," Ty said. "I'm going home."

CHAPTER 35.

KAYLA'S PHONE WAS STUBBORNLY DARK and silent. She'd woken up to a text from Ty, telling her he'd landed safely and would reach out later in the day. That had been six hours ago. Since then, she'd met dozens of musicians—people Kayla never thought she'd share the same bill with, much less the same bowl of backstage M&M's. She should have been mingling like Toni, networking like Seb and Jordan, or at least taking a ton of selfies like Tiff, for her nonexistent Instagram account.

Instead, she paced along the outer wall of the hospitality tent, worrying about things over which she had no control.

"There you are." Tiff's head popped around the corner of the tent. She walked over and leveled her with a look. "What are you doing out here? All the action is inside."

"Needed some air," Kayla lied.

"Oh, I thought it was because your boyfriend hasn't called you yet today. Silly me." Tiff pursed her lips, and a bright pink bubble pushed through them. Chomping down, she popped it.

It was on the tip of Kayla's tongue to say Ty wasn't her boyfriend. Not because he wasn't, but because she'd never called him that.

She hadn't called anyone that in longer than she could remember. After his impromptu declaration, Kayla hadn't had time to process her own feelings, much less respond. They needed to talk, needed to establish parameters or whatever. That would be the adult thing to do, even if her heart was fully onboard with the whole falling hard and fast thing.

Tiff sighed. "Come on, you know I'm only teasing. I'm happy for you." She slid her arm around Kayla's waist. "Having second thoughts about staying for the rest of the festival?"

"No," Kayla said, putting her arm around Tiff. They were about the same height, with just enough of a difference for Kayla to rest her cheek against Tiff's hair. "I think it's good for the band to be seen here and to meet people."

"Everyone is talking about us, especially Lilly," Tiff said. "They keep coming up to her. Some of them just want to fuck her, I can tell."

Kayla released Tiff and looked at her. "What do you mean, you can tell?"

"You know what I'm talking about." Tiff put her hand on her hip and made a show of checking Kayla out. "They have an entire conversation with you but never look you in the eye?"

Kayla snorted. "I can't see Lilly putting up with that for long."

"Not for one minute," Tiff said, laughing. "It's been fun watching her shoot the poor souls down one by one." She pulled lightly on Kayla's arm. "Come back inside. There's a rumor Queen B might show up."

"Wait, is she playing?" Kayla's heart skipped a beat.

"No, but she's in LA this week, and someone said she told the festival she might come hang out today or tomorrow."

"No shit," Kayla said.

"Come inside," Tiff begged, pulling a little harder. "Keep me company. You know I hate being alone."

It was a big tent, but it still made Kayla feel claustrophobic once they were back inside. It was one of four hospitality tents spread out in the area designated for performers. As far as festival facilities went, it was definitely nicer than most of the places they'd played on the tour. But some things were ubiquitous—like the unpredictable weather.

This time, it wasn't the rain but the wind that caused delays in the programming. Everywhere Kayla wandered, people complained about playing through flying debris.

"I swear, that goddamned tower almost fell on my head!" one guy exclaimed. "Thank Christ for the crew. Fucking saved my life, I swear. I should find those guys and fly them to Hawaii or something. Shit."

Tiff had abandoned her not long after they entered, so Kayla walked around until she spotted Toni and Lilly, who waved her over.

"This is…" Toni looked around at the clumps of people drinking, smoking, toking, and laughing all around them.

"This is nothing," Lilly said. "I once went to a post-Grammys party in Santa Monica that lasted for three days."

"Three days?" Kayla asked. "What did you do for three days? Or do I wanna know?"

"Oh, I didn't stay past the first night." Lilly shook her head, her gaze following a trio that stumbled by, arms around each other. "But the stories that came out of there are epic. Ask anyone here about Malone's NoMa party. It's become legend."

"I heard Malone was here somewhere," Tiff said as she bounded over to them.

"Let's go check out the other tents." Lilly nodded toward the exit.

"I'm gonna go find Seb and Jordan and see who they've been talking to," Toni said. "Catch you later."

The rest of them walked down the lane to the next tent. It was just as loud and overcrowded as the one they'd come from, so they moved on to the next.

"Is that Billie Joe Armstrong?" Tiff asked, her eyes wide.

"Yeah," Kayla replied, wishing Ty were there. On their last night at the resort in Sedona, he'd told her about the Green Day poster he had on his wall as a kid. "You think he'd let us snag a photo with him?"

Lilly gave her a slow blink. "Only one way to find out." She linked arms with Kayla and Tiff, and they walked in together.

The air was blessedly cool inside, and it wasn't wall-to-wall people like the other two. Music from the main stage played on wireless speakers that sat in the back corners, but at a volume that allowed actual conversation.

"This is, like, the adult tent," Tiff said as they passed the food and drinks tables. "Look, they have wine and cheese." She let Lilly go and grabbed a toothpick, stabbing a cube of white cheese and popping it into her mouth, already scanning for her next morsel. "Oh my God, mini quiche!"

Lilly smiled and shook her head.

"Leave it to Tiff to flip out over the food and not the fact that Billie and Finneas are sitting right over there," Kayla said, trying not to stare at the famous brother-sister duo.

"Oh, *faen*," Lilly cursed under her breath.

"What?" Kayla took in the suddenly blazing fire behind Lilly's eyes and followed her gaze across the room.

It didn't take long to spot Candi Fairmount. Their former guitarist had changed her look up a bit, but the neon pink hair that had been her staple ever since Kayla had met her remained. "Shit," Kayla muttered.

Candi looked thin, and even her flawless makeup couldn't completely hide the bags under her eyes. A sliver of compassion threatened to uncurl itself in Kayla's heart. Deep down—very, very deep down, somewhere inside Candi's twisted soul—Kayla knew there was a decent person. She hoped, anyway. She hated the idea that someone she'd once considered a friend, someone gifted with that much raw talent, could be such a horrible human being.

Unsurprisingly, a small group of photographers followed Candi and her new bandmates through the area. The heiress-turned-rock-star was right in her element, chin high with an extra swing in her step.

Kayla had to hand it to her: like a cat, Candi always seemed to land on her feet.

As if on cue, Candi's step faltered as she registered the Lillys' presence, but she recovered quickly, adopting an air of disinterest that Kayla could almost admire.

"I was kind of hoping she wouldn't show, or at least not until tomorrow."

"Same," Lilly said. "But she's here, so we should say hello. The last thing any of us want is to give any fuel to feed Andre's girl band rivalry bullshit."

Kayla squared her shoulders. "Agreed." She reached for Tiff, who had picked up two hunks of cheese, one in each hand.

"I don't know the difference between Manchego and Brie." She frowned at the labels. "And someone mixed these all up."

"Brie's the soft cheese," Kayla replied. "But never mind that, we have a situation."

"What sort of situation?" Tiff shoved a chunk of Brie into her mouth.

Stepping behind her, Kayla took her by the shoulders and directed her to turn. She knew right away when Tiff spotted Candi because her shoulders went tight under her hands.

"Fucking fuck," Tiff said, tossing the chunk in her hand aside and turning to Lilly with a nervous expression. "Are you okay?"

"I'm fine," Lilly said. Her voice was even, her expression neutral. "Let's go say hi."

Kayla and Tiff exchanged a look but followed Lilly across the tent to where Candi sat with a group of people.

"And I'm like...mate, you've got it all wrong. Me and him, we ain't trying to do nothing untoward. We was just having a bit o' fun."

The storyteller was a tall, lanky guy with sickly pale skin who had somehow folded his spindly limbs into a lotus position on one of the beanbag chairs. Around him, the group of listeners laughed, including Candi.

"I can't believe you made it out of there alive," she said.

"It was close, especially since I had me bollocks out swinging in the breeze!" The guy finished to more raucous laughter.

"Hey, you played early yesterday, right?" a woman asked Lilly. "Great set."

"Thank you," Lilly replied, her eyes on Candi, who seemed to take a deep breath before she looked up at her.

"There she is," Candi said. "Guys, this is the soon-to-be famous—or so they say—Lilly Langeland, bandleader extraordinaire." She made a snide sound, much to the amusement of her hangers-on, before turning back. "Lilly and I go way back, don't we, babycakes?"

"From your old band, right?" the storyteller said. "The Lillys?"

"You used to play with them?" the other woman asked.

"Before Andre, he's the head of YMI Records, literally begged me to start my own group, yeah," Candi replied, waving a hand in the air. "I got my start with these gals. By the way, where's your new guitarist? Tammy? Tanya?"

"Toni," Kayla said. *Oh, it's going to be like that?*

"Is she still here?" someone asked. "I wanted to tell her that solo she did on your last song was ridonkulous."

"Are you the band with the Black chick that plays guitar?" another guy asked. "That was *wild*."

"Wild, why?" Lilly asked, one golden brow arching.

The guy's grin faltered, his eyes darting around the group

looking for support. "I just meant...you know...she's terrific." He gave a nervous laugh.

"Well, I'm super sorry I missed it," Candi said as she got to her feet. "The label booked us on a photo shoot for the cover, and it ran way too long."

"What cover?" Tiff asked.

"Oh, hey, Tiffany. I didn't see you!" Candi said, blowing her an air kiss. "The album cover, of course."

"When's it due out, Can?" the storyteller asked.

"We're thinking late fall or early winter." Candi held a finger up to her lips. "But don't say anything to anyone, okay? Cone of silence." She turned to Lilly.

"Looking forward to hearing it," Lilly said. "And your set tomorrow."

Candi blinked. "You're sticking around for that?"

"Of course," Lilly replied. "Wouldn't miss it for the world."

"Can't wait," Kayla said.

"Yeah," Tiff said, stepping around Candi to get back to the food. "Break a leg." When they were out of earshot, she added, "Or both arms. Same diff."

CHAPTER 36.

TY SAT ACROSS THE DESK from Rami Hamed and let out a deep breath. It felt like the first he'd taken in nearly two years. After feeling…well, not much of anything at all for so long, it was strange to experience everything all at once.

Pain, anger, and disbelief, but also hope and the joy he'd found with Kayla. God, he wished she were with him now. He wished he'd asked Van to come, but he'd been afraid of more disappointment, despite everything Jordan had said the day before.

"You doing all right?" Rami asked. He was around the same age as Jordan, early thirties, with ink-black hair, smooth copper skin, and Hollywood good looks. Like a young Omar Sharif in his granddad's favorite classic movies. "Do you want some water? Or maybe something stronger?"

Ty shook himself. "I'm fine, thanks, I, uh…" He ran a hand over his face. "It's a lot to take in. I feel like I'm in the lost pilot of *Law and Order: College Campus.*"

Rami made a disgusted sound. "Unfortunately, things don't always tie themselves up in a neat little bow in real life." His British accent was more clipped and precise compared to Jordan's rounded drawl. "For one thing, it isn't as simple as identifying the good guys and the bad ones. Rather it becomes a matter of distilling truth from opinion. Or from bias. In your case, well…you are a victim of some regrettable circumstances, some of which are criminal and others systemic. Which, I suppose"—he seemed to think about it—"can often be one and the same."

"What are the next steps?" Ty asked, bracing himself for the answer. "Do we need to request a...hearing with the board of directors at the university? Or do I go back to the police?"

Rami burst into action, pulling his keyboard close and attacking it with quick, nimble fingers. "Honestly, I don't think you'll need to see the inside of another chamber. I have a friend at the DA's office, and I think I might know someone at the university. As much as people are slow to right the wrongs of a system that's been broken for too long, they also don't want to invite the spotlight if they can just as soon avoid it."

"But my case wasn't exactly a quiet one for either the department or the school."

"Most of the press was localized," Rami said. "Believe me, if it had garnered more national attention, you would most assuredly become the poster boy for this new fair play initiative. From what you and I have discussed this afternoon, that isn't something you want. Yes?"

"Yes. I mean, no. I don't want that. I want...the opposite of that. No press, no...nothing."

Rami nodded once. "Then that's what we will aim for. All right? But, Tyrell, if it's unavoidable, do you still want to pursue this?"

Ty could already feel his pulse racing at the mere thought of reporters knocking on his door again, of them tracking his granddad down at River Willows. He'd have to warn Van.

"I need to discuss this with my grandfather. Could I call you later today?"

"Of course." Rami plucked a business card from the small brass holder on the desk and flipped it over. "I'm writing down my personal mobile," he said, scribbling. He handed it to Ty. "Ring me if you have any more questions, or just shoot me a text."

"Thank you, I..." Ty's throat thickened, choking off his words as he took the card with shaking fingers. "I'm really grateful for this, for you, and for Jordan."

Rami's eyes softened. He leaned across the desk and put a hand on Ty's arm. "You seem like a good guy, and Jordan doesn't vouch for just anyone. I know this has all been...rather difficult for you. And for that, I'm truly sorry."

"Why?" Ty asked. "It's not like you had anything to do with it."

Rami sat back and sighed. "I love the law. I must, or I wouldn't have spent the best years of my youth studying two entirely different judicial systems." He laughed softly. "In theory, the law is pure. It is indifferent. It is—at the sake of sounding like an acolyte—just. Its application should be blind, but of course, it isn't. Hasn't ever been, despite all our efforts to make it so. Any chance I get to help Lady Justice find her way, I take. And your situation will help with that. You will help others, simply by standing up for what's right."

"You make me sound like some sort of freedom fighter," Ty said.

"Well," Rami said, smiling. "You are still fighting for your freedom, are you not?"

Ty opened the front door expecting to play his usual guessing game of "what's Van cooking today?" It took a moment of standing in the empty, silent kitchen for him to remember Pop-Pop didn't live in their Nicetown rowhome anymore.

He braced his hands on the back of one of the kitchen chairs and took a moment to get his bearings. Ty had never been able to sleep much on planes, and last night—this morning?—had been no exception. Exhaustion made his limbs heavy and, evidently, had fogged up his brain. He needed to speak to his grandfather, and a phone call wouldn't do.

After a quick shower, he walked the few blocks to the Broad Street Line and headed downtown. Forty-five minutes later, he was signing in at the front desk. River Willows was a nice place, with great amenities and clean, modern architecture and decor, but Ty couldn't shake the feeling that this might be where his granddad drew his last breath. Or that he might not be there for him when that happened. That, in Van's last moment on earth, he'd be surrounded by strangers.

God. Ty needed sleep before his thoughts truly spiraled out of control.

"You made good time." Pop-Pop's voice went a long way toward lifting his spirits, and Ty met his granddad with a big smile and an extended hug. "I just signed up for swimming lessons."

Ty released him, eyeing him carefully as concern overtook him. "You already know how to swim," he said. "You taught Dad, didn't you?"

"Of course I *know* how to swim. Could've been born a fish." His granddad started walking, and Ty fell in step beside him. "I taught your dad when he was around seven or eight. Used to take him to the Y on North Broad. Kept him off the streets in the summertime."

"Then why are you taking swim lessons?"

Van stopped and gave Ty a baffled look. "They're SCUBA lessons. They're bringing in an instructor from the aquarium. Why would I take swim classes if I already know how to swim?" His granddad shook his head and resumed his trek toward the elevators.

"But you said..." Ty scrubbed his hands over his eyes. "Never mind. That sounds awesome."

"Swimming lessons," his granddad muttered when they stepped onto the elevator. "I could teach that class myself."

"I'm sure you could." Ty leaned against the wall and watched the numbers go up. It was a mid-rise, so the journey was quick. He followed Van through his new, sleeker front door.

It was odd, visiting. Van had gotten new furniture to fit his new life, his new space. The couch was light beige instead of dark burgundy. The walls were eggshell white, rather than the hunter green and canary yellow his grandmother had picked out before he was born.

It was…nice. But Ty didn't know where to sit or where to drop his bag. Or whether he should take off his shoes, as Van had when they walked in. He decided to err on the side of caution and left his Docs by the door.

They still had some dust from the festival fields he'd been on. That reminded Ty he hadn't gotten back to Kayla.

"You look dead on your feet," his granddad said.

"I'm all right." Ty walked over to the island and leaned against it, afraid that if he sat down, he'd fall asleep.

"If I'd known you were coming, I would have asked you to bring a box from the house." Pop-Pop poured Ty a small glass of orange juice. "Drink this."

"You know I hate this stuff." Ty grimaced but drank it anyway.

"Oh. Right. Well, come, sit."

They moved to the couch, and Ty was already regretting that choice. Its oversized, fluffy cushions sucked him down, and his head fell back. He stared at the ceiling.

"What's this about a lawyer?"

Blinking, Ty lifted his head and tried to focus. "The band I've been working for, their lawyer has a friend here in the city who wants to take up my case."

His granddad sat up and turned to him. "I thought you were dead set against a lawsuit."

"I was. I am. No lawsuit, at least not if we can avoid it." Ty explained everything that Rami had said, including the likelihood of him being thrust back into the public eye.

"Seems to me that might happen anyway," Van said. "That

reporter won't be the only one looking your way, especially if you and that girl of yours get serious. What's her name again?"

"Kayla," Ty replied, unable to keep the grin off of his face.

"Kayla," Van repeated. "You met her folks yet?"

"Uh, we're a little new for that. It's only been, like…" Ty thought about it and couldn't believe it hadn't even been two months since they met. "A minute."

"When you know, you know," his granddad said sagely.

"Besides, I get the feeling I wouldn't be their first choice, at least not her mother's."

"Well, then she's not too bright. You're the best man I know." His granddad patted his knee. "But about this lawyer, you trust him?"

"I told you. I trust Kayla. She trusts Jordan. Jordan trusts Rami." Ty shrugged.

"That's quite a circle of trust."

Ty met his granddad's gaze. "Before I move forward, I need to know how you feel about this."

Van barked out a laugh. "Me? Son, I've been trying to get you to hold those folks' feet to the fire since you got home from the halfway house. I'm all in, don't worry about me."

"I don't want to disrupt your life again, not now—when you're settling in here. Making new friends."

Frowning, his granddad turned to him. "Tyrell…you honestly think I could live here, live—what do you kids say? Live my best life? You think I could be in here going about my business, knowing you could finally get out from under this shadow that's been hanging over you, and not want to do everything in my power to help?"

Ty was tired. Too tired to stop the tear that slipped down his cheek. He didn't trust his voice, so he shook his head.

"Aww, son." His granddad pulled him into a hug, rubbing his back the way he did when Ty was a kid, sick with the flu. He rocked him gently and murmured soothing words in his ear. "You've been through so much." His voice was thick with emotion. "If someone can help, let them help. Don't worry about me. I'll be fine. Okay?"

Ty nodded and sat up, wiping at the wetness on his cheeks.

"When's the last time you slept?" His granddad stood up and went to a closet by the door.

"Um..."

"That's what I thought. Lie down." Pop-Pop didn't give him a chance to object, and Ty didn't think he had the energy to fight him.

He stretched out on the couch and let his granddad cover him with a throw.

"Don't let me sleep too long," he murmured, letting himself sink into the darkness.

Ty missed his reply. He was out within seconds.

CHAPTER 37.

"THE SYSTEM IS SO FUCKED," Ty grumbled. "You wouldn't believe the stories I found online. Jordan's friend, Rami, does pro bono work for a nonprofit that does nothing but help people trapped in bad circumstances. Some are innocent. Others are guilty of small infractions but have been handed down harsh sentences for no other reason than the whims of a prejudiced judge or the work of an incompetent defense."

"Sounds familiar," Kayla said.

"No kidding. The more I learn, the angrier I get." Ty let out a harsh breath. "I can't believe I thought it was okay not to push back on what happened to me. It could have been so much worse."

"Are you planning to bring a case against the school? Or the department?" Kayla asked.

"Rami expects everyone will want to settle out of court," Ty said. "The new DA is actually trying to clean up some of the mess left behind by her predecessors."

"Not that any of this could ever be considered good circumstances, but at least there's someone in office who acknowledges the problem and wants to fix it."

"Exactly," Ty said, then sighed. "I miss you."

Kayla melted a little. "I miss you too. I'm actually sitting in your seat."

"In my seat?" There was a smile in his voice.

"I'm on the bus."

"Are you guys leaving early?" he asked. Kayla didn't miss the hopeful note in his question.

"Nah, we're resolved to stay and support Candi's new band, or at least appear to."

"Oh."

"But I missed you, and the bus is sitting out here in the field, empty and quiet, and..." Kayla blushed.

"And?"

"And I kinda wanted to be in your space."

Ty shuffled on the other end. When he spoke again, his voice was low. "Kayla, are you telling me you're sitting in the driver's seat of the coach because you wanted to feel closer to me?"

"No, silly!" Kayla laughed, then whispered, "I'm telling you I think about you all the damn time, but especially in this big leather seat. Remember my fantasy?"

He groaned. "Kayla...you're killing me. That's it, I'm heading to the airport."

"Aren't you visiting your grandpa today?"

"Yeah, but... Jesus. He's a grown man. I should have caught the next plane back out there."

Kayla actually giggled for the first time since she was twelve. "You are incorrigible."

"Me?" he asked incredulously. "You're one to talk, got me three thousand miles away thinking about you sitting on my lap. Okay, okay." Ty cleared his throat. "I need to focus on something else before Van gets back from his doctor's appointment. How was it seeing Candi again?"

Kayla sobered. "She's still Candi."

"Sounds like I'm not missing anything, not having met her."

"Nope," Kayla agreed. "Not a damn thing. Get some rest."

"Will do. Later, Red."

Kayla leaned forward on the big steering wheel, one hand on the console, her other hand supporting her cheek. She tried to think about the work the band needed to do when they got back east, but all she could see in her head were images of Ty sitting in the driver's seat, the dark cab swallowing his smiling face as he leaned toward the display to check the map.

She spied Ty's notebook, the one she'd given to him, in the pocket on the door and picked it up. After a moment of hesitation, she opened it and found the first third had already been used, the pages full of Ty's neat, elegant handwriting. His poetry.

I woke up this morning strong and fast
Realized you're who I've wanted
I want this to last
And I've known it from the start
And you've seen me from the start
And we've felt it from the start
You revived my dying heart

Kayla was wrong; this wasn't a poem.
These were lyrics.

Indio Fest had areas cordoned off on either side of the main stage where performers and their guests could watch the act currently on the deck. There was a snack bar and a drink bar. The bank of port-a-potties put all other port-a-potties to shame. Clean and spacious, with little flower vases and scent pods, it was almost as nice as the bathroom in her North Jersey apartment.

The last artist wasn't one Kayla was familiar with, but she'd enjoyed their set. It had been a little bit disco, a little bit rock-and-roll, and a whole lot of catchy hooks.

"Here you go." Seb handed Kayla a hard seltzer. "All they had was mango."

"It all tastes the same," Kayla said. "I like to think of it as adult soda."

"That's just—"

"Excuse me!" A short girl with green hair ran up to Kayla and Seb. She wore a blue festival crew shirt and a frantic look on her face. "Sorry, are you with the Lillys? You're in the band, aren't you? Please tell me you're with that band."

"Yeah," Kayla replied.

"What's up?" Seb asked, switching over to his manager's voice.

"Oh, thank Darwin." The staffer exhaled with apparent relief. She lifted the walkie to her mouth. "I found them."

"What's wrong?"

"Nothing if you tell me your band can be onstage in ninety minutes," the staffer said.

"What do you mean onstage?" His gaze narrowing, Seb raised a hand and waved Jordan over.

"The Flaming Threes had to pull out, something about a trashed hotel room, a baby tiger, and the cops. I dunno." She waved it off as if it were nothing. "Anyway, if it were the B stage, it wouldn't be a big deal. We'd just throw an extra DJ set in there. But this is the main stage, on closing night, and we can NOT have an empty slot. We just..." She took a deep breath.

"Calm down." Jordan handed her a bottle of water.

After cracking the seal, she took several big gulps. "Thanks. Okay, as I was saying. Sorry, can we walk and talk?"

Seb grabbed Toni's and Lilly's attention and beckoned them to follow as the staff member lead them around the back of the stage to the performer area. They skirted around stacks of equipment cases and stepped over enormous ropes of bound, black cable. It was chaos.

"You want the Lillys to perform again?" Jordan asked.

"We can do it," Lilly said, jogging alongside him. "Not a problem."

"But not for free," Jordan added.

"Of course, not," the girl said. "Nothing in this world is free, least of all filling a main stage slot at a festival this size. You'll basically get to name your price. Anyway, we'll send some of our people with some of your people to get your gear." She stopped abruptly, and Tiff almost ran into her.

Kayla shot out a hand to steady her.

"How long is the set?" Seb asked.

"We'd love fifty minutes, but we'd be okay with forty-five."

"Do we have fifty minutes' worth of material?" Toni asked only loud enough for Kayla and Tiff to hear.

Tiff shrugged. "If we add a couple of the tunes we haven't played out yet."

"We can do forty," Lilly announced.

The girl bit her lip, then lifted the walkie. "The Lillys are up for a forty-minute set, and possibly an encore?" She looked up hopefully. Lilly nodded. "Copy that. We're en route."

The next hour was a blur. Toni, Kayla, Tiff, and Lilly were driven back to the bus to hash out a revised setlist and change, which they did in record time, thanks to them sticking to the basics. They didn't have time to fuss over preselected outfits. Ripped jeans, their favorite tees, hair wild—totally rock-and-roll. It reminded Kayla of when Zach first started playing in bands. This was all about the music and the opportunity that had just fallen into their laps.

"Thank you so much for stepping in last-minute." Julian Gadea, the director of Indio Fest, met them at the largest of the hospitality tents. He was tall and thin, with bright gray eyes and olive skin that had seen way too much sun. "It's actually a blessing in disguise for me. Everyone has been talking about your set Friday afternoon, and I've been kicking myself for switching you out."

"Yeah, that wasn't cool," Toni said, narrowing her eyes at him.

He held up his palm. "It was totally my bad. Though, to be fair, YMI didn't make it easy for me to say no. They were adamant that Sugar Habit go on today." He added, "Which is fucked up, if you ask me. Not one but two bands full of hella fine chicks? You'd think they'd want to flaunt that shit. But nope." He shrugged.

"Fucking Andre," Tiff muttered.

Seb gave her a warning look.

Kayla wanted to double back to that *hella fine chicks* comment but let it drop. It didn't matter that he was only giving them this opportunity because of what they looked like rather than how good they sounded. It only mattered what they did with the moment.

"Won't YMI give you shit for putting the Lillys on today anyway?" she asked instead.

Julian shrugged. "I had no choice. I sold a fuck ton of tickets, and these people want nonstop music. But also, dude, you guys... I heard your single on the radio last night. It is fiyah! I want to be able to say I called it when you break big."

"Thanks," Lilly said. "And thanks for giving us this chance."

"It's not a gamble," Julian said. "And it's worth the extra five grand to see you guys live since I missed you on Friday. Lilly, I heard you were practically naked up there." His gaze swept over her. "Shame I missed that."

Before Lilly could unleash her vicious tongue on the asshole, one of the stage managers hopped down the steps. "Hey, Jules."

"My man! Good job this weekend," Julian said as they bro-hugged. "This is Brian. He'll hook you up."

"Weekend's not over yet," Brian said. He turned to the group. "Hey, Lillys. I'm looking forward to hearing you guys again. A couple of things to note—if anything goes wrong with any of the equipment, raise your right pinky finger above your head like this. Someone will take care of it. Security has been instructed to keep anyone who isn't in the band or wearing credentials out of the wings and out of the pit. Sundays at Indio, people get a little..." Brian circled his finger near his temple.

"They're all saturated by then," Julian said.

"Saturated?" Toni asked.

"Booze and drugs," Seb replied.

"That's pretty much it," Brian said. "Have fun. This will be a little different than Friday afternoon. Oh, and when you get the signal for your last song, finish up and get off stage as quickly as you can so that..." He looked at the tablet in his hand. "Sugar Habit?" He shrugged. "Don't know 'em, but there's not much turnaround time between you, so try not to crash into each other as they prep."

"Wait, we're on before Sugar Habit?" Kayla asked. She hadn't had time to do the math.

Julian grinned. "Don't you just adore irony?"

CHAPTER 38.

UNKNOWN: Hey, it's Jordan.

TY: Yo, is everything okay?

UNKNOWN: Can you get online right now?

TY: Sure

UNKNOWN: I'll text you a link. Do it right away!

TY: You're kind of freaking me out

UNKNOWN: Sorry mate, it's all good. Here's the link.

TY OPENED THE URL ON his phone, not knowing what to expect or what it had to do with Kayla not answering his texts. He figured she'd been busy.

The link led him to the YouTube channel for Indio Fest, and he was surprised to find it was streaming live.

"Seriously? I could have watched some of it," he grumbled. "Hey, Pop-Pop? Do you mind if I cast some music to your TV?"

"Go ahead," Van said. "I've already seen this finale. Alistair wins it all with his tasteless healthy recipes."

Chuckling, Ty sent the signal to Van's flat-screen. He did a double take when he read the title card at the bottom of the screen.

COMING UP NEXT ON THE MAIN STAGE—THE LILLYS—SPECIAL ENCORE PERFORMANCE

TY: Is this live?!

JORDAN: Yes. Long story. They're about to go on. 🤞

Holy. Hell.

"Van!" Ty yelled. "Come here! Hurry!"

"What in the world?" His granddad rounded the kitchen island and came to stand beside him, alarmed. "Is something wrong?"

"Sorry, I didn't mean to…" Ty scooted down on the couch and patted the seat next to him. "Sit down. I want you to see something."

"Boy, you scared the living daylights out of me."

"Sorry, sorry." Ty turned up the volume on the remote. He was on the edge of his seat, literally. This was huge! "The band is playing the mainstage any minute."

"What band?"

Ty glanced over at his granddad, only then noticing the apron around his waist and the dish towel in his hand. "Were you in the middle of cooking something?"

"It's fine. Good thing I set a timer." He let out a breath and sat back. "Is this the band you were traveling with? Is your girl gonna sing?"

"I told you, she's a drummer, but yeah."

A roar from the crowd sent Ty's pulse through the roof. He clutched the remote in one hand and his phone in the other, wishing he could text Kayla and tell her she was about to go on. Which was ridiculous because she was about to go on!

He shook his head but couldn't help the wide smile that split his face when Toni, Tiff, and Kayla walked out onto the stage. It was a wide shot, and he wished the lens would zoom in on Kayla's face.

The shot was from somewhere in the middle of the field. Thousands of bodies filled the space in front of the stage. An ocean of arms, banners, and flags greeted the girls, so much bigger than the smattering of people they'd performed for on Friday. He wondered if they were nervous and how they'd landed this undoubtedly coveted spot.

So many questions swirled through Ty's mind, but there Kayla was—behind her drum kit like a deity surveying her devotees.

The band opened with a song Ty actually knew. It was one of his dad's favorites, "Driven to Tears." He couldn't remember the original band but had clear memories of his father singing along while working on their car in the garage.

His dad had called it a protest song. Ty hadn't paid much attention to the lyrics as a child, but as Lilly took the stage, he finally listened.

As she sang about shirking responsibility and turning a blind eye to the injustices of the world, Lilly seemed to hold eye contact with several people in the front rows. The camera zeroed in on her. To Ty, she had often come across as impermeable and a little removed from everything and everyone around her. The only time she seemed to come alive was when she was onstage, and her expression now was full of fire.

The view switched to Toni, who wore large, black sunglasses that hid her eyes completely. She stood at the edge of the stage—legs wide and feet planted—with not even a hint of a smile. She was pure attitude, and the crowd was eating it up.

Tiff drifted into view, as animated as ever. She gave the audience all the rock-and-roll antics they could ever want as she swung her hair and gyrated her hips, using her bass guitar like a sex doll as she straddled it.

"Well, now," his granddad said. "She's got it going on, doesn't she?"

"Tiff is a badass," Ty agreed.

"Where's your girl?"

Ty pointed her out in the back, cursing the lack of camera time for her.

When the song ended, they segued right into the next one, picking up the tempo. The camera cut back to midfield. The view from there was a veritable sea of arms clapping in time.

"That must be quite the rush. Look at all those people."

"It's amazing," Ty agreed. "I only got to stand in the wings, or in the pit, but the energy they put out—and what they get back when the audience is into it—it's unlike anything I've ever experienced. I can't imagine what it's like for them right now."

"They're damned good."

Ty turned to his granddad and smiled. "They are, aren't they?"

"Is that her?" He pointed, and Ty turned.

Kayla filled the screen, her hair wild and her hands flying. She looked thoroughly in her element—like she was born to be doing exactly that.

Watching her, Ty's heart swelled with pride, love, and he ached to talk to her. Touch her. Just be with her.

The camera stayed on her throughout her solo, then cut away as Lilly addressed the crowd.

"Thank you, Indio! We are so happy to be here with you again so soon. Are you having a good time?" There was a collective yeah, and Lilly shook her head. "Come on, I know you can do better than that. I said, are you having a good time?" She cupped her hand against her ear.

This time, there were screams and shouts and earsplitting whistles. The scene shifted to the audience. People were jumping up and down while others crowd-surfed. One woman climbed up onto the shoulders of a guy standing next to her, waving her arms in the air when she settled on them. It was such a wonderfully clichéd moment, one the band deserved.

When the camera went back to Kayla, this time a side shot that actually managed to get closer to her face, Ty felt a hand smooth down his back.

"You look at her the way your daddy used to look at your mama," his granddad said.

Surprised, Ty tore his gaze away from Kayla. "Really?"

Pop-Pop nodded. "It happened fast for them too, you know. I wasn't for it at first, but anybody could look at the two of them and see it." He rose slowly to his feet. "I'm gonna go check the oven. Can't wait to meet your lady, though. She must be something special."

"She is," Ty said. He was disappointed to find the camera had switched back to a wide shot, but the band sounded incredible. He realized they were all essentially dressed the same, in jeans with black logo tees—though each one wore the look differently.

They were jamming, guitar, bass, and drums locked into a groove that had the audience in the palm of their hands. Above the stage, Lilly stood perched on one of the monitor speakers. Hands by her side, her gaze sweeping over the writhing throngs, she looked like a huntress scanning for prey.

Lilly pointed to a back section of the field and raised her arms in the air, bringing them together in time with Kayla's kick drum. The people there cheered and raised their hands to clap in time above their heads.

The blond pointed to a section opposite them and gave them a different beat to emphasize, this one in time with the snare.

One by one, the singer dissected the crowd into parts until the whole became a separate instrument. One she commanded.

"Give me more!" Lilly shouted and the sound grew deafening.

Ty could only imagine what it was like on the field and wished like hell he could be there.

The camera cut back to the other three women, and Ty zeroed in on Kayla. The breeze from a set of large fans blew her curls around her head. With the light behind her, her curls glowed like wisps of flame.

God. She was glorious.

Tiff ripped into a run that Toni chased with one of her own, and then the band launched into the next number.

Lilly raised the mic to her lips, threw her head back, and sang a note that seemed to reach the clouds above.

The crowd went absolutely bonkers.

It was a powerful, triumphant moment, and Ty was thrilled for them.

A crash sounded from the kitchen.

"You need any help in there?" he asked.

"M'fine" came his granddad's typical response.

Ty shook his head, chuckling to himself. Van's kitchen was always a wreck when he was in the middle of one of his experiments, and Ty hoped he was more mindful when he used the commercial kitchen in the main building.

But at the sound of breaking glass, Ty shot to his feet, craning his neck to try and see into the kitchen. Sighing, he paused the stream. "Pop-Pop, what in the world are you doing in there?"

No answer. "Van?" Ty walked over to the kitchen, ready to tease his granddad. But when he stepped around the island and saw Pop-Pop lying on the cold, tiled floor, Ty's heart stopped.

CHAPTER 39.

AFTER THEIR SET—DURING WHICH THEY totally rocked the Indio crowd—they were rushed offstage to give the crew time to do the changeover for the next act. After stashing her sticks and grabbing her towel, Kayla jogged over to the wings and right into the middle of a situation. She stepped close to Toni, who was at the edge of a group gathered around some commotion she couldn't see in the middle.

"What's up?" she asked before she heard a familiar voice.

"Admit it, you got Andre to put you on tonight. This was supposed to be *our* big moment but you just can't stand to share your precious spotlight, can you?"

Candi.

"You're making a spectacle of yourself." That was Lilly, her voice tightly controlled.

Kayla could only make out the top of her blond head and pulled Toni toward the pair, bystanders making room for them as they moved.

"Me?" Candi's laugh was artificial. "Hardly. You can't stand the fact that I found something better."

"We're not the competition."

"As if. Baby, we're not even in the same *league*," Candi boasted, overloud. She stepped closer to Lilly, who didn't back down an inch.

Instead, she observed Candi like she was a riddle she was trying to decide whether it was worth or not it to solve.

Beside them, Seb hovered as if it might come to blows.

Toni leaned close to Kayla. "Should we, I dunno…do something?"

"This is between the two of them," Kayla replied, even as she was ready to jump in if Lilly needed her. "It's always been about the two of them."

Candi had always been a diva, but this was a lot. Even for her.

Around them, the festival staff seemed frozen, confusion on every face.

"Don't act like it doesn't bother you, *Lil*." Candi took another step, lifting her chin to meet her eyes. "I know you like to pretend you don't have a heart behind that gilded armor of yours, but I know better. I know it stings that I can do this without you."

"Wow, you really are delusional if you think Lilly uses up any of her energy thinking about your sorry ass," Tiff spat back as she hovered by Seb.

Candi turned her head to glare at her before turning back to Lilly. "The ice queen can speak for herself."

Lilly studied her for a moment, then leaned in close. "Maybe you should spend more time practicing with your new band than worrying about your old one. It sounds like you need it." She stepped around her and headed for the stairs.

When Candi grabbed her arm, Kayla and Toni both braced themselves, but in a flash, Seb slipped his arm around Candi's waist and pulled her back. Behind him, a crew member shouted for everyone to get out of the way as Lilly marched down the steps.

"What the hell was that about?" Kayla asked Lilly when they got to one of the hospitality tents.

"*Drittseken*," Lilly hissed, her face scrunched up and so red that her hairline was a glowing white streak above her forehead.

"Draaaamaaaa," some dude singsonged as he jogged into the tent. He went straight to the bucket of Coronas and popped one open, holding it out to Kayla when he caught her watching him.

She shook her head. "No, thanks."

Leave it to Candi to bring them all down from such an amazing high. Kayla leaned against the back of a sofa and took several deep breaths.

Being in this band meant wild, wide swings of emotion. High highs and low lows. It was...a lot. Zach would have loved every second of it. Kayla did too. Most of it, anyway.

She was tired. And she missed Ty. And she still had to figure out a way to talk to her mother without one or both of them derailing the conversation they both needed to have.

"You're the drummer that was last on, right?" said a voice behind her.

She turned, and the Corona guy downed half his beer before Kayla could nod. "I thought so!" he exclaimed and then reached forward with his palm in the air.

Kayla high-fived him, hoping he wouldn't turn around and see Lilly pacing circles in the corner, still clearly pissed, with Jordan patiently trying to calm her down.

"Glad you liked it," she said to keep him occupied.

"Liked it?" he said aghast. "Baby girl, the four of you tore the fucking roof off this place. Did you hear them chanting your name? Or uh..." He lowered his voice as he leaned in. "Did that pink-haired train wreck distract you from your moment?"

"Candi just likes to make an entrance," Kayla said, hating that she had to defend her.

He pursed his lips. "Aww, aren't you the diplomatic one? I know who she is. Everyone does, darling. But you four?" He brought his fingers to his lips and kissed the tips. "Bra-fucking-va."

Kayla grinned despite herself. "Thanks."

The guy plopped down onto a beanbag and pointed a finger in the air. "You hear that?"

Kayla tuned in to the music, realizing it was live and not a recording. "The next act started already?"

"They've been playing for about ten minutes." He looked around as more people drifted in. "See that? People are bored. They're roaming."

Kayla followed his gaze, surprised to see several performers and other celebs filtering in. Some went for food or drinks. Others sat down and pulled out their phones.

"Shit," Kayla said, remembering she'd left her phone charging in her bunk. In all the hullabaloo, she hadn't had a chance to catch up with Ty. He wasn't going to believe they'd played Indio again.

"Shit is right," the dude across from her said. "Who the hell thought it was a good idea to put them on the main stage?" He laughed, shaking his head before he finished his beer. He let out a loud belch and smacked his lips. "They sucked when I saw them in Baton Rouge. No cohesion at all. Nothing to latch on to."

"They who?"

"The guitarist is that chick with the rich family," he said. "Pink hair."

"Sugar Habit?"

He drew back as if he'd smelled something foul. "Is that what they're called?" He snorted. "Jesus, that's…bad."

Kayla strained to hear the music overhead. It wasn't great. It wasn't horrible, but there was nothing to latch on to. And Candi's guitar sounded slightly out of tune. Kayla wondered how the techs hadn't caught that yet. Or maybe they had. She hadn't been on her best behavior. Maybe not telling her was payback.

"What's your name?" The guy held out his hand.

"Kayla." His handshake was firm and surprisingly professional, as was his demeanor. No leering, no innuendo.

"Tomin Hale, editor for *Spinwire*."

"The magazine?"

"What's left of it," Tomin said. He pulled a vape pen out of his pocket, rolled his eyes as he groaned, and shoved it back. "Nasty habit. I'm trying to kick it."

Kayla sat up a little straighter, glad she hadn't told him to go away when he sat down uninvited. She wished Toni or Tiff were there, or Seb. Or that she could get Lilly's and Jordan's attention. She'd never spoken to the press by herself. And no matter how casual the setting, she understood enough to know nothing was ever really off the record.

"You look spooked," Tomin said, a grin tugging the corner of his mouth. "Relax. I don't bite. And even if I did, you're not my flavor." Kayla frowned, and he laughed. "I didn't mean it like that, sugar. You're fine as hell, and you know it."

Tomin looked around the room, leaving Kayla to wonder what the hell he was talking about until he zeroed in on a petite redhead in the tiniest shorts Kayla had ever seen. She had to admire his confidence, wearing that.

"Now, *that's* more my speed," Tomin said, tilting his head to the side as his gaze followed the person across the room. Turning back to her, he sighed. "Alas, I have someone waiting for me back in NYC, though I'm not sure if that's going to last."

"Uh…" Kayla had no idea what to say. "That's too bad."

Tomin shrugged. "C'est la vie. But enough about me, tell me more about the Lillys. You're signed, right?"

She nodded, her gaze darting to the corner and back. *Why am I the one left alone with a reporter?* "Yeah, YMI."

His eyes lit up. "That's riiiiight." He waved a hand in the general direction of the stage. "The singer, or whatever, from what's-its-face out there, she was in your band, right?"

"She was, yeah," Kayla replied, trying to keep her answers as brief as possible. Maybe if she stuck to the facts, she wouldn't say anything that could come back and bite them on the ass.

He narrowed his eyes knowingly. "I'm not interviewing you, babes, just being nosy."

"Sure." Kayla sat back and crossed her legs, hoping to convey an air of confidence when, inside, she was a coiled spring.

"I'm harmless," Timon said. "But it's smart to be wary. Seriously, though, I'd like to know more. Maybe interview the band when we're all back in New York?" He fished into his back pocket and pulled out a card. "Take this and call me, or have your people reach out."

Kayla took the card. "We will, thanks." She smiled at him.

"There she is," he said, winking. His attention snagged on someone behind her, and he got up. "Sorry, Finneas just walked by, and I need to have a chat with him. Talk soon, okay?"

Timon gave her shoulder a pat and Kayla watched him weave through the crowd. She stood and made her way to the corner where she found Jordan, Lilly, and Tiff.

Lilly's mouth was tight at the corners, and she had her arms folded across her abdomen. Kayla had never seen her look so vulnerable.

"Shake it off," Tiff said.

Kayla ran a hand down Lilly's arm and cupped her elbow. "What did Candi say after we left?"

"You don't want to know," Jordan replied, taking out his phone.

"Apparently, she's back on her bullshit," Tiff said.

"Tiff." Jordan was using the tone he used when he was about to lecture her on minding her tongue.

She huffed. "Well, it's true."

"It doesn't matter what she said, you guys rocked it. Look." He held his phone out for Lilly. "Indio Fest Twitter is lit up with your mentions. They loved you even more today than on Friday."

"Because we are awesome," Tiff added. "And Sugar Habit sucks balls."

Dropping her arms to her sides, Lilly exhaled a deep breath. "They're not that bad."

"They're not connecting with the crowds the way you do," Jordan said.

"He's right," Kayla agreed. "Look around. The tent is practically full. For us, the wings, the pit, and the VIP space were packed. They really liked us. Plus," she said, pulling the card from her pocket, "we impressed the editor of *Spinwire*."

"What?" Jordan said, swiping the card from her fingertips. "Did you talk to him?"

"Yeah." Kayla turned to try and spot Timon in the crowd. "He said he wants to interview us."

Jordan's jaw dropped open before snapping shut. He smiled. "I could kiss you," he said. "And I should have before you met your new beau."

Right. Ty. She really needed to get to her phone.

Tiff bumped her with her shoulder. "Damn, Kayla. You're, like, our good-luck charm. First Broken Pilot, now this?" She hugged her waist. "I think I'll keep you."

"Mind if I hold on to this?" Jordan asked, slipping the card into his wallet.

Kayla nodded as she started to back away. "Please do. I need to head to the bus. I left my phone charging, and I want—"

"We know," Jordan said, grinning.

"Tell him hi," Tiff added. "And tell him he missed all the fun."

"Actually, I don't think he did," Jordan said. "I texted him the link to the live stream."

"There was a live stream?" Kayla heard Tiff ask as she jogged away.

CHAPTER 40.

A MEMBER OF THE FESTIVAL crew was kind enough to run Kayla back to the bus, and Kayla used her remote to unlock it. Closing the door behind her, she took a deep breath once she was inside the quiet, secluded space. She walked back to her bunk and flopped down, closing her eyes for a moment that somehow turned into twenty minutes.

Her phone lit up the small space and she blinked awake, picking it up. She was anticipating a message from Ty and there were several from him, but also a missed call.

She read the texts first.

TY: So much to tell you. Call me when you get a chance. 🖤
TY: Hey babe. I'm guessing you're busy. I heard the single on local radio. So effin cool!
TY: Watching the live stream, holy fuck!!! 🤘 🤘
TY: on way to hospital with van. will call when i can

Kayla's blood went cold. She sat up, nearly bumping her head on the ceiling, and hit the call button at the top of Ty's text. When he didn't answer, she jumped to her feet.

"Fuck, fuck, fuck." She didn't know what to do. She shot him a text.

KAYLA: Do you need me there?

She waited, watching for the arrows at the bottom of the screen to turn blue, signaling that he'd received her text. They remained stubbornly gray.

"Fuck!" she yelled into the silence of the bus.

Of course, she should go to Philly. That's what significant others did, right? He'd want her there for support, wouldn't he?

Pacing wasn't going to help, so Kayla texted Jordan.

KAYLA: I need to grab a flight to Philly tonight.

Her phone rang within seconds.

"You that anxious to get to your—" he began.

"Jory, something's happened to Ty's grandpa. I need to be there," she said.

There was a beat of silence. "I'll take care of it. Where are you?"

"On the bus."

"On my way to you. Pack what you need, it's going to be tight."

"Thank you," Kayla said. Not that she couldn't buy her own plane ticket, but she appreciated Jordan's help. No one was cooler under pressure than him, and she didn't want to take any chances.

Turning her ringer all the way up, Kayla pocketed her phone and went to the cockpit. She released the lock on the cargo hold and unlocked the door to the bus. She was searching through the luggage for her bag when she heard voices.

Kayla took a quick glance over her shoulder but focused on finding her suitcase.

"Hey," someone called out, but Kayla didn't think they were talking to her. "Damn," they said. "I think she's ignoring us."

"Nooooo," another voice replied, closer now. "That can't be. Kayla and I are *family*."

There was laughter, and Kayla froze. She recognized Candi's sickly sweet whine.

Torn between ignoring Candi, not giving Candi another excuse to make a scene, and wanting to clear the air between them, Kayla stood up and turned around.

There were three men and another woman with their former guitarist. Candi had her arm wrapped around one guy's waist, while the rest of the group clumped together.

"Hi," Kayla said, scanning the area behind them for someone from Sugar Habit group. There was no one, and she wasn't sure if that was a blessing or a curse. In the distance, she could hear music. Out here, it was much quieter. "What're you guys up to?"

One of the men stumbled toward her, stopping a few feet away. "Post gig after-party, wanna come with?" His words slurred a little, but his eyes were sharp. He smiled. "I know you, don't I?"

"She's a Lilly," Candi said. "You know, my old band. The one that kicked me out."

"It was a little more complicated than *we kicked you out*."

"Ohhhh yeah," the one in front of her said, tapping his lips. "I remember. You're on drums, right?" His gaze took a lazy tour over her body. "You beat the hell out of those skins."

"Thanks," Kayla said, crossing her arms. She kept her eyes on Candi, wondering what she wanted.

"Yeah, Kayla is a badass drummer," she said, grinning.

"You guys sounded great out there." They hadn't. Kayla was shocked by how ill-prepared Sugar Habit had been for their set. She had a feeling they hadn't practiced much.

"Well," Candi said, rubbing the back of her neck, "we haven't been together long, but give it time. We're going to blow everyone else out of the water. Including the Lillys."

Oddly enough, there was no bravado this time, and Kayla smiled. "You're welcome to try."

Candi brightened. "Hey! You should defect and come join us."

"Uh, don't you already have a drummer?" Kayla scanned the people with her but didn't recognize any of them. "Where is your new band, by the way?"

"Around." Candi made a pfft sound, waving her hand. "And Natalie's all right. Not as good as you. Besides, you were always my favorite." As if sensing an opening, Candi's eyes sparkled. "Come on, you know we'd make a great team. With your lead foot and fast hands? And my, well, everything else? We'd rule the world."

"Thanks for the offer, really, but I'm cool where I am," Kayla replied. Candi was an incredible musician, but she came at a cost. One Kayla wasn't willing to pay, even without her own drama looming over her. She made her way toward the front of the bus where the door stood open.

"What's wrong, you don't like the name Sugar Habit? It's dumb, isn't it? Andre made it up. We could start something brand-new." Candi's voice followed her, and Kayla turned back.

"I didn't say that, Can. You guys have a lot of potential. You could be great one day."

"Potential?" she said, incredulous. "We're sure as shit gonna burn up the charts when our album drops. You'll see," Candi said as if she'd been in the middle of an argument.

"I'm sure you will. Good luck with everything."

The guy with the woman draped over him lifted the bottle in his hand. "Right on. Gotta love mutual admi...ad..."

"Admiration," the one closest to Kayla finished.

Kayla turned to open the door. "Well, it was...good to see you, Can."

"Hey," Candi said, cutting her off. "That's it? That's all you've got to say to me?" She peeled away from her entourage. "The four of you, Seb, Tiff, and—God!—Lilly... You're all so full of shit."

"Candi," Kayla began, stepping back when Candi spun on her.

"Don't *Candi* me, like I'm some kid and you're my mom." She looked at Kayla with utter disgust. "All of you are fake as hell, all that talk about family. Complete bullshit."

"We gave you a million chances," Kayla said, struggling to keep her voice even. "You blew every one of them and gave us the finger while you did it. What did you think would happen? Yeah, we're a family, but this is also our livelihoods."

"Oh, so it was just business, then? Good to know that's all I meant to you, you fucking hypocrite."

"What the hell. Really, Candi?"

"Ladies," the taller of the men said, holding his hands up in placation. "C'mon, we're all friends here." His smile creeped Kayla out, and she wondered if he was part of Candi's other pastime.

"Sorry, Lonnie," Candi said, blowing out a breath. "They just get on my nerves. Such goddamned snobs. Lilly barely looked at me all damn day. Then, when she did, she shit all over me."

"Seriously? Is that the lie you're telling yourself?" Kayla heard herself ask. Before Candi could launch into one of her trademark tirades, Kayla held up her hand. "You know what? Never mind. I've got shit I need to do."

"Sure you don't want to party with us?" Lonnie asked, pulling a tiny plastic bag from his pocket. He dangled it between them, and Kayla didn't miss the way Candi's eyes lit up.

"No thanks," Kayla replied. "That shit's not for me. And you shouldn't have it on festival grounds anyway. I'm pretty sure security is patrolling out here."

He gave Kayla an exaggerated pout, moving between her and the door a couple of feet away. "Aww, come on. Don't be like that." His voice dropped low. "I don't know about you, but a bump and a good hard fuck after a gig is just what I need to get rid of all that excess energy. You feel me?"

Kayla dropped her arms and straightened her back. Lifting her chin, she said, "If a good hard fuck was what I needed, I wouldn't want it with someone I don't know."

"You got somebody waiting?" He glanced at the bus. "They in there? They up for a party?"

Candi laughed and Kayla's gaze shot to hers. "She ain't down, Lonnie. Saint Katherine is never down for anything."

The shock of hearing her first name drop from Candi's lips made her next words sound thready and uneven. "What do you want, Candi?"

The guitarist's shoulder dropped. "I wanted to bury the hatchet. I miss you, K," Candi said, a hint of hurt in her voice. It was probably intended to play on Kayla's sympathy, but all it managed to do was piss her off even more. Everything was a game with Candi. It always had been.

"What are you even talking about? There is no hatchet to bury." Kayla gestured around them. "You've moved on, we've moved on, and we're all getting on with the business of making music. What more do you want?"

A flash of a different emotion moved behind Candi's eyes, gone before Kayla could decipher it.

"The Lillys aren't YMI's golden goose anymore," Candi said coldly, all traces of vulnerability gone. "Sugar Habit took your throne. *I* took it, and I'm gonna own that shit. We'll be on the Grammy stage before your first album is out of the gate."

"Whatever," Kayla said. "Can we be done? I'm so over your bullshit."

Candi's eyes went wide. "Mine? Where the hell do you get off—?"

"Whoa, bitch. I don't care who you are, you don't talk to her like that," Lonnie said, crowding into Kayla's personal space.

"Okay, now *you* need to back the hell up," Kayla yelled. This situation was spiraling out of control. Her heart hammered in her chest and her knees began to shake.

It was Lonnie's turn to put his finger in Kayla's face but whatever he'd been about to say got cut off by a flying shoe smacking the back of his head.

"Ow!" he yelled, his hand going to the spot. "What the—?"

"Get the fuck away from her!" In a blur, Tiff launched herself at Lonnie, wrapping both legs around his torso and both arms around his neck.

He lashed out, swinging while trying to protect his face as she clawed at him. "Get this bitch off me!"

"Lonnie, stop!" Candi yelled just as Kayla called out, "Tiff!"

She tried to grab her but narrowly missed getting punched herself.

"You freaking maniac!" Lonnie twisted and turned, trying to dislodge Tiff, who had locked her legs around him like a vise.

Candi pulled at Tiff. "Girl, get off of him before you hurt yourself!"

Kayla and Jordan tried to pry their bassist free, but Lonnie had a fistful of Tiff's hair in his hands. Kayla hauled off and kicked him hard in the shin.

Lonnie and Tiff fell to the ground in a heap, Tiff really whaling on him now.

"Tiff!" Jordan shouted, trying to get her attention, but she was in a rage. "Tiffany!"

"Stop it!" Candi screamed. "Someone get security!"

"Tiff," Kayla said, daring to get close as she spotted Jordan running toward them, just ahead of security. Lonnie was on the ground, covering his face as Tiff pummeled him from above. "I'm okay, Tiff, stop! Please!"

Kayla grabbed her elbow, and Tiff's arm froze in midair. She blinked, her chest heaving as if she'd been in a daze. Looking around, Tiff seemed to come back to herself. She pushed off of Lonnie, and Jordan helped her get to her feet.

Security arrived just as Lonnie stood up. "Dude, I want these cunts arrested."

"Hold on," one of the guards said. "You're bleeding." He examined Tiff's forehead. "That might need stitches. You should go to the med tent."

"I'm fine. It's this asshole who's gonna need stitches," Tiff spat, yanking at her disheveled clothing. "Great new friends you've got there, Candi." Her voice cracked.

Kayla pulled her into a hug.

"I didn't cause all of this," Candi said, sounding dazed herself. She took a step toward Tiff. "Are you okay?"

"The fuck do you care?" Tiff shot back. "You *left* us." She was shaking.

"God, you and your issues," Candi sighed. Her gaze sharpened, and Kayla didn't like the gleam in her eye. "Wait until Andre hears about this."

"About what? *Your* pusher friend got all in *my* face," Kayla shot back.

"I didn't do nothing except invite her to a party," Lonnie said, backing away from the security guard who eyed him suspiciously.

The security guard rounded on him. "Julian told you about slinging your shit here, man. You need to start walking."

"Do you know who I am?" Lonnie said, his voice menacing. He jabbed a finger in Tiff's direction. "Sweetheart, you just fucked up big-time."

"You might want to slow your roll, buddy," Jordan said. "I don't care who you are. You threatened my clients and, if they want me to, I'll take your arse to court and strip you of everything that makes you *whoever* the fuck you think you are."

Even Kayla shivered at the implication. Jordan turned to her, his expression severe but concerned as he looked her over before turning to Candi.

"The next time you hassle one of my clients, I'm going to the label. A little band rivalry is one thing, but I doubt even Andre will put up with shit like this."

"But I..." Another flash of *something* passed behind Candi's eyes, but then she shrugged. "Go to him all you want, you guys are yesterday's news. I have a new family now."

She stalked off after Lonnie, and Kayla glanced at the others that had been with them, surprised when she realized the woman had been taking photos or video with her phone. Kayla shook her head.

"Some family," she muttered.

"You talking to me?" the woman said. "'Cause I didn't say shit to you."

"Learn when to shut up, Gina," her friend said. "C'mon, let's go." He gave Kayla a look she supposed was meant to be apologetic, but she turned away. He hadn't done anything to stop the mayhem, so he didn't get any brownie points from her.

The security guard turned to Tiff. "Let's get you looked at."

"You sure you're okay?" Tiff asked Kayla.

"I'm fine, you little hellcat. I didn't need rescuing but, damn. Remind me to hire you as my bodyguard."

Tiff grinned. "Nah, I'd do that shit for free."

"Do I need to talk to Julian about this?" Jordan asked the guard.

"Nah, man. Lonnie's been on thin ice for a while. I'll fill him in. He'll probably slap him with a lifetime ban." He lifted his walkie-talkie and mumbled some sort of code into it. "I'll make sure he's off-premises within the half hour."

"Thanks." Jordan shook the man's hand.

"Sorry this happened," the guard said. "I was on the other side of the lot when I got the call about the disturbance. Guess we need more bodies out here to keep an eye on things."

He wandered off when someone pinged his walkie, and Jordan

ushered Tiff and Kayla inside. "I shouldn't have let you come back here alone," he said.

"Don't beat yourself up, I'm okay." Kayla hugged him, and he squeezed tight before letting her go. The truth was, she was shaken. She'd known Candi held some bitterness toward the Lillys for everything that had gone down before, but this had unnerved her and left her feeling jittery.

"By the way, your flight's booked."

Kayla's adrenaline surged for an entirely different reason as she remembered why she'd come to the bus in the first place. "Thanks. I still need to pack."

"Let me help," Tiff said.

"You already have," Kayla replied, giving her a quick kiss on the cheek.

CHAPTER 41.

KAYLA TRIED TO REACH TY before the plane took off, but he hadn't picked up, so she was relieved to get a text from him right after she landed at PHL.

> **TY:** Sorry, my phone died. We're at the hospital. I'll fill you in when you have time.
> **KAYLA:** Which hospital?
> **TY:** Penn General, but don't send any flowers or anything. I'm hoping they'll release him this afternoon.
> **KAYLA:** I'm on my way to you. Just landed.
> **TY:** Kayla...
> **TY:** Fuck. You're amazing.
> **KAYLA:** See you soon 🖤
> **TY:** 🖤 🖤 🖤

The nurse at the desk directed Kayla to a room at the end of the corridor. She'd always hated hospitals and could still remember the smell of the antiseptic they used in her grandmother's room. She'd only been seven when her nonna had passed. But that was old enough to remember the pain of watching her slip away, and she didn't wish it upon anyone. Considering the special relationship she knew Ty had with his grandfather, she was especially worried about him.

The door was open, so she slipped quietly inside, grateful there was no occupant in the nearest bed.

As she'd expected, Ty held a vigil at Mr. Baldwin's bedside. He'd pulled a chair as close as he could probably get it and held his grandfather's hand between his, his head bent over them.

He and Kayla had never discussed religion or faith. Kayla herself had never subscribed to anything in particular, but she wondered if Ty was praying now. And to whom. Not wanting to intrude, she set her bag on the floor and leaned against the wall.

Several minutes passed, and Ty didn't move.

A nurse entered the room, smiling as she passed her.

"Is he still sleeping?" she asked Ty.

He looked up and nodded. "Kayla?" he said, noticing her for the first time. He gently laid his grandfather's hand on the bed and came to her. "How long have you been here?"

Pulling her into his arms, he wrapped Kayla in a warm hug that smelled of rubbing alcohol and fabric softener. Underneath it all, though, was Ty's unique and familiar scent. Kayla breathed deep and sank into him, feeling guilty for the relief she found in his arms at a time like this.

"How is he?" she asked when he leaned back.

Ty rubbed up and down her arms. "He had a mild stroke."

Her stomach clenched. "Oh...Ty."

"The doctors think he'll be all right, but they wanted to keep him here and run some tests," Ty said, turning back to the bed.

"His vitals look good," the nurse said, looping her stethoscope around the back of her neck. "We love Mr. Baldwin. He always brings us cookies when he has an appointment."

Ty smiled. "I hope they aren't the ginger blueberry ones."

Laughing softly, the nurse shuddered. "Once. And we told him we'd pawn him off on another hospital if he ever brought those in again." She patted Ty on the shoulder as she passed. "The doc will be in shortly to update you, but I'd say you'll be able to take him home tonight. Tomorrow morning at the latest."

Ty's shoulders rounded with relief. "That would be amazing, thank you."

With a wink, the nurse left.

"I'm sorry you flew all the way here," Ty said, taking Kayla's hands in his. She leaned up to kiss him, and he drew back, sheepish. "I've been here all night. I probably have the worst morning breath."

"And I just got off of a plane." She shrugged, stepping even closer because she needed to.

Kayla's heart fluttered in her chest as Ty wrapped his arms around her and tilted his mouth over hers. The kiss was warm and soft. And tasted stale, but she didn't care. It was him. And he was home to her now.

"Maybe you should get your own room," a scratchy voice said behind them.

Ty spun around, a smile lighting up his entire face before he tempered it with a wry grin. "We would if someone wasn't an attention hog, demanding that it be all about him."

His grandfather smiled and scratched his nose, a sound of annoyance escaping his throat when he felt the plastic tube attached there.

"I don't need you to help me sleep, son." He reached for his glasses on the bedside table, and Ty darted over to get them for him. "I can reach."

"You're not supposed to move around too much," Ty scolded him gently.

"I'm not gonna jump outta bed and run a marathon," his grandfather said, laughing. "I just wanted to get a better look."

He beckoned Kayla over, and she went, suddenly shy about meeting this man who meant so much to the guy she'd fallen for.

But when he smiled up at her, warm and bright, she could see Tyrell in him.

"Sorry we had to meet like this," he said, holding up his hand for her to take. "Vanderbilt Baldwin. I'm this knucklehead's grand-pop." He nodded at Ty, who smiled and rolled his eyes. "What's your name again, sweetheart?"

"My friends call me Kayla" she replied, blushing at the term of endearment.

"Well, then, Kayla," he said, squeezing her hand with surprising strength. "People call me Van."

"It's so nice to meet you, Van."

"You sure this is your girl, Tyrell?" Van said, winking at her. "She might be too pretty for you."

"All right, that's enough." Ty laughed and pretended to pull their hands apart. "Get your own. She's mine."

She's mine.

A shiver of a thrill coursed through her.

"Sorry, Van, I'm taken." Kayla leaned in. "But if it doesn't work out, you'll be the first to know," she stage-whispered.

"I think introducing you two may have been a mistake," Ty said, teasing.

They were laughing when the doctor entered the room. "That's what I like to hear," she said, smiling brightly as she walked to the end of the bed and pulled a tablet out of a pouch there. Glancing at it, she swiped down a few times, scanning the info on the screen. "I see we're feeling much better today."

"I'm fine," Van said, sitting up in the bed a little. Kayla guessed he was trying to look as hearty and hale as possible so the doctor would release him as promised.

"Yes, you are. Mostly," the doctor said, putting the tablet back. Pushing her glasses to the top of her head, she looked at Van. "We need to talk about your heart."

"What about it?" Ty asked.

Hesitating, the doctor glanced at Kayla.

"I can wait outside," Kayla said.

"No need," Van said. "Go ahead, doc."

"I think it's time we schedule an ablation," the doctor said.

Van made a sound of disgust.

"A what?" Ty asked. "What's wrong with his heart? What's wrong with your heart, Van?"

"Your grandfather has arrhythmia," the doctor explained. "It's been causing episodes of tachycardia, or rapid heartbeat. We've tried medication, which seemed to contain it for a time, but Van isn't responding to those anymore." She looked at Van. "Your grandfather insists he doesn't want a pacemaker..."

"I don't want that thing in me," his grandfather snapped.

"Van," Ty warned. "Is there another option?"

"An ablation," the doctor said. "We essentially shut down the tissue in his heart that's triggering the abnormality. I know it sounds scary, but it's a fairly routine procedure. I've performed dozens of them. I use a catheter, so it's minimally invasive."

"I've never been under the knife," Van complained, "and I don't want to start now."

The doctor sighed. "And round and round we go."

"Can we have a minute?" Ty asked. The doc nodded and stepped outside.

"I'll go too," Kayla said.

"You don't have to."

She kissed Ty on the cheek. "I think this is really between you two. I'll just be outside."

In the hall, Kayla found a seat by the door. She'd silenced her phone when she arrived and woke it to check her messages. It vibrated in her hand, and Siobhan's name popped onto the screen underneath a photo. It was Siobhan, Derren, Zach, and Kayla, all smiling on a beach somewhere when Kayla was in high school. It was an old memory but a happy one, and one of the few she had that didn't cause her chest to ache.

Kayla spotted a waiting room a little farther down the hall and headed for it as she accepted the call. "Hiya."

"I know a guy who can get you a whole new identity and smuggle you out of the country," Siobhan said by way of greeting. "How do you feel about shipping containers? You should probably brush up on your Spanish. Have you had your shots?"

Kayla blew out a breath. "Siobhan, not that I don't love bearing witness to your flights of fancy, but this isn't a great time."

"Yeah, no kidding," came her reply. "I've seen your mother go nuclear before, but this is going to be epic."

"Wait, my mom? Jesus, what has she done now?" Kayla's question was met with silence. It went on so long, she thought the call had dropped. "Are you there? Bonnie?"

"Kathy," Siobhan began slowly, "where are you? I hear beeping."

"I'm at a hospital in Philly. And before you ask, I'm fine."

"You might want to fake an illness of some kind and get them to check you in."

"Uh, why would I want to do that?"

"Shit, you really don't know?" she asked.

Unease prickled along Kayla's skin. "Know what?"

"Shit," Siobhan muttered again. "Okay, all kidding aside, you need to check your Twitter feed."

"I don't have a Twitter account, you know that."

"The band does, doesn't it?" Impatience had seeped into her tone, which was even more worrying.

"Lilly handles that."

"Dammit, Kath," she sighed. "Open a fucking web browser and go onto Twitter. Search for the hashtag IndioBrawl."

Kayla's stomach dropped. "Can't you just tell me?"

"Honestly, no," Siobhan said. "Because the video is grainy, I can't really tell what's happening. But you're there, and some girl is beating the life out of a guy on the ground. She looks like the one who plays bass in your band."

"Oh, fuck," Kayla whispered.

"Indeed," Siobhan said. "Apparently, reporters started calling around not long after the video went viral. They asked me about you, wanted to confirm I knew you. I didn't tell them shit, by the way."

"Bonnie, I need to call home."

"Are you sure you want to do that?"

No, she didn't. "I have to."

"Okay, but I'm here if you need anything."

"Thank you." Kayla hung up and took a deep breath. She dialed her dad.

"Kathy, I was just about to call you. What is going on? There's a video—"

"I know, Dad. I wanted to let you know I'm okay and that things are getting blown way out of proportion."

"Who is Tyrell Baldwin?"

Kayla felt like the wind had been knocked out of her. "Wh-what?"

"A reporter contacted your mother's publisher. She said she found out you were her daughter. I didn't know that was a secret. And you're in a band?"

"Daddy, there's...a lot I need to tell you. Nothing bad, just..."

"What's going on? You've never kept things from me before. Not things that mattered." Her dad sounded uncharacteristically frayed around the edges. Kayla squeezed her eyes shut. "Mom's not happy and, frankly, neither am I. One reporter said you're dating a man who was arrested for *assault*? I know you're an adult, and you can make your own decisions, but really sweetheart. Don't you think that's risky?"

Kayla checked the anger that flashed through her like a lightning strike. "I should have told you about Ty, about a lot of things, but it's not what you think. He's not a criminal, and he is completely innocent of any wrongdoing."

Her father sighed. "Did he tell you that? What am I saying? Of course, he did. Come on, baby, you're smarter than that."

"I can't explain everything to you right now, but it's true," Kayla said, fighting to keep her voice down. "Ty was a victim of some pretty sh...er, crappy circumstances, but this reporter—was it a woman named Sara Marsh?"

"I don't know, you'd have to ask your mom, but, Kathy? She is very upset. I'm surprised she hasn't tried to call you."

"I was on a plane," Kayla said, thinking it wise not to mention the hospital. "She may have." She took a quick look through her recent calls and found four from her mother. Christ. "Yeah, she did try."

"Well," her dad said, "call her back before I'm forced to replace the carpet because she's paced a hole in it. You know how much I hate home reno."

Despite the fear sending Kayla's heartbeat into overdrive, she laughed. Leave it to her father to lighten the mood, if only a little.

"I'll explain everything to you and to Mom when I get there. Don't talk to any more reporters. Mom's publicist should be fielding those calls anyway. Someone will handle the story on my end."

"All right, sweetheart, I'll wait for you to fill us in, but your mother has been on the phone with her publisher all day."

"How bad is it?"

He made a sound of discomfort. "Well, it's not good. They want to meet with her in New York."

Shit.

"I'm so sorry."

"Hey, now, you listen," he said. "Whatever is going on, we'll manage. Take care of whatever you need to there and get home. We can get through anything if we're together."

"Okay, Daddy." Kayla blew out a breath. She'd pretty much given up on living up to her mother's expectations. Her dad, however, was a different story. Kayla didn't think she could bear it if she lost his respect.

"This young man, Ty, it's...serious?"

Kayla thought about how much she enjoyed being with him. How comfortable she felt in her own skin when Ty was around. Glancing toward Van's room, she smiled. "He's...amazing, Daddy. He's a poet, like you."

CHAPTER 42.

KAYLA HADN'T WANTED TO LEAVE the hospital, but she had to deal with her mom in person. Needed to explain. Apologize. All of the things.

She knew exactly what her mother was going to say. That she was irresponsible, naive, and thoughtless. That she should be more careful when choosing her friends. That she put herself in this situation with no thought to her mother's career and reputation.

If she only knew *how* careful Kayla had been her entire life.

This time, she'd trusted her heart, and her heart hadn't led her astray. But her mom wouldn't see it that way. She never had.

KATHY: 16 YEARS OLD

"Back later," Kathy said, kissing her dad's cheek.

"Where are you off to?"

"Movie with a friend." She bent to kiss her mother, who sat on the sofa, a stack of books in front of her on the coffee table and her laptop open on her lap.

"Which friend?"

"Eddie." Kathy turned for the door, but her father caught her arm.

"Who is Eddie?"

She turned obediently. Kathy knew her dad wouldn't care, but her mom was a different story. "His parents own the garage on Third and Main."

As expected, her mother's eyebrows rose.

"How old is he?" her dad asked, his tone so fatherly it made her chuckle. She knew he was half-teasing.

"He's a year older, seventeen, a junior at Grange High, and we aren't going alone. A bunch of his friends from school will be there."

"Grange?" Her mother's nose wrinkled. "That place should be turned into a charter school, it's so far below national standards."

"Mom, please don't start."

"Only stating facts. Anyway, I think you should stay in tonight."

"What? Why? Because Eddie doesn't go to the right school?"

Her mom turned to look over her shoulder at her. "Did you clean your room?"

Kathy cringed internally. "I was going to do it tomorrow."

"No, you'll do it right now."

"But, Mom." Kathy turned to her father. "Dad, please?"

"Normally, I'd be on your side," he said. "I've met Eddie, and he seems like a nice young man. But if your mother asked you to clean your room, you need to go do it. If there's still time to catch the movie when you're done, then you can go."

"But—"

The look her father gave her cut off her protest. He rarely put his foot down like this, and when he did there was no changing his mind. "Okay, but then I can go meet up with my friends?"

"When you finish, we can take a look at some of the classes you can take this summer." Her mother turned back to her work.

"What? I told my friends I'd be there. Why can't we do that tomorrow?"

"You barely know those people, Kathy. Be careful who you're

quick to call your friends. It's best to be around people who enhance you, not diminish you."

———————

That had always been the crux of her mother's disapproval. You were only supposed to surround yourself with people who could enhance your public image. It was an arcane concept that made Kayla cringe.

"Do not look at me like that," her mother said while they stood around the kitchen island, her voice clipping on the consonants. "You cannot possibly expect us—expect me—to be *happy* about any of this. A rock band? Really, Kathy. Do you have any idea what this will do to your fans?"

"My...fans?" Kayla's head throbbed. She'd rented a car and driven straight to her parents' and she was exhausted. Hungry. Angry. Already over this conversation.

"Yolanda is such a role model for young people. They look up to you."

"Mom...I'm not..." She grit her teeth and took a deep breath.

"When this gets out, and it will thanks to your antics, it will *ruin* Yolanda," her mother said. She sounded almost distraught. "My publisher is worried the TV show won't proceed. That the network won't risk it."

"I'm sorry." This was everything Kayla had been afraid of happening. "There has to be a way to—"

"And that boy you're seeing," her mother continued. "He's a criminal! The things he's done—"

"Hasn't done," Kayla said sharply.

"God, you're just like your father. He was *arrested*. Charged with assaulting one of his female classmates after she turned him in for cheating. And then she...she *died*. Oh, Katherine." Her mother held up a hand to stave off Kayla's response as if she'd been interrupted during one of her presentations. "Who knows what else he's capable of? Even if he wasn't a hardened criminal when he was arrested, being in jail had to have changed him, darling. Don't you see?"

"He was only there for a few weeks, Mom." Which probably seemed like a lifetime to Ty, but Kayla knew a little about the impact it had on him.

She drew in as deep a breath as she could. She'd known it was going to be like this. Ty had tried to convince her everything would be all right, that her mother would understand. He was such an optimist, he'd even offered to come with her. Kayla loved him for it, but he had never met Gisele Larrington.

"I'm going to explain one more time," Kayla began, her eye already twitching.

Her mother sniffed and turned her head away. "You can explain a hundred times. It won't change the facts. Thanks to your secrecy, I may be retiring right alongside your father. Do you think the university will want a president with these kinds of scandals hanging over her?"

"You really think they would fire you over something so trivial?" Kayla had been worried about book sales. She never considered her mother might lose her job. This was a nightmare.

"Trivial?" her mother asked, turning back to her. "You're consorting with...with prostitutes who fight like alley cats. I've seen the video. And that Candi Fairmount, you're in a band with her?"

"Was."

"And you're sleeping with degenerates who think violence is the answer when they don't get their way."

"That's not—!"

"The facts speak for themselves, Katherine."

"Facts? *Facts?*" Kayla's voice bounced off the granite countertops and travertine tile floor of her parents' spotless kitchen and she paused to take a breath and get herself under control. When Kayla spoke again, her voice was tight with rage.

"You aren't interested in facts. You've made your mind up based on the shoddy reporting of one woman. The only thing you care about, other than your image and your precious Yolanda, is being right."

Her mother faced her, her eyelashes fluttering dangerously. "Excuse me?"

Kayla shut her eyes, wondering if she really wanted to finally get into this with her mom. She thought about all the times her mother made comments about her friends, especially the musicians she hung out with in high school and college. They were never the right kind of people from the right kind of families or neighborhoods.

"If you're going to make a statement like that, you had better be prepared to defend your position."

Kayla pinched the bridge of her nose. "This is not one of your lectures, Mom. I am not one of your students."

"That's an understatement," her mother muttered. "My students *finish* their education."

It was a blow low enough for Kayla to open her eyes and really look at her. She took in her sour expression and judgmental body language—nose in the air, arms crossed in defiance.

"You're prejudiced," Kayla said.

"What on earth are you talking about?"

"You are. You're prejudiced against anyone who doesn't travel in your circles."

Eyes widening, her mother opened her mouth. Closed it. Blinked. "I can honestly say, I don't think I've ever heard anything so...so...utterly ridiculous in my life."

"I don't doubt it."

"You're calling me a, what? A—"

"A snob," Kayla supplied, wanting to use a much harsher word.

"Good Lord, Katherine," her mother exclaimed. "What has gotten into you since you moved away?"

"Do you remember Trevor?"

Her mom frowned. "Who?"

"Trevor Gramm," Kayla said. "He was the little boy I met at summer camp when I was seven. We were fast friends, and I was so excited that we didn't live very far apart. I wanted to invite him to my birthday party, but you told me he wasn't able to come."

"I don't know what that has to do with this conversation." She wrung her hands, discomfort all over her beautiful face.

"I think you do know. You want me to support my statement? That's what I'm doing." Kayla pulled out a stool and sat at the counter as if it were a real debate prep. "You told me you'd called Trevor's parents but that they had another birthday party to go to. I was upset, but I tried to have fun anyway. Even though I didn't know most of the people you invited."

"Really, Kathy." Her mom turned and opened a cabinet, taking down a glass. "Have some orange juice."

"I don't like orange juice. You never called them," Kayla continued. "When I saw Trevor at Lara Kern's party a month later, he wouldn't speak to me. You know why? Because I hadn't invited him to my party."

"I'm surprised you remember something so…" Her mother pulled a carafe of juice from the fridge. "You were so young."

"Do you remember Miriam Smith?"

Her mother pursed her lips. "How could I forget that little thief?"

"Miriam wasn't a thief, Mom. I told you a million times that I borrowed your silver cuff bracelet without asking," Kayla said. "I lost it in the woods behind the school. *Me*. Miriam had nothing to do with it, but you blamed her anyway and forbade me from seeing her outside of school."

"She was a bad influence," her mother argued. "I did what was best for you. I always have."

"Were you doing what was best for me when you called the dean of students at Claremont and told him I'd changed my mind about attending?"

Her mother took a sip of the juice.

"Trevor. Miriam. Bryce Joyner, who wanted to take me to prom," Kayla said, her blood boiling with each memory card she laid on the table for her mother. "Do you know what they all had in common?"

Her mom straightened. "I know where you're going with this, and I'd advise you not to say another word."

"You've spent your entire career celebrating the achievements of the African American community. I just don't understand why"—Kayla paused to take a breath—"why are you so quick to believe the worst of people just because they didn't grow up with your privilege?"

"I won't even dignify that with an answer."

"But you know it's true."

"It's nonsense!" she replied in as close to a shout as Kayla had ever heard from her. "Why? How could you level such an infantile accusation? Because I don't want my daughter associated with a miscreant who should have gone to prison for assault? Who tried to plagiarize the work of a legacy student who isn't even here to defend herself? I know the Stanwicks. They're upstanding people. Richard Stanwick is a great supporter of higher education." Her mom set the glass down so hard, Kayla was surprised it didn't crack. "My God, I cannot believe you. This is what makes me a bad mother?"

"No," Kayla said, trying to remain calm. "What makes you a bad mother is that you never listen to me. You never *hear* me."

Her mom actually rolled her eyes.

"Am I not your daughter?"

She frowned. "Of course you are, though I know you wish it weren't so."

Kayla ignored that comment. "If I'm your daughter, if I am the child of Geoffrey and Gisele Larrington, if I grew up under this roof and under your tutelage, what makes you think I would associate with someone capable of doing the things you think Ty is capable of doing?" She wanted to take issue with her mother's dismissal of Tiff, even though the rumors were unfounded. One chunk at a time.

"Sometimes, nurture isn't enough. It certainly wasn't enough to keep you in school."

She had a point, but Kayla wasn't about to concede it. She opted for a different tact. "Mom, I'm...I'm not blinded by hormones. You know I have never been one to walk around looking at the world through rose-colored glasses. That's your handiwork—yours and Dad's. You taught Zach and I that life isn't always fair. It isn't always kind. Sometimes it's shitty—"

"Language, Katherine."

"Sometimes, it's awful," Kayla rephrased. "But we adapt. We fight for what's right, but we get on with it. Am I wrong?"

"No, you're not wrong," her mother admitted.

"Did you ever stop to wonder *why* I left the way I did?" Kayla asked. "Why I left school, left home?" *Left you.*

"You were headstrong and willful," she offered, but there was no bite in her words.

"Mom, I was *suffocating.*" Uncomfortable silence followed her confession. "You... After Zach... You kept me under a microscope, and it was all too much. You were too much, Mom. The extracurriculars, and the tutors, and the book tours, and the clothes...the hair. Being your project, being Katherine Yolanda Larrington, prodigy, your...archetype. Your Little Miss Yolanda. All I wanted was to be your daughter. I wanted you to be my mom."

"I only ever tried to mold you into the woman you were meant to be." Her mom's voice cracked a little, her shoulders sagging an inch.

"Do you get to decide who that is?" Kayla needed to make her understand. "Or do I get to choose the person I want to be?"

"I'm your mother. It's my job to help you achieve your potential, especially being who I am, your father and I both. Anything less would feel like failure."

"I get that, I do. But honestly, I think I spent more time with Dr. Larrington than I ever did with my mom," Kayla said. "I needed *you*. Just you. And you weren't there for me." She cursed under her breath when her mom visibly flinched.

"I…"

She reached across the counter and covered her mother's hand with her own. "Mom, I love you. I do, and I know I haven't said that enough over the years. And I know I've put you in an impossible situation. I never wanted that, and I'm so sorry, but I was afraid to be myself around you."

Her mother's eyes filled with unshed tears. "Kathy, sweetheart, I love you. I hope you know that."

"I do." Kayla tightened her hand around her mother's. "But sometimes, you've really disappointed me. I needed you to support me, not turn me into some perfect ideal. I needed you to encourage me. But it was like you didn't see me, you just saw Yolanda and the Larrington legacy."

Her tears spilled over. "Oh…Katherine, *no*. I never meant to make you feel like you were anything less than extraordinary. I was hard on you both because I didn't want you to take all your gifts for granted. You can't afford to in this world."

Kayla could feel her own eyes start to prickle. "I know. And I know you meant well."

Her mother's gaze was steady on her, but she drew her lips in, blinking as if trying to decide whether or not to share her thoughts.

"Do you know why I resisted the idea of you playing the drums?"

Surprised by the question, Kayla shook her head.

"It was because of Zachary."

"Zach? Why? He loved teaching me. We—"

"I *know*," her mom said. She pulled a stool out from the island and sat down. "He adored you, and you him. And he would have sliced the moon into small pieces if it would have helped you to hold it in your hands when you were a little girl. Zachary thought the world of you, and you thought he hung the stars in the sky. I was worried..." She paused, and it only then occurred to Kayla how tired she looked.

Her hair, though pulled back into its usual style, was mussed. As if she'd run her hands over it again and again. There were faint circles under her eyes, and her bright eyes were a little dull.

"I failed you, didn't I?"

"No, Mom. No. I turned out okay." She smiled, relieved when her mom returned it.

"It's just that, Zachary was everything to you. Your father and I knew that, and we cherished how close you were. And when Zach... when he...was no longer with us, we worried... Well, *I* worried that you would try to emulate him. He died...he *died* because I indulged him. Because he wanted a life in music, and I didn't insist. I didn't... and that night, he...we argued." The words were stilted, as if it physically hurt her to say them.

It hurt Kayla to hear the pain in her mother's voice. She'd tried so hard to prevent it, had tried to keep her two worlds from colliding for this very reason. She reached out to clasp her hand and found warm, dry fingers that trembled only slightly.

Their gazes met. "I thought playing the drums was your way of staying connected to Zachary, and I didn't want you to...commit your life to mourning. I didn't understand that your passion for playing isn't about him."

"It is," Kayla said. "Some of it is, you were right. I do feel close to Zach when I play. I know we weren't twins, but he felt like a twin. He…"

"I know." Her mother gave her a watery smile. "Truthfully, I'm glad you have something so…creative and tangible to keep him close to you."

"What do you have, Mom? You never talk about Zach. We never—"

"What? I have you, Katherine." She smiled and it was full of both sorrow and sympathy. "We have *you*."

They looked at each other across the island, her mother's fingers warm and fine in her calloused hand. Kayla had never felt so *other* in her life, and yet it was the first time she thought, maybe, her mother saw her.

"Tyrell…" she said carefully. "He's sweet and gentle, and so fu…freaking smart."

"Is he?" There was only a small percentage of her mother's usual judgment in her tone. Kayla took that as a promising sign.

"He's an avid reader, loves his granddad more than anything in the world, and was in the middle of getting his degree when this…horrible thing happened to him. It happened *to* him. It was nothing he did."

Her mother's brow creased as she considered Kayla's words. She leaned forward on her elbows and stared deep into Kayla's eyes, searching, perhaps, for the truth.

"That reporter who called the house, Marsh, she had some damning things to say against him. And what in the world was that video of you in a fight? Heavens, I'd almost forgotten about that."

"It's not what it looks like, trust me."

Her mother raised a skeptical brow but nodded. "I'm trying, Katherine. You don't make it easy. So much like your brother."

"I know, and I'm sorry, but I'm not Zach. Listen," Kayla said. "Things are changing for me, Mom, which means they'll likely change for you too. The Lillys, my band, they have a lot of potential. A lot of buzz. But if…" She swallowed hard. "Do you want me to…walk away? From the band? Would it help?"

"What?" Releasing her hand, her mother sat back, alarmed. "Why on earth would you ask me that? Of course I would never ask you to do that."

"I know you don't approve."

"I don't. But your father played your song for me this morning," her mother said, surprising Kayla once again. "I must say I was rather impressed. You've come a long way since I used to find your pounding away on your brother's drum set."

Kayla laughed, feeling lighter. "I should hope so."

"Well, you always were an overachiever when it was something you were passionate about."

Kayla didn't miss her mother's pointed look, remembering the arguments they'd had over piano practice, math homework, and all the other things she'd hated doing as a kid.

"Didn't you write that the difference between mediocrity and excellence was passion?"

Her mother blinked with surprise. "You've read my books?"

"Of course I have, Mom," Kayla replied softly.

Her mother reached across the island and grasped both of her hands. It felt like they had reached a long overdue understanding, and Kayla feared her eyes were going to start leaking, so she looked away, blinking rapidly as she fought back the tears.

"Ty is reading the new one. He didn't even know you were my mom when he bought it."

"Katherine," her mother tone was teasing. "Don't tell me you're ashamed of Yolanda."

"No, not that. I wanted to… I was trying to…" Kayla didn't know how to explain. "I wanted to see if the world would want to know me as *me*. Ty does."

"You really like him, don't you." It wasn't a question.

"Yeah."

Her mom's smile was a little sad. "Then I suppose we'll have to meet him. And learn more about your band. The Lillys?"

"That's them. They're a great group, Mom. They're like a second family, and we all look out for each other."

"I'm so happy you have that in your life," she replied. "I do worry. Though I know you have an iron will, and you don't suffer fools, you have a soft heart. But you're right. I should trust your judgment more, and I promise to try, but I need you to meet me halfway. Even when we disagree, I'm still your mother and you're my only..." Her voice faltered and she cleared her throat. "I want to be a part of your life. Please don't shut me out again."

"Oh, Mom...I promise." Kayla's heart swelled. She was full of love for this woman who had given birth to her, who had sometimes pushed her, who had always loved her, even when she'd chosen to show it in frustrating ways. Covering her mother's hand, she squeezed as their gazes locked. There was so much in their silent exchange. Regret, hope, and love—so much love—shone in her mother's eyes.

She was under no delusion that things would magically change overnight between them but her mother was trying. She was listening. Even more surprising, she seemed to hear Kayla. It was all she'd ever hoped for.

"There are my two favorite girls."

Kayla's dad entered the kitchen and dropped a kiss onto her head. Picking up the glass of orange juice, he winked at her mother before taking a giant sip.

"Hi, Daddy. I'm sorry I can't stay longer. There's a lot to deal with," she said, standing.

"Anything I can help with, sweetheart?" her father asked.

"My people will handle things on our end," Kayla said.

Her father grinned at her mom. "Listen to her. My baby has *people*."

"Didn't you know? I'm a rock star now. Sorta," Kayla teased, putting on her sunglasses. "Are you sure you're okay with this, Mom?"

"I will be." Her eyes were clear, her expression determined. "We won't let some second-rate shill ruin your momentum. If this is what you really want for your life, we support you. Even if the university and I part ways and I never publish another book, I'll simply find a new path to conquer while I watch my daughter bring her dreams to fruition."

There was Dr. Gisele Larrington. For once, Kayla was thrilled to see her. She kissed her dad's cheeks and then went to her mom.

They hugged for a long moment before her mother took Kayla by the arms and held her back a little. "You've...given me some food for thought, Kath...*Kayla*. Thank you for opening up to me."

Kayla smiled. "I'm just glad there was room on your plate."

CHAPTER 43.

IT WAS UNUSUAL FOR TY to go more than a few hours in Van's presence without finding himself drawn into an hours-long conversation on his granddad's topic of the day. Be it cars, politics, or his thoughts on who produced the best butter, Pop-Pop was always up for a good talk. It was disquieting, to say the least, these last few days of near silence.

Intellectually, Ty knew it was due, in part, to the anesthesia. Van's doctor had warned him that it affected people his age a bit differently. And that it might take a few days to work its way out of his system.

The staff at River Willows was well-versed in the aftercare for the heart procedure, but Ty hadn't felt comfortable leaving his grandfather in the care of virtual strangers. He'd spent the last two nights on the pullout sofa in Van's living room. The facility had a policy of no guests for more than three consecutive nights and only once per month. He'd have to leave soon, and it made the eggs on his plate taste like cardboard.

"I can hear you worrying from all the way over here," his grand-dad said from his position on the couch. "I already told you I don't need you hovering over me. I'm fine."

Ty hadn't gotten a full night's sleep in days. He was tired, he missed Kayla like mad, and he'd just about had enough.

"You know, I'd be more inclined to believe you, old man, if you hadn't lied to me about your arrhythmia." It sounded harsh but, damn, it had really been eating at him.

"I was handling it," Van snapped back. "I had regular appointments with the cardiologist, tried all the meds they prescribed, and agreed to have the procedure on their recommendation. I'm not sure what else you would have had me do."

Ty got up and stalked into the living room. "Maybe tell me? That would have been a start."

Van glared up at him. He seemed a little smaller, somehow, practically engulfed by the sofa cushions and the throw blanket. And yet, his eyes blazed with anger.

"All you would have done is fuss over me and put your life on hold trying to be some sort of caregiver," he said, his lips twitching when he pressed them together. Ty realized he was holding back tears. "You need to understand that *I* am not your life, Tyrell. I am not your responsibility."

"But you are!"

"No," Pop-Pop said sharply.

Ty sank into the armchair and put his head in his hands.

"Is this why you didn't look into the circumstances surrounding your case?" his granddad asked, his voice softer. Sadness dripping from every syllable. "Because finding a resolution there would have freed you to become what you were on your way to becoming?"

"Which was what?" Ty raised his head to meet his granddad's gaze. "I didn't have a path. I had an idea. I still don't have a path, even though I'm going to get closure on this whole mess."

"Well," Van said. "I'm glad for that. Have you heard anything?"

"Rami said he'd call when he had news. He reached out to the DA's office first thing Monday about getting my record expunged."

His granddad nodded. "You'll find your way, Ty. I keep telling

you. But you have to let go of this idea that I need... Look, I love
you, son, but why you think I moved to this place?"

"For the kitchen?" Ty joked, grateful when Pop-Pop smiled.

"Exactly." Van nodded. "And also, to give you a push." He
studied Ty for a moment. "Could you get something for me?"

Ty shot to his feet. "What do you need?"

"Go to my desk, the center drawer, and bring me the big envelope there."

Ty fetched the envelope. It was thick, legal-sized, and his heart
clenched at the thought he might be holding his granddad's last will
and testament. His hand shook when he handed it over.

"Sit," Van ordered. Ty obeyed, feeling all of fourteen years old
again, like when his granddad gave him *the talk*.

His granddad opened the envelope and pulled out a stack of
papers. A few sections were flagged with brightly colored sticky
tabs, and he flipped to those.

"Find me a pen."

Ty handed him one from the coffee table.

"And give me a dollar."

"A dollar?" Ty asked, not sure where Van was going with this.
Was he loopy from the meds?

"One dollar," Van clarified, looking up at him. "Or are you
one of those millennials that don't carry cash? I've got the Venmo,
you know."

Ty snorted. "I've got cash. Some old man I know insisted that I
always have some on me, just in case." He pulled out his wallet and
handed his granddad the newest, crispest dollar bill he had.

"Good, now sign here." Van put the stack of papers down and
turned them toward Ty.

Ty frowned. He scanned the page in front of him, confused,
until he realized what he was looking at. "You're...selling me the
house? For a dollar?"

"Happy birthday."

"My birthday already passed," Ty reminded him, incredulous.

"Happy belated birthday, then. Sign the papers." He held out the pen for Ty to take.

"I can't accept this," Ty said, shaking his head. "What would I do with a house?"

"Live in it? Sell it? It's up to you."

"Is this even legal?"

His granddad's smile was more like the old Van than Ty had seen in days. "Oh, it's legal. Happens all the time in Philly. Sign."

"But..."

Sighing, his granddad dropped his hand to his lap. "Tyrell," he said, waiting for Ty to meet his gaze. "Let me do this for you. And if not for you, then for me. Let go, son."

Kayla wandered through Ty's childhood bedroom as if she were in a museum, hands clasped behind her back as she leaned in to inspect something. Reaching out to run a careful fingertip across an old poster.

"Billie Joe Armstrong," she said, glancing at Ty over her shoulder. "He did it for you, huh?"

Ty turned and wrapped his arms around her waist, peering over her shoulder at the poster. "I didn't know if I wanted to be him or just wanted him," he said. "It was a very confusing time, but a light bulb went off when I read that he was bisexual."

"I'm pretty sure most of the band is bi." Kayla kissed him on the cheek and pointed at a trophy on his bookshelf as he nuzzled his favorite spot on her neck. "You won a writing contest?"

She stepped out of his embrace and picked up the brass and marble figurine. It was supposed to be a man hunched over a desk with a plume in his hand, but to Ty, it had always looked more like a dude falling asleep at work.

"It was nothing."

Kayla arched a brow at him. "It says National Beecher Prize for Poetry."

"Honestly, it was between a bunch of high school kids. I was fifteen or sixteen."

Pursing her lips, Kayla put the trophy down and picked up the slim volume beside it. "Can you read it to me?"

She sat down on the bed and beckoned him to her.

Ty blinked. "Read what?"

"Your award-winning poem." She looked so enthused, bless her.

"Yeah, I don't think I want to jeopardize what we've got going on here," Ty said, laughing at her puppy dog expression. He dutifully followed her direction as she patted the space next to her.

Kayla pushed out her bottom lip and held the book out for him. "Please? I'll make it worth your while."

It was impossible to miss the spark of want in her eyes. The implication of her words smacked into him like a wrecking ball—his desire for her suddenly a third presence in the room. "Well," he said. "If you insist." Ty took the paperback from her and settled his back against the headboard.

In one smooth move, Kayla straddled him. She gathered the hem of his T-shirt and rucked it up.

"What are you doing?"

"What am I doing?" Her laugh was soft and full of heat. "I must be doing it wrong if you don't know."

Ty lifted his arms, and she pulled the shirt over his head.

It was difficult to concentrate on the words in front of him with someone peppering his face and neck with kisses. Particularly when that someone was the person he most wanted to be with for any foreseeable future.

Kayla whipped her tank top off. Underneath, the bra was black lace and the tops of her breasts threatened to spill over the cups.

Ty couldn't breathe.

"You're not reading," she said as she reached between them and pulled his kilt up his thighs. She wore a pair of cutoff shorts, and the blast of heat from her bare skin against his was unbearable.

"Sorry."

Every kiss an ember, every look a flame.

"Every touch steals my breath and curls it around your name."

"Jesus," Kayla muttered as she went still. "That's...hot."

"Yeah?"

"Yeah. Don't stop. I love the rhythm of your words."

Her praise lit him up from the inside. Suddenly, Ty could imagine all the things they might do together. Travel to places he'd only ever dreamed of going, get into heated arguments over their favorite books, and, yes, this.

When she rolled off him and shoved her shorts down and off, Ty's mind filled with other things they might do. Imminently.

"All I ever wanted is your everything."

But not in this bed.

Ty moaned when she straddled him again, shifting to get comfortable so he could sink into the pleasure of the moment. Had his mattress always been this lumpy, or was it the weight of two people too much for the ancient twin box spring?

"You're into this, I can tell." She grinned, putting pressure where he needed it most. "But something's off."

"It's this bed," Ty said, setting the book down beside them. He reached up and ran a hand over Kayla's hair to her cheek, running a thumb across her swollen lips. "Trust me, you're incredible. But this room..."

"Isn't it every teen's fantasy to sneak someone into the house for this very thing?" she asked, flashing a wicked grin.

This time, she pressed herself right up against his growing length. Ty's eyes fluttered shut as she ground her hips against him. Taking her waist into his hands, he tried to still her movement.

"If you keep doing that, this is going to be over before we can start."

"Can't have that," Kayla said. Her voice was husky in his ear, and Ty wasn't sure how he was supposed to prevent the inevitable. It was akin to stopping a runaway train by adding grease to the wheels.

"We need to... I don't even know what," he croaked, his fingers tightening on her hips when she nipped at his ear. "Fuck...Kayla..."

"Condom," she rasped.

Ty fumbled open the drawer, ready to rip the thing off its railings, before it finally opened. He pulled out a strip of three and tossed them on the bed.

Kayla's eyes flashed with delight, and she snatched it and tore one off. She glanced down at the tented fabric of his kilt. "Please say yes."

"Yesssssss," he groaned. "Fucking yes, whatever it is, please. Need your hands on me, mouth, whatever you want. Just yes." It was an incoherent torrent of words, and Ty would have been embarrassed if Kayla hadn't slid off his thighs and knelt between his open legs.

"I've wanted to do this for weeks." She flipped up the kilt and sat back on her heels. Staring. "Whoa. Tyrell Baldwin. Do you always go commando when you wear a kilt?"

He snorted. "Are you kidding?"

Kayla grinned and smoothed a hand up his thigh to his groin, where she circled her fingers around the base. His body gave a warning jolt, and her grin widened even further.

"You're saying this is just for me?"

"All for you." *All because of you*, he wanted to say but couldn't, because her lips grazed the tip and his vocabulary was reduced to *God, yes* and *do that again.*

Kayla swiped her tongue across his slit, and every muscle in Ty's body clenched. She kissed down his length, and he swore. "Kayla," he warned.

She made quick work of the condom and went up on her knees before him, stripping off her bra. She was gloriously naked except for the scrap of fabric that served as her underwear. Ty had expected her to take them off, but she straddled him with them still in place.

"In my bus fantasy," she began, straddling his hips. "You're driving, and I'm sitting on you just like this."

"Dangerous," Ty murmured, his entire body humming like a live wire.

"Indeed." Kayla reached between them and stroked him. "And we're kissing. I love kissing you by the way. Love the way you put your whole body into it."

"I love kissing you too," Ty confessed. "Love your mouth, love touching you. I really love your hands on me."

"In my fantasy, I…"

Kayla lifted up and, shifting her underwear aside, sank down onto him, agonizingly slow but fast enough to push the breath out of his lungs. She went blessedly still when she was fully seated, and Ty took a moment to collect his brain cells and put them back where they belonged. Roughly.

He skimmed his hands up her body and pulled her against his chest.

Kayla leaned in and kissed him, desperate and greedy, and Ty gave as good as he got. It had been forever since he'd connected with anyone like this.

When she began to move, he gently pushed her back so he could see. Because he needed to see her, see this. He bunched the fabric of the kilt up as much as he could, wishing he'd taken it off. There was no time now.

"Ty," she panted, rising and falling as she gripped his shoulders.

He wanted to hold on for her, tried to make it last. It was unreal, being inside her, being held by her. Wanted by her. Ty forced himself to breathe, to look at her.

He watched her face, watched her ecstasy play out across her gorgeous features as she chased her release, fulfilled her own fantasy because she was his. She was the only one he'd ever had come true.

A low groan tore from his throat. "Kayla…"

"I know." She made a helpless, intoxicating sound. "Fuck, I know."

Her hips stuttered.

"Oh, God," she panted, her head thrown back and her eyes squeezed shut.

Ty pulled her close and bent his head to latch on to one of her nipples. Kayla cried out brokenly. Her name spilled from his lips like a prayer when his own release hit a moment later.

Kayla's head dropped forward, and she locked her gaze with his. She wore the same awestruck look of contentment in her eyes Ty was sure she saw in his. She wrapped her arms around him, and Ty held her close, breathing in her scent.

They sat like that, both heaving in ragged breaths until their racing hearts calmed down. Kayla stroked his hair, his shoulders, his back as Ty rested his cheek against her shoulder. He smoothed his hand up her back and into her hair before drawing her into a languid kiss.

"If I were a teenager, I wouldn't have lasted three seconds," Ty confessed.

He kissed her again, working hard to ignore the way his feet dangled off the end of the bed when he stretched out his legs. This really was ridiculous, but it was also kind of hot.

Kayla settled into the circle of his arms, their tongues dancing—little sighs escaping from her mouth into his—and he was content to stay in his lumpy, too-small bed forever if it meant he got to hold her like this.

"I'm surprised Van didn't buy you a bigger bed when you got older."

"Can we not talk about my grandpop right now?" Ty said.

Kayla laughed softly against his neck.

Ty ran a hand down the curve of her spine, and she sighed.

A loud crack split the air as the bed frame gave way, and one corner of it hit the ground.

Kayla lifted her head, her eyes wide on Ty's, and they both burst into laughter.

"Okay, maybe I do need to shop for a new bed," Ty said when they quieted.

"Uh, you think?" Kayla grinned. She rolled her lips as if she wanted to say something more.

"What?" Ty ran the top of his finger across her brow, which was damp with sweat with a few tiny curls clinging to it.

Kayla propped her hands under her chin, resting them on his chest. "Don't freak out, because this is just a suggestion. I know we're new and haven't really known each other that long, but…"

"Kayla," Ty said, his heartbeat ticking up again. "Just say it."

"Move in with me," she blurted. She seemed to hold her breath, awaiting his answer.

Ty thought about making her suffer a little longer, but it had been on his mind too. He'd just thought it was too much, too soon.

"Okay," he said shrugging. He would have said it a thousand times to put the smile on her face that was there now.

"Really?" Her eyes were so soft for him, it made Ty's heart grow three times its size.

"Yeah, really. Van wants me to sell this place and use the money for…I dunno…life. A place to live that's not here. School. Whatever."

"That's quite a gift," Kayla said.

"Right? Turns out, he bought shares in some app start-up a while back, and the company just sold for a bazillion dollars," Ty said, still not quite believing it himself. "He'd pretty much forgotten about it until he read an article about how well they're doing. Then he cashed some in."

"Seriously? That's… Wow, Ty, that's wonderful!" She smiled. "I'm happy for Van. And I'm happy for you. You both deserve it."

"It wasn't a ton of money, but he has enough to cover his expenses, plus a good amount left over for whatever he might need or want."

"Very cool." Kayla pecked his lips.

"So, yeah, let's do it."

Kayla rolled off him and got to her feet.

"Hey, where are you going?"

"To get my laptop," she replied, throwing on one of Ty's T-shirts. And, yeah, he could get used to that sight. "I'm not giving you a chance to change your mind."

Kayla left the room, bouncing on the balls of her feet like a kid on Christmas morning.

Change his mind? Not a chance in hell.

CHAPTER 44.

EXCERPT FROM INTERVIEW "THE SECRET
LIFE OF LITTLE MISS YOLANDA"

TOMIN HALE EXCLUSIVE FOR
SPINWIRE MAGAZINE

If you're in your late twenties or early thirties, chances are you've read—or had read to you—*Dream to Be*, a story about a gifted young girl who dreams of growing up to be a teacher like her mother. It's book one in the Little Miss Yolanda series, one of the bestselling series of children's books in half a century.

Little Miss Yolanda, instantly recognizable by her bronze skin, bright red hair, and constellation of freckles, is the ideal child. She's well-mannered, obedient, and yet curious about the world around her. To many, she feels as real as the kid that lived next door. As real as you or me.

Because she is.

But why am I writing about a board book in a music magazine? You'd be forgiven for not making the connection. I hadn't, not even when I met Little Miss Yolanda in real life. In fact, had she not come to me and asked for this interview, I might never have known.

The Lillys are a band out of Philadelphia, via New York City. You may have heard some of the buzz around them, a lot of it tied to their former guitarist, Candi Fair (Sugar Habit). Bands don't always live up to the hype, but I was blown away by their set at Indio. Don't let the marketing copy fool you, these women rock hard. None of them harder than drummer Kayla Whitman, whose flaming red curls can be seen from the back of the largest festival crowd.

That's right, folks. Little Miss Yolanda is living the dream.

Tomin Hale: You went to seemingly great lengths to hide your identity. What made you out yourself now?

Kayla Whitman: I was tired of lying to my family. Tired of hiding parts of who I am. I owed it to all the kids who read Little Miss Yolanda. I want them to know that every dream is valid, even if it isn't the one others might want for you.

TH: And your mom? Do you worry how you being in a band like the Lillys will affect her? Those books were her first bestsellers, and she built her career off of their success.

KW: I did worry, but I underestimated my mom. She's resilient, which is where I guess I get that from. My dad is the diplomat; my mom is the fighter.

TH: She's okay with your life choices, then?

KW: (pauses) We're…getting there.

———————

"Just so we're clear, Ty's record is wiped clean, correct?" Jordan asked around a bite of pizza.

It had been a week since the band—minus Tiffany—had returned from the West Coast. An eventful week for Kayla, Ty, and their respective families. As they sat around the table at the Electric Unicorn, the couple tried to catch them up on current events.

"I'm free and clear," Ty said, smiling. He moved through the world as if a weight had been lifted from his soul, and she supposed it had been. "The DA examined my case and sent it to the chief of police, who did an in-depth review of all the documents. He tore the captain at that precinct a new one, actually. The DA is reviewing some of his other cases."

"I'm kinda kicking myself." He shook his head. "I can't believe how…well, not easy but… I mean, it all came together so quickly. I shouldn't have waited."

She didn't know what to say to that. He'd been through so much. "You had your reasons, babe."

Ty inhaled a deep breath. "The bottom line is, it's over," he said. "I can move on with my life, my granddad can retire in peace, and…" He glanced at Kayla. "For the first time in a long time, I'm looking forward to tomorrow."

"I'm so happy for you, Ty," Toni said, giving his arm a squeeze. "And I'm glad your granddad's doing okay."

"Okay?" Kayla laughed. "He's living the dream. You should see the place he moved to. It's a goddamned luxury resort."

"It is," Ty agreed. "I'm still pissed I can't live there myself."

"You already have a place to live," Kayla reminded him. He grinned. "Though my hotel isn't exactly home. We need to step up the search for our apartment before we have to hit the road again."

"Speaking of which," Seb said. "I got the itinerary from Broken Pilots."

"And?" Lilly asked.

His mouth twisted into a wry grin. "Twenty-two cities," he said, pausing for effect. "That's the U.S. leg."

"What do you mean, the U.S. leg?" Toni asked.

Jordan wiped his mouth and sat back. "It's thirty cities, in total. Twenty-two here, three in Canada, four in South America plus Mexico City. YMI will split our touring expenses with Broken Pilots' label—which happens to be their own, of course, so they're covering the other half."

"We can go over the logistics in more detail since we're still hammering out some things," Seb said.

Jordan nodded. "Indeed. But still, it's exciting stuff." He turned to Ty. "Fancy being our driver again?"

Kayla met Ty's gaze. "I think he has other plans."

"I'm going to go back to school," Ty said, smiling shyly. "And I've got to get the house ready for market, put some of my handyman skills to good use."

"You have handyman skills?" Kayla asked, loving the mental picture of Ty shirtless in a pair of overalls, his tool belt around his hips, sweaty and glistening and...

"Earth to Kayla," Toni said, laughing. "I think we've lost her."

Ty nudged Kayla's shoulder. "I'd like to come check out some of the shows if I can."

"You're always welcome," Lilly said, surprising Kayla. Ty, too, evidently—judging by the look on his face. "Kayla told me about the lyrics you've been working on. I'd love to see them."

Kayla felt herself blanch.

Ty turned a questioning brow to her. "Lyrics?"

"I forgot to mention your notebook," she said sheepishly. "You left it on the bus, and I...uh... In my defense, your poetry is phenomenal and so lyrical, I just thought..."

His smile, his eyes, everything was so soft for her that Kayla wanted to melt. "It's cool." He turned to Lilly. "I think she's biased, but if there's anything of mine that you want to use, I'd be more than flattered."

Lilly's smile sparkled. "Thank you, Ty."

"I told you." Jordan clasped Ty's shoulder and shook him a little, beaming at him like a proud big brother. "Once we let you in, you're family."

"Speaking of family, I need to run some things over to Pop-Pop's," Ty said, standing.

Kayla moved to get up.

"Stay," he said, dropping a kiss to the top of her head. "I'll see you back at the hotel."

Fuck. She loved this person so hard.

"Oh yes, you will," Kayla replied, waggling her eyebrows lasciviously.

"I thought we were bad," Seb said to Toni.

"Oh, you are," Kayla and Jordan agreed simultaneously.

When Ty was gone, the table fell silent. Kayla wondered if she was about to be subjected to another lecture. But she'd gotten through her talk with her mother, so she could handle whatever this was.

"Okay," she said when no one broke the stalemate. "Just say what you're going to say."

Toni and Seb shared a look.

Jordan examined his pizza crust.

But Lilly met her eyes. "I like Tyrell, but don't you think this is a little fast, moving in together?"

Kayla took a breath. Sitting back in her chair, she tried to summon the words to express what she had with Ty. How he'd filled a space in her life she hadn't known was empty. How they didn't complete each other, they complemented each other—which was an important distinction. How they fit perfectly. So perfect, it was frightening. How loving him was as easy as breathing and as freeing as playing the drums in front of a crowd of thousands.

She opened her mouth to say all of this. Instead, she asked Lilly, "Haven't you ever met someone, and the moment you met them, your heart suddenly made sense to you?"

Lilly swallowed. Her gaze darted to Seb before she dropped it to the table, and Kayla blinked, unsure of what she'd just witnessed.

Seb sat with his arm around Toni, their attention on Kayla.

"I've always wanted a little brother," Lilly said. She lifted her eyes to Kayla and smiled.

"And he deserves a family like ours," Kayla replied. "A sister like you."

And a love like theirs.

EPILOGUE.

THREE WEEKS LATER.

KAYLA TAPPED THE PATTERN AGAINST her thigh so she wouldn't forget it, cursing herself for not bringing a notepad into the booth.

"Why are we stopped?" she asked into the microphone.

"Tiff had a phone call," Richie replied in her headset.

Figuring it would be a few minutes before Tiff was done, Kayla took the headphones off and climbed from behind the drum kit. The chill from the AC swept over her as she opened the door and stepped into the live room. She made sure to close the door firmly behind her, giving Richie the thumbs-up to crank the AC in there while he could.

"Is it me," Kayla said. "Or has Tiff been...a little subdued lately?"

Toni propped a hip against the windowsill. "She has been kinda quiet ever since she came back from LA."

"How did it go with Peaches, did she say?"

"Only that she handled it," Lilly replied. "I didn't push."

"You never do." At Lilly's sharp look, Kayla held up her hands. "It wasn't criticism, only an observation."

"I prefer not to impose myself," Lilly said as she cracked open a can of Dr Pepper.

"Since when do you drink soda?"

"She has a special relationship with DP," Toni said, smirking. She and Lilly exchanged an amused look.

"Hey, I'm going to need more details on that," Kayla teased as she opened the door to the control room. "Richie, you don't happen to have a spare notepad, do you?"

"I might," Ty replied, and Kayla spun around.

"Hey, you!" She ran and jumped into his arms, wrapping her legs around his waist and kissing him soundly. "I thought you had an open house today."

"I did," he confirmed, grinning. "A couple put a cash offer on the house."

"It sold?"

"It sold."

"Aww, babe." Sliding to her feet, Kayla pulled Ty back into her arms. "I'm sure you have mixed feelings about all of this."

"Nah," he said. He smiled, but it didn't reach his eyes. "I have everything I need."

Ty planted a soft kiss on her lips, and she let out a happy sigh.

"I'm calling it," Lilly said as she emerged from the live room. "I don't know where Tiff went, but it's not clicking today anyway."

"Maybe we need a break," Toni said.

"I'm here, I'm here," Tiff jogged back into the room. "Sorry."

"Everything okay?" Toni asked her.

Tiff shook out her shoulders and picked up her bass. "Peachy. Let's do this."

There was a beat of silence before Lilly said, "All right, let's try again."

Kayla pecked Ty on the cheek and made her way back behind the kit. Once everyone settled, Tiff's voice came through the headset.

"Kayla, give us a new beat. Something driving."

"I'll try." Kayla checked her sticks. One was chipped at the tip, so she swapped them for a fresh pair.

"There is no try," Tiff replied and Kayla grinned, happy to see a little of the old Tiff.

"There is only do." Kayla started with a simple 4/4 that somehow tripped into a variation of John Bonham's "Ramble On," but it felt good and loose. She leaned into it, playing the syncopated kick along with the ghost notes on the snare. At the end of each measure she added an accented sixteenth note on the hi-hat. For a few moments, things were quiet except for her drums, and she noodled for several measures before looping back around to the top.

"Ooo! I like that," Tiff exclaimed, thumping in time on her bass. "Do it again."

Kayla pressed her mental rewind and went back over the pattern she'd casually tossed out without realizing it. Somewhere along the way, she had developed the ability to mimic herself. She didn't know where or when or how, only that it had come in handy at moments like this. She knew she'd found the groove again when Tiff's eyes lit up on the other side of the glass, and her noodling coalesced into something solid and complementary.

Toni strummed along, quietly working her way through chords as she tuned in to Tiff and nodded along to Kayla, who had settled into the pattern by now.

Once Tiff found the pocket and landed on the line she wanted to play, Toni finally worked out her part.

Kayla sat in awe, watching the two women work. Her own hands were on autopilot. So lost in the moment that she startled when Lilly's voice rang out over the earphones.

"Are we recording this?"

"Fuck yes," Seb replied from the control room. "Don't stop."

For the next twenty minutes, they jammed, playing with no particular direction in mind. Kayla loved these moments almost as much as she loved performing in front of crowds. The synergy she had with these people floored her at times. By the time they stopped, every cell in her body was buzzing with possibility.

"Hot damn!" Tiff exclaimed.

"That was great stuff," Richie said through the headphones. "I hate to cut you off, but we have another session booked in the A room in fifteen minutes."

"Oh shit, man. Sorry," Seb said. "I should have been keeping an eye on the time."

"No worries."

"My stomach is about to eat itself anyway," Toni whined as Kayla left the ISO booth. The air in the main room smelled faintly of sweat. They definitely needed to get out of there.

"I have all of this energy now," Tiff said.

"I don't suppose I could talk you guys into helping us paint?" Kayla asked hopefully.

"As long as you feed us," Toni said. "I'm starving."

———

The doorbell rang, and Kayla stepped around a few stacks of boxes to answer it, checking her pocket for the money she'd stashed there.

"Food's here!" she called out, getting a round of *finallys* from the rooms where Lilly, Jordan, Seb, Toni, Richie, and Toni's BFF, Yvette, were busy painting.

The group could not decide between Korean BBQ or American BBQ and had ordered from two different restaurants. Bets were taken on who would arrive first. Kayla thought it would be the bulgogi. Then again, Ty had run to the hardware store to get more brushes. Maybe he'd forgotten his key.

When Kayla opened the door, she did a double take.

"Mom?"

"Hello, sweetie. I hope we didn't come at a bad time." She smiled nervously, her gaze darting into the apartment and back.

"Uh…" Kayla's brain struggled to catch up. "No, of course not. Is Daddy with you?"

"He's parking in the garage next door." Her mother held up two shopping bags. "We thought we'd come down for the weekend and help you get settled. And we…well, we wanted to meet your young man."

Kayla snapped out of her stupor and stepped back. "Sorry, come in. Let me take those."

They carried the bags into the kitchen, and her mother walked straight over to the floor to ceiling windows.

"What a lovely view. What bridge is that?"

"The Ben Franklin," Kayla explained, emptying the contents of the bag. "What is all of this? You guys didn't need to get us groceries."

"I'm your mother, Katherine. Knowing you, when I open that refrigerator, I will be lucky to find a carton of milk and half a loaf of bread," she said, casting enough shade for a full-sized oak tree. It was impressive.

"I have some grapes. Tofu too," Kayla countered, smirking.

Her mother chuckled. "I stand corrected."

"Hey, babe," Ty called out. "There's a man in the hall who claims he's your dad?"

"Oh!" Kayla darted to the front door. She pecked Ty on the cheek before opening it. "Daddy?"

Her father was halfway down the hall. He turned around. "Hey, pumpkin! I wasn't sure if I had the right apartment number."

Kayla hugged her father tight. "You're in the right place."

"Was that your Tyrell?" he asked, his voice barely above a whisper. "He's very young, isn't he?"

Kayla laughed and pulled him toward the kitchen. "Ty is twenty-five, Daddy."

"He does look very young," her mother said as she put the groceries away.

"It's that baby face." Kayla made a mental note to check where everything was since they hadn't gotten around to filling the cabinets yet. She only had one week to help get the place in some sort of livable shape before the Lillys were to hit the road. Which reminded her...

"Did you guys get the itinerary I sent?"

"We did, we did," her father exclaimed. "New York, Atlanta, Miami, Toronto... Could we come see your show in Boston?"

"You really want to?" Kayla asked her mother. She had no doubts her father wanted to come, but Mom was a different story.

"Of course," she said, her expression sincere. "Not every parent gets the chance to watch their child become a bona fide superstar."

"Let's not get carried away," Kayla said, blushing a little.

"Oh, no. Get completely carried away." Ty joined them in the kitchen, wiping his hands on his kilt.

He wore a ratty black T-shirt that was splattered with paint. His utility kilt wasn't faring much better. Kayla suspected he would have liked a heads-up before meeting her parents. He fidgeted, tugging at the hem of his tee and brushing imaginary dust from his clothes.

She took his hand in hers, and he smiled, inhaling deeply as she met his gaze.

"Mom, Dad...this is Tyrell."

Her father wiped his hands on his thighs and stuck one out to shake. "It's a pleasure to meet you, young man. Kathy speaks very highly of you, and I—we—are looking forward to getting to know you."

"It's such a pleasure to meet you too, sir." Ty shook his hand with a little more enthusiasm than was probably necessary.

Her dad grinned. Then he and Kayla both turned to her mother, who put down the bunch of arugula she'd been rinsing and dried her hands on a towel.

As her mother looked at Ty, Kayla could practically see the data set running through her mind. Inner-city. Lower middle class. Not Ivy League educated. Brush with the law. Locs in his hair, piercings in his ears and nose, rings on his fingers. The kilt.

She braced herself for her mother's usual unguarded disapproval and faux sincerity.

Instead, her mother rounded the counter and stood in front of Ty.

His hand tightened almost painfully on Kayla's as her mother studied him for what felt like an eternity but was probably only a few seconds.

"It's lovely to finally meet you, Tyrell," she said finally. "Katherine, you didn't tell me he was so handsome." She turned to her daughter and smiled. "Shame on you."

A bubble of laughter ripped from Kayla's throat. "I mean, I thought that was a given."

Her mother tsked. "Don't be so shallow." She looked at Ty, who seemed to find his tongue. Mostly.

"You're...you're Gisele Larrington. I mean, I knew you were *you*, but it's really you. Sorry, it's great to meet you too," he added. "And please, call me Ty."

"Ty it is." Her voice was warm and welcoming, and it was breaking Kayla's brain. "And you may call me Gisele. Or Gigi, as my friends do."

Kayla's mouth dropped open. "Who? Who on this planet calls you Gigi?"

Her mother gave her a rare, soft grin. "People do."

"Seriously, name one," Kayla said, laughing.

Gigi went back to the vegetables. "You don't know everything about me, darling."

"I'm beginning to think I don't know anything about you," Kayla teased.

"Do I smell food? I'm fucking—" Tiff stopped mid-track and

midsentence, her eyes wide. "Oh. Hi, Kayla's parents. I'm Tiff. I play the bass." She gave Kayla's parents a little wave.

Yvette steered her away. "Sorry for my friend's mouth. It has a mind of its own. I'm not technically in the band, but I offer moral support. Or I would if I had morals." She paused. "Shit, I think Tiff is rubbing off on me. Sorry! Hi, I'm Yvette. Forget everything I said before hello."

After a beat of silence, Kayla's dad threw his head back and laughed. "Hello there."

"Aren't you going to show me around?" Kayla's mother asked, smiling.

"Oh, of course." Kayla wiped her hands on a towel. She turned to find her father engrossed in introductions with Tiff. "Should we rescue Daddy?"

"He'll be fine." Her mom took her arm. "You can give him the tour later."

Kayla led her through the apartment, pointing out the features she loved and giving her an idea of what it would look like when she was finished decorating.

"Are you sure you want to paint the walls such a dark color?" Her mother looked aghast at the paint samples taped to the wall of the room Kayla and Ty had designated as her studio. "Wouldn't something...brighter be more conducive to creativity?"

"Mom, it's my space. I think I know what will help me feel more creative," Kayla chided gently.

Her mother was quick to nod. "Of course, of course. I wasn't trying to...impose my will."

"I know." Kayla squeezed her hand before letting go.

"All right, good." Her mom stepped into the space and did a slow turn, taking in all the natural light and high ceilings. "This is going to be quite nice. Quite nice, indeed. I'm proud of you, sweetheart."

For a moment, Kayla was stunned. Her mouth hung open, and she blinked back tears. Her mother hadn't said that to her in longer than she could remember.

"Mom, I hope you know I'm proud of you too." Her voice cracked, and her mother walked over to her. "I'm so glad your publisher is sticking by you."

"Thank you, dear." She ran her fingers down Kayla's cheek before cupping her face in her hand. "I couldn't ask for a better daughter."

They shared a quiet smile.

Later, after the introductions, after the groceries were all put away, and after the takeout arrived, they all sat down wherever there was space—her mother sat on the floor!

Kayla leaned against the wall, her head on Ty's shoulder, and took it all in.

She had her past, her present, and her future right here in this room. It was incredible, being surrounded by all the people who meant the most to her. The only one missing was Zach.

Her phone pinged.

SIOBHAN: Guess who broke the glass ceiling?!

KAYLA: What are you on about? Btw, my mom and dad are here in Philly for the weekend.

SIOBHAN: Babe, that's great! But did you know your song just went to #10 on the alternative chart? I just heard it on satellite radio.

KAYLA: What?

"*What*?!" she said aloud.

"Something wrong?" Her mother's eyes filled with concern.

Kayla looked up. "A friend just told me we're number ten on the alternative chart."

Jordan's eyes went wide. "Hang on." He pulled out his phone. "Hot damn!"

> **KAYLA:** We had no idea. Thank you!
> **SIOBHAN:** Congrats, babe! How is your mom handling everything?
> **KAYLA:** Better than anything I could have imagined.

She snapped a photo of her mom and dad eating BBQ on the hardwood floor, smiling at each other like a couple of teenagers, and sent it.

> **SIOBHAN:** Did you get her drunk or something?
> **KAYLA:** Disturbing, right? But also kinda cute.

She snapped another photo, this time a selfie of her and Ty, who smiled for the camera and then kissed her temple.

> **SIOBHAN:** Uh... At the risk of losing you as a friend 🔥💦💦
> **KAYLA:** Stop macking on my man 😄

"Fuck me," Jordan muttered as he thumbed away on his phone. Looking up, he winced. "Sorry, parental units."

Kayla's mother gave him a stern look but ultimately waved him off. Once again, Kayla had to wonder who this pod person was— not that she was complaining.

"Your friend is right. You broke the top ten in alternative." Richie held up his phone as if to show her.

"You're also sitting at number one-twenty-three on the Hot 200 chart. With a bullet," Jordan added, grinning wide. "I can't wait until Andre gets the news."

"What does that mean exactly?" her father asked.

"It means the Lillys have done what no other all-female rock band in the history of...everything has achieved. It means we just added another chip to the bargaining table. And, pardon my language, but it's fucking phenomenal!"

"Oh my God!" Tiff exclaimed, jumping to her feet.

Seb threw his arm around Lilly, who seemed stunned.

Jordan pulled Toni up into a full body hug.

Ty turned to Kayla, utter joy and pride etched in his gorgeous face. "Fucking hell, babe..."

"Oh my God" was all she could say before he yanked her into a hug. "We're actually doing this."

"I'm not sure what's happened, but I feel like we should have brought champagne or something," her mother said.

"We'll run down the street and score some hooch," Yvette offered, grabbing Richie's hand.

"I don't quite understand either, but it sounds like you've made history." Kayla's father was practically beaming.

"That's exactly what it is, Kayla's daddy," Tiff said, grinning and sounding more like herself than she had in days.

Tiff climbed up onto one of the boxes, and both Jordan and Seb reached for her when she wobbled, but she steadied herself.

"We are the motherfucking Lillys," she said. "And we're gonna take over the goddamned world. Who are we?" she prompted.

"The Lillys," Kayla, Toni, Seb, and Jordan replied.

Tiff rolled her eyes. "You can do better than that, Kayla and Ty's apartment. I said, *who are we?*" She cupped her hand to her ear as if she were hyping up a concert crowd.

"We're the motherfucking Lillys!" Toni said, laughing.

"Yes!" Tiff smiled wide, pointing at her. "Again!"

"We're the motherfucking Lillys!" Toni, Seb, Jordan, Ty, and Kayla yelled.

"Who?" Tiff asked.

"The motherfucking Lillys!" Gisele and Geoffrey Larrington exclaimed, giggling when Ty high-fived them both.

Good lord. Her mother was now throwing f-bombs.

Kayla needed that drink.

Stat.

Ty slipped an arm around her waist and snuck in a kiss while the others reveled. "Love you. I'm so proud of you," he said before brushing a soft kiss against her temple.

Kayla looked up into his fathomless eyes. Thunder rolled its steady rhythm in her chest as he smiled down at her. "I love you too." Turning to the room, she said "Well, gang. It looks like it's time to take over the world."

BONUS MATERIAL

Enjoy your exclusive VIP backstage pass as Xio Axelrod takes you on a tour of the world of the Lillys, including:

1. About the Band + links to their music

2. Sheet music for an original song

3. The Lillys' festival tour schedule

4. The Lillys' current set list

5. Questions for your next book club meeting

6. A conversation with the author

ABOUT THE BAND

Ask any fan of the Lillys to describe them and you'll hear words like "hypnotic," "fierce," and "unapologetic." This uber enigmatic, all-female unit isn't interested in labels. They are utterly unconcerned with image, status, or style.

The four members of the Lillys—Kayla Whitman on drums, Tiffany Kim on bass, Toni Bennette on guitar, and Lilly Langeland on lead vocals—came together through chance and no small amount of karmic intervention.

Some think the Lillys exploded onto the New York music scene with their cover of the Toadies alt-rock classic "I Burn," but they first paid their dues playing in small clubs and dive bars. Known for their raw and raucous performances, fans have wondered aloud what will happen to the band's signature sound now that they've been picked up by a major label like YMI. Rest assured, the Lillys are here to melt your brain and upend any preconceived notions you may have about girl bands. These women rock.

To learn more (and hear their debut single "Hurt U"), follow the Lillys on:

Their Website thelillysrock.com
Facebook: thelillysrock
Instagram: @thelillysrock
Twitter: @thelillysrock
Spotify: spoti.fi/3nTNbMU
Apple: music.apple.com/us/artist/the-lillys/1522235126
Youtube: youtube.com/@thelillysrock6457

Hurt (U)

I hear you breath-ing so I know you're there,
you should stop wor-ry-ing I know you care sur prise sur prise,
you made an-oth-er sac-ri-fice.
And if you nev-er mend your brok-en heart,
you will al-ways live your life in parts, o-pen your eyes,

RUNNING SET LIST

Hey Lillys, here are the songs for your upcoming set list. You get 3 picks each ("Hurt U", "Burn", & "Rooster" are already in). Go ahead and slot your picks into the doc.

KAYLA:
Driven to Tears
Seven Nation Army
Sick Muse

TONI:
Transparent Soul
Sick of You
Gold Guns Girls

TIFF:
This Town
Antagonist
Get Free

LILLY:
Go with the Flow
Way Out
All Is Soft Inside

FESTIVAL TOUR DATES

Be sure to catch the Lillys LIVE at these upcoming festivals!

06.25	DragonFest,	**Dover, DE**
06.28	Live on the Lake,	**Syracuse, NY**
06.29	Park Life,	**Ann Arbor, MI**
07.19	Neon Fest,	**Savannah, GA**
07.20	Future Music,	**Memphis, TN**
07.27	Hot Town,	**Austin, TX**
08.03	Phoenix Fest,	**Tempe, AZ**
08.09	Indio Fest,	**Indio, CA**

www.thelillysrock.com

READING GROUP GUIDE

1. As an all-woman rock band, the Lillys are already fairly notable, but Kayla is particularly unique as their drummer. For many in the music industry, playing the drums is still considered a "man's profession." How do you think that has colored how Kayla interacts with the world? Can you name three prominent female drummers?

2. Kayla views her drumming as a connection to her late brother, Zach. Would she have pursued a career in music had she not lost him? What do you think her life would have been like if she'd listened to her mother instead? Were there any "crucible" moments like that in your own life, where a single event changed everything?

3. Ty and Kayla form an instant connection when they meet. What do you think they recognize in each other that clicks for them?

4. Both Kayla and Ty eschew traditional gender roles and expectations. Do you think this affects the way others treat them? How do you think most people see Ty in particular?

5. Kayla is described as the heart of the Lillys. Why is that? Do you think she views herself that way? What is it about the way she was raised that might drive her to slip into that role?

6. Kayla almost always has a pair of drumsticks in her hands. Do you think this is a coping mechanism, a way to channel nervous energy, or a manifestation of the music running through her mind at any given time?

7. Ty has a very close relationship with his grandfather but feels guilty about relying on him. Why do you think that is? Is it admirable that Ty tries not to rely on others, or should he be more willing to accept help freely given?

8. Candi is the toxic, complicated former lead guitarist of the Lillys whose fame as a socialite brought major (often negative) media attention the Lillys' way. Why was it so important that she be cut loose? What similarities and differences are there between the attention Candi brought the group and the attention Kayla fears she will bring?

9. Why does YMI insist upon pitting the Lillys against Candi's new band? Is this a sexist double standard, or can you think of any other bands a label deliberately pitted against each other for attention?

10. It's revealed that Kayla is the inspiration behind an internationally famous kids' series. How do you think that notoriety has shaped her life? How would you feel if everyone you ever met thought they knew you because they'd read the books loosely based on your life?

11. The Lillys are gaining national recognition. What do you think is in store for them as they embark upon their first world tour?

A CONVERSATION WITH THE AUTHOR

You grew up in the music industry. What real life inspiration did you draw upon as you created the Lillys?

A: There are so many phenomenally ground-breaking female bands in rock, it was easy to tumble down the rabbit hole. In addition to my experience of life on tour, I read memoirs by Cherie Currie (the Runaways) and Gina Shock (the Go-Gos). Both provided valuable insight into life on the road. I also drew from childhood memories of hanging out with my "cousins," Sister Sledge. Their tour bus was like a wonderland for little Xio.

The Lillys are still early in their career but are starting to make a name for themselves on the touring circuit. What's most important about this stage in an artist's career? What kind of advice would you give them?

A: This is the point when the band needs to solidify its sound, as well as tighten up its stage show. They're opening for more established acts, which will give them exposure to much larger audiences. They'll have to distinguish themselves and become unforgettable. Better get those songs written and recorded, ladies!

You're a recording artist as well as an author. Have you written any songs with the Lillys in mind?

A: I have! Some of the new lyrics make an appearance in this book. The pandemic placed my plans on hold, but I'm really looking forward to returning to the studio to record new Lillys material.

Which of the Lillys do you feel most strongly connected to? If you were a member of the Lillys, which part in the band would you play?

A: Of course, I feel connected to all the members of the band. I own several instruments and wish I had the proficiency that Toni and Tiff have. Plus, I've always wanted to play the drums (sadly, no room in our home for a set) and Kayla might be me in another life. But Lilly is who I identify with the most. Lead singer might seem like the easiest position in a band—we typically don't have a lot of gear to set up and we get a lot of attention—but the pressure to engage the audience night after night can be immense. The entire band could perform the show of their lives or barely make it through a set, but if the lead singer is off even the slightest, the set will fall flat.

The Lillys rock. What are some of your favorite all-women rock bands? Why do you think it's so (comparatively) rare to see an all-woman band?

A: Some of my favourite classic, all-female groups include the Go-Gos, the Runaways, the 5.6.7.8s, Le Tigre, and Bikini Kill. And I love female-fronted acts like the Noisettes, Hole, Metric, Skunk Anansie, and Savages. During my research for the series, I discovered an unsung act called Fanny that everyone should check out. I've also been super excited about some newer bands like the Linda Lindas, the Warning, and Nova Twins, as well as solo artists like Willow. Unfortunately, rock is still a male-dominated genre. Search for a list of the best rock drummers or rock guitarists of all time, and you'll be lucky to see a woman listed among the greats, even if they deserve to be there. I do think we're seeing more girls and women finding their way into the space. I credit entities like School of Rock and fabulous social media darlings like Nandi Bushell, Guitar Gabby, and the Pocket Queen for inspiring tomorrow's rock stars.

Both Kayla and Ty are non-gender-conforming. Why was it so important to show them (and how the world reacts to them) in *Girls with Bad Reputations*?

A: Now that the long overdue conversation about gender is finally taking place, I felt it was important to show how gender expectations can affect one's sense of self. While Ty's grandfather was very supportive and accepting of him, he experienced pushback in the wider world. And rather than respect her choices, Kayla's mother tried hard to mold her into the person she wanted her to be. It's so easy to take people as they are, and I've never understood why so many find it difficult. I can only attribute it to fear of the unknown or the unfamiliar, and the only way to push past that—to learn and to grow—is to listen. And to read.

Kayla and Ty bond over a shared love of reading. What are some of the books that most influenced you throughout your life?

A: Too many to mention, but growing up, my favourite authors included Anne Rice, Edgar Allan Poe, and Sir Arthur Conan Doyle. Later, I discovered the work of L.A. Banks, Jim Butcher, and Diana Gabaldon. If you're sensing a theme here, you're right. I was all about gothic fiction, sci-fi, and urban fantasy. However, it wasn't until I started to write myself that I discovered authors like Beverly Jenkins, Kristan Higgins, and Christina Lauren. Talk about eye-opening!

If readers wanted a sample of what the Lillys sound like, which bands/songs would you recommend?

A: Well, the Lillys themselves. Ha! Sadly, they only have a few songs available right now, so I've added many bands I mentioned earlier to their Spotify playlist, including Metric, Hole, Nova Twins, the Go-Gos, the Runaways, Savages, Willow, and many more. I also have a soft spot for alt-rock from the aughts, so you'll find groups like Yeah Yeah Yeahs, the White Stripes, and Paramore.

What's next for the Lillys?

A: They have an album to finish, a world tour to prepare for, an old rival, and a manipulative label to contend with. Who knows what else I have in store for the band? Okay, I do. You'll have to wait and see. *wink*

ACKNOWLEDGMENTS

Like an epic rock anthem, this book pulled my heart in so many directions. Luckily, I had a generous and patient editor in Mary Altman. She gave me the time and space to discover Kayla's story. Thank you, Mary! More thank-yous go to my right hand, Ann R. Jones; to my magnificent agent, Nalini Akolekar; and to my pioneering publisher, Dominique Raccah, for believing in the Lillys.

Each of you has inspired qualities in my girls.

I tend to write in a vacuum, but I've received incredible encouragement from some incredible people, including Roan Parrish, Avery Flynn, Christopher Rice, Helena Hunting, Susan Scott Shelley, Kwana Jackson, and Dena Heilik. Backstage passes for all of you, forever.

Finally, to my ever-supportive (though slightly stupefied as to how I managed to become a novelist when music was supposed to be my jam—still is, babe!) husband, Mr. X, you're the real rock star in the family. Thanks for being the best roadie I could ask for.

Rock on,

Xio

ABOUT THE AUTHOR

Xio Axelrod is a USA Today bestselling author. She writes different flavors of contemporary romance and what she likes to call, "strange, twisted tales."

Xio grew up in the recording industry and began performing at a very young age. A completely unapologetic, badge-wearing, fic-writing fangirl, Xio finds inspiration in everything around her. From her quirky neighbors to the lyrics of whatever song she currently has on repeat, to the latest clips from her favorite TV series.

When she isn't working on the next story, Xio can be found behind a microphone in a studio, writing songs in her bedroom-turned-recording-booth, or performing on international stages under a different, not-so-secret name.

She lives in complete denial of the last five minutes of Buffy with one very patient, full-time, indoor husband, and several part-time, supremely pampered, outdoor cats.

Website: xioaxelrod.com
Facebook: XioAxelrod
Instagram: @XioAxelrod
Twitter: @XioAxelrod
TikTok: @xioaxelrod